THE WITCH COLLECTOR

CHARISSA WEAKS

CITY OWL
PRESS

THE WITCH COLLECTOR
Witch Walker, Book 1

CITY OWL PRESS
www.cityowlpress.com

Cover Design by MiblArt. All stock photos licensed appropriately.

Edited by Tee Tate.

For information on subsidiary rights, please contact the publisher at info@cityowlpress.com.

Print Edition ISBN: 978-1-64898-044-2

Digital Edition ISBN: 978-1-64898-043-5

Printed in the United States of America

PRAISE FOR CHARISSA WEAKS

"This book left me completely breathless in the best sort of way. Honestly, I don't feel like any review I can type can accurately portray just how incredible this story is and how brilliant Charissa Weaks is. Her writing is sumptuous and vivid, building a stunning world for the reader to escape to...It is perfect for fans of Jennifer L. Armentrout and Sarah J. Maas —trust me, you will not be disappointed."
— *Ashley R. King, Author of Painting the Lines*

"Gorgeous, well-written fantasy with all the peril, fighting, magic, and romance you crave! This read drops you into a new world and sends you on a journey where you never know what you're going to get around the next bend. If you love fantasy romance, enemies to lovers, super evil antagonists, hero with a tough backstory, ferocious mute heroine who's reluctant to love (or like), then this is for you."
— *Poppy Minnix, Author of My Song's Curse*

"The Witch Collector is a magical, enchanting, fantasy romance whose pages are filled with threads of love, loss, and healing. Highly, highly recommended for anyone who loves fantasy romance, fantasy with strong female leads, unique magic systems, and beautiful writing."
— *Alexia Chantel/AC Anderson, Author of The Mars Strain*

"The Witch Collector is a finely woven tapestry of everything one could desire of fantasy—compelling characters, intricate world-building, gripping action, and burning romance. The threads of this story sing in Weaks' skilled and passionate hands."
— *Annette Taylor, Early Reviewer*

"The Witch Collector will immerse you in a magical world filled with intrigue. An unlikely and surprising alliance will make you fall in love."
— *J Piper Lee, Contemporary Romance Author*

"Lush prose, beautiful world building, and sexual tension for days, and trust me, you want to add this one to your TBR."
— *Jessa Graythorne, Author of Fireborne*

"First off this is an enemies to lovers with such fantastic world building, a strong heroine, a true VILLAIN and a swoon worthy love interest. Add in an intriguing plot and a slow burn romance and I'm sold... The ending had me wanting to read the next book immediately and I can only imagine how much better the story gets from here."
— *The Bookish Journal*

"The Witch Collector has everything you want in a fantasy story —characters with depth, cool magic, political intrigue, ancient gods, a sinister villain, and exquisite romantic tension building. Up there with the best!"
— *Emily Rainsford, Bookstagrammer @coffeebooksandmagic*

"This story is so beautifully crafted. The journey it takes you on is so gripping and intense, it has you on the edge of your seat. I could not put it down!"
— *Paulina De Leon, Bookstagrammer, @bookishnerd4life*

"I haven't read a novel so quickly—I thoroughly enjoyed it! The Witch Collector is my new favourite book."
— *Marcia Deans, UK Bookstagrammer, @itsabookthing2021*

"This story is so unique which was refreshing. The book is well-paced and I found myself unable to put it down!"
— *Emily McClung, Bookstagrammer, @busybookreporter*

"Raina utterly captured my heart and made it impossible to put this book down. I wish I could live in this book with these characters. A must read!!"
— *Gabrielle Perna, Bookstagrammer, @fantasybookobsessed*

To my family.
You are my light in the darkness.
I love you all to the moon.

And to all the writers who worry
that they aren't good enough,
that they can't keep going,
that they won't succeed.
You are. You can. You will.

AUTHOR'S NOTE

Signed languages are languages that use a visual-manual approach to communication. There is no universal signed language. For instance, BSL (British Sign Language) is a different language from ASL (American Sign Language). Sign languages have their own grammar and use hand movements, sign order, and body and facial cues to create that grammar, as well as gaze direction, blinks, and rests. For ease of reading, the fictional sign language in this novel reads as if it were SEE (Signing Exact English).

COLLECTING DAY

It's been eight long years since the Witch Collector took my sister.

Every harvest moon, he rides into our valley, black cloak whipping in the wind, and leads one of us to Winterhold, home of the immortal Frost King, to remain forever. It's been this way for a century, and today is that day—Collecting Day. But the Witch Collector will not come for me. Of this, I'm certain. I, Raina Bloodgood, have lived in this village for twenty-four years, and for twenty-four years he has passed me by.

His mistake.

Some women long for a husband. A home. Children. Others desire feverish kisses in the shadows, whispers of seduction against their skin. Me? I want my family. Together and free. I also want the Frost King and his Witch Collector.

Dead.

And today I make my wish come true.

❧ I ❧
THE FIRE

RAINA

U nder the bruised light of early dawn, I sneak through the rear door of the baker's hut, swipe two loaves of fresh bread off a cooling rack, and slip into the silvery fog creeping through our sleeping village. No one sees me. No one hears me. I've been quiet and stealthy all my life, used to being the overlooked witch without a voice. But I've never been a thief, and I've never been a murderer.

People change, I suppose.

With the bread bundled inside my apron, I rush into the empty cottage that I share with my mother and drag my pack from beneath the bed. That sweet yeast-and-honey aroma makes my empty stomach grumble, but I must stay focused. The stolen bread might save us in the coming days.

The last few weeks have given me reason to believe that those I love can have a different future than the one that has stretched before us for so many years—one of fear, dread, and loss. Finally, we can leave Silver Hollow and this valley, find a new life far away, someplace safe from the heavy hands of immortal rulers. I just need to kidnap the Frost King's right-hand man first, force him to guide me through the forbidden Frostwater Wood, ambush the kingdom's guarded castle at Winterhold, kill my enemies, and take back my sister.

Alone.

Once I've added the loaves to the other items I've prepared for our flight, I shove the pack back to its hiding place. Most young witches in the village are probably huddled with their families, worried about being taken, while I'm plotting a one-woman uprising.

But unlike the other witches in the vale, I've never feared being chosen. Witch Walkers sing their magick, in Elikesh, the language of the Ancient Ones. Born without the ability to speak, I learned to weave magickal constructions by translating Elikesh using the language Mother taught me —a language of signs spoken with hands.

Creating magick in this way is a difficult skill. Sometimes, I get it wrong. A word here, a refrain there. That struggle, and the fact that not a single witch's mark lives on my skin, has made me invisible for the choosing. The chosen Witch Walkers help protect the northernmost borders and Winterhold itself. What would Colden Moeshka, the Frost King, want with an unskilled witch like me?

A grin tempts my lips.

If only he knew all that I can do.

A hard *thud* smacks the door, and the sound reverberates through my bones. At first, I think it might be Mother, her arms overloaded with apples as she toes the door for me to let her inside. But the unmistakable scent of death wafts beneath the threshold. The smell is weak, but it's there.

When I drag open the door, a dove lies on the ground, its wings splayed and unmoving. With a gentle touch, I cradle the bird in the bend of my arm, trail my fingers over her head and breast, and carry her inside. Her neck looks damaged, but she's still alive, though barely. I have a few minutes to save her, but that's all.

More often than not, the chance to help passes me by. It's safer if no one knows that I'm a Healer. I've never dared tell my parents or anyone else. Not even my friend Finn. Only my sister, Nephele, knows that I have this skill. She always said to be thankful that I have no witch's marks, because the power living inside me makes me valuable.

And valuable things get locked away.

As the scent of death grows sharper, I sit in Mother's chair near the hearth and nestle the dove in my lap. Her death smells like pine needles and damp moss mixed with a hint of chilly rain. On a deep inhale, I close my eyes, absorbing that scent, and watch as the shimmering, coiled strands of the dove's life unravel like a spool of thread.

I'm not sure this is my wisest decision given what I must do today. Healing can be tiring, depending on how near death is and the size of the life I'm weaving back together. A tiny dove should be a small effort, though. I can't just let her die.

Concentrating, I imagine the dim strands becoming a gleaming braid, and the dove soaring over the valley. This is the first part of every rescue— to manifest a vision of my will. Next, I drudge up the ancient song I've known since the first time I saw the threads of life in a dying doe and form the lyrics with my hands.

"Loria, Loria, anim alsh tu brethah, vanya tu limm volz, sumayah, anim omio dena wil rheisah."

The strands glow and tremble, drawn together like iron to lodestone. I keep singing, repeating the words until the strands have entwined and the gilded construct of life is once again solid and resplendent.

The dove's wings flap and ruffle. When I open my eyes, her heart pounds so hard that her breast moves with each beat. Her little eyes open too, and she's up, flying from wall to wall. I shove open the shutters and watch her take off into the cold, vanishing in the distance near the forest's boundary.

I'm a little tired and dizzy, and cold sweat slicks my brow, but I'll recover. The strangest part of healing a life so close to its end is that the stolen death coils inside me like a shadow. I only have a handful of deaths tucked away, but I feel the tiny darkness of each one.

I begin to close the shutters, but instead, I pause and take in the view of morning in the village—possibly my last. To the west, where Frostwater Wood curves over the hills, the midnight shift of Witch Walkers moves along the forest's edge near the watchtower, gliding through the gloom like ghosts. And in the mist, just beyond the village green, a few women appear from the east. They carry baskets of apples on their heads, surrounded by clouds of their own breath. All else is calm, for now, a village on the cusp of waking for the most dreaded day of the year.

After stoking the fire, I exchange my cloak for a shawl and head to my worktable. The sun is almost up, which means that Finn will wake soon, and like the others carrying their apples, Mother will return from the orchard any moment. There's work to do, a plan that I must see to the end, though it's hard to imagine leaving all I've ever known.

But I cannot stay. We live in a world where wars simmer between two of Tiressia's continental breaks—the Eastland territories and the Summerlands to the south. For centuries, every eastern ruler has tried to conquer the southern lands, longing to claim the City of Ruin—a citadel believed to hold the Grove of the Gods, and the burial ground of Tiressia's deities.

Or so says the myth.

To the Frost King's credit, I've never known war. The Northlands have remained neutral, but our citizens—whether protecting the coast, the mountains, the valley, the Iceland Plains, or the king himself—must live according to the Frost King's wishes, guardians above all else. I believe I have the power to change that, to end his immortal life and make us a free land governed by its people, free to live as we choose.

And that's what I aim to do.

Father's old whetstone sits at the bottom of his trunk. I gather it from beneath his other work tools and scoop a cup of rainwater from the wash bucket for the grinding task. Just as I sit to work, Mother bursts into the cottage carrying a bushel of apples. She kicks the door shut, but not before a bitter wind out of Frostwater Wood follows her inside. With a grunt, she drops the laden basket.

The cold wraps around me, and I tug my shawl tighter, the colorful one Nephele knitted ages ago. Lately, her memory is everywhere. Even the rime-covered apples at my feet make me think of her. Nephele loved the orchard and enjoyed the Collecting Day harvest. She also didn't mind living on the Northland break of Tiressia's shattered empire, nor was she bothered by the touch of winter that clings to our valley after every harvest moon.

I'm the opposite. I hate living in the Northlands. I hate the Collecting Day harvest, and I hate this time of year. Each passing autumn day is another reminder that the Witch Collector is coming and that Silver Hollow, with its rolling green hills and sun-washed flaxen fields, will soon be buried beneath winter's suffocating frost.

Mother wipes a strand of graying hair from her brow and props elegant hands on her wide hips. "I know you'll think me foolish," she says, "but this will be a good day, my girl. I feel it in my bones."

Mother's witch's marks are few, her magick simple. The swirls of her ability glisten under a fine sheen of cold sweat, faint silver etchings curving along the tawny skin of her slender neck.

Setting the cup of rainwater aside, I force today's first smile. My fingers are stiff with cold when I sign. *"I am sure you are right. I should get to peeling."*

A beat later, I spin on my stool, turning away from her and those knowing eyes.

My smile vanishes as I light the candles that illuminate my work area. I want to avoid this conversation. It happens every year, and every year the Witch Collector proves Mother's intuition wrong.

Still, I would never call her foolish. Though a dreamer with her head in the stars, my mother is the wisest person I've ever known. It's just that this day is never good, and this year it might be worse than ever before.

Because of me.

I unlock the worktable drawer and retrieve our salvation, the reason I've found such bravery for taking back our lives: Father's old knife. *The God Knife*, he called it, said to have been fashioned by an eastern sorcerer from the broken rib of a long-dead god. It had been missing since the winter after my sister was chosen, lost in the snow-covered fields the day Father's heart stopped beating.

A few weeks ago, a group of farmers found the blade during harvest, half-buried in the soil of a soon-to-be fallow field. One of them, Finn's father Warek, recognized the knife by its unusual white granite hilt, strange black blade, and the amber stone set into the pommel. He made sure the farmers returned the find to my mother.

"What's so special about a God Knife?" I asked one night when I was still small enough to sit on Father's knee. My father carried that knife everywhere he went. There was no question that it was important.

He'd just come in from harvest. I still remember the way he smelled— like musk and field. I traced the veins in his hand, following his witch's marks—the marks of a reaper—that branched like tree roots over his knotty knuckles.

"The God Knife is a god remnant," he answered. *"God bone, fashioned by the*

hand of Un Drallag the Sorcerer. It harkens to the soul of the god from whose body
the bone was taken. It can kill anyone and anything, the blessed and the cursed, the
forever living and the risen dead—even other gods."

"*Yet you keep it,*" I'd said, not understanding the depth of his words or
the fact that they would one day change my world.

His only reply had been: "*Yes, daughter. I keep it. Because I must.*"

Like Nephele, thoughts of my father are never far from my mind. Why
he went to the fields the day he died—in the dead of winter—will forever
remain a mystery, as will the question that might haunt me until my last
breath: If the blade is so all-powerful, why didn't he use it to save us? To
save Nephele?

He had possession of the knife for years—a god killer, an immortal
slayer, a divine weapon. Never once did he use it against the Frost King to
change our circumstances.

Mother leans over my shoulder and unties her cloak as she eyes the
knife. The scent of cloves, fallen leaves, and smoky coldness floats from
her skin and clothes.

"You're sharpening that old thing?"

She holds no faith in Father's tales of finding the God Knife along the
Malorian seashore. Though she's kept the blade hidden away since its
rediscovery, Mother still doesn't believe in its myth and claims it has no
power.

But I believe. Because I feel it.

In answer, I hold the dull, black edge to the candlelight. I need this
knife sharp enough to penetrate sinew and bone, and I only trust one pair
of hands to make sure that it can.

Unfortunately, those hands aren't mine.

"Carry on, then," Mother says. "But we have better knives for peeling
apples, Raina."

I need to get the knife to Finn. He usually works with iron mined near
the Mondulak Range, but his hands are the hands I trust. I just need an
excuse because Mother is right. We have other blades for the day's work.
I've no reason to be so focused on this one, none that she'll believe anyway,
and it's not like I can explain my plan. Something tells me she wouldn't be
too keen to learn that her daughter means to kidnap the Witch Collector
today at knifepoint.

Mother hangs her cloak by the door and crosses to the hearth to pour a mug of mulled apple cider. When she returns to my side, she watches over my shoulder as I position Father's whetstone on a piece of oiled cloth. She says the knife isn't made of bone. What bone is black as night and cold as ice?

But it's bone. God bone. Not flint or steel. I'm so sure of it. Something deep inside that old marrow vibrates with every pass, as though I'm bringing it back to life.

More sweat beads on my brow as I work, sliding the edge along the stone with careful measure. What if I damage it? Can god bone *be* damaged? And what if the Witch Collector bests me today when I hold this blade to his throat?

My hands tremble at the thought of standing against him, enough that I falter in my work. Bone catches against stone—a nick of my fingertip. I gasp and suck the wound.

Gods' death. Only *I* would accidentally kill myself with the very weapon that could save me.

"Raina, careful." Mother sets her mug aside and studies the cut. She touches my chin, love softening her eyes. "I know you consider this knife a connection to your father, but maybe Finn should have a look at the blade if you're so determined to use it. I prefer your beautiful hands intact."

My pulse quickens. I feel like a child again, a little girl hiding something from her mother. But this is the perfect moment. I couldn't have designed it any better.

"Finn is probably on his way to the shop," I sign. *"I will take it to him, and I will finish the apples long before noon. I promise."*

"Go." She smiles. "But don't be long. The harvest supper won't prepare itself."

I throw on my cloak, wrap the knife in a piece of animal skin, and head for the door.

"Daughter."

I glance over my shoulder, and Mother crosses the small distance between us.

"You try so hard to hide it," she says, "yet a mother knows her child better than all else. Do not let your loathing lead you—or us—to trouble, Raina. If you're going to promise me anything, promise me that."

Her sharp, indigo eyes dart to the bundled knife like she knows my every intention, and guilt and shame squeeze my heart for what I'm about to do. What I *must* do.

I lean in, kiss her soft cheek, and lie anyway.

"*I promise,*" I sign, and slip into the cold, gray light of day.

RAINA

The Owyns' blacksmith shop sits on the eastern outskirts of Silver Hollow, near the orchard and vineyard. It's a long walk, but I'm brimming with enough nervous energy that I should arrive in a short time.

As I make my way across the green, I memorize the village's every detail. Frost glistens on the thatch of each cottage and hut, and the last thin breaths of nighttime fires curl out of chimneys. Gardens are dying back, and the wildflowers lining the path to the fields have turned to colorless husks. Soon, snow will pile on the eaves and creep knee-deep over every door, and life here in the vale will grow bitter and difficult.

I think a lot about how much I hate this place, but the truth is that I only hate my circumstances—not having a choice. Because life could be worse. I could live in a barbaric clan in the Eastland Territories or deep in the sweltering Summerland sands, or I could live along the Northland Coast, constantly worrying about the war and danger across the sea. Instead, I live in a peaceful village filled with good people—Witch Walkers, halflings, and those with no magickal ability at all.

The guardians of Frostwater Wood.

Our Witch Walkers, along with those from Hampstead Loch, Penrith, and Littledenn, serve as the second line of defense in the Northlands, second only to the Northland Watch who protect our southern borders. Hour after hour, Witch Walkers' voices carry magick into the ether along Frostwater's rim to reinforce a barrier we keep intact at all costs.

I've walked that boundary many times, helping to strengthen the protection with my silent song. To a stranger, the barrier is nothing more than a shimmer in the trees, dew sparkling on a spider's web in morning light. But it's much more than that. It's an impenetrable fortress with a single guarded entry point to the west near Hampstead Loch, through which the king and his entourage—namely his Witch Collector—are said to travel.

Sometimes, I wonder if we're keeping intruders out of the wood and therefore out of the Frost King's mysterious Winterhold.

Or if we're keeping something in.

On the other side of the stone wall that separates the main village from the farmers' steads, a handful of elders exit the temple after their customary morning prayer. Several villagers follow, including Finn's mother, Betha, and his four younger sisters.

The Owyns are loyal Northlanders, dedicated to their worship of the ancient gods, especially the last Northland god in recent memory—Neri, a selfish bastard who's been dead for three hundred years. Sometimes, being around the Owyn family makes me feel blasphemous, but then again, I'm anything but pious. I haven't stepped foot inside the temple since Nephele was chosen.

And I never will, ever again.

"Raina!" Helena, the second-to-the-oldest Owyn child, starts my way.

Not a day goes by that I don't talk to Hel. I've known her all her life, but when I lost Nephele, Helena wouldn't leave my side. She filled an emptiness in me that not even Finn could reach.

I wave, and the girls pick up their steps to meet me, their light brown faces drawn tight against a cold wind. Betha seems reluctant, and she wears a grim expression on her face.

The twins, Ara and Celia, are unfazed. They run and cling to my legs while Saira, the least of the Owyn family, leaps into my arms and hugs my neck. She pulls back and signs the only phrase her tiny hands have mastered, thanks to her mischievous brother.

"Raina needs a wash."

Saira giggles, and a genuine smile spreads across my face. She's a small wedge of joy in an otherwise joyless day.

Helena approaches, her black hair fighting the breeze. The dagger her father and brother gifted her last year when she turned eighteen is forever strapped to her side, even during prayer. She's tall and strong like her father but soft in the ways of her mother.

The Owyns dabble in fire magick—wise for blacksmiths—though the bulk of their skill lies in common magick like the rest of the villagers. Helena's silvery witch's marks are bold today against her fire-gold skin, though, outlined in a pretty shade of ocher.

When I meet her stare, she pokes my side and smiles, but her wild spirit doesn't stir, not even in her eyes.

"Morning, Raina," Betha signs. She flashes a tight smile and glances at her small daughters, a silent way of saying she doesn't want them to hear the worries so evidently etched onto her face.

After all the years she's known me, Betha still hasn't learned how to sign anything more than the most basic communication, nor have the others—save for Finn and Hel.

I look up into Helena's deep, brown eyes. *"Everything all right?"* I sign.

Whatever's bothering them has nothing to do with Collecting Day. The Owyns are Witch Walkers, and Finn and Helena are still of age for the Witch Collector's choosing. The Owyns believe the Frost King does what he does for a godly reason, a man gifted with insight from Neri's eternal blessing, a leader who means to protect our lands. I know they'd be saddened to lose any member of their family today, but they view sacrifice as duty—unlike me. Something else must be wrong.

"The feast hunters should have returned from the mountains last night," Helena signs, *"in time to prepare their kills for the harvest supper. There has been no sign of any of them. Not even Da."*

I set Saira on her feet and watch her skip toward the village. Every autumn, the feast hunters journey south toward the Gravenna Mountains, hoping to trap and kill a few Great Horns for the harvest supper. Scattered steads and small villages lie between our valley and the mountains, but other than that, the land is a stretch of rolling hills and open grassland. It's certainly not a dangerous trek for hunters who've traveled that ground for years.

"I am sure they only lost track of time," I reply. *"Warek will return with his merry band on his heels, as though he is the greatest hunter of them all."* I squeeze her hand in comfort because her unease is visible, tightening into twin lines between her eyes. I don't know if I'm right, but later, after I've talked to Finn, I have a way to find out.

Healing isn't my only gift.

Helena bites her lip. "I hope you're right, but say a prayer to Loria just in case?"

"Of course."

Helena knows me well enough not to include her Northland lord in her request. Loria is the goddess of all creation, and though I can't say that I believe the Ancient Ones listen anymore, Warek was my father's closest friend, and so—impious as I might be—I will pray to our maker.

Just not to Neri. Never to him. He's the reason we must deal with the Frost King in the first place.

Helena and I bump forearms. She presses her forehead to mine and manages a soft smile.

"Tuetha tah," she says, an Elikesh phrase that means *My sister.*

I press the signed form of the words against her chest, feeling guiltier with every passing second. I keep little from Hel, except the story of the knife. But I haven't mentioned my plan, or that I'm leaving the vale—for real this time. Helena loves me, but she would never understand.

She gathers her sisters and mother and herds them toward the stone wall. Although her face is still shadowed with worry, her smile brightens, and she winks playfully over her shoulder. "Finn is in the shop if that's where you're going. See you on the green at noon?"

I nod. As if I'd be anywhere else.

Outside the forge, I step over Tuck—the lazy, golden shop dog I adore—to reach the entry. A stroke behind his soft ear garners a beady-eyed glance, but other than that, he doesn't move. Such love for the woman who stole death for him once when no one was looking.

Inside, I'm not surprised to find Finn sitting in a dark corner, leaned back in a chair with his feet propped on a worktable, sipping from a steaming mug of mead. This used to be Finn's father's shop, and it shows. Tiressia's green and indigo flag hangs from the rafters while Neri's pennon covers the wall above Finn's head. The image of a creature more wolf than man stares at me, embroidered in ash-colored thread on blue and white silk.

The sight disgusts me.

The door creaks and Finn glances up. His wild black locks are mussed and hanging over his forehead, his eyelids heavy. In better light, his skin—like Helena's and his father's—appears marked with silver, save for the outline of dim amber.

"From that look you're wearing, I take it you saw my family." He downs a long drink and lets out an irritated sigh. "Father is fine. They'll make it back in time for supper. They're hunters—the best. I'm not worried."

That's Finn's way of stopping a conversation he doesn't want to have before it begins.

I don't mind this time. I agree with him. The feast hunters know our lands better than anyone. Besides, what could've gone wrong that all seven would not return?

"*Yes. No need to worry,*" I sign. Crossing the space between us, I set the wrapped knife next to Finn's feet and flip the skin back. "*Could you sharpen this for me?*"

Finn looks at the God Knife, then back at me, and furrows his brow. "What for? That's the knife my father found, right? A bit large for peeling apples." He takes another sip of mead, watching me with a curious eye.

"*It is not for apples. I need it to help clean the Great Horns for the feast. It must be sharp enough to cut through flesh and bone alike.*"

Gods, what a terrible excuse. There won't be any Great Horns for the harvest supper if the hunters don't return in time.

Finn drags a hand through his thick hair and tilts his mouth into a smirk. "You are Tiressia's worst liar, Raina Bloodgood. You're up to something."

I move to stand with my back to the heat of the forge, trailing a hand along a row of finely crafted dagger and knife belts Finn sells to his customers. Last night, I considered what it might be like to tell him every detail of my plan to set Nephele and the Northland peoples free of the Frost King's rule. To plead with him to be brave and help me.

But now that the moment is here, I can't bring myself to be honest. He may know how to form and wield every weapon created, but Finn is a lover, not a fighter. He's content where I'm restless, sated where I starve. He will call me ten kinds of foolish and try to stop me.

He could very well succeed.

"I am not lying." I form the words steady and sure, hoping that I'm convincing. *"Mother sent me. We are using the knife to clean the wild deer for tonight's supper. The hunters will return."*

Better to cling to a terrible lie than reinvent another.

He narrows his brown eyes, and the need to cower behind something sweeps through me. Deceiving Mother was bad enough, but deceiving Finn might be even more challenging.

Finn has been my first everything. My first friend. My first fight. My first kiss. My first lover. My first heartbreak. He's the only person with whom I ever shared the knife's story. He's also the man I decided not to build a family with because he refused to leave the vale, and I didn't want to stay. My life's moments are filled with him. He reads me as plainly as any book.

After a groan and pointed glare, he rests his chair on all four legs and reaches for the God Knife. He's still half asleep, and he's either grown disinterested or annoyed.

Or both.

"Wild deer, huh?" He twists the pommel in his hand, and the amber stone reflects the forge's firelight. He looks up at me, narrowing his eyes again like he's sorting me out. "You wouldn't happen to mean a Witch Collector instead, would you, Raina? Perhaps a Frost King?"

Annoyed it is.

I take a seat in the chair across from him. *"Finn, stop. Please do not make this difficult. I need your help."*

Finn returns the knife to the table and speaks to me with his hands. *"Help with what? Killing the Witch Collector? Bringing the Frost King's rage down upon all our heads? I remember your father's tale. Surely you do not believe that this knife will change everything. Or anything, for that matter. If it could, do you really think Rowan and Ophelia Bloodgood, of all people, would not have tried?"*

My chest tightens at the sound of my parents' names. When they met in the Northland's southernmost city of Malgros, my father was Head Sentry for the Northland Watch, a guard witch assigned to protect the port. My mother was also a guard, often stationed near my father's territory. A short time after Mother became pregnant with Nephele, tensions between the southern queen, Fia Drumera, better known as the Fire Queen, and the East's King Regner, created unrest. As the southern and eastern breaks prepared for war, the Northland peoples along the coast feared the conflict might finally spill across the sea to our shores. Then Fia Drumera killed Regner, and soon, in the east, a mystical prince with no name rose to power.

My parents were granted leave to raise their family but were required to head north and help protect the vale. They were never loyal to the king. But they *were* loyal to their land and their people.

"I cannot say why they never tried," I tell Finn. *"Only that I am not them."* I grab the knife and animal skin and set them in my lap. *"Will you help me or not? I need the blade sharpened. That is all I ask."*

"You want me to hone a killing blade." He folds his muscled arms across his chest. "That is, at its essence, what you said when you walked in here. Something to cut through flesh and bone alike. And I know you do not mean wild deer."

I tighten my fingers into fists of silence. Every blade he forges is used to kill, and that's saying a lot. People come from all around the Northlands to purchase the beautiful and deadly work of Finn Owyn, to seek his expertise. He's only conflicted now because it's me who's asking for his help.

"I want you to sharpen a God Knife," I reply. *"And believe in me."*

"A God Knife." Finn scrubs his hand down his face, his frustration evident. "Made by the great sorcerer Un Drallag, a figment of Eastern lore. Forged from bone and the essence of a deity, yes? Which god, Raina? Which god do you think this bone belonged to? Neri? Asha? Urdin? Thamaos? One of the ancients? Loria herself?"

"I..." My fingers still. Father never mentioned that part. I always figured he didn't know, though I've always wondered. *"He never said,"* I reply, *"but it does not matter for the task at hand."* I pause and add, *"Wild deer and all."*

A grin tests one corner of Finn's mouth but fails to reach completion. He pushes off his knees and stands, skirting the table between us, a weary expression shadowing his face. Crouching at my feet, he rests those strong, black-stained and blistered hands on my thighs like they belong there.

When he looks into my eyes, I taste the bitterness that has lived inside my heart ever since he refused to run from the vale with me three years ago. I could've loved him the way my parents loved each other. We could've had so much more than this. Then again, if we'd left, I wouldn't have had this chance to save my sister and maybe every single person living in the Northlands from enduring lives they did not choose.

Gently, Finn tucks a loose strand of hair behind my ear. "You know that I believe in you, in all things. And I'll sharpen this knife until it can flay flesh and penetrate bone if that's what you want. But you are no match for men like the Witch Collector, Raina. And certainly not the Frost King. I hate them too—more than you believe or will ever know. But if I think, even for a moment, that you're about to do something foolish once the Witch Collector arrives today, know that I won't stand there and watch it happen. I can't. I will always save you, even if it means saving you from yourself."

I clench my fingers again. There are so many things I want to say, none of them kind. Instead, I hold Finn's stare until he takes the knife, slips on his leather apron, and steps to the forge.

"*Fulmanesh, iyuma.*" He speaks the words over the low flames and they rise, supplying more light.

After a moment, I follow, silently swiping one of the dagger belts I noticed earlier while he's not looking. Shoving the leather into my skirt pocket, I watch over his shoulder. I'm more nervous than I want to be now that he holds the God Knife. He could so easily take it from me.

Finn studies the weapon. "Why is it so cold?"

I shrug. *"It has been like that since I can remember."*

He tests the knife's heft in his hand, bites the blade between his teeth, and drags the dull edge across a piece of thick hide, which slices far easier than I would've guessed.

He cuts a sidelong glance. "Feels like bone. Tastes like bone. But it doesn't look like bone, and it doesn't cut like bone."

Of course it doesn't resemble the kind of bone we're used to handling. Gods were practically indestructible. It took the last of them killing each other three centuries ago to end their reign, after all. Surely killing a man Neri only gifted with immortal life and rule won't be as impossible a task as Finn makes it seem. I imagine one good thrust to the Frost King's heart will do the trick.

As for the Witch Collector, he's human—perhaps cursed to his duty unto death. At most, he's a Witch Walker dedicated to his king. Helena thinks he's an older man, and I agree. He keeps his head buried beneath his cloak, but he's the same collector who has come to the vale since I was a child. I know his voice, and I know his tall frame. He won't expect me to attack—no one ever challenges him. The element of surprise and a holy knife held to his throat should render him easier to overpower.

If I'm faster than him.

"I'll try the grindstone first," Finn says, the edge in his voice receding. "Then we can go from there. All right?"

I link my arm with his and nod, resting my head on his shoulder. The coiled tension in my muscles ebbs. Finn and I aren't together anymore, not in the way we once were, but he's still my comfort, even when he's impossible. I don't know how to live life without him, but I fear I'll have to. When the moment arrives today, I'll still give him—and his family—a choice, but if I'm honest with myself, he made that decision three years ago.

He presses a tender kiss to my forehead. "Don't thank me, Raina," he whispers. "Just don't make me regret this."

ALEXUS

"I have a bad feeling. Don't you understand that?"

Colden Moeshka leans against the small hearth of my hunting shelter, picking at a loose thread dangling from the gold-ribboned cuff of his blue velvet coat. I can smell the cold on him—that constant, crisp scent of winter that has clung to his skin for ages now.

He squats, tosses another log into the fire, and stokes the flames until the wood catches and sparks dance. I can't help but stare. His alabaster skin glows golden under the firelight, and his dark eyes shine like black onyx mined from the Mondulak Range. Much of his flaxen hair hangs loose from its tie, lending his features an air of innocence that he does not possess.

Shifting on my wooden stool, I rest my elbows on my knees and rub my tired eyes. "Bad feeling or not, I have to go. I've never missed a Collecting Day. The villagers' lives must go on as normal, at least until we know the truth. And the only way we can know the truth is if I go to the vale and get the girl."

Already, I'm several hours late. Every Collecting Day, I wake near midnight to finish the last leg of a week-long journey through Frostwater Wood. I usually reach Hampstead Loch—the closest village to my cabin and Winter Road—around sunrise, and end my day at Silver Hollow by noon.

But last night, I woke to Colden slipping through my door in the darkness, alone and travel-weary from trying to catch up with me, all to deliver what I consider less than trustworthy news.

"We've heard rumors from the East along the spy chain before," I remind him. "Nothing has ever come of them."

"Yes, well, this rumor is different." Colden holds a chilled hand over the rising heat from the fire, a useless effort to chase away the cold that lives in his veins. "There's only one reason the Prince of the East would break King Regner's peace agreement with me, and that's if he's learned that I'm much more valuable as a weapon against Fia than as an ally."

Fia. I think of the Summerland queen often and wonder if she worries for Colden the way he worries for her.

"Everything I've ever done has been with Fia and all of Tiressia in mind," he says. "If the prince knows my secret, they will come for me. You know they will. And they will destroy anyone who stands in their way."

"Our borders are protected," I tell him for what feels like the hundredth time. "Even without our Witch Walkers, the Iceland Plains and eastern range are impassable this time of year. The Eastlanders never have and never will survive sailing through the White Tides, nor can they make it past the Summerlander fleet to enter via the Western Drifts. The coast is well fortified. You're safe, Colden."

And Fia is safe. No king—and certainly no nameless prince—has bested her yet. She doesn't need to deal with the Prince of the East getting his hands on her former lover, but if anyone can take care of themselves, it's the Fire Queen.

Colden slices that black gaze across the room and arches a perfect brow. "As well as you know me, do you really think I fear the Eastlanders for myself? If they come for me, I'll turn their army into ice statues for courtyard decorations, hang the Prince of the East's icy balls on Winterhold's gates, and dance on the shards of his pathetic, frozen bones." He turns back to the fire as though some answer to our predicament lies in the flames and ashes. "It's the Northland people I'm concerned about, Alexus. I can't be everywhere at once."

His words sound so assured, but they're lies. The truth that Colden won't admit is that the Prince of the East scares him. The prince is said to bear the stains of walking in the Shadow World—another rumor, and one I don't believe. It's been centuries since someone crossed the Shadow World's dark shores. He was no mere man and wouldn't have survived otherwise.

I hold my hands up in mock defense. "I'm only trying to ease your mind. It's hearsay. There's no need for upheaval until we have more evidence."

He drops into the chair beside me, and his irritated expression morphs into concern. "I also worry for *you*. I've had dreams. No, not dreams," he clarifies, his brow pinched. "Nightmares. For a while now."

We've been back and forth about this situation since he arrived, but this is the first time he's mentioned nightmares.

I gesture toward him. "Go on."

"It's like the Ancient Ones are warning me that danger is coming," he says, "yet I don't know how to stop it. All I know is that I fear the East-landers have discovered what I've been hiding, and that you don't need to be in the vale tonight."

Though I consider asking what he saw in his dreams to lead him to such conclusions, I lean over and rest my hand on his bouncing knee instead. His foot stills.

"You can't have it both ways, my friend. We can't get the truth without a Seer, and we can't consult a Seer if I don't go to the vale. I must get the girl. It's the only way to end this worry."

The girl with no voice and no witch's marks. The so-called *Seer*.

Raina Bloodgood.

Of all the names I might've written on my list, hers has never been a possibility. Not until this morning anyway, now that Nephele has decided to turn her sister into an asset.

Nephele has always been honest with me, or so I believed, but although she's told me much of her younger sister, she's never mentioned this valu-able and hidden talent. Rather, she's done everything in her power to protect Raina from ever making the journey with me along Winter Road. I've always understood and agreed to leave Raina alone. In truth, I've never sensed strong enough power inside her to make her useful—not a witch's mark one. But gods know a Seer would've been a precious addition at Winterhold.

Why would Nephele deny the entire kingdom such rare protection? And if the girl is all Nephele claims, why isn't her power visible with one glance?

I remind myself that Raina has long been a woman, not a girl. A woman whose face lingers in my mind when it has no reason to.

Colden fists his hand against his mouth for several long moments, knuckles tight and white as snow. "She'd better be worth the risk I'm taking by allowing this."

I pull my hand away from his knee. "You don't trust Nephele's word?"

I can't blame him if he doesn't. I even find myself doubting her, though the thought twists my insides. The truth I can't ignore is that if Raina held that sort of power, her skin would show it.

Unless there's greater magick at work.

"Of course I trust Nephele," Colden answers. "But time blurs reality, or have you forgotten? Her and Raina have been apart for a long time. What Nephele remembers of her sister may not be the truth that exists now."

Colden isn't lying about Nephele's wishes—I would sense it if he were —but it would help if Nephele were here. After eight years of swearing on my life to spare her sister the fate of duty at Winterhold, I don't know how to feel about breaking my word.

I drag my hand over my beard. "The question is, are you willing to ignore the possibility that Raina has Sight, thanks to a bad feeling and a bad dream? If she *is* a Seer, and if the rumor about the Prince of the East betraying your agreement holds even a grain of truth, then we need her. Unwarranted concern for my safety cannot stand in the way of that. I've faced far worse things than another Collecting Day. I'll be careful."

"I could ride with you," Colden offers, eyes unguarded. "Alone, you're formidable. Together, we're a force of nature."

"Absolutely not. If there's danger, we're both safer if you're home, and all of Tiressia is safer if you're shielded by the Witch Walkers' protections. Please do not argue with me on this. You will not win."

He leans forward, resting his forehead on steepled fingers, and exhales a long, chilled breath that hangs in the air before floating away. I know his dilemma. I can feel his turmoil. It's impossible not to worry about someone with whom you've shared so much. We are, after all, like two halves of the same whole.

"Go then." He lifts his head. "Ride fast. Go straight to Silver Hollow. Find the girl and get back to the forest as soon as possible. I don't want you in the vale after full dark."

He likes to think he rules me, but we both know I'm only still here because he needed me to be.

"Yes, my lord and mighty king. I was born to grant your every desire." With as much of a smile as I can muster, I stand and give a spurious bow, hoping to lighten his mood before I go. When I rise, I half expect Colden to roll his eyes at my antics, but his face is still serious, perhaps more so. Any humor in my voice vanishes. "Fine. But tell me you'll head back to Winterhold. Don't wait for me. I want you as safe as you want me."

"I know you do." He gives me a look I know well. "And yes, I'll go. I won't like it, but I'll go."

We stare at one another for a long beat, then I put out the fire and set to strapping on my baldric, scabbard, and blades.

"At least all you must do is get the girl." Colden stands, sounding like he's convincing himself. "Easy enough task."

"That is the hope. I can't imagine the woman I remember causing me any trouble."

Colden gives me a dark half-smile. "If she's anything like her sister, you might be very wrong about that."

We head outside and mount our horses, facing one another under the weak light filtering through the forest's canopy.

Colden wraps those deadly fists in his animal's reins. "Before I left, I instructed Nephele and the others to focus their attention on the boundaries come sundown. If anyone enters the wood, my Witch Walkers will know. If they sense a threat, they'll make sure the enemy regrets ever stepping foot in our vale." Ice branches over the leather straps within his grasp. "They won't leave Frostwater Wood—at least not until they've endured me."

His eyes are black as soot, his face stone. Any vulnerability he permitted to creep beneath his skin moments before has now been buried in his bones.

Colden Moeshka, frigid Frost King, has returned.

"I'll see you soon," I tell him, and after he pounds a fist to his chest, his way of saying, "Until we meet again," we part ways.

I dig my heels into my horse's sides and bear down for a stealthy ride. "Like the wind, Mannus. Let's find Raina Bloodgood."

4

RAINA

With the sharpened knife and stolen dagger belt tucked in my pocket, I return to the cottage and spend the rest of the morning helping Mother prepare for the harvest feast. After dumping the last of the apples into a pot, I place them over the fire.

"I'm sure the hunters are fine." Mother stands from her chair and wipes her hands on the towel cinched at her waist. With a slight frown, she glances out the window. "Probably enjoyed a little too much ale and wine last night."

A few hours ago, I would've agreed, but I find myself less sure with every passing minute.

Gods, I need to be alone with my scrying dish. The thought to look for Finn's father has struck more than a few times, but Mother is constantly at my side. I can't risk her catching me, even now. The hurt she'd feel—the betrayal at knowing all I've kept from her—might undo my resolve.

Later, I occupy my nervous hands by making myself useful outside. I help Mr. Foley haul wood for the bonfires and assist old Mena in setting stones for our ceremony circle. Mena moved here from Penrith after she lost her daughter many years ago on Collecting Day. She has no family now, but she and I have always shared a sort of kinship.

As we press the rocks into the ground, she eyes me more keenly than I like. Her wrinkled, pale skin is covered in witch's marks—blue like veins, shimmery like fish scales. With age, her skill has developed, but the degree of magick supposedly required at Winterhold is said to be too depleting for the old. I have to think that means the Frost King finds the elders useless because the only other option is that he and the Witch Collector actually care what happens to the Northland people.

I know better.

Mena goes to the cart, and I hold out my dirty hands for another stone, but she hesitates.

"Your palms are calling to me today." She winks.

Mena reads palms, something I've let her do a handful of times. She knows I'm reluctant and doesn't press, but she likes to tease. She's a dear friend, so I tolerate her prying mind.

I snatch a rock from the cart and place it on the ground, giving her a light-hearted smile. *What do they say?*

"That there are two things you need to learn. Or perhaps, not *learn* but come to accept. One," she comes closer, smiles, and taps me on the nose, "is that you are more capable than you believe, dear one. Your strength is in your heart. And two..." She kneels beside me and pushes my hair over my shoulder, letting her hand rest there. "Victory only comes through sacrifice, Raina. I don't know what's weighing on you, but I know you're in turmoil. I can see the burden. Most battles are hard-fought. Something must always be lost if you're ever to gain. Don't fear this. You will never move forward if you never leave things behind."

Crying is the last thing I want to do right now—I've cried enough for all of Silver Hollow—but tears rise unbidden anyway.

I take a deep breath and blink them away. *Thank you,* is all I can think to say. I don't know what her words mean for me, but they're likely the last words of wisdom I'll ever take from Mena, so I tuck them away. Something of her to keep forever.

A short time later, after Mena and I finish the stones, Finn finally arrives with Tuck trotting at his heels. Together, we stake torches and Tiressian flags around the green, but Finn is quiet, wearing a perpetual frown. I know him so well. Behind that heavy brow, his mind is tearing apart what-ifs. I also know that—while much of his concern is for me and what he fears I might do today—most of his worries are for his father's whereabouts. Whether he can admit it or not.

If I could just get a moment to myself for scrying, I could ease him. But the village green is full of people, our cottage overrun, my mother's friends darting in and out. And Finn? He's my shadow.

The sun is warm enough that most of the dew has burned away, so when all the tasks are done, we sit on the grass, shoulder to shoulder, knee to knee, staring at the noon-day sky to the west. After a while, Tuck curls against my side, and I slide my fingers through his fur, though the act doesn't hold its usual calming antidote. My thoughts about the feast hunters dissipate, replaced with enough anticipation that my heart begins a steady thumping against my ribcage.

"I love you, Raina," Finn says out of nowhere.

My thudding heart all but stops. I snap my head around, searching his boyishly handsome face. Why is he saying this to me *now*?

The second that thought hits me, I realize that I know why.

"I felt you needed to hear that before doing something rash," he says. He takes my hand and presses a tender kiss to my fingertips. "I love you, Raina Bloodgood. Forever."

At first, I'm without words. I want to be giddy, like hearing him say he loved me *used* to make me feel. I want to be moved, so much that his confession changes my mind. It doesn't, though, and I don't know what to think about that.

"I love you too," I sign and rest my head on his shoulder. Those words are true, and I need him to know they're true, but I can't look at him with this other truth no doubt shining in my eyes. The one that says our love is not enough.

It never has been.

"Do you want to know why I hate the Witch Collector and the Frost King?" he asks.

I nod. His words from this morning haven't left my mind. *I hate them too*, he'd said. *More than you believe or will ever understand.* Finn's reasons for loathing the two men are clearly different from mine. He still worships Neri, and I can't understand why. Then again, no one from Finn's family has ever been taken. He doesn't know how much it hurts or how much the need to blame all those responsible can shatter the strongest faith and harden the most devout heart.

He leans closer and lowers his voice. "Because they took *you* from me. Maybe not physically, but we can't have peace thanks to them."

I lift my head and hold his gaze. *"Then why not help me? Why not fight? Why not—"*

He folds his hand around my fingers, silencing me. "Because I would rather have *this* life, with *you*, taking my chances in a land I know, than a life out there—" he jerks his head south "—where I have no idea what dangers we might face. You think you want freedom, yet you never consider that maybe the kind of freedom you long for doesn't even exist." He tilts his head, like nothing about me makes sense. "You and I aren't capable enough with magick for the Collector to ever choose us, Raina. It takes the most talented of the vale to protect the far reaches of the northern borders. That is not us. Yet you're willing to walk away from everything. For a dream."

I yank my hands from his grasp, any moment of tenderness lost. *"You cannot know who he will choose. And you are complacent. Willing to walk away from me for the safety of a prison. Fear rules you."*

"Of course fear rules me," he snaps. "There is no love without fear, Raina. You'd understand that if you thought about anyone besides yourself and what *you* want."

His words strike me hard as a fist. We stiffen, and the inch between us becomes a chasm.

Fixing my watering eyes on the horizon again, I do my damnedest not to think of all I could lose. I'm not only doing this for me—for a *dream*. I'm doing it for Finn and Hel and Saira, and anyone sweating with dread as we bide our time.

The God Knife is strapped to my thigh, and it's so cold it burns. Tuck's warm body presses it tight to my skin, frigid as an ice stake. I like the chilly reminder that it's there. The cold focuses me. Any moment, the Witch Collector will ride over the western hills, and if I can be strong enough, if I can just out-move Finn and the Witch Collector and anyone else determined to stop me, everything will change.

For the better.

Except noon arrives and vanishes without any sign of the Witch Collector.

Finn and I sit for a long while, staring past the village outskirts to the valley beyond. Everyone else on the green stares too. A village holding its breath.

"Where can he be?" people ask. "He's never late."

"Something's wrong," others whisper. "First the hunters, now the Collector."

Even when the sun lowers in the sky, he still doesn't come. Neither do the hunters.

The halfling and human families grow tired waiting for the spectacle of Collecting Day, so they begin preparing for the harvest supper. The Witch Walkers still linger, watching the horizon with a mixture of exhaustion and hope in their eyes.

I shake out of my daze, press a kiss to Tuck's head, and get to my feet. Finn squints up at me, his face hard.

"I need some time," I tell him. *"Alone."*

He glances at his family sitting a few strides away, such worry on Helena and Betha's faces that my chest tightens.

"Me too," he replies.

I spot my mother and avoid her as I weave through the crowd and head toward the cottage. Inside, I snatch my scrying dish off the worktable and fill it with clear rainwater collected from the garden bucket. With a quick jab, I prick my fingertip using a sewing needle and squeeze a single red pearl into the liquid, focusing on the first question at hand.

"Nahmthalahsh. Where is Warek, Finn's father?"

The water will only show me the present—not the past and never the future. I must also know what I'm looking for. Exactly.

Staring at the glimmering surface, I conjure a thought of Warek. The water turns violet, then ripples like a puddle disrupted by a stone. An image forms, and I let out a deep breath. Warek sits near his horse with his back to a large boulder. He's slumped over, legs outstretched, an empty flask lying in the dirt, inches from his hand. Mother was right. Too much drink.

At least that's a worry I can forget. For now.

After changing out the water, I prick another finger and perform the simple ritual again. This time I envision the man I plan to kidnap and eventually kill.

"Nahmthalahsh. Show me the Witch Collector."

The violet swirling slows and changes, stretching out and around until the surface grows still and flat, reflecting my answer. The Witch Collector rides his dark horse through Frostwater Wood, head ever hidden beneath that black cloak. Nearing the clearing outside Hampstead Loch, he's surrounded by the day's fading light and autumn color in the trees.

With a shuddering sigh, I toss the water out the window and steel myself for the night as quiet rage sparks to life inside me. I cling to it. Thrive on it.

Because the Witch Collector is still coming.

It's only a matter of time.

ALEXUS

The Witch Walkers guarding Frostwater Wood allow me passage, reconstructing the break in the boundary the moment Mannus has all four hooves on the valley side of the forest. I considered obeying Colden's wishes about riding straight to Silver Hollow. It would be faster, and I'd avoid the coming dark that's settling over the valley in a dusky light, but I can't, even with Colden's worries about my presence in the vale tonight. I'm late, and I owe the villagers the relief of knowing that —for this day at least—they're safe from me.

When I arrive at Hampstead Loch, people scurry around the green. I lower my hood, hold up my hand, and ride through the masses.

"It's all right," I shout over their murmured voices. "I'm only here to tell you I'll take no one from your village this year."

What must be four hundred folk stand frozen, though they thaw once my intent registers. Others pop their heads out of doors, the disbelief on their faces turning to elation.

An elder approaches, pressing his heavily marked hands together in thanks. "My lord, join us for the harvest celebration. Let us feed you. Give you a place to rest."

The offer is tempting. He cannot know how much so. I'm tired from a week on Mannus's back and little rest thanks to Colden's late-night visit. One look around has me considering, but I know better.

"Much thanks, but I cannot stay," I tell him.

A little light-haired boy appears at my feet—a halfling child who's likely been taught to fear me yet is too young to understand why. Smile bright and green eyes shining, he tugs on my boot, uprooting precious memories that take over my rational thought. Before I can decide better of it, I dismount, grab the little one, and whirl him in the air as though I'm a father and he's my son. It's a foolish action. The *most* foolish.

Slowing to a stop, my smile fades. A woman stands at my side, face pale and tight with alarm. She's the boy's mother, I assume, and my presence is not a welcome sight. I hand over the child.

The villagers gawk as confusion twists their expressions, but their glimpse of the real me quickly dissolves from their minds. Thunder rolls in the distance near the loch, followed by the sudden cacophony of horses screaming.

The entire village looks westward.

At first, there's nothing but the terrible sound coming from the animals and an odd heartbeat in the air. But soon, smoke rises from the stables, the earth trembles underfoot, and fire-tipped arrows cascade in burning arcs across the bruised sky.

I blink, sure that this can't be real. There's no denying, though. Not when people begin wailing, thatch starts burning, and wardens run to save the beasts in the fired stables.

I mount Mannus and yell for the remaining elders and wardens, but they can't hear me over the frantic voices of four hundred villagers. I turn to the woman with the little boy. Their eyes are wide and terrified.

"Run!" I shout. "Get to safety!"

As the woman bolts away, I ride west, determined to meet whatever fate awaits—until a wall of Eastland warriors on horseback comes into view at the southwestern edge of the glade.

Garbed in dark bronze leathers from head to foot, a flock of cawing crows accompanies them, a shrieking cloud blotting out the sky. Some Eastlanders carry pine-knot torches while a few dozen wave crimson flags —golden wings and an ever-watching eye embroidered in the silk.

The symbol of the old king blended with that of the new prince.

Most Eastlanders carry swords, hatchets, or bows, aiming their blades and arrows with deadly precision. Leading the charge are three men and a woman whose faces I can't discern, but they ride hard and swift.

I yank Mannus around and head back toward the village. The promising rumble of hooves strikes the earth, and the eerie echo of a thousand wings beats at my back.

The reins bite into my palms as I draw back hard, pausing, uncertain. Hampstead Loch is a lone flower in a field surrounded by a swarm of bees. There's no time. No way to run or call anything to order before warriors and their summoned predators are upon us.

And just like that, they are.

A screaming shadow of crows swoops low over the village, beaks tearing at flesh and plucking at hair and eyes. Behind them ride hundreds of horsemen, spreading through the village like a plague.

For a moment, I see nothing but the flash of blades, hear nothing but screams and swords meeting flesh, remembering too well the melody of battle, the tune of war.

Mannus rears on his hind legs. Coming to my senses, I cling to the reins with one hand and fight off a crow with the other. The second my horse's hooves touch the ground again, an Eastlander rips past, vermilion war paint coating his braided gray hair. The blade of his curved knife catches my right arm and cuts through my traveling cloak. The pain is searing and shocking, but no more than the scene unfolding around me. There's blood. Death. Fire.

So much fire.

The Eastlander doubles back, his silver eyes focused. He's important—one of the four leaders. Modest armor covers his shoulders and chest, and his horse is barded, the red and gold flag of his land hanging beneath his saddle. I shake off my daze and charge toward him, cutting down any enemy I can manage along the way.

He exchanges his short blade for a sword and, when we meet, slashes it in my direction. I block his attack, but the hilt of my blade turns in my hand. Still, I land a hard blow with the flat of my sword where I know he'll feel it.

The back of his head.

He jerks forward and falls from his horse. I should dismount and kill him, but there isn't time, and he'll be trampled soon enough.

I spin Mannus around, only to come face to face with another Eastlander—a red-haired beast of a man who stares at me so pointedly that I almost feel a hint of familiarity. His sword is raised, but the blade bears no blood. Yet.

My pulse pumps in my veins. I'm certain we're about to clash, that I'll be his first attack, yet the warrior does something most unexpected.

He turns and rides away.

I start to drive my heels into Mannus's sides so I can take the man from behind, but the peoples' cries for help swallow my attention. We're so outnumbered. Villagers of all kinds fight, and Witch Walkers sing, but I fear it's too late to turn the situation in our favor.

In the chaos, the woman from earlier tries to enter the shelter of a small cottage. She shields her little boy all the while, but two Eastlanders trap them. I point Mannus in that direction.

We race through the crowds, and I slash my sword across the first warrior's neck. Blood splatters and his head topples, kicked away by a fleeing elder. The second Eastlander falls just as quickly, only because the elder finds his bravery and runs the enemy through with a blade.

Fearful that she won't accept, I reach for the woman. She hesitates a single second, then grabs hold of my forearm. I don't know what I mean to do with them, but I lift her and the boy onto my horse and nestle them in front of me. I cannot leave them in this disaster.

The elder seizes my wrist and points to the east. "My lord! You *must* warn the others. You must!"

"I'm not leaving you! It would be better to die here than to abandon the innocent."

"You are abandoning two thousand more if you do not go! Now!" He chants magick into Mannus's ear and smacks the animal's hindquarters. The stallion flees the village at a rapid pace, ignoring my commands to turn back. The elder controls Mannus now.

The wind rips angry tears from my eyes, and devastation crashes through me. Once such a comfort to me, Hampstead Loch is being destroyed to ash—its people with it—while I head toward Penrith, carrying a weeping mother and child in my arms. Have I saved them? Or only extended their execution?

As Mannus storms across the vale, I grow cold with knowing.

This is the rumored attack. This is why Colden couldn't look away from the fire.

I'm in his nightmare.

The Eastlanders *did* come, and they will not stop until they reach Winterhold.

⚜

HAMPSTEAD LOCH AND PENRITH'S WATCHTOWERS ARE EMPTY BECAUSE it's Collecting Day. I'm sure that every watchtower across the valley sits unoccupied.

When I arrive in Penrith, I send a young messenger to the other villages in warning, along with a herd of women and children, including the mother and child from Hampstead Loch. They're guided by a group of guardians to see them safely to Littledenn.

One group of Witch Walkers still patrols the forest's edge, singing magick, attempting to keep the barrier strong, but I command another group to form a protection around the village. Because of this, Penrith is prepared, though barely, when the Eastlanders breach the boundaries of their lands.

It's not enough.

The Eastlanders' arrows—and their ruinous crows—penetrate the Witch Walkers' veil of magick like it isn't even there. The people, at the sides of their wardens, must fight.

It's a valiant effort, one that cuts the enemy's numbers, and for a short time, I have faith that we might survive. But soon, I'm riding with a band of villagers toward Littledenn—Eastlanders and that flying flock of death on our heels, Penrith burning in our wake.

Mannus's strides eat the ground, and I glance over my shoulder. Dusk has fallen to full dark now, but the sky behind us glows, the horizon aflame. The Eastlanders' torches are everywhere, scattered across the valley, chasing us like a raging fire through a dry field.

Some drift north toward the wood, a thought that sends a chill down my back. The Witch Walkers manning the barrier are about to be slaughtered. Frostwater Wood will be left vulnerable.

And there's nothing I can do to stop it.

With a racing heart, fury lights my blood, and I tighten my grip on the reins. Go or stay. Colden and Winterhold? Or the innocent people of the vale?

I mutter a prayer to the Ancient Ones, hoping with every fiber of my being that Nephele and the others have done as Colden asked, and that it's enough to prevent the Eastlanders from breaching the wood. I must believe they have. I know their power and determination. I know their hearts.

And I know their magick.

Littledenn is ready when we arrive. Its children, along with those from Penrith and Hampstead Loch, have been hidden in the village's root cellar. However, my messenger from Penrith and a stray Eastlander lie dead in the middle of the village green.

I grab the hood of a passing elder. "Did you send someone to warn Silver Hollow?"

He pales as awareness strikes him all at once. "We didn't, my lord. We..." He scrubs his face, tears falling. "We were too overtaken. We had so much to do. We failed them!"

It's too late to send anyone now, because the second I look away from him, Eastlanders descend.

Littledenn's numbers are small in comparison to the other villages. Still, they hold their own, setting fire to any savage crows that dare cross their path. Highly skilled archers—perched atop cottages—shoot arrows into enemy hearts while others fight with swords, spears, and even reaping hooks. They edge up enough of an advantage that I glance eastward, Raina Bloodgood heavy on my mind.

At this rate, the people of Littledenn might annihilate the remains of this army, but I can't take the chance they won't. The Eastlanders are here to kill, though they may also take prisoners, and the possibility that a Seer could fall into enemy hands is too dangerous a thought. The Prince of the East has larger plans of destruction than this. He must. I won't make it easier for him.

I want to save everyone in Littledenn, but I can't. I *can* save the loved ones of a dear friend, a friend who has rescued me from my own darkness so many times before.

So I wrench Mannus around and head for Silver Hollow and Raina Bloodgood.

The problem is, I am not alone.

❧ 6 ❧

RAINA

The harvest moon hangs like a pearl in the night sky, and the tang of smoke floats heavy on the air. Torches crackle beneath the evening's silver glow, a circle of warmth blazing around the chilly village green.

Feasting tables are laden with summer's final blooms and boast more food than I've seen in years past. In the center of the green lies the roasting pit, which *should* be empty, but a boar hangs on the spit—thanks to the animal's poor decision to flee the western hills and head toward Silver Hollow not long after sunset.

Surrounding the pit are barrels of ale and fermented wine, men singing and making music, and a crowd of villagers losing their senses to the drink. Everyone is dressed in whatever finery they own, our traditional homespun put away this one night of the year. Some are happy, while others are sad, worried for their loved ones who never came home from the hunt.

I stroll to an empty table and sit. Earlier, when I returned to find Finn, he and his family had gone. I'd wanted to ease his worry about his father, to assure him Warek is all right, but Finn is bitter with me, and I cannot blame him. I'm leaving, and I think he knows.

The day's events have left me with a sour stomach, but the sweet scents of stone-fired bread and baked apples awaken my hunger. I break off a chunk of the loaf, dip it in the soft fruit, and savor the warm bite.

I turn when a herd of children runs behind me, laughing and playing war. One snatches a torch, and they disappear into the valley's darkness. Smiling at the children, my mother walks up and sits her wooden custard bowl beside a spray of stardrop blossoms and jasmine.

"Don't you look beautiful. I knew you'd be lovely in blue." She runs a hand over the sleeve of the dress she made me and begins braiding some of the stardrops into my hair. "There. That's perfect," she says when she's finished. "All this white is so pretty in your dark hair."

I look up at her, at her tender eyes and kind face. Am I doing the right thing?

She pinches my chin. "Do try to be happy, Raina. You look as though you carry the moon on your shoulders. There's no collection this year, and tonight we say goodbye to the light, a night of celebration and balance. Let us show the Ancient Ones our thanks for the giving season. They've blessed us."

She's wrong, but it isn't like I can tell her that.

In time to the music, she dances around the table and toward the roasting pit where she plunges a mug into a barrel of wine. Smoke from the torches and bonfire twirl around her while little glowing embers flicker and float toward the night sky.

My mother is sun and warm breezes, always comforting, and tonight, in her white gown, with her graying hair waterfalling down her back, she shines brighter than moon or flame. Her joy is a living thing. I stare in amazement as the villagers become enthralled with her laughter and merriment. She's life and light and love, and for a moment I do as she asked. I smile and allow myself a few seconds of true happiness. Because if I'm thankful for anything, it's her.

Mother's stare finds mine, and she catches my smile. She grabs a second mug, dunks an amphora into the barrel, and dances over to me.

"*There* she is." Face glowing, she fills the mug with rich, ruby liquid. "Drink, my girl."

One glance at the wine's calm surface makes me think of my scrying dish and what I *should* be doing right now—watching for the Witch Collector and Warek. When I look up, I notice Helena and the Owyn family walking with Tuck across the crowded green, and my guilt only deepens. Finn is stopped by friends, but Helena spots me and heads my way.

How gorgeous she is in her golden gown, the silken fabric draped over her statuesque frame. Her dagger is sheathed in a black and gold leather belt that I'm certain Emmitt, the tanner's son, made for Helena and Helena alone.

As she strolls toward me, an image drifts across my mind's eye, one of Helena wearing a golden crown. It's a fitting picture. If I didn't know her parents, I'd think she was half-goddess, half-warrior, born from a line of ancients.

Her face is downturned, though, her distress and concentration obvious. I should be pricking my finger every hour, asking to see her father. Instead, I'm at this celebration wearing a fancy dress with pretty paint on my lips and eyes, a dagger burning ice cold against my leg while I fill my belly. I'm an awful person, because my mouth waters with want the second the wine's scent tickles my nose, and I suck down a drink.

Helena slides onto the bench in front of me.

"Here." Mother hands Hel her mug of wine and pats her back. "You look like you need this more than I do. I'll leave you two to talk."

"Still no word about your father?" I ask once Mother has gone.

Helena downs a gulp of wine and shakes her head. "Nothing." She lowers her voice. "I'm thinking about heading south to look for him later. Before dawn. Before Mother wakes. Want to come?"

Gods. I would, and that's the only way I'd let Hel take to the Northlands' open land alone, but I don't plan on being here.

I lean forward. *"Hel, give Warek more time."*

"I *can't*, Raina." She glances around with wary eyes. "I swore that if I wasn't chosen for Winterhold this year that I would convince my father to take me to Malgros to enlist in the Watch. If something happened to him... If he doesn't return..." She sets her mug aside and frames her face with her hands. "I can't leave my mother and sisters."

My mug hits the table harder than I intend. I need two hands for this. *"The Watch? Surely you are not serious. Why are you only now mentioning this?"*

The moment the words leave my hands, it hits me that I have no right to chastise Hel for not sharing this news. As much as I don't understand it, this is her choice. One I know she's made willingly.

"I didn't mention it because I knew how you'd react." She gestures at me. "And I was right."

"The Watch is a difficult life," I sign. *"My parents lived it. You never know who or what might sail into port. It is a life of constant worry and fear."*

She shrugs. "Only if you're scared of the Eastlanders or the Summerlanders."

I widen my eyes at her. *"As anyone should be."*

"I don't expect you to understand," she says. "And it's all right that you don't. But I believe that I can find purpose in protecting my land and my people. I could learn so much in Malgros. No one will look at me and hope to keep me safe by sticking me behind a forge or in the fields or harvesting apples. More is meant for my life than Silver Hollow, Raina."

I don't doubt that, but I still don't know what to say. We spar by the stream every week, Helena giving me covert fighting lessons, and still, I had no idea she wanted any of this. I'm one of the people so protective of her, but I can sympathize. I know what it's like to want a different life. But where I want a life of peace, Helena wants a life of duty.

To a king who doesn't deserve it.

Emmitt strolls up to our table, brown eyes glittering. His smile is like a strike of lightning across his ebony skin.

"Raina." He tilts his head in greeting, then turns to Helena and extends a calloused hand. "Care to walk with me, Hel? The bonfire is warm."

Helena takes one last sip of wine and slips her hand into his. "Sure. Why not?"

They stroll toward the fire, leaving me to wallow in wine. Drenching my body with drink feels foolish but necessary. I'm weary from days of anticipation, but I also fear I might need the liquid courage for what lies ahead—especially once my eyes lock with Finn's. Dressed in a forest-green jacket, white tunic, and dark trousers, he pulls away from his friends and walks toward me like a man with a purpose.

I tilt my mug and drain it, relishing the earthy bite. After a refill to the rim, I down another.

Finn stalks around the table and captures my hand. Hair perpetually in his eyes, he tilts his head toward the green where my mother and other Witch Walkers move to the music. "Come on. Dance with me."

My every muscle tenses with irritation. It wasn't a question but a command, and I don't take well to commands. Still, I find myself following him toward the stone circle I helped Mena cast today.

Helena stands at the fire with Emmitt and a few of her friends. She looks away from them long enough to give me a small smile and arches a sharp brow when I pass. I roll my eyes and glare at the back of her brother's head.

It's just a dance.

We pause at one of the torches we set today, one whose flame is dying.

"*Fulmanesh*," Finn whispers, and the flame comes back to life.

I should've harnessed the power of fire magick. I could've simply burned my way to Winterhold.

Finn pulls me close, and after a stiff moment or two, I relax in his arms. We begin moving in the ways of our people, bodies arching and swaying in time, softly at first. But his movements become more dominant.

He turns me around, my back to his chest, reveling in the music and cool night air. Taking a stardrop from my hair, he trails the white petals over the delicate lace trim at the top of my bodice before grazing the soft flower against my sensitive skin.

"You look stunning, Raina."

My breaths come faster, and I can't fight back a shiver. He slides his hand lower, down my bodice, tucking me against him.

Something in my stomach curls like a question needing an answer— something that shouldn't be affected by Finn Owyn at all. He and I haven't been intimate in such a long time, but I recognize the sultry tone of his voice, the familiar way his fingers rub circles below my navel, the way his body molds to mine.

A chill rises when his voice rushes hot across my neck. "So beautiful," he whispers, pressing a kiss there.

I almost draw him even closer, almost urge him on, but from somewhere deep inside Frostwater Wood, a white wolf lets out an echoing howl, like a signal for the celebration to truly begin. We kick off our shoes, and our dancing becomes something more. The music changes from strumming strings to softly pounding drums, and the revelry gives way to ceremony.

Helena, Emmitt, and several other Witch Walkers join in. The shift in every mind reverberates through me, instinct taking over, our bodies flowing in a circle around the fire. For the first time in so long, I feel free.

I close my eyes and will my dance to keep time with the drums, with the internal heartbeat of the earth as I sway and spin, reaching toward the stars to call down the moon. Finn glides against me. I'd be lying if I said the contact didn't make my heart race, my blood heat.

But here, beneath the moon, with the pounding rhythm of life beating in my veins, the world falls away, any thought of the Witch Collector along with it. Through ritual, we witches are connected, conduits between the Ancient Ones whose power radiates through the soil into the bare soles of our feet and the deities in the heavens who shine down upon us. For a time, that's all I feel. There's no Finn. No desire. No anxiety. No cold.

Nothing. Just connection.

It doesn't last, though. From beyond my consciousness, worry drips a tingle down my spine, luring me back to the here and now. A smell floats on the wind—familiar and cloying.

Blinking at the stars, I dance harder, trying to reconnect, refusing to let anything poison this moment. It'll all end soon enough, and I may never experience this again.

On the edge of my vision, Helena kisses Emmitt and leads him toward the darkness to the east. The pair disappear into the shadows, hand in hand.

Live. The word forms in my mind, but I send it across the village to my friend. Maybe one of us will find the kind of peace that stays tonight.

Finally, reality dims once more, until I'm so close to deep connection that I see nothing but a kaleidoscope of colors and light, feel nothing but power and Finn's touch and a strange warmth radiating down my outer thigh.

Finn's hands are everywhere, but then he's discreetly gathering and lifting my skirts between us, his fingertips tickling the back of my thigh, drifting—

The connection snaps, the heat vanishes, and Finn lets go. For a moment, it's like I'm falling, coming down from a high I'd forgotten existed.

Then I sense it—the absence. The source of the heat I'd felt is gone.

I spin around, only to find Finn Owyn slipping into the crowd.

With my knife.

He glances over his shoulder. A smirk curls one side of his mouth as he flashes the white granite hilt of the blade now hidden in his jacket pocket.

Come and get it, he mouths. Then he runs toward the orchards, vanishing in a mass of villagers.

I ball my hands into fists. Damn that man. This is *not* a time for teasing or games. According to what I saw in the water and given the time it takes to ride from village to village, I expect the Witch Collector to arrive within the hour. I *must* get that knife.

I head in Finn's direction, but in a single breath, everything changes. Over the drumbeats and howling guffaws, a strange sound shatters the night.

I stop. Listen.

The sound mingles with the revelry and ceremony chanting but soon builds into a clamor that brings everyone—even the musicians and dancing folk—to a standstill.

Heart hammering, I shove my hair away from my sweat-dampened face and turn my gaze on the night sky to the west. My hands grow clammy with a cold fear that clings to my skin like the mist rolling in around our feet. I know that sound, those voices.

The children from earlier—the ones playing war.

They're wailing.

Little screaming figures burst from the darkness at the edge of the village, red faces tear-stained and carved with panic, hands waving as if to swat us away.

Every person on the green stumbles around, stunned and confused, whether by ale and wine or from calling down the moon. Still, many parents gather their wherewithal and lunge toward their crying children. Everyone is focused on the little ones, on their nonsensical words, but I glance back to the darkness. This time, I pay attention to the scent saturating the air.

Death.

Something moves in the shadows outside the village. Beyond, along the horizon, shines what looks like giant fireflies in the deep bend of the valley. Mother stands on the other side of the fire pit. She bristles with energy, her skin glistening in the moonlight. I force every ounce of emotion I can onto my face and motion west.

"Elders! Wardens!" she screams. The tendons in her throat strain with effort, but the people tasked with guarding our village sit at a table wearing lost expressions.

"Look! There!" A little girl points past the farrier's cottage.

A horse, dark as night, charges into the light, hooves pounding the ground so hard that clumps of grass and earth fly up behind him. Villagers scramble out of the way. It's as if the horse means to storm right through the green.

But the horse has a rider—a rider who jerks the reins and brings the looming animal to a halt.

A rider hidden beneath a black cloak.

The Witch Collector whips the beast around. "Get your feeble and young to the orchard!" His voice is so deep and commanding that every drunken villager sobers, including me. "Wardens, gather your horses and weapons and all the torches you can find! Witch Walkers, prepare your magick! Fill every bucket and pitcher with water from the troughs! Dowse the thatch!" From his side, he frees a sword that carries the stain of blood and aims the blade toward the fiery amber moons growing to the west. "Eastlanders are coming! And they're going to set this village alight! Hurry!"

Parents scoop up their babes, and wardens finally run to find their blades and beasts. Elders and Witch Walkers chant the opening refrains of protective songs, all while rushing to the troughs to fill buckets. Families scatter into the night, some heading for the orchard and vineyards while others stumble around bewildered.

Mother rushes toward me and takes me by my arms. "We have to help! Let's get to the well!"

We start across the green, but I look over my shoulder. Panic crawls down my throat and grips my heart as I scan the sea of faces for Finn, but I don't see him. I need that damned knife. I also need *him*. I need to know he's safe, but there's such disorder, such confusion.

Gods, I should've watched the waters. I should've stayed true. I could've seen. Could've stopped this.

I can't go to the well. I must stand and fight.

Mother stares at me in confusion when I jerk her to a halt. I glance around, searching not for a bucket but for anything to use as a weapon. There's nothing save for musical instruments, drinking vessels, and too many dishes of food. I know where to find what I need, though.

Something sharp. Something deadly.

With that thought, I grab my mother's hands, too scared to let her far from my sight, and run barefoot toward our cottage.

7

RAINA

I storm through the back door and rush across the garth to the small outbuilding where we keep our harvest tools. Heart pounding, I snatch my scythe from its mount and spin around to find Mother gaping.

"No." She holds up her hands as if that alone will stop me. "You are not a warrior, Raina."

She's right. I'm not a warrior. I'm a witch, and not a very good one on most counts, but I'm not helpless. All my life, at least until he died, Father taught me to use a scythe in nearby meadows. And though no one knows, Helena has taught me so much in the last year. Hel *is* a warrior, if anyone cared to pay attention to the blacksmith's daughter. Her lessons alone have made me skilled enough that I don't fear facing a sword if I must.

Resting the scythe in the crook of my arm, I bring my hands together. *"I can swing a blade,"* I sign. *"An extra weapon could mean saving our home. I cannot stand by while you sing magick and hope it is not met with greater magick."*

I think of the stories Father used to tell me, the lessons about the world beyond the vale. Of all the kingdoms, the one I least want to fight is the Eastland Territories. The Summerlanders, brutal as they are, fight for life and land, but the Eastlanders fight from a place of greed, a place of sheer privilege and perceived domination. Their sovereign, the Prince of the East, is more like a mythical figure than a true leader. Father always assured me he exists, a man who somehow steals life and magick from others to grant himself immortality and power his own dark desires.

A man made of shadows, souls, and sin.

The Eastland armies have never invaded the Northlands, though, and I can't imagine why the prince would deploy them here now.

Hurt flashes across Mother's face. She opens her mouth to protest, but hoofbeats resonate, accompanied by war cries. We race through the cottage where she snatches one of her kitchen knives, and we hurry to the green, which has descended into disorder.

Turning in a circle, I search every terrified face one more time and let out a familiar whistle. It's a little bird call that Finn taught me so I could summon him from a short distance. But he doesn't rush to my side. He's nowhere to be found.

Surely he and Hel did the same as me. Surely, with all their weapons, they'll stand against what's coming. I just pray they stay safe.

Mena leads a chorus of voices, chanting a curtain of magick around our village, even while those same singing Witch Walkers haul water from the troughs. Mother tucks her knife into her corded belt, grabs a pail, and joins the crowd in their song. Sadly, the protective construction struggles to rise, a silvery veil lifted by distressed witches.

A western wind slips over the failing construct. I bury my nose in my elbow, nearly gagging from the eye-watering stench of death. It reeks like a thousand fading souls.

Gods. Am I smelling death from other villages?

I stare at the many flickering flames coming nearer and nearer, a strange pulse beating in the air, bringing a sense of doom I've never known.

Then I see him—the Witch Collector. He rides right past me, his uncovered head turned the other way.

One glance at him and all the hurt, pain, and fear inside me twists into rage and loathing. Armies don't attack innocent people for no reason. The Frost King had to have done something to cause this. More loss I can lay at his feet.

The Witch Collector turns his stallion this way and that, scouring the village like he's searching for someone. He shouts at a man who shrugs and shakes his head before running away. He yells at another man running past, but there's too much noise to hear them.

A thought flutters through my mind. I flex my fingers around the scythe and stiffen my spine. We're so close, the Witch Collector and me. Only a few feet between us.

And he's distracted. I could kill him now, a blow from behind. Rid the world of his dreadful presence.

With my jaw clenched tight, I take a step closer. Another. And another.

A girl points at me, and my last step comes up short. The Witch Collector twists in his saddle and meets my gaze.

I swear the air between us becomes electric.

Heart stuttering, I freeze as his attention drifts to my scythe. He spears me with a piercing look and tilts his dark head. Those green eyes narrow, shining under the blazing torches and bonfire light. I've never seen his face. His head is always shielded behind the hood of his cloak. Even if I could have, I've always been too afraid to look him in the eye.

Helena was wrong. He's so much younger than I imagined, less than a decade older than me. He wears a short, neat beard, and his face is all dangerous edges and sharp lines. He's handsome in a wicked, dark way. Beautiful, even. He must've been younger than me when he took Nephele.

The moment stretches between us—whisper-thin, taut, and unbearable. His stare is so penetrating that it's like he's peering into my soul, prying through the cobwebby corners I show no one. I blink and remind myself that he's the enemy and that he's *right here*, within my reach. One swipe to his neck is all that death requires. He'd never take from us again.

Reality washes over me. The king will replace him, and if we live through this night, I will have murdered my only way to find Nephele. More than that, the Witch Collector is trained, a warrior with a weapon, and thus very likely our best defense.

Survival must come first. Revenge later.

Resigned to fight at his side, at least for now, I form the sign of peace against my chest. He can't know what it means, but he nods like he understands.

I take a step back and lay the scythe at my feet. Turning toward the western hills, I close my eyes in prayer and lift my hands to sing, forming every lyric, careful to make no mistakes.

The Witch Walkers' voices raise, loud as they can manage. I focus on Mena's words which radiate the clearest, until I feel the wall of magick rising over us.

My movements slow, my fingers relax, and I open my eyes. A dome of protection hovers above, glittering beneath the moonlight. In that heartbeat of time, I feel safe, believing that we can keep the Eastlanders from entering Silver Hollow with just our song.

But the first flaming arrow soon arcs across the sky and pierces the veil. Then the next, and the next, until hundreds of balls of fire fill the night.

The black sky shifts, as though darkness can come alive. From within that darkness, a swarm of crows descends, followed by arrows stabbing into the cottages' summer-dried thatching, setting our village ablaze like a pile of parched kindling. With them comes a horde of Eastlander's on horseback, carrying death in their eyes.

8

ALEXUS

I should take Raina. Take her and run.

I glance beyond the demented birds raining down on the village to where the enemy's hoofbeats pound loud and sure and where the first fires catch hold and flare. It's a single moment of indecision, but when I turn back, Raina's gone.

"Damn the gods!" I jerk Mannus around and swing my sword at crows, looking for her. That long hair and blue dress. Those sapphire eyes. It's like she vanished.

I face west where the Eastlanders charge straight for us, the darkness that lives inside me swelling like a storm. I long to let a fraction seep out, let it settle over me—a second skin. Magickal armor. Such a thing is impossible, though, and even if it weren't, it's been so long since I've tasted that power.

I might kill everyone.

Instead, I draw my sword, the ring of metal sending a rush through my blood. The man in me will have to be enough.

Eastlanders blow through Silver Hollow like a flaming wind, too numerous and fast on their mighty horses for the wardens who never made it to the stables. I slice my weapon across one Eastlander's middle, spilling his innards, then plunge my blade into another's mouth before yanking back to land a fatal hit across the throat of one more.

All around, villagers fight on foot, struggling to hold off the crows and Eastlanders at the same time. Witch Walkers run and fight and chant all the while, but it's no use. The Eastlanders' arrows, cast with a magick strong enough to penetrate the veil, strike many and kill them in a manner I'd been too panicked to notice at the other villages. I tell myself it couldn't have happened there. Surely I would've seen such terror.

Beside me, a man falls to his knees. A fiery arrow sits lodged deep inside his abdomen. Flames billow unnaturally from his mouth and eyes, melting skin and sinew from bone—burning him alive from the inside out. Crows gather and pick at his flesh before his body explodes into dust like he'd been made of ash.

Fire magick—the devastating kind only ancient Summerlanders like Fia Drumera know. It's happening everywhere, one after another, villagers shot down and incinerated. Even the children who didn't manage to leave are not spared.

"Watch out!" A young man holds a wooden platter in front of me, catching a fired arrow before it penetrates my chest. A small girl clings to his leg as she sobs with fright. Weaving around them both is a small dog, barking and yipping in fear. The young man glares at me. "You don't deserve to live, you big son of a bitch. But I'm giving you a chance for redemption. Now, you owe me."

I narrow my eyes at the brave little bastard. I've seen him and the girl before—the blacksmith's kids.

The boy tosses the platter aside. With one protective hand clutching his sister, he swipes a dagger at an approaching Eastlander with the other. He misses and drops his blade.

A colorful curse leaves his lips, and fear twists his face as the Eastlander lunges.

I slice a diagonal, cutting the warrior in half before it's too late. With a stunned look fixed on his face, the Eastlander's body slides apart, the two pieces falling to the ground.

The little girl screams a painful shriek that splits the night. The smithy jerks her into his arms, hiding her face in the crook of his neck. He looks up at me, eyes wide and wet, chin jutting out, his fine moss-colored tunic and dark britches painted with the dead man's blood.

"*Now* we're even," I grit out between clenched teeth.

I don't know what it is about this kid, but I can't decide if I'm impressed by his bravery or if I can't stand him.

"We'll *never* be even." His dark face hardens, and he's shaking, from fear or anger—I can't tell which. He glances around, desperation in his eyes, then exhales a trembling breath and adds, "I tried. I did. But I must get my family to safety."

Those desperate words are meant to persuade himself to leave, and I can't imagine why he's even still here, so I jerk my head toward the hills. "Go south or west. It'll be easier."

He'll find ruin either way, depending on how the Eastlanders got here in the first place. But his death is waiting in Silver Hollow, not back at Littledenn, Penrith, or Hampstead Loch—not even in the valley or near the southern mountains. I sent all those other villagers east earlier, to the orchards, a mistake made in the heat of the moment. Now a band of killers —led by the gray-haired general I fought back in Hampstead Loch—rides in that direction, on the hunt for fresh blood.

They'll find it, thanks to me.

The boy runs with the little girl and his dog. The three of them disappear through a cloud of smoke and cawing crows. Throughout the village, fire races from thatched roof to thatched roof, chasing along any piece of wood it touches.

In the ashy haze that too soon settles over the green, I see Raina again. It's impossible to turn away. In all the years that I've looked upon her face, I've only ever witnessed nervousness. Dread. Fear. Even repulsion, and maybe hatred.

Like tonight.

Tonight, she'd stared at me like she could kill me. Brutally.

But I've never seen her cloaked in pure rage. It rolls off her, hot and bright as the fires around us, lighting her up like a virago. A fury among men.

An upward swing of her blade catches an Eastlander in the chin, his end gruesome. She spins, and her next strike lands in the bend of a warrior's neck. In *her* hand, a farmer's scythe is deadly as any sword, her movements so swift and precise that I'm momentarily mesmerized, even in the midst of such devastation.

I'm brought out of my admiration by a flash of silver through the air. I twist to miss an Eastlander's sword, but not before it slices deep into the meat of my wounded arm.

Pain fuels my anger, and though the weight of my weapon makes it feel like I'm holding the world on the ends of my fingertips, I swing the tip upward and jab, piercing the Eastlander's throat where I'm certain it will end him.

I withdraw, and he slides from his horse, lifeless, like the sack of bones he is.

My sword arm falls limp. The wounds burn and throb as blood streams to my fingertips. Mannus wanders around the green's rim, confused by the thickening smoke and cries for help. The number of crows and Eastlanders has thinned, but villagers are still fighting, and so many lie dead or dying, burned or burning.

And I no longer see Raina.

A few feet away, an enormous Eastlander struggles to rise out of a daze. He fixes his eyes on me. With a groan, I draw my injured arm up and sheathe my blade before retrieving my dagger from my boot. I don't know how I'll win this fight if he heads in my direction.

I glance toward the stone wall to the east where more Eastlanders ride, followed by a flock of deadly crows. Could that be where Raina's gone? To help the helpless? If she's anything like Nephele described, that's something she would do.

With my good hand, I yank the reins and turn Mannus toward the east, but the sight of Raina and Nephele's mother standing in the middle of the ceremony circle, surrounded by a translucent smoke cloud, stops me. I recognize her silvery gray hair and lovely face. She's the older version of Raina, though I see Nephele in her features too. The power emanating from her body is the one thing I *don't* recognize.

Her lips move with earnestness as she sings magick, her hands and eyes lifted in prayer. Dead birds drop at her feet, and the raging fires engulfing nearby cottages dim. The flying sparks fade, the smoke clears, and a rain cloud rumbles overhead.

Gods' teeth. *She's* doing that. Her alone.

In all my years, I've never sensed such power in this woman, Just like I never sensed it in Raina, and only once in Nephele—the year I chose her. Now I think I understand why.

Ophelia Bloodgood did the impossible. She hid her family's power.

An Eastlander stalks toward her, teeth bared and dagger raised, and at her back, another assassin appears. He forms from a plume of red smoke, a smiling wraith stepping from a scarlet shadow, testing the heft of a spear in his hand. Darkness swirls around him, and a crow sits on his right shoulder.

I know those shadows, and I know him. We met once, after King Regner died. He seemed so innocent at the time. I never dreamed I'd see his face in this valley, let alone with murder burning bright in his eyes. He's the man who rose from nothing and nowhere and no one to become the leader of an entire continent.

The man who broke his word.

The man with no real name.

The Prince of the East.

9

RAINA

The Eastlander crushing my throat in her elbow is as strong as a bear, but I'm slippery and quick. I spin and bring a knee to her gut, and she staggers back enough that I'm able to break free of her hold.

I stand crouched, arms wide, in front of Mena. She sits huddled behind me, chanting in the smoke-filled corner of her cottage. Powerful as she is, her magick is too weak for any weaving now.

She's bleeding. From where, I don't know. I didn't have time to look. I only knew I had to help her when I saw this behemoth Eastlander woman shove her inside her cottage. That same woman blocks the open doorway —and the path to my scythe.

She picks up my blade, and with a snarl, lunges at me. In the same second, she freezes, face blank. It takes a moment to understand why.

The woman crumples to her knees and collapses face-first on the slatted floor. Blood flows from a puncture wound to the back of her blonde head. Behind her stands Helena, bloody sword still raised, on guard.

Lowering her weapon, Hel steps over the Eastlander and throws her arm around my neck, her words coming out in a rush. "I was so scared I wouldn't find you! Meet Finn and me at the fallow fields! I have to find my mother and the twins!"

And just like that, she's gone, a flutter of blood-stained golden silk flying out the door.

I turn to Mena and kneel before her, uncertain what to do.

"Leave me." She lifts a hand from a gash in her stomach. "My time is here."

But it doesn't have to be. There's so much death in the air that I can't tell if hers is as close as she believes or not.

Not caring if she learns my truth, I begin signing my song. *"Loria, Loria, una wil shonia, tu vannum vortra, tu nomweh ilia vo drenith wen grenah."*

These are the words for healing, for when death hasn't crossed too near. I start to repeat the lyrics, but she grabs the fingers of my right hand.

A faint smile tilts her lips. "I *knew* there was more to you. But I won't let you waste your energy on me." She jerks her chin toward the door. "Go. Find your precious mother. Get to the fields."

I ignore her and try again.

"Loria, Loria, una wil shonia, tu vannum—"

"Go, Raina!" she yells. "Your mother needs you more than me. Go!"

Something in the tone of her voice penetrates. I don't want to leave her here to burn, but I can't carry her, and she won't let me heal her. If I drag her out, someone will surely kill her.

She shakes her head. "Do you not remember what I told you? There is no victory without sacrifice. I'm ready. Now go."

"I will come back for you," I tell her. *"I swear."*

And I will, as soon as I'm sure Mother is safe.

Determined to be fast, I storm out of Mena's cottage and battle my way toward the green. With every clash of blades and every slash of my scythe, I'm reminded that my life might end any minute. Though I owe as much to every single person in Silver Hollow, death cannot come for me yet. I cannot allow it.

Like the weapon in my hands, I become hammered and honed, my movements severe as I slay with blow after blow. The fires—are they dying? And is that thunder? Rain could snuff the remaining blazes and give us a chance.

The sight of my mother snags my gaze. She stands in the middle of the stone circle, still singing her magick. I move to go to her, but every muscle in my body seizes when an Eastlander appears in the corner of my vision, stalking through the smoke on the western side of the green. His long strides are calculated and sure.

I glance at the dagger clasped in his grip and connect his line of intent.

Fury courses through my veins.

Gathering my skirts, I run, calling on the power of the moon still flowing within me, and climb a feasting table in two leaps. The third leap takes me off the other side, and with a downward swing of my scythe, I land a blow that sends the Eastlander's head rolling into the embers of the roasting pit.

Mother hasn't moved, her gaze still cast to the sky, and relief hits me like a crashing wave.

I saved her.

In the next heartbeat, a spear juts through her stomach from behind.

Time stops.

I can't move.

Can't breathe.

Her eyes meet mine, and she clutches the spear. An expression of confusion twists her beautiful features.

"No," is all she says as blood pours from her wound, staining the white gown we stitched together last summer. I read the single word on her lips, just before those lovely eyes of hers, with such bright light, go dark.

Disbelief tears through me, hot and raw. When Mother slumps to the ground, the scent of her coming death carries across the space between us, and a flood of deepest sorrow fills me. My mother's death smells like her. Cloves and fallen leaves and smoky coldness, tangled with the memory of sun and warm breezes.

The killer presses his booted foot to her back and pushes her off his weapon as though she means nothing.

Then he sets his sights on me.

I did this. *Me*. I could've saved her. Gotten her out. Gotten *everyone* out. All those little children. Finn. Helena. Betha. Saira. The twins. Tuck. Emmitt. Mr. Foley. Mena.

I want to tear my hair out, pound my fists against the earth, beat the pain from my heart. Oh *gods*, why did I not look at the waters? Why didn't I keep my eyes on the Witch Collector all day?

The Eastlander stalks toward me, spear in hand and a crow perched on his shoulder. With a flick of his wrist, the bird flies away. Blood splatter decorates his leathers. The blood of my people, of my mother, and if he has his way, of me.

I blink, clearing away the tears from my eyes and the shock from my mind. There's something unsettlingly different about this warrior. Wisps of crimson shadow writhe around him like they're trying to get away, growing redder and redder as he nears. His short hair lies swept back, neatly in place, making it noticeable when his face and eyes redden too. Even his hands hold orbs of blood-colored shadows, like malevolence leaks from his every pore. The whole of him becomes such a sinister thing to behold that I'm certain he is evil incarnate.

I retreat and falter over my skirts, my scythe dragging the ground. The cottage fires catch hold again, so fast and devouring, and the storm cloud disintegrates. I no longer thrum with the moon's power or hope or even infernal rage. Instead, I'm numb with guilt and grief.

In that sliver of time, I don't care if I live. All around me lie the dead and dying. Warriors raid the orchard and vineyards. I hear the pounding of their horses' hooves, the fading screams of those hiding in the grove, see the billowing smoke of fires to the east, even while my village—*my home*—burns to nothing.

The Witch Collector rides on the fringes of the green, fighting like a devil. He is but one man, though, and he's wounded, right arm dangling as he struggles to hold off a giant Eastlander with a dagger.

Did this happen to the other villages? Is that why the Witch Collector was late? Did all the valley's people endure this brutality? In my gut, I know they did.

I drop to my knees, swallowed by the magnitude of loss and devastation. And death. In the swiftness of an arrow's flight, this valley was erased.

The mysterious Eastlander approaches. I want to tell him that killing me will haunt him, that he will see my face in his nightmares, but a disturbing glimmer sparkles in his eyes and he smiles, rolling the spear in his hand.

"What's your name?" He tilts his head, studying me with a curious stare.

Something clenches inside me, some instinct that screams at me to get up and fight. But it's too late. He's so close, close enough that I spit at him.

He laughs. "Fiery little thing, aren't you? Pardon the play on words. I couldn't resist."

What a despicable creature. He isn't the kind of man who will be haunted by *any* of the lives he's taken.

"Pity to kill such a fighter," he adds. "But, much as I'd like to see you in chains, you'd only be a distraction."

A shiver chases across my skin as he takes his aim and rears his arm back. I inhale a deep breath and glance beyond him, needing one last moment with my mother. Her face is a blank mask, her eyes empty of life, but...

Her face and neck and hands are covered in witch's marks, glowing with soft light, like nothing I've ever seen, especially on my mother. I must be imagining things...

But...no. The marks are there, and her dead stare is fixed on me. And her mouth... It's *moving*. Her effort is weak and waning, but she's chanting magick.

If even a faint whisper of life remains, I can bring her back to the light.

Just as the Eastlander thrusts his spear toward my heart, I summon enough strength to swing my scythe one last time and blunt the death-end of his weapon. The dulled tip strikes my breastbone like a siege engine pounding a castle door, knocking me across the green.

The wind leaves my lungs until I manage a stinging gasp of smoky air that forces me to double over and cough around the shocking pain.

Through the amber and gray haze filling the night, I see the Witch Collector. He stands between my attacker and me, back turned, his sword sheathed. His right arm hangs limply at his side, but he holds a dagger in his left hand.

"I won't let you have her!" He maneuvers his blade in a swift, wide arc.

The Eastlander jerks back and dodges the attack. "Hello to you too." He laughs, and this time it's an awful sound—low and deep but shadowed by faint high-pitched shrieks, like demons live inside him. He tosses what remains of his spear aside. "And I don't *want* her," he says. "Not really. I want to *kill* her. Very different things."

The Witch Collector moves closer, blade ready, but in a flurry of that black cloak, he's facing me. The Eastlander holds him ensnared around the neck, the Witch Collector's dagger in his hand.

The Eastlander grins like a sick bastard. "Now what? I get to kill you too, old friend? It's been so very long."

A perplexed look passes over the Witch Collector's face. "We are *not* friends." He grits out the words, jaw clenching.

"Right you are. Which means I don't have to be nice. Let the fun begin."

The Witch Collector stares at me with eyes so green they shine through the caliginous night. "Run!" he yells, and the warrior plunges the blade into his side. Once, twice, with a twist between the ribs.

Crying out, the Witch Collector slumps to the ground—just like my mother—and again, the Eastlander comes for me. This time there's no sick, playful gleam in his eyes. Only wrath and determination.

I force myself to my feet and dart around him, barely missing the swinging edge of his stolen dagger. The Witch Collector is kneeling, resting the dying weight of his body on one hand. His gaze is still on me, bewildered as I charge him and rip his sword free from his baldric. The weapon is lighter and sleeker than I imagined, so I rage forward and drive the blade toward the Eastlander's chest. I hope I gore his heart.

Wearing that evil smile, he explodes into a gust of crimson smoke.

I run right through him, or what *was* him.

Stumbling, I fall to my knees, the sword's hilt bruising my palm when I land. A strange feeling comes over me. A release, like some unnatural pressure—one that feels like it's been with me always—lets go. A surge of power rushes through me, heavy and consuming and altogether foreign.

My hands. They look like my mother's. Covered in witch's marks that I've never had before. I blink, gasping, sure that I'm dreaming. That I've dreamed *all* of this.

But also because, right there in the grass, right within my reach, lies the God Knife, like Finn left it here for me on purpose.

A presence at my back makes the hair at the nape of my neck rise.

"Miss me?" The Eastlander's words flit across my ear.

I grab the God Knife and flip over, slashing, praying I catch any part of him on the end of this blade. Blood sprays from the gash opening across his face, from his left temple to his right jawline, right through his lips. He all but howls, the sound an unholy thing.

"My lord!" someone cries.

The man straddling me only holds up his hand to silence them. "Go!" he screams.

I don't know what I expect of the God Knife's damage. This killer already morphed into smoke before my eyes, but I half imagine he might rupture like the villagers he and his men killed with whatever evil magick on which they thrive.

Wait. *My lord. He and his men.* He's a leader. But...gods. This is no normal Eastlander. Not a commander. Not even one of their sorcerers.

I've just destroyed the face of their prince. Maybe even killed him if the God Knife is as deadly as Father claimed.

It *has* to be.

The prince presses his hand to his bleeding cheek, holding his face together at the seam. Dark eyes lit with violence, he glances at the God Knife, the blade slick with his blood. Everything about him changes, the deep red of his entire being blackening.

He reaches for the knife, but my grip is relentless. He grabs my wrist and slams my hand to the ground, but I don't budge, keeping a death grip on the hilt.

With one last wicked roar, he lowers his heinous face an inch from mine. Blood drips from his gaping lips onto my chin, into my mouth.

"We'll meet again, Keeper," he mutters. "And when we do, I'm going to drive that knife into your heart and inhale your pathetic little soul."

He won't if he's dead.

I thrust the blade toward his heart, but again he transforms into curling tendrils of darkness and fades away.

I lie there, blinking at the sooty sky. Shock rolls through me wave after wave. The God Knife is so oddly warm, all but humming in my hand.

Was that the God Knife's power just now? Erasing the Prince of the East from existence? Or was it just him vanishing? Will he die from the wound to his face? How can I know?

It hurts to sit up, but I make myself. There's not an Eastlander in sight anymore. I slip the knife into my belt and struggle to my feet, stumbling past the Witch Collector to my mother's side where I fall to my knees. Her lips no longer move, but those marks...

I have to help her.

Eyes burning from the looming smoke, I plead to the Ancient Ones

—*"Loria, Loria, anim alsh tu brethah, vanya tu limm volz, sumayah, anim omio dena wil rheisah"*—casting the song of life into the night like so many prayers, calling upon the moon from which I descend, willing my magick to repair the damage done to her gentle soul, all to breathe life back into her witch's blood.

I can feel the power inside me, feel it growing.

"Loria, Loria, anim alsh tu brethah, vanya tu limm volz, sumayah, anim omio dena wil rheisah." I envision my beautiful mother living, laughing, dancing, and I try so hard to weave the glimmering strands of her precious life back together again. *"Loria! Loria! Anim alsh tu brethah! Vanya tu limm volz! Sumayah! Anim omio dena wil rheisah!"*

She never stirs.

I sit there, stunned and in anguish. There's no sound but the crack and creak of burning wood and the hiss and whipping roar of fire spreading from stead to stead. I sweep a tear-filled glance across the village.

No one moves. Not anywhere. Not even in the fiery shadows. If Mena or anyone else remained in the cottages, they've been burned to nothing now.

With agony gripping my heart, I force myself to stand and run into the night. The smoke is so thick that I can't see the moon, much less the stone wall on the outskirts of the village.

But I could find my way to Finn's shop blindfolded.

It's burning, like everything else. The temple. The tannery. The orchards and vineyards. There are so many dead, and the whole world is on fire.

Struggling to breathe, I cover my mouth with my sleeve and scour the area for any sign of life. Any sign of Finn or his family or even sweet Tuck.

I run toward Finn's home, trying to whistle, praying he might hear my call, only to see three bodies lying near the door, burned and blackened.

I stumble back, tears streaming down my cheeks. Two of the bodies are so small.

Betha and the twins.

After a terrible groan, the house crashes in on itself. A family, a history, people I loved—gone.

But then I remember.

Helena. Finn. The fallow fields.

I turn and bolt in that direction, but when I reach the clearing, there's nothing save for empty land and a blanket of smoke. I don't know how long I stand there—staring, waiting—but eventually, I head back to the village, so very numb. My chest aches, hollowed out, a cavern where my heart used to be. I can't think around the pain of knowing that death by flame is how Finn and Helena likely met their end as well. Gods, I would've killed them myself to spare such torture. I would've done anything.

But I didn't do enough, did I?

Exhausted and choking on smoke and tears, I return to Mother's side. There's no one left. Just me. This was probably the Prince of the East's plan when he didn't kill me, to punish me with the fate of emptiness and utter aloneness. To take *everything* from me but my breath.

Someone touches my shoulder. I jerk around, God Knife raised, prepared to be cut down like everyone else.

The Witch Collector's valley-green eyes meet mine. He's on his knees, holding his bleeding side. He opens his mouth to speak but collapses before any utterance leaves his lips.

After a moment, I crawl nearer and press my blade to his throat, its edge ready to slice through skin and bone—exactly what Finn prepared it for. I'm so angry, so devoured by the pain in my heart. Gods, I want to blame him.

The Witch Collector lifts his chin, staring at me in a way that causes guilt to swirl in my gut. I can't stop crying, and I loathe that he's seeing me this way—consumed with grief. I've lived in terror of the Witch Collector my whole life, and now I have the chance to kill him. Yet under the glow of this terrible firelight, I see not a man to be feared or destroyed, but just...a man.

Struggling to breathe, his every breath gurgles in his throat. He looks to the black sky, but his gaze finds mine again, and he asks the unthinkable.

"Sing me alive." He glances toward my mother. "I saw you. Heard you. I know you can. D-don't...let me die here. We can't...let them...win. Sing me alive."

He watches me, a helpless plea hidden inside the fine lines fanning from the corners of his eyes. He's the last person I should save, but he still carries the breath of life, and I'm surrounded by death, and I just want someone else to be with me when the sun rises.

But this isn't someone else.

He's the Witch Collector.

And so, with a heart that feels hard as stone, I stand and turn to go.

10

ALEXUS

For a heartbeat, I'm certain Raina Bloodgood might help me. It's a false hope, because a moment later, she rises and turns to leave.

She's not only a Seer. She's a Resurrectionist.

And she's going to let me die.

At least the last thing I will ever lay my eyes upon in this long life is a powerful woman of both beauty and fury. A soul delicate yet wild and so deeply moving—even if she does wish me dead.

In the last few years when I've visited Silver Hollow on Collecting Day, I've been incapable of preventing my gaze from lingering on her face, though she has never so much as lifted her chin to look me in the eye. I can't blame her. In another life, I would've tried to know her. I would've admired her and read her poems written by my own hand. I would've walked with her through fields of stardrops, danced with her in the stream.

This is not another life.

She turns back and casts a long look over her shoulder. I watch her, standing in her bloody, soot-stained dress, the wind tearing stardrops from her long hair, white petals drifting through the smoke like snowflakes.

If I could speak, I'd tell her I came here to help her. To help us all. I'd tell her that I'm not evil. That I'm not entirely good, but I never meant to bring her sorrow. I'd tell her I'm terrified of what my death means, and that

I'm worried about leaving her alone, because she doesn't realize how alone she might truly be or what evil is yet to come.

I would tell her to go to Littledenn. To see if all those women and children in the root cellar survived. I'd tell her to get them out of the vale, though where they might go I cannot fathom.

I fear war is coming, the likes of which Northlanders have never seen. The Prince of the East has indeed walked inside the Shadow World. He also has power he should not have, a living amalgam of all the things people claim: shadows, souls, and sin.

In truth, my death will weaken the Eastlanders' chances of success at conquering the Summerlands, and I tell myself that I'm ready to sacrifice all.

But it's what I'll leave behind that Tiressia must fear. I am salvation and damnation. There cannot be one without the other.

Something in Raina's eyes shifts from dark to light. She returns to me and kneels in the grass, ash falling all around. Conflict swirls in her irises, but as the last breaths of life slip from my body, she lifts her slender hands, and with the most graceful movements I've ever seen, begins to sing.

11

RAINA

The first time I rouse, I see nothing but a smoke-filled sky, and it hurts to breathe. I'm lying next to a body that folds around mine, warm and comforting, and for a heartbeat, I think it's my mother. But a little death thrums against my chest, nestled away in a deep corner of my heart. It isn't hers, and that thought brings overwhelming sadness that sweeps me back to darkness. At least the stolen death feels like it's exactly where it belongs.

Inside me.

A deep voice meets my ears. "Come, little beauty," it whispers, and I'm dimly aware of being carried away, the crumbling cinders of my village fading from sight.

THE SECOND TIME I OPEN MY EYES, A LONG, BLACK CLOAK SWEEPS OVER me like a blanket. The world no longer burns, and I think I'm in the vale, the pale light of morning breaking through the clouds. I'm atop a horse, strong arms cradling me while holding fast to the reins. I hear the *chink chink clink* of a bridle, the soft thud of hooves, and I notice an unmistakable sway rocking me back to sleep.

Before I succumb, I look at the bearded face of the man who holds me, and he meets my stare. My head rests on his shoulder, his mouth so close that the warmth of his breath drifts over my lips.

"It's all right. Rest."

My heart pounds, something inside me screaming *Get away,* while another part of me wants to be closer. I shouldn't be with him, but I am, and I'm too tired to question where we're going. My eyes close—I've no command over them—and I drift, curling against the Witch Collector's heat.

⚜

THE SOFT MURMUR OF THE STREAM FLOWING ALONG THE OUTSKIRTS OF our valley wakes me the third time. I lie on a bed of crushed, tall grass beneath the canopy of a great oak tree. Its leaves flutter and rustle overhead. I'm folded in a dark cloak that smells like spices and sandalwood, and maybe juniper and the sheep fat used to protect material from rain. The fabric also carries the scent of smoke and a thousand deaths, a scent that rattles my brain awake.

I bolt upright and flinch, bracing my breastbone with my hand. My chest aches like a god pounded it with their fist.

Wary, I take in my surroundings. A warhorse—black as a moonless night—drinks from the stream that moves on lazily as ever, as though the rest of the world has no notion of the devastation that transpired in the night.

And at the water's edge squats the Witch Collector.

His jet hair—damp and untied—hangs down his back in waves. He wears fitted leather britches, cracked with age, and a loose linen tunic marked by ragged tears and faded bloodstains at the side and sleeve. He's a contradiction—that's the thought fluttering through my mind. A towering, intimidating Collector—hard, unstoppable, and unyielding. Yet here in the valley, he kneels, wide shoulders soft, hair lifted just so by a breeze. That dark head bows in reverence, and in his hand rests a bundle of plucked stardrops.

I think of the way Finn touched me with the flower Mother braided in my hair and lift my hand to feel for them. They're gone.

One by one, the Witch Collector casts petals into the unhurried current where hundreds of blossoms float away to the river.

"A stardrop for every soul," he says, whispering the words like a prayer.

It isn't lost on me that he's performing a ritual of *my* people. In Silver Hollow, Littledenn, Penrith, and Hampstead Loch, it's customary to say a prayer to the Ancient Ones for the newly dead and provide a simple offering of the valley's most beloved bloom.

He turns to look at me, and a charge sparks the air between us again. Though I wish it weren't so, a shiver dances across my skin. I want to dismiss it as disgust, but that would be a lie.

It's his eyes. Something about them makes me want to look closer, like I might see a whole universe if I peer hard enough. But it's just the color. I didn't think it could be any bolder, any more penetrating. Yet here in the vale, with daylight rising, his eyes shine like emeralds.

"How do you feel?" His voice is soft and kind, not like it sounded when he shouted his warning through the village.

I don't know how to answer. I feel like I'm floating in a dream. Any second, someone will shake me awake. It will be the morning after Collecting Day, and my shattered world will piece itself back together again. But my throat is raw and dry from soot, and my blue gown is now the color of a stormy sky with brown splotches covering the skirt and bodice.

And my hands...

They're trembling, and they're caked in ash and old blood. Blood that belongs to the warriors I killed. Blood that belongs to my mother. Blood that belongs to a vile prince.

The Witch Collector exchanges the stardrops for a half-scorched wooden bowl filled with stream water and reaches me in three long strides.

I quake harder. Mother used to say that grief always strikes when we least expect it, and that we rarely realize how those we love inhabit even the most seemingly inconsequential parts of our lives. It's in those moments that the pain of their absence strikes so much deeper, because the time we took for granted suddenly shines in sharp relief.

Like right now—as I stare at Mother's dish.

The Witch Collector sets the vessel in the grass and unsheathes a knife from his boot. He cuts a strip of his tunic from the hem, returns the knife to its hiding place, and with a dip in the clear water, washes my face with a tender touch.

"*Shhh*. There now, don't weep. It's over. You're safe." His voice is still so warm, so gentle. It's the kind of voice a woman could find solace in, a voice that could conquer even the strongest will.

I should pull away from him—from his touch, his aid, his nearness— but my tears flow fiercely, uncontrollably, and the shaking...

I killed so many people.

The Witch Collector strokes my hair away from my face and stares deep into my eyes, anchoring me. "Come to the water. We can clean your hands."

With an arm tucked around my waist, he helps me to the stream where we kneel next to his abandoned flowers. Already clean, his skin smells crisp and earthy. He must've bathed while I slept.

"You exhausted yourself with magick," he tells me, scrubbing my hands in the lapping waves. "It requires much strength to save a life from the brink of death. I woke at dawn, and you lay collapsed beside me."

Of all the people to learn my secret, it had to be him. This seemingly kind-natured man my mind can't even comprehend is here—alive—much less because of *my* doing.

Those green, soul-searching eyes flick up and hold my gaze. "Thank you for what you did. I owe you my life." He turns back to the stream, still gently washing my hands, but the blood and soot don't seem to leave.

In a daze, I pull away from the water and stare at my skin. Silver swirls etched with hints of crimson, violet, and gold vine along the backs of my hands, from wrist to fingertips. The sleeves of my dress are tight, but I push them up, as much as I can, only to find more intricate detail. Startled, I sit back and yank up my skirts. My legs are covered too.

Witch's marks—that I've never had before. Vaguely, I recall noticing them when the Prince of the East came after me. Gold for life magick, red for healing magick, silver for common magick—like the protective magick we build at the wood's boundary. The violet must be for Sight.

All I can do is stare, disbelieving.

"It was your mother," the Witch Collector says. "She was far more powerful than anyone knew. She hid your marks, as well as her own, but..." He pauses, and compassion fills his eyes as he takes my cold hand, folding it inside his warmer one. "When she passed, the magick fell apart, and your marks became visible. I watched them appear on the green, Raina."

My body is so heavy and my mind so sluggish, like my thinking needs to catch up to the moment. Nothing he said makes sense. He called my entire life a lie, my mother the master of deception, and me a fool.

But also...

I yank my hands away. The Witch Collector knows family names, but even those must be difficult to recall. The Owyns. The Bloodgoods. The Foleys. There are hundreds of surnames across the vale. But first names? Of a woman forever overlooked?

"How do you know my name?" I mimic the words with my mouth as best I can and force the question into an expression as I touch my throat and lips, shaking my head, making sure he understands that I cannot speak.

Did he hear my mother call to me?

He *must* have.

He studies my face before doing the strangest thing: He moves his hands and fingers in the way Mother taught me.

"I have known your name for many years," he signs.

I scramble to my feet and stumble backward several steps, finally steadying myself against the oak tree. The Witch Collector rises as well, hands lifted in placation.

"It's all right," he says and switches back to speaking with his hands. *"You have no reason to trust me. You may even hate me. But please do not run. There is nowhere to go anymore."*

My spine goes rigid, and a long moment passes before I can make my hands work. *"How...how do you know this language?"*

The answer creeps into my mind before he replies. He's collected dozens of Witch Walkers from our valley over the years, but there's only one who could've taught him how to speak with me so adeptly. Still, I watch fervently as his right hand spells the word.

N-E-P-H-E-L-E.

My thoughts rage, as does the rest of me. The word *liar* screams in my mind. I charge him, shove at his chest. And though it feels like I've run into a wall and I'm still so weak, he falters. In that slice of time, I spot his discarded baldric and sword. It's too far away, so I lunge for the knife sheathed in his boot instead.

He twists out of my reach, and when I begin whaling on him, clawing, he grabs my wrists and drives me back to the oak tree.

Pinning my arms against the low, thick branches, he presses the weight of his heavy body against mine—chest to chest, hip to hip, thigh to thigh. I wriggle to get free but quickly decide better of that idea. We're breathing so hard. The friction between us is unbearable and unwanted, so I jerk my head forward and headbutt him. He yanks back, but I catch his mouth with my forehead before he can get away.

Bottom lip bleeding, he eyes me like I'm some kind of savage. Perhaps I am, in this moment at least.

"You need to calm down," he grits out, pressing his forehead to mine, holding even that part of me at bay. "I am *not* your enemy. Not anymore. If you want answers, I suggest you stop trying to kill me and let me explain."

Pressing against me once more, he jerks, a movement meant to punctuate his words. It only makes me far too aware of the body touching mine. His hot breath on my lips, those long, strong legs standing firm, that thick chest rising and falling against my own, and his rough, powerful hands holding tight.

Neither of us moves for what feels like an eternity as an unwelcome and unexpected heat coils between us. He tightens his grip, though the action doesn't elicit pain. I unfurl my fingers, steady my breathing, and let the tension in my muscles relax, softening against him—all signs of relenting.

Because if I've ever needed anything, I need him to let go.

Now.

Finally, he draws his head back and peers at me, his big body still trapping mine. My surrender registers in his eyes.

He turns his head and spits blood on the ground. "No kicking, no hitting, no biting, no attacking. We talk. That's it. All right?"

When I nod, he releases me and steps back a few paces. Eying me, he wipes his mouth on his sleeve, looking a bit rattled. Maybe he needed distance too.

For too many long moments, he studies me again. This time, his gaze traces my every line. Slowly. Eventually, he looks away, drags his fingers through his long hair, and sighs.

Why am I staring at him? Noting his every move?

I rub my wrists where his touch still lingers and push away from the tree on shaky legs. I'm just exhausted and bitter and grieving, my mind and body spent from what I've been through and from saving his godsdamned life. That's all. I'm not thinking clearly.

"Thank you for not behaving like a feral animal," he snaps, groaning when he touches his thumb to his wounded lip. He switches to speaking with his hands. *"Ask your questions. I am sure you have many."*

Gods, he has no idea. Questions form so fast I have to fist my fingers in my dress while my mind sifts through which one to ask first. An exhale shudders out of me.

"Why would Nephele teach you my language?" I shape each word with force.

"Because she is my friend," he signs. *"Hard as that might be for you to believe."*

Friend? My sister is *friends* with this man? This man—this *Witch Collector*—the likes of whom we've dreaded the whole of our lives? More impossibility.

"Nephele taught me years ago, a way to pass time," he signs, moving his hands with flawless precision. *"And because she missed you. She made me swear I would never choose her sister on Collecting Day. Your mother needed at least one of her daughters to care for her with your father gone. I promised that Raina Bloodgood would never leave Silver Hollow. Not by my hand."*

His words are a shock to my entire being. I've never been chosen—not due to my lack of skill and witch's marks—but because my mother shielded me and my sister asked the Witch Collector to spare me. I can't wrap my mind around any of it. The thought that Mother knew what I was capable of and that my sister could ask the Witch Collector for my protection and have her wish granted seems so very wrong.

"I should have known," I sign, pounding out judgment with my hands, every jolt making my sore chest ache. *"On top of all the awful things I have come to know you to be, you are also a liar."*

The menacing way he stares at me in warning and the way his entire body stiffens almost makes me flinch. But I hold fast.

"Be sure, I am many things." The veins in his temples and forearms stand out in relief with every sharp word. *"But I am no liar."*

I motion to the valley around us. *"Yet here we are. So much for your promises."*

It's a weak accusation. He could've ignored his agreement with my sister and left me in the ruins of my village, alone. My anger needs release, though, and he's my only target right now.

"Yes." He scoffs. "Here we are." Another infinite moment passes, his glare a hard, sharp thing. "I owe it to your sister to get you to Winterhold without harm," he continues. "But, as I said, I am no liar, and we are running out of bloody time, so I must be honest with you about what we face. A sennight past, word reached Winterhold that the Prince of the East planned to break King Regner's treaty with the Northlands. To be certain the news was correct, we needed a certain kind of magick. The kind only you possess. You were to be my choice for Collecting Day because your sister claims you have the true gift of Sight. But I was too late."

He looks toward the west where blue sky fades into cloudy gray as the dying embers of Littledenn, Penrith, and Hampstead Loch release their final breaths.

I press my fingers to my temple. Too many thoughts swirl inside my mind. For one, I pray that I sent the Eastland prince to the Shadow World —for good—so he can harm no one else in whatever evil quest has possessed him. I hope that bastard is reduced to no more than a shadow wraith, lurking through the deepest, darkest pits of the Nether Reaches.

But secondly, the part I can't make my brain process is that Nephele *sent* the Witch Collector for me. Told him my secret. Even if she overestimated me, she still revealed something we swore to never tell—to our greatest enemy no less.

She left the village a short time after I learned I could see things through scrying. It had been a game, a joke, until the waters spoke to me. We didn't truly understand such magick then, and I didn't learn the rules for some time. She's been gone for eight years, but has she changed so much that she would sell her sister's soul to the king?

I glare at the Witch Collector. *"She would never do such a thing."*

But clearly she did, even if Sight isn't so easily wielded as she made it seem.

The Witch Collector takes a long step in my direction. His torn linen tunic billows in the breeze, revealing a thick, corded arm and the flexing muscles covering his ribs where terrible stab wounds should exist. Instead, I glimpse perfect, lightly bronzed skin—thanks to me.

"With your gift," he says, "we could've foreseen an attack. Maybe we could've found a way to stop the Eastlander army before they became a threat. Maybe we might've saved everyone in the vale. Nephele knew that and knew she had to tell us what you were capable of. She was only doing what anyone who loves their homeland would do. She was trying to protect it. Do not fault her."

My flaring temper cools and chills into a ball of ice as his words settle deep. The Eastlanders didn't come to the vale to kill villagers and leave. It was never about us at all. We were only in the way. A deterrent to remove. A threat to silence.

"They want to reach Winterhold," I sign. *"Why?"*

The muscles in the Witch Collector's jaw tense, and his eyes turn hard as river-worn stones. "They want the Frost King. They are on their way to capture him now. They breached the forest last night."

Unsure which rising emotion to hold onto, I glance toward Frostwater Wood in the distance. In truth, I don't care about the Frost King's safety. But my sister, and all those Witch Walkers...they're the strongest of the vale. Will their voices be enough against the Eastlanders? Or will they be cut down for protecting an unworthy king?

"There were so many," the Witch Collector continues. "They obliterated Hampstead Loch. The elders and wardens at Penrith cut the Eastlanders' numbers, but the enemy had only been reduced by half when they reached Silver Hollow. And not because they all fell to the blade. At Littledenn, the army divided further when most of their number took off into the wood. Those Witch Walkers manning the boundary were slaughtered."

Again, I glance toward the forest and back to the Witch Collector. My pulse races and my palms dampen.

I take an angry step toward him. *"Why are we here, then? We have to help them. The Eastlanders are so far ahead of us."*

A twinge of dizziness sets the world to spinning.

We.

I can't believe the Witch Collector and I are on the same side. A day ago, I planned his end. Envisioned it. Tasted the sweetness of revenge and wondered if I was brave enough to take the life of a man who threatened all I hold dear. Now I stand here with the deaths of dozens painting my hands, speaking with one of the three people I hate most in this world, forced to be his ally because we share a common goal.

At least I think we do.

I blink to steady my dizzy head and move to step past him. He blocks me, his green eyes shimmering in the dappled sunlight filtering through the leaves. He's so tall and broad, casting me in his shadow.

Instinct sends my hand to my thigh, reaching for the knife I haven't thought of until now. The God Knife isn't there, and its absence hits me so strongly. I can't recall when I held it last.

Images flip from one to another in my mind's eye. They're hazy, like my brain is blurring them from memory. I glance back at the cloak on the ground. Maybe it's there.

"Listen to me," the Witch Collector says, and I face him. His eyes dart toward my hand, which is still pressed against my empty side. "Nephele and the others protected themselves and Winterhold," he continues. "They were to enchant the boundaries around the king's land so that if anyone infiltrated those lines, a difficult journey was ensured. Those Eastlanders might have traveled through the wood undeterred for a short time, but at some point, they will meet with magick the likes of which they have never seen, and they will regret ever coming here."

I cock my head and arch a brow. *"You do not imagine Eastlanders can unravel Witch Walker magick? A trap? Silver Hollow's magick was no match for them. They wiped us away like no more than an annoyance."*

I have to hope that, at the very least, the Eastlanders are now without their leader. I *did* cut him with the God Knife.

"The Witch Walkers of Silver Hollow had but minutes to sing," he replies. "There was no time to walk magick around the village to strengthen it. I'm certain that Nephele and the others have been singing and weaving vast magick since last night at sundown. I do not doubt the king's witches. I know their skill."

Vast magick? That knowledge should soothe me, but it doesn't. It's one thing for elders waiting near the barrier to unweave a small portion of magick so the Witch Collector can pass and then put it back together again. It's another for witches to control their magick from miles away. Vast magick is an arcane form of power. I've never seen it. There's never been anyone in the vale skilled enough to teach it. Such ideas are legend— the stories of witches projecting their magick and will across space and time.

I don't know how practiced the witches at Winterhold have become, obviously enough that they've learned inscrutable forms of magickal ability, but if the lore is true, vast magick has limitations. The sheer magnitude and number of required voices limits control. Even beyond that concern, something Father used to say remains: *With the right hands, most any magick can be undone.*

"*I am not as talented as my sister,*" I confess, "*but I have never heard of vast magick being selective. If the forest offers harrowing passage, then we will face the magick in the wood as well.*"

He wants to take me to Winterhold, and I want to go, but what will we endure to get there? The Eastlanders are skilled as well, but at least there's a good chance they no longer have the Prince of the East on their side. Something tells me he possessed the sort of magick we all should've probably feared more than we did.

With his hands resting on narrow hips, the Witch Collector leans close. "I will let no harm come to you, Raina. The wood will let us pass. The Witch Walkers' magick knows me, especially Nephele's." His face darkens, and a gloomy shadow drifts across his pupils. "I can't say it will be easy or fast, but a way will make itself clear. Your sister is more capable than you give her credit for."

Irritation roils inside me. The Witch Collector has a bond with my sister, the kind of bond I once had, but that has since faded.

Because she was *stolen* from me.

Shoving my loathing down deep, I focus on Nephele and the need to save the only family I have left. My head feels fuzzy, made of clouds, but I push past him, not sure what I plan to do—steal his beast and flee into an enchanted wood?

I don't make it far. His stallion seems a million miles away, and the world tilts, right as my knees buckle mid-step.

The Witch Collector folds his arms around my waist and turns me to face him, holding me flush against his body. The movement makes me more lightheaded, and instinctively, I grab hold of his tunic.

He stares down at me and glances at my mouth, the knot in his throat moving on a hard swallow. When he speaks, his voice falls from his lips with softer edges. "I'm afraid we aren't going anywhere until you can craft magick again. We can't get inside Frostwater Wood without it."

Eyelids heavy, I shake my head, not understanding, and manage the words, *"Why not?"*

"I tried to enter the wood after we left the village. The Eastlanders threaded a wall along the perimeter. There's no following unless you can summon enough power to break through their construction." The pressure of his hand at the small of my back makes me cringe and heat up at the same time. "Somehow," he continues, "I don't believe you're up for the task yet, much as you would probably like to disagree."

He lowers me onto his cloak, hovering above me. I don't know why I notice, but his lips—even though the bottom one now bears a swollen cut —are a perfect, scarlet bow nestled inside his short, dark beard.

"You need to recover," he says. "We'll ride once you're able and pray to the gods we're not too late."

I want to argue, because I need to get to my sister. Now. Instead, I let go of his tunic as the world around me dims. I struggle to cling to awareness, only to be pressed down by impossible darkness.

Nephele is my last thought as consciousness gets carried away by an unstoppable tide.

12

RAINA

The next morning, I pace the water's edge, awaiting the Witch Collector's return. The memory is unclear, but I recall him kneeling beside me, loose, dark hair framing his face. Behind him, the sky had been bruised with the first rays of morning light. He said something about going to Littledenn for food and clothes and that he would come back soon, but I was still too heavily in sleep's grasp for his words to stay.

Wrapped in his cloak, I hunt for the God Knife in the grass with no success, then watch the sun rise as thin mist rolls over the vale. I've been to this stream many times, stared over the land as hearth smoke rose from chimneys to the west. For too long, I gaze at the horizon, hoping those gray curls and wisps will rise once more. When the sky lightens, the only smoke in the distance is what remains of the Eastlanders' fires.

Tired of so many reminders of the attack, I remove Finn's dagger belt from my thigh, trying not to think about his last moments alive, and wade into the stream at the deepest spot behind two boulders. I'm anxious, wanting to leave, yet I'm trapped here—waiting when there is no time to wait.

The water is cold, but it washes the scent of fire and death from my dress and hair well enough. As I bathe, I marvel at the new marks coloring my skin. All this time, Mother was protecting me, hiding what I am from everyone. I understand, but I wish I'd been able to share my magick with her, to learn about my abilities without the threat of being chosen hanging over us like a dark cloud.

With one last dip under the water, I finally feel awake, my thoughts clearer, my sorrow and denial fading. In their place resides only determination. If I plan on finding Nephele, there's magick to breach, so I need to focus.

If only I could remember what I did with the God Knife. I recall slashing it through the Prince of the East's face, and I remember him vanishing as I held the weapon in my hand. But after that, all I see is death and fire and...the Witch Collector.

When I finish bathing, I wring out my hair and clothes, wishing it was warmer out. Too soon, my restlessness returns, so I take my mother's wooden bowl and dip it in the stream. If the Eastlanders are trapped in the wood, and I pray to the Ancient Ones they are, perhaps we can circumvent them and reach Winterhold first—*if* the Witch Walkers' vast magick lets us pass.

A thorn pricks my fingertip nicely, and once my blood swirls in the water, I center my every thought on the Eastlanders' whereabouts.

"Nahmthalahsh. Show me the Eastlanders from last night."

A faint scene forms on the water's violet surface, a band of men riding on a narrow road through what looks like the dark of night in a forest. Wariness wafts off them. They look confused or lost, and I sense magick—strong magick.

I tilt the bowl, and the image remains. At least I don't see the Prince of the East, and his warriors aren't invading a castle or fortress—*yet*. That alone eases me.

I clean the bowl and prepare the water again. *"Nahmthalahsh. Show me the God Knife."*

Though I can't see the black blade, I can make out the white hilt. The knife is surrounded by darkness, making it hard to discern. Did it end up in the fire? Can god bone burn? Is it buried in Silver Hollow's ashes? How will I ever find it if it's in Silver Hollow's ruins?

Frustrated, I toss the water and stare at the bowl. I could look for Finn and Helena, but the thought terrifies me. I know what I'll see—piles of ash or something far worse—and I feel too raw. I cannot endure the images of their suffering imprinted on my memory. Instead, I decide to look for the prince. He wasn't in that band of Eastlanders, but I need to know if the God Knife worked, if it's even worth searching for. I'd so believed that it was.

A third time, I fill the bowl and bleed into the water. *"Nahmthalahsh. Show me the Prince of the East."*

The water swirls longer than usual, and the violet-tinted clearness becomes nebulous. Shadows and smoke roll over the bowl's edge like a bleeding mist. I lean closer, pulse racing.

Surely I'll see a dead man.

His face forms and stares back at me with wide, unblinking eyes. I can't tell if he's alive and watching me from the other side of the waters or dead somewhere, staring into nothingness. The sight of his open wound makes me shudder, and again I toss the water, watching as the smoky mist floats across the grass and melts away.

Dead, I tell myself. The God Knife's power is real.

I'm standing beneath the great oak wringing out my skirts again when the Witch Collector returns, riding at a quick pace. Though he's leading a strong-looking white mare behind his glossy, black stallion, something in me dies when he approaches. His face is pale and expression bleak, his broad shoulders not so high and strong anymore.

Earlier, while I watched the sun rise, I let go of any faith he might return with survivors, but I can see that he went to Littledenn with a double-edged shard of hope in his heart.

He dismounts, and I help him lead the animals to the stream.

"Mannus, eat." He smooths a comforting hand down the horse's side and clicks his tongue. The beast's ears prick back, listening, and the animal does as told, chomping on clumps of grass.

The Witch Collector says nothing to me, though. I'm a little unnerved by his silence and the fact that he hasn't looked at me since he arrived.

I set to inspecting the even-tempered mare he's brought me so we can leave. Stroking her head, I decide her name is Tuck. I spell the word against her shoulder, needing to hold on to something from my life before this disaster. She lifts her muzzle from the stream and presses her nose against my thigh, almost as if in recognition. I pat her back, confident she'll provide a safe journey.

The Witch Collector leans his sword against the great oak and kneels in the grass. With quick hands, he unloads clothes and boots from a bundled blanket crammed with rope, an iron-framed oil lamp with amber glass on the sides, a small tinder box, a couple of skins of water, a flask (probably of something stout enough to down a boar), a tin mug, several apples, and a loaf of stale bread. It makes me think of the pack I hid beneath my bed.

At random, he grabs a tunic and holds it between us. Finally, he looks up, and his eyes lock with mine.

A moment later, his gaze skims down my body like a touch. "You're wet. And calm."

He says it like I'm some sort of freakish creature.

"I bathed," I reply, damp hair drying in a cool breeze. *"And I consulted the waters."*

His gaze catches on Mother's dish, and he lowers the tunic. "Did you see anything?"

I nod. *"The Eastlanders had not reached the castle. Yet. They were traveling. A dark road. Lost. Worried. Confused. Magick surrounded them. Powerful magick."*

"And the prince?"

Hesitating, I consider telling him about the God Knife and that I'm fairly certain I killed the prince. But what would he do if he knew such a thing as the God Knife exists? That with one slice, he and his immortal lord could be destroyed? Even with the dim chance that the blade isn't as powerful as Father said, the Frost King wouldn't risk having such a weapon out there somewhere, ready for the taking. There'd be more than one of us trying to figure out how to find it, and so I keep that information to myself.

"Lost as the rest of them," I lie.

Hands pressed to his thighs, the Witch Collector relaxes, like a yoke has fallen from his neck. "At least the forest is guarded, and we haven't run out of time," he says. "That means everything."

He isn't wrong. The image of the Eastlanders is the only thing keeping me composed.

Clearing his throat, he gestures with the tunic. "For you. I couldn't find any armor your back can bear. There's a quilted gambeson here, though. Bit large, but still better than a dress."

"*I fight fine in a dress.*"

A small smile curves one corner of his mouth. "That you do. I cannot argue. But a tunic and britches will make riding easier."

I press my hand to my bruised chest. The boning Mother sewed into the bodice provides support. The summer-linen tunic is thin and loose. Too thin and loose for a woman to wear while jaunting across the valley and through a forest. As for the gambeson—it looks made for a giant. It would swallow the Witch Collector, let alone me. Still, the softer armor will provide modest protection from a blade and arrows if it comes to that.

But I can't ride in such garb.

The Witch Collector seems to understand my thoughts. His cheeks flush, and a strange kind of tender innocence fills his eyes.

"Oh. Right." He drops the tunic, sits back on his haunches, and studies my gown.

After a moment, he snatches a pair of leathers from the pile—much like his own though smaller and less worn—likely belonging to a boy who hoped to one day break them in. Another thought that makes my heart hurt, yet also stokes my fury.

With a toss, the Witch Collector says, "Slip these on and come here. I have an idea."

He looks away, and I hurry into the bottoms. I wear britches when working in the fields and orchards or when training with Helena. This pair is snug and a little long but otherwise perfect.

With my dress covering the leathers, I approach him, feeling awkward as he faces me and looks up, still on his knees. He pulls a knife from the sheath fashioned inside his boot and begins cutting a line up the middle of my skirts. It's tedious work. The layers of wool and linen are thick and waterlogged, despite my earlier efforts.

Again, I think of the God Knife. The Prince of the East vanished while it was in my hand, and when I got up to go to Mother, no one was around, save for the Witch Collector, but he was dying. Had I even carried it with me then? Gods, I need my memory to clear.

I study the Witch Collector's body. His wide, wing-like back stretches the fabric of his tunic, tapering to a narrow waist. The material clings to him, not only because he fills the garment so completely, but also because a cool breeze plasters the linen to his skin. His long legs are folded under him, his leathers hugging every muscle and curve like a second skin. I don't see anywhere he could hide another knife, perhaps save for his other boot. There's certainly no hidden belt beneath that shirt.

Did I even have the God Knife around him? My mind's last image of the weapon is the blade clenched in my hand, the bone dripping with the prince's blood as he promised to one day kill me.

The Witch Collector sets his knife aside in the grass and stares at me, resting his hands on his knees. He's made it halfway up my skirts.

"I'm trying to be gentle-mannered," he says, "but sometimes a rough hand is best."

I take a deep breath. *"Do what you must, Witch Collector."*

Tears sting the backs of my eyes, and I swallow the tightness forming in my throat. My mother made this dress for the harvest supper. She worked so hard harvesting the woad and extracting the dye. Other than her wooden dish, it's all I have left of her.

The Witch Collector takes hold of the fabric on each side of the cut, and with a grunt, rips the layers clean to the bottom of the bodice. Stumbling under his strength, I grab his shoulders, and he grips the backs of my thighs to steady me.

Our eyes meet, and he studies my face, no doubt seeing my sadness. Again, I find myself too aware of him, of the taut muscles rounding his shoulders beneath my palms, the firm feel of his fingers clutching my legs, of how comforting it is to be close to another person.

Even him.

We release one another like we touched something hot, pulling back as much as possible. The Witch Collector takes up his knife again and begins separating my skirts from the bodice.

"Turn around?" he asks, and I obey.

My traitorous heart flutters when he slides his fingertips along the bare skin above my britches.

When he's finished, I'm fashioned in a way I think can't be improved, but then he rises, picks up a pair of boots and hosen which he drops at my bare feet, and moves to stand behind me. Still a little on edge around him, I glance back as he pushes my hair over my shoulder.

His calloused fingertips graze my collarbone, sending a rogue chill along my arms as he begins loosening my laces.

"So you can breathe better," he says, and I have to look away.

My breasts fall, and my lungs and ribs expand on a blissful inhale. At my back, however, he leans close. When he speaks, his warm breath grazes the curve of my neck, and it's all I can do not to shiver.

"My name is Alexus. Alexus Thibault. *Not* Witch Collector." He comes to face me and says it again, this time with his hands.

Cheeks burning, I sign his name too. The feel of it is as odd on my fingertips as it would be on my tongue.

After giving me the tiniest appreciative smile, he turns, leaving me standing there, drenched in foreign and overwhelming sensations I need to ignore. Because moons and stars, I don't trust him. Not in the least. But I'm beginning to think I could, and that's the most unfathomable notion I've ever imagined.

While he gathers our things, loads the pack on his horse, and hangs the oil lamp from the saddle, I slip on the too-small boots and socks and strap the gambeson on the mare. I hand the Witch—no, *Alexus*—his cloak, which he accepts, but he whips the garment around *my* shoulders instead of his own.

"It suits you. As does this." He retrieves Finn's dagger belt and produces a fire-singed blade he must've taken from Littledenn. "You're good with a scythe. Hopefully, you're good with a small blade too."

Good enough to slice open the Prince of the East's face, an act I suppose Alexus couldn't have seen from his vantage point during the attack.

"Why do they want the king?" The thought blurts from my hands before I accept the belt and weapon and strap them to my thigh.

He stares down at me, black hair catching in the wind. "Long story. Just know that the Eastlanders need him, so if they manage to get their hands on him, they won't take his life. Not yet. But there's an excellent chance we'll regret letting them succeed."

I want to tell him that my last concern is the Frost King. That he could melt into a puddle, and I would feel nothing but satisfaction. I'm only curious why the Eastlanders want the king *now* when all has been silent here for so long.

"We could always use your gift with the waters before we go." He extends the bowl between us. "To determine where the king is."

I take a deep breath, dreading my next words. Another glimmer of hope shines in Alexus's eyes, and I'm about to dash it to pieces.

"I fear I cannot help. Not in that way."

His brow twists. "Explain."

I shake out my tired fingers. *"I cannot see whatever I choose. I must form an image in my mind, and I only see things as they are happening. Like Nephele. I did not become skilled at scrying until a year after she was taken. I mastered the art, but the image of her no longer matched the woman she had become. I could not see her."*

He flinches at that, and in truth, so do I. It all makes sense now that I've said it. Nephele really *has* changed, and it happened so soon after leaving Silver Hollow.

It makes me despise the Frost King even more.

"I have never laid eyes on that cold bastard you call a king," I add. *"I do not know what to look for when it comes to him. The most I can do is watch for East-landers and hope I see the right group."* I'm rambling, and my words have clearly shaken his faith, so I lower my hands.

Alexus scrubs his face, half-smothering a groan. "All right. Let's do that, then. One last look before we go."

I take the dish and refill it at the stream's edge, squatting low. This time, I use my new dagger to pierce my finger.

My blood runs into the water and, once again, the forest at night appears. The faint glow from a snowy wood outlines the silhouettes of tree limbs and horses and men. I can sense the Eastlanders' distress, feel their racing hearts.

Alexus stands over my shoulder, clearly curious.

"I cannot see their faces, but at least one band of warriors is still in the wood," I tell him. *"Cold and worried about never getting out."*

He stares down at me. "You can tell what they're feeling?"

"Sometimes." I shrug, empty the dish, and stand.

"Is that...normal for you? Reading people's emotions?"

I raise a brow. *"Why? Worried?"*

Alexus opens his mouth to speak but shakes his head instead, as though clearly thinking better of whatever words tempted his tongue. He bends to help me mount the mare.

After he climbs astride his horse, we sit facing the foreboding tree line in the distance. I look at him, still stunned that we're here, together. The weight of all the things neither of us can seem to say hums between us.

"To the forest, then," I sign.

He nods once, eyes gleaming with new and eye-opening clarity. "Yes. To the forest."

II

INTO THE WOOD

13

RAINA

Save for their magick-cast arrows, I've never seen Eastlander witchcraft. In truth, I've never seen witchcraft of this magnitude at all.

We're a half-mile away on Borier Hill, overlooking a foggy Littledenn, staring at a complex tangle of trees and thorny branches stretching east to west for miles. Frostwater Wood spans the valley's length, from the base of the snowy mountains near Hampstead Loch to the glade below the rugged eastern range that can be found a short journey from Silver Hollow. The entirety of the wood now lies hedged by this barbed, malevolent barricade.

Though similar to the valley's Witch Walkers' construction, this wall is different because it is tangible. Our barrier was a force we had to maintain day in and day out, a repelling boundary that made passage impossible.

This one is real, something created from nothing—unless the Eastlanders used the forest in some form of magickal alchemy. Such a thing isn't impossible. It's just not something I've ever been able to do.

There's also no one left behind to prevent the construct from crumbling to a pile of sticks and briars, unless there are dozens of Eastlanders on the other side of the blockade—another possibility, though unlikely. There weren't enough Eastlanders remaining last night for that task, which makes this level of craft even more terrifying. Someone must be maintaining this magick.

I swallow hard and look to the sky. A dark cloud moves above us, the sun bathing us in gentle midday heat as it burns away the crawling mist.

Alexus squints. "This is a sorcerer's doing. A powerful sorcerer. Or perhaps more than one."

It can't be the Prince of the East. I keep telling myself that the God Knife ended him.

It had to.

"Can you break through such a monstrosity?" Alexus asks. "You can conquer death, see through time, and feel people's emotions from miles away. Perhaps this won't be the task I fear."

I curl my fingers around words unspoken. Saving him was the grandest magick I've ever worked. I've saved a doe, Tuck the dog, a bird, and a few other small creatures, and I've performed a few minuscule healings, but stealing death for a person? Last night, thanks to desperation, I'd held enough faith that I could save Mother and Alexus, but there was never any guarantee.

"We shall see," is my reply.

A half-hour later, we ride along the forest's thorny fringe, headed toward Littledenn. We pass so many fallen Witch Walkers that I stop, wanting to bury the dead, or at least build a pyre piled with bodies and ashes and pray to Loria for their souls.

Alexus slows his horse and gives me a long look, a hint of sadness lining his brow. "I'm sorry. It goes against all that I am to leave them here, but there isn't enough time."

I know there isn't time, but my heart still breaks all over again, a crevice forming in my soul that might never heal.

Alexus dismounts anyway and retrieves a trampled flag that lies rumpled and dirty on the ground. Neri's flag—ice blue and snow white, with a white wolf stitched in silver thread. He hands it to me, an offering, a piece of my home he thinks I might wish to keep. To cherish.

I accept, but I take the dagger he gave me and stab it into the fabric, tearing the blade from one end to the other, over and over, until the material is nothing but shreds, and the rising pain inside me has abated.

A lone tear escapes down my cheek, but Alexus is watching, so I ignore it. Instead of wiping it away, I toss the flag to the ground and sign to him.

"I hate Neri."

He plants his hands on his hips and raises his dark brows. "I see that."

Concern flashes across his face, and something more as well, but he turns away and mounts his horse before I can place it. I'm sure he finds me sacrilegious, but I don't care.

"Look for any weakness," I tell him. *"Broken limbs. Thin vines. Missing bramble."*

He eyes the thorny barrier with diligence as we ride on, but the wall is so perfectly intact, the magick crafted with flawless precision. For Witch Walkers, if a refrain is chanted wrong or a lyric left unsaid, it manifests as a damaged thread in the fabric of our construct. I cannot imagine a horde of warriors creating magick as sure as this, without even one imperfection.

Soon I'm reminded that *nothing* is perfect.

We come upon a weak spot in the barrier along the outskirts of Hampstead Loch, a place where the thick limbs are sparse enough to see through, providing a glimpse of the green and brown expanse that is Frostwater Wood. I dismount to sit at the forest's edge and begin trying everything within my power—which, decidedly, isn't much—to get inside.

First, I try conjuring a wood-eating blight. Once upon a time, when Finn and I were young, we managed to cast such a disease on Betha's favorite flowering bush, all because she made us collect its buds for her soap, and we'd grown tired of bloody fingertips from its thorns. We were barely ten years old and didn't give an owl's hoot about such things as smelling fresh. This isn't a bush, however, and Finn isn't here to craft his part of the song.

My heart squeezes around the empty place he used to inhabit, and I force myself not to cry.

Later, when the afternoon sun sits lower in the sky, and I've tried the handful of magickal designs that exist in my arsenal, I'm ready to give up.

Then I think of lightning.

I've always been drawn to thunderstorms, the way the air pulsates with power beforehand, making me feel like—if I just stand outside long enough—I can absorb it. Sometimes storms tear through the vale mid-summer, leaving behind a path of destruction for us to heal. But other times—the times that thrill me most—lightning bolts arc across the sky, white-hot light tinted in lavender, fracturing fevered nights, wild and restless as me.

Unfortunately, I've never been able to capture lightning. And when I try my hardest to craft a song built from ancient words, begging Loria to imbibe my spirit with a bolt of energy—the kind that can split even the heavens, that I might part this godsforsaken wall—nothing happens.

Not a damned thing.

Alexus crouches beside me, watching the tiny construct of my magick fall apart. He's been silent as I tried and failed and tried again, which is a lot given that we needed to get through the wall hours ago.

Sensing his growing disappointment, I let the final silver strands of my spell collapse, my hands along with them.

He drops his head and lets out a quiet sigh. When he looks back up, he says, "Might I give some instruction?"

I start to roll my eyes but remember who I'm with. This is the Witch Collector, a man who—much as it pains me to admit—seems to truly know the Witch Walkers in his care, as well as their talent. Yesterday, the thought of allowing him to teach me anything would've likely made me implode from the sheer absurdity of it all. But now I nod, annoyed and embarrassed that my lack of skill is so painfully visible, regardless of the marks decorating my skin.

"You're thinking too hard." He taps his chest. "Magick can be created from a song, but it isn't required. In truth, the most powerful magick is conjured from the deepest parts of our souls, not with voices or hands or anything else. But, no matter how a conjurer builds their magickal constructs, it must come from the heart. You know this, yes? Born of emotion, love, hope, sadness, desperation, all tied to ancient commandments of the old gods. The words are easy. Reaching for the emotion is what's hard."

"*Easy?*" I give him an incredulous look. "*You cannot fathom how hard the words are for me.*"

Everything about the ancient language of Elikesh is different from how we speak in Tiressia, down to the way the words in each sentence are ordered. I don't have the luxury of mimicking sound. The emphasis on certain syllables must be correct as well, something I do with precise movements, or else the entire construct fails.

It's *anything* but easy.

I glance down, but Alexus tilts my chin, forcing me to look into his bottomless eyes.

"Forgive me. It was wrong of me to say that. I only meant that I could give you the words. I may no longer have power at the ready in my blood, but I know Elikesh like no one else in the Northlands. I know the right words to say if you can translate them."

I nod, slipping my chin from his touch. I've never thought about what kind of magick the Witch Collector possesses. It's never mattered. He's the king's man, which gives him power regardless. I wasn't even sure if he had magick until now. There are no marks on his skin, which leaves me curious. *I may no longer have power at the ready in my blood,* he'd said.

Which means that he did, once upon a time. What happened to it?

I lock that nugget of information and question in the back of my mind for later.

"You saved me because of all the feelings that flooded your soul," he says. "Fear. Anger. Grief. Suffering." He stabs a finger at the wall. "*This* magick is no different. Those who created this barrier did so with their hearts, corrupt as they might be. Hatred, greed, and vengeance are not to be ignored. The Eastlanders understand how to harness that emotion and channel it into their work, like Witch Walkers infuse feeling into song." He taps my chest and, much as I know I should, I don't flinch from the contact or pull away. "You must listen to your soul, Raina. Listen to the emotions boiling deep and *use* them." He stands and holds out his hand, motioning with a flutter of his fingers. "Up."

He stares down at me when I hesitate, and gods, that face is persuasive in ways I wish it wasn't.

I slip my hand into his and stand, trying not to think about the held-back strength in his grasp or the way he folds his fingers so delicately around mine when I look him in the eyes. He lets go, and with a firm touch takes me by the shoulders, aiming me toward the weak area in the wall. I force back a shiver when he comes closer, standing behind me.

"Like I said, I can give you the words." Gently, he grips my wrists and brings my palms together. "Close your eyes and keep them closed. Now think about that night. Think about what the Eastlanders did to your friends, your family, your home. Think about the fires. Remember the devastation. Do you see it?"

I don't want to remember, but at his mention, images appear in my thoughts. Flames and smoke. Mother bleeding. Others lying dead. Alexus staring at me when death approached.

"How do you feel, Raina? Listen to your misery. Listen to your rage. If you're angry, let it boil. If you're heartbroken, let your heart shatter." His lips graze my ear, sending a rogue chill down my spine. "And if you hate, hate with the fire of a thousand suns."

My pulse pounds, and memories drift in and out of my mind, one horrific event after another until fury rises inside me like the storms I always wished I could harness.

"That's it," Alexus whispers. "Now weave your magick. *Lunthada comida, bladen tu dresniah, krovek volz gentrilah.*"

Bladen. I know that word. It means sword.

The ancient chant falls from his lips so naturally and so beautifully that the tiny hairs on my neck and arms rise. I listen as he repeats each word, memorizing the intonations and soft rolls of his tongue, his voice stirring my blood. This chant—falling from his lips—sings to me.

I form the haunting song now echoing within my heart, no longer trying to give life to a weak bolt of hope but what I know is a sword of intent.

"Lunthada comida, bladen tu dresniah, krovek volz gentrilah."

Alexus walks me forward, still reciting the words, and I imagine the wall of thorns and wood before us, blocking our path. I can't help but falter and tense.

"Relax. I've got you." He runs his rough hands up and down my arms and wraps his fingers lightly around my wrists once more.

I swallow and build *my* song, focusing on the silver strands of my magick, blending it with the words he's still reciting against my hair.

But then his mouth touches my ear. "Think the words. Carry the song in your heart. Hear it. Don't let it fall silent."

An involuntary shudder ripples through me, but I cling to the words, even as Alexus's fingers thread with mine, stilling my fingers.

I flinch. Finn always silenced me like this, and though I don't feel like that's what's happening now, the reality is that I can't work magick without my hands.

"Trust me, Raina," Alexus whispers, and I try. "Hear the song. Sing it in your mind. *Lunthada comida, bladen tu dresniah, krovek volz gentrilah.*"

With a firm and steady touch, he begins guiding my movements in a different manner. He might as well be teaching me to swing a blade against bracken and undergrowth. A downward arc here. An upward slash there. Over and over as we move, his body flexing and tensing behind mine, one fluid stroke after another. A dance that I feel in my bones. A connection I cannot deny. I'm beginning to feel like I did at the harvest supper, linked to something far more powerful than myself as I become a conduit—thrumming and alive.

We come to a standstill. My heart races as I stand there, hearing the song, my body wrapped up in Alexus Thibault.

"Open your eyes." His voice is soft and warm at the shell of my ear.

I obey, just as his touch slides away, only to find that I'm holding a sword made of amethyst light.

In my awe, the song in my mind stops, and the magickal weapon evaporates like stardust on a breeze. Nevertheless, relief washes over me, and I take in the surrounding wood.

When I turn around, Alexus stands flanked by our horses, wearing a proud, closed-lip smile. The Eastlanders' wall still stands behind him, a truly mighty work, only now a path exists through the blackened thorns and twisted trees.

"*I...I did it,*" I sign, half-believing.

Alexus's smile brightens, and a dimple dips deeply into his left cheek, unobscured by his beard. I bite my lip and silently damn him, because that smile is a lovely sight that I want to hate but somehow can't.

"Be proud," he replies and then signs, "*You conjured the perfect song, and your magick delivered us.*"

Much as I want to feel powerful and excited, the thrill of conquering the wall fades. For one, I didn't truly conjure the perfect song. He sang it to me. Secondly, I have a feeling the hard part of this journey is only beginning.

With a worried eye, I study the landscape around us, feeling so small and insignificant in comparison. I've never seen the forest's immensity from the inside. It's always been a mystery realm lying at the edge of my world. Witch Walkers never cross the tree line, never step foot in the wood's shade. Frostwater is as foreign to me as Winterhold will be.

If we ever get there.

The trees here appear as ancient as Tiressia, colossal and mostly evergreen, though there's plenty of timber showing autumn's burnished shades, bearing soon-to-be naked limbs. Thousands of trees stretch as far as the eye can see, creating a sense of confusion I'm certain could trap anyone here.

Though the wood is intimidating, it's also a wonder. Gnarled roots sprawl across the forest floor, twisting beneath soft moss and winding around verdant ferns with retreating fronds turning brown for winter. It's darker here and cooler, the sun struggling to stretch through the forest's thick canopy. Frost has settled and survived on exposed branches and in windswept dunes amid fallen leaves.

I don't know what I expected, but it isn't this. Perhaps monstrous trees that come to life or shadows that can swallow a person whole. Beauty, quiet stillness, and archaic mystery aren't descriptors I imagined.

Alexus drops to one knee and grabs a stick. "We're a day and a half behind the Eastlanders, a week from Winterhold without the enchantment ahead to endure." He clears a swath of moss to reveal the soil beneath and begins drawing a crude map that means absolutely nothing to me. "Nephele and the others will do their best to keep the Eastlanders far from Winter Road." He draws a double line for the road, sharp slashes in the dirt. "That's where you and I need to go if we plan to journey north with any sense of direction. We just need to avoid the ravine."

Winter Road. Another part of my world that feels more like a myth than reality. It's supposedly the only clear route between the valley and the king.

What if we cross paths with the Eastlanders before we reach Winter Road? I ask.

The Witch Walkers' magick might not harm us, but the enemy is another story.

"It's a possibility," Alexus replies, drawing another odd line and an X to mark some random spot in this never-ending wood. "Which means we need better weapons than what we have." He pauses, scrubs his brow. "But

I can't remedy that until we get to Winter Road. We have to hope for the best between now and then."

Hope for the best? All the sexy dimples in the world wouldn't still my hands at that remark.

"Wonderful. Sounds like a great plan." This time, I do roll my eyes.

He arches a brow at my cynical remark. "I'm not sure what you want from me, Raina. This is a game of chance we're walking into. I'm trying to give you some idea of where we're going should we become separated." He carves out a tower and stabs the stick in the ground before sitting back on his haunches. "We may already be too late to stop the Prince of the East and his men from reaching the castle. There's no way to know. We have no idea if your vision is showing us the only band of Eastlanders or if there are more. More than one group rode into the wood last night. And this wall? This wall and the fire magick we saw in the vale could be the simplest of their power. The prince is all but infected with the Shadow World. We can't know what we face."

Words blurt from my fingers before I have time to think them through. *"I thought you held no doubt for your Witch Walkers' skill."*

"I don't," he snaps. "Between them and our king, the Eastlanders are in trouble. But I've seen things in the last day and a half that I never imagined. The Eastlanders don't know this type of magick, or at least they haven't before now, and the Prince of the East is..." He sighs. "I don't know what he fucking is anymore, but I can't help worrying that we've highly underestimated him."

Another *we.* This time it means him and the Frost King, I'm sure.

And maybe Nephele.

"If the Eastlanders make it to the castle and take the king," he says, "then there's a chance we can intercept them on their trip back through."

I frown, questioning this man's strategy and mapmaking skills, but also our logic.

"There is more than one way out of the Northlands," I remind him. *"The Mondulak Range. The Western Mountains. The Iceland Plains."*

The second the words leave my fingertips, I realize that if there are other ways out, there are other ways in. Maybe we should've tried another route.

"If they conquer the Witch Walkers' magick and take Winterhold," he replies, taking his stick and forming rugged ranges, "they will avoid both stretches of mountains when they leave. As will we. There are too many fatal passages on either side this time of year. As for the plains, they would never survive the trek to the northernmost villages. I'm sure they realize that. Frostwater Wood is the only possible way in or out." He pauses and glances toward the sky before meeting my eyes. "So the plan is simple. We get to Winter Road and save our king, one way or another."

He stands and turns to help me mount the mare again, bending with cupped hands. When I make no move, he straightens to his full height, and with those big, strong hands planted on his hips, narrows his eyes like he senses something wrong.

Something *is* wrong.

The Witch Collector and I have indeed found ourselves on the same side, but now that my mind isn't so clouded, I fear we have very different objectives.

"What is it?" he asks. "Say what you mean to say. Your face hides nothing, Raina."

As though I'm unaware.

"Your king is not *my king,"* I reply. *"He never has been. He can rot in an Eastlander pit for all I care. I do not want to intercept anyone, certainly not someone who might have taken your pathetic, helpless king. I want to go to Winterhold to get my sister before they attack the castle and kill her like they killed my mother. There has to be a way to bypass the army. I aim to find it."*

Something like anger flashes across Alexus's face, and he dips his head low, ensnaring my gaze. "You shouldn't be so quick to doom a man you've never met. You know little about him."

His words aren't as sharp as mine but edged all the same.

"I know he brought the Eastlanders to our door. I know I would not have spent the last eight years without my sister if not for him. My mother would still be alive. I would still have a home. If the Ancient Ones listen at all, I hope they let the Eastlanders have their way with him."

Alexus steps forward, closing the remaining distance between us until his nose is less than a finger's length away from mine. "You have no idea what you're saying."

"I know I am going to find my sister," I continue, undeterred, *"and that I am not running to the king's rescue. You will find me kissing the Prince of the East right*

on his disgusting mouth before that happens." I pause, stretch my fingers, and shake away the fact that I just brought that murderous bastard back to life in my mind. *"I thank you for your help,"* I add, *"but consider your debt to me cleared. I will go my own way from here."*

He assesses me, disbelief clouding his expression. "You are foolish. You will never find Winter Road without me. And know this. That is the only way you hold any chance of ever reaching Winterhold. Second..." He shakes his head on a laugh, peering at me from beneath the hood of those dark, feathery lashes. "If the Eastlanders take the king, who is about as pathetic and helpless as you, my dear, understand there's a great chance that your Nephele, the Frost King's high servant and paramour, will be found ever at his side. Lovers are often protective like that."

A wave of nausea threatens. Lovers? That word ricochets through my brain, and black dots swim across my vision. I ball my hands into fists, the prickle of angry tears stinging my eyes.

"You lie. She would never."

I feel like that's all I've said regarding my sister today.

"Oh, but she would." He smirks, and his scarlet mouth falls into a tight, thin line. "But do it your way. Go off on your own like a heedless child. Not only will you find yourself lost, but you'll also risk any chance of ever seeing your sister again, because if the Eastlanders take Nephele and the king, I will *not* have time to hunt for the likes of your stubborn arse, which means you will likely die out here. Alone." The tendons in his neck go rigid. "You write your future now, Raina Bloodgood. Make up your mind."

He hauls himself up onto his horse and snatches the reins, waiting for my answer. It doesn't seem that patience is a virtue for Alexus Thibault, or perhaps I've tested his limits. Because after an annoyed scoff and one last irritated glance, he says, "I don't have time for this," and rides into the wood, weaving through the trees, leaving me standing in an infinite forest with no more than a lone white mare and a decision.

14

RAINA

The day passes with Alexus riding just within sight, a speck in the distance. Over more miles than I can count, he never looks back. I decided to follow him for as long as possible, then figure out how to find Winter Road myself, because I can't let him win. He's all but shattered my memory of Nephele. I fear I won't recognize my sister in the least when I see her again.

He's also made me weak. The Witch Collector is more than handsome, his face created to slay with a glance, kissed and blessed by the gods themselves. That face, combined with that gentle way of his, delivered from beneath all that tempered power, does awful things to my mind. Even when he's angry with me, my body responds. I hate everything about it. I feel like a youth again, incapable of controlling whatever it is that puts such fire in the blood. More than anything, I don't want to *need* him.

I don't want to need anyone anymore.

The further I travel, the more my plan disintegrates. The thick trees become even more densely spaced, and the air gathers a bitter chill, the dim light of day falling to twilight. At times, if it wasn't for Mannus's steam and breath or the chinking bridle or the clanking of the oil lamp strapped to Alexus's saddle, I would be lost as to which way to go. I'm no tracker, and I was right about one thing: Frostwater is a confusing place, even without enchantment. No matter which way I turn, it looks the same, especially under the gray cloak of dusk.

Shadows creep, coming to life like forest wraiths crouching and crawling along the edges of my vision. Eerie sounds drift from behind me, sending an invisible touch trailing along the back of my neck, enough to make me shiver. All too soon, the Witch Collector will melt into the darkness, and then I'll truly be on my own.

It's what I thought I wanted, but now, with night descending, I must admit that I was—*am*—being foolish. There are many things I cannot do, and I fear crossing Frostwater Wood alone is one of them.

As much as I would rather eat tree bark the entire time we're here, I have no choice but to go along with Alexus's plan. I need to catch up to him first, while there's still a hint of light.

I urge Tuck onward but lose Alexus when he cuts a hard left around a tangled thicket. Mannus, familiar with the wood, rides hard and swift, but my mare, even if obedient, is slow and unsure of every trot. I can't blame the poor girl. It feels like we're heading into some unholy world. The boughs are silhouetted by the coming dark, and night creatures wake and stir in the undergrowth and shadowed treetops. When a cold breeze snakes through the wood, a fine frost settles over the world.

We won't make it much further, Tuck and me. Not before we must stop and bed down on the cold ground until morning. By then, we might never find the Witch Collector again.

I bury my nose in the hood of his cloak, thankful for the warmth, but his smell—like rich spices, dark wood, and—honey, perhaps—is all over me. It makes me push Tuck harder.

When I round the bend at the thicket where Alexus disappeared, I yank the reins and bring Tuck to a stuttering halt. I listen for Mannus's hooves and glance around the darkening wood for any glimpse of my former companion. He's nowhere to be found, and I've no notion where I am. Bitter, I wish I could tell Alexus that his drawing of Frostwater Wood was sorely lacking in detail and wholly inadequate.

A terrible, eerie howl echoes through the forest, sending a burst of crows from the treetops. Gasping, I duck low, covering my head, and clamp my legs against Tuck's sides when she stamps and snorts.

I'm not so fearful of being thrown from her back or of what sounded like a white wolf. What I fear are demented crows. I'd forgotten about them. Are these the prince's winged demons? Were they left behind without their master? If they are, they don't attack.

The cawing fades, the trembling treetops still, and Tuck settles. I sit up, heart racing, and peer at the foliage blocking most of the moonlight. With a sigh, I rake a shaky hand through my hair, clearing the strands from my eyes, and will my heart to slow. I inherited my father's hot head, something that has often led me to quite the predicament, but perhaps none such as this.

"I didn't take you for such a difficult student."

Startled, I whip Tuck around only to find Alexus sitting casually on Mannus's back, both hands resting on his saddle's pommel. A shaft of silver light splinters the forest's canopy, illuminating him enough that I can make out the smug look on his face. Though I want to throttle him, I cannot deny the overwhelming sense of deliverance I feel in his presence.

I ride into the soft light.

"And I did not take you for a trickster teacher," I reply with quick hands, *"so I suppose we were both wrong."*

One dark brow rises, and he lifts his chin. He gives me a once-over that —if I'm not mistaken—holds a twinkle of admiration despite his eyes being filled with barely bridled irritation.

"You have fire in you. I don't despise it."

I scoff, but he continues.

"I *don't*. I'd rather have a fighter with me, even if she *is* scared of her own shadow."

My anger flares and I ready my hands to land a harsh retort, but he stops me with a glare.

"No. You need to listen. I don't like being challenged when I'm only trying to help. Your actions have done nothing but slow us." He presses his heels into Mannus's flanks and walks the animal forward until he's alongside me. With a penetrating look, Alexus raises a fist and extends his finger. "This was a lesson. Winter Road shouldn't be far now, but if your head was where it should be, you'd sense that magick isn't far either. I've no idea what we're about to face, but there's a good possibility it won't be pleasant, and it won't be anything you want to endure by yourself. If your self-serving independence is a problem again, know that I will not be so kind as to rush to your aid. The people we care about need us, and I will not be deterred anymore. Do you understand?"

I hesitate to reply, and his voice deepens.

"I said, *do you understand?*"

Pride is difficult to swallow when it comes to him, but darkness closes in all around, so I do it anyway. Though it kills me, I give the Witch Collector a single, stiff nod.

An annoying half-smile graces his lips. "Good. See how easy that was? I might tame you yet." He thrusts his chin toward the west. "Now let's find a place to rest."

⚬⚬⚬

FROM MY SEAT ON AN OLD TREE STUMP, CURLED IN ON MYSELF AGAINST the cold, I glare at Alexus Thibault, wondering if looks can kill. I don't want to spend the night with him. I don't want to even be in his presence, and he knows it. I certainly didn't want to stop riding, but it's so dark, and the horses are tired. I know that it's best if we sleep for at least a few hours before facing what lies ahead, but god all, I am not happy about it.

After what happened earlier, it isn't like I can argue.

"Look," he says from where he's crouched, knees spread wide as he adds twigs and sticks to the fire he built in a small clearing. "I reacted harshly earlier. It's just that, over the course of my life, I've spent countless days and nights in this wood. Even without being enchanted, Frostwater is no place for anyone who hasn't traveled its ground many times. I only wanted to keep you safe, and you were being impossible."

A flush rushes up my chest and neck. I like to think that I could've kept myself safe, but sometimes, whether I care to admit it or not, experience trumps daring.

"Also," he continues, "there's a very good chance that we might be forced to spend several nights together, so you should get used to me. I don't bite." A flicker of humor flashes in his eyes. "Not hard, anyway."

"Hilarious," I sign, doing my best to keep my face expressionless.

A smile tugs his mouth. "I'm only saying. There are a lot of dangerous things in this wood besides me. Wolves, boars, venomous snakes. Ghosts, wraiths. You never know what might come crawling out of the dark."

He tosses a small pebble at my feet, the movement so quick that I almost miss it. I still jump half out of my skin. The thought of wolves, boars, and snakes terrifies me, that's true, but at least the other creatures he mentioned don't exist. Not anymore, that is.

"You are a child."

"I thought I was a trickster teacher. A liar."

"You are those as well. And more."

Again, he smiles, and it's irritating how devastating it is, even with a busted lip. His lone dimple makes an appearance, too, making matters even worse. It's hard to despise someone who lights up the world when they smile.

Damn him to the Nether Reaches.

Though I'm oddly glad the tension between us has dampened, and though I'm struggling to stop looking at him, I don't find his joking about the wood funny at all. The leaves and limbs in a nearby tree keep rustling like something's climbing or walking up there, making me shiver. I was raised in a vale. I'm used to all sorts of creatures wandering into the village, climbing on the thatch, scurrying into the cottage. But the wood has forever been contained. It's still too new for me. Still feels forbidden—for a reason.

The thought makes me shiver.

Gods. The best thing I can do is go to sleep.

The ground is hard and frigid, but I lie down and turn on my side anyway, my back to Alexus. The moment I close my eyes, his voice drifts over the fire.

"I haven't had a chance to tell you that I'm sorry for the loss of your village. And your mother."

The moment he speaks those words, I see her smiling at me, so real.

I sit up, heart racing, and hug my knees to my chest. After a few minutes, I face him. I don't want to talk about last night, especially with him, but he seems sincere, and I haven't had time to process the enormity of the disaster. The loss feels so great that I don't think it's hit me yet, like reality will arrive in cresting waves.

I remember what it was like when I lost my father. I walked around in a daze most of the time, the ghost of him following me everywhere. I would even hear him laughing sometimes, or see him from a distance, or run into the cottage with news on the tips of my fingers that I needed to tell him, only to realize that he wasn't there.

"Did you have a partner?" Alexus asks.

I shake my head, then nod and end up shaking it again. Finn was never my partner, not like my parents were partners, but for a time, I'd believed he was everything.

"I had someone. It was...complicated."

And that's all I say about that.

"Well, losing everyone you love is something no one should be forced to endure. It leaves an indelible mark on your soul." Alexus stares into the fire but then meets my eyes. "I truly am sorry, Raina. I would change it if I could."

Again, his words are so sincere—like they're coming from a man with experience or a load of guilt. Or maybe both.

My stomach twists into a tight knot. He's partly to blame for my loss. He took Nephele, though it sounds like she's been just fine living at Winterhold. I still can't grasp how that's possible, thinking maybe I'm being tricked, because if she holds so much sway over the Witch Collector and the Frost King, why has she not come home?

"Tell me about my sister," I sign, needing to take my mind off last night. *"What is she like now?"*

At first, he looks like he's not sure how to reply, but he finally does, with an amused grin. "She's a wolf in sheep's clothing, that's for certain. She has an affinity for clashing swords—with me, in particular. Sometimes I win, but I won't lie. Much of the time, she beats me, fair and square."

I can't help but allow a faint smile at that. *"Nephele used to beg Father to teach her the sword."*

Father did teach her too. I was so small—she's six years older than me —but I remember. However, as we aged, more important duties took precedence, and the playtime of pretend sword fighting had to be cast aside.

Another reason for my smile is that Alexus speaks of her with such familiarity and admiration. It angered me so much before, but now it brings me a sliver of comfort. Even if I don't yet know the details of Nephele's situation, it seems like she's made the best of it.

"Nephele cares for the children at Winterhold too," he continues.

"Teaches them." He switches to signing. "*She even teaches your hand language. We have two deaf children who benefit from it greatly. I cannot tell you how many times she has smacked my hands for getting something wrong one too many times.*"

I laugh, but it makes my heart hurt for a reason I can't place. I'm glad she's had this other life. A rich life, it seems. I truly am.

And that she hasn't been unhappy like me.

The stars are out, so I lie down and stare at the sky, unexpectedly brutally aware of the empty cavern inside me. I've no reason to speak to Alexus openly, to confide in him, but that emptiness aches so much, and words rush from my fingers anyway.

"*I have never killed anyone before.*"

There's a moment of quiet. I'm not sure if he was even watching me, but then...

"You did what you had to do."

He *was* watching.

"*But it was not enough,*" I reply after a long moment. "*I killed everyone in my village.*"

He stands and comes to sit on the stump beside me, elbows on his knees. "That isn't true. Why would you think that?"

"*I could have watched the waters. I could have seen you coming, seen you fighting, seen the Eastlanders chasing you. I could have gotten them out.*" I fold my shaking hands together, and a hot tear slides down my temple. I scrub it away, but another takes its place.

This is one of those cresting waves. I can't let it drag me under, but the truth is that Finn was right. I only think about myself.

Alexus leans over me, hair falling around his shoulders, and looks me steadily in the eyes. "You cannot carry that responsibility. We all face moments of decision, and when we look back, it's so easy to think what might have been. But you didn't know to look at the waters, Raina. *You didn't know.*" He pauses. "If either of us is guilty, it's me. I left an entire village to fend for themselves."

"*Littledenn?*"

He nods, and his throat moves on a hard swallow. "You and I needed supplies, but when I left you at the stream this morning, it was because I had to know if they made it. They were all dead, and that is a loss I will never forgive myself for."

I'd figured as much when he returned with the horses, and I see that same sadness all over him now. Much as I wanted to blame him and the Frost King—for everything—the tragedy we experienced in the vale lies in the hands of one man.

A man I pray is dead.

We're silent for a long time, until my eyes are so tired I can't hold them open any longer. I want to sleep, but it's too cold, the ground too hard, bumpy with roots.

Alexus strides to where the horses are tied and removes the gambeson from Tuck's back, along with the blanket from Littledenn. He spreads the quilted armor on the ground near a fallen tree and sits, leaning against the log, the blanket ready to spread over his legs.

With a gesture, he nods to the space beside him. "If you can stow away your dislike of me for a short while, we might both get some rest. The Eastlanders are far ahead of us, but I'll still keep an eye out. And I will be ever honorable."

Of all the events I could've imagined happening on this night, *this* was never one of them. But I'm tired, and a crow caws, and the leaves in that damned tree rustle once more. In the next breath, I'm there, half an arm's length away from the Witch Collector, thankful for the giant who owned such a blessed garment as the gambeson.

Alexus spreads the blanket over us, and though it doesn't stave off the cold completely, it's enough.

I drift, watching the fire's flames dance. When I finally close my eyes, a face appears in my mind's eye. It's distant and dim, but I know it.

The prince looms there, a bloody nightmare, watching me.

And from the abyss of sleep, he smiles.

15

ALEXUS

Frostwater Wood is my home. I've crossed its grounds hundreds of
times, taken rest beneath its cool shade, hunted from within its
shadows, traversed its floor in search of special herbs. It's as much
me as I am myself.

And yet, this morning, the wood is foreign.

Ahead lies a tunnel of trees and thorny brambles I can only discern
thanks to daybreak's weak light. Hundreds of interwoven branches arc
across a leaf-covered path that leads to utter obscurity.

Or so it seems.

The magick radiating from the tunnel is so strong that the power
prickles against my skin. The entrance all but writhes, like the branches
only remain open to draw us in.

I pull back on Mannus's reins, slowing him to a stop. So much for
making it to my hunting shelter for better weapons before things get trou-
blesome. This is certainly vast magick—a massive construct nestled in the
wood.

A trap.

Mirroring me, Raina halts her mare. Both animals fall still with little
effort. I'm sure they sense the magick too.

"This is not Winter Road," Raina says.

"No. That it is not. It's the darkness you saw in the waters, I imagine."

She nods, but when wolves howl in the distance, sounding their morning wake-up call, she twists in her saddle.

"Aren't you glad you didn't run off alone?" I ask. "This *is* the land of the white wolf."

I need to let it go, but even after our conversation and a few hours of sleep, I'm still bristling. It wasn't Raina's defiance that angered me. I like her fire—too damn much. Enough that it'll burn me if I'm not careful. It was the idea of having to leave her to her fate that rattled me, and for no other reason than she's too stubborn for her own good.

She glances to the right and left of the tunnel, where the wood appears ordinary and calm. Shafts of soft sunlight stream between the leaves and bare branches of the deciduous trees, glistening in the frost clinging to the evergreens. The morning is marked by birdsong and skittering animals, but I have a feeling that it won't remain this innocent once we cross into the construct.

"I suppose you are going to tell me we cannot go another way."

"There's only *one* way, and that's through," I reply. "Even if we'd gone our separate ways, chances are we would've still ended up here. We just wouldn't be together. This is the part of vast magick that can't be changed if it's meant to hold. The larger construct. It's the smaller things within that the witches at Winterhold can manipulate as we pass."

I know my witches. They're cunning and strategic. I only hope they can hold this construct long enough to snuff out the Eastlanders. Vast magick is challenging to sustain for long periods. *That* is the true flaw in the plan.

Raina's brow tightens with mistrust, but I'm right, and I know I'm right, so I turn Mannus to the left and guide him toward the peaceful woodland—an act of compromise and education. The tunnel shifts, heading me off, a gaping, lightless cavern waiting to swallow me whole. I redirect and head in the opposite direction, but again...

"The tunnel is everywhere," I tell her. "That's the magick's design. To give the Eastlanders no other choice than to find themselves within the enchanted darkness of a hopeful tomb."

Raina's face hardens, and her hands—lovely as they are—move in an almost threatening manner when she signs. *"You said the wood would let us pass. That the magick knows you. Why does it not allow safe passage now?"*

"I also said this might not be easy or fast," I reply, keeping my voice steady. "But we *will* get through. Winterhold's witches are trying to contain an army from many miles away. Their construct cannot distinguish between invaders and us. Not until we're inside, anyway. Their magick must taste us first for the Witch Walkers to know we're here, and even then, they have to single us out amid the chaos of this type of construction and manipulate the right strands—out of thousands—just for you and me. They'll deal with us the best they can."

None of this is a lie, but what I don't say is that it isn't the Witch Walkers' magick that I'm worried about hurting us.

It's the enemy lurking within.

She glances at the tunnel, then back to me. From her measuring look and the annoyed expression on her face, my words have provided little convincing. She stiffens her spine, sets her hands firmly around the reins, and jerks her chin toward the intimidating path anyway.

The horses require urging into the tunnel, but the moment we cross beneath its archway, a looming cold grows ahead. The sure way out begins closing behind us.

Raina peers over her shoulder, her attention drawn to the unnatural creak and moan of wood groaning like the tunnel trees have come alive. I turn in my saddle too but say nothing as I watch her. In the corner of my vision, a mass of trunks begins braiding across the entrance, shutting us in and slowly shutting out the daylight.

"The lamp?" she signs.

"No. If the construct still stands, that means there are Eastlanders still trapped here. We can't light ourselves for all to see, and there's only so much oil. Communication is more difficult this way, but I'll ride close. If you need me, can you whistle?"

She signs the word, *Yes*, melancholy softening her features when she whistles quietly. It's such a lovely sound, like the trill or warble of a nesting bird. Still, she looks so forlorn.

I'm not sure what I said to cause such a reaction, but I give her the best reassuring look I can muster under the circumstances, and we ride on, side by side as the tunnel darkens.

We move deeper into the construct, still encouraging the horses, and I study a flicker of movement along the path. Little white flowers—similar to stardrops—pop up from the leaves of meandering vines, opening wide and shining dim light along the path. It's just enough illumination that the horses can see where they're going, and the lines of Raina's face and hands are outlined in a diffused silver glow.

When she looks at me in wonder, I smile. "Told you. Their magick knows me."

She gives an exaggerated roll of her eyes, but I also note a smile teasing her lips.

We keep moving.

The tree trunks lining the path are so numerous that if we needed to find cover amongst them, we couldn't. Dense briar bushes grow in every gap, covered in thorns, long and sharp as bear teeth. At the tops of the trees, little eyes watch us, like birds are perched on the limbs, much like the crows last night. This part of the construct has to be Nephele's doing. Over the years, she's developed a tendency toward more... *intimidating*...magick.

I can't say I don't appreciate it now.

My thoughts drift to Raina's magickal sword. It's possible she could cut through the tunnel walls, but I doubt that would do any good. The tunnel would only find us again.

My attention is drawn back to the path. As we ride, the autumn cover changes, the dirt and rotting foliage becoming marred by branching veins of crystallized frost. The awaiting cold reaches for us, clawing at the ground to drag us closer.

Ahead, light snow swirls in a coming breeze, depositing a white dusting over a forest that only held a bit of frost before. With flurries dancing, I almost miss the second flicker of movement along the path's edge.

Turning a glance over my shoulder, I look more closely as we pass. Snow clings to a thick patch of curled briar vines that have been hacked away, leaving a barbed hole big enough for a man to crawl into if he were desperate enough. Beyond, I think I see the whites of eyes. An animal perhaps, but I can't be sure.

To be wise, I wrap my fingers around the hilt of my sword and look down as Raina reaches across the small distance between us. She closes her hand on my wrist a moment before the white flowers begin withering on the vine. The blooms fight their unwanted death, trying to open again, straining to glow. Most lose the battle, but a few stay strong, barely illuminating the path at our horses' feet.

Only two things can be causing this. Either my witches are already too exhausted to maintain a change like these flowers, or someone else is killing the light.

Someone capable of fighting vast magick.

I swallow hard and hold back a shiver, unease coming over me, the way a stare makes the skin crawl.

"It's all right," I whisper, squeezing Raina's hand as the world grows colder. Her touch falls away.

In time, the soft hoofbeats of our beasts change, the snowy ground crunching under their weight. I focus on guiding the horses. They falter and balk, no doubt sensing wrongness, but they thankfully obey and carry on.

There's no way to know what lies ahead. No moon shines here. No stars. Just night and more lightless night.

My eyes adjust, and though our horses have excellent night vision, heading into an abyss is still unsettling. Enough time here would drive someone to the brink of despair and desperation.

That's likely the point.

Raina grips my forearm hard, digging her fingernails into my skin. I can hardly distinguish her outline now, but I feel her energy. It pulsates into me, and an unmistakable tension fills the air.

We are not alone anymore.

Again, I reach for my sword, but the icy bite of a knife buries deep into my thigh before I can free my weapon. Too stunned to do anything else, I roar and wrap my hand around the blade's protruding hilt.

Mannus rears, kicking wildly. I try to regain control with one hand on the reins, but my thighs instinctively tighten around his sides, and the knife digs deeper.

I cannot breathe around the pain. For a moment, all I can think is that I'm fucking tired of being stabbed. My shock passes swiftly, though, and my thoughts shift to Raina. I yell her name, but the only sound that meets my ears is that of two bodies colliding.

She's fighting an Eastlander, and I can't see her.

The parts of me that I keep locked away jerk against the prison of my ribs, longing to be free, tasting a fight, tempting me for release. I grab the hilt of the knife instead and yank it free from my muscle.

The wet heat of fresh blood courses down my leg, but I can't let a little cut slow me. I turn, ready to swing off Mannus's back, and pray the blade in my hand finds an Eastlander heart and not Raina's.

A sound splits the night, freezing me in the saddle. It's a sound I know far too well—the slick slice of a dagger's edge through thin flesh, followed by the gurgling of blood in a choking throat.

"Raina!" Her name tears from my lips, and a hand grabs my knee, making my pulse ratchet higher. I don't know whether to attack or hold back. If it's the Eastlander or Raina.

The blackness around me is all-encompassing, and my head swims, but I ready myself to strike a deadly blow.

A tender intake of breath is what stays my hand. Even in this short time I've been with her, I've learned the way Raina shudders out an exhale, memorized the sweet taste of her sighs. I recognize that breath. Feel it. Know it.

I reach out and find her arm, then slide my hand down to her trembling fingers. Relief floods through me, though I worry there might be more Eastlanders waiting in the briars.

I think to dismount, or maybe I should haul Raina up on Mannus with me and ride hard. But I don't get the chance to do either one, because suddenly I'm tilting, head light as air, and tumble from my horse.

16

RAINA

I don't know much about Alexus Thibault, but I do know he's as heavy as a fucking ox.

My blood is still alight from the fight with the Eastlander, and though I'm half Alexus's weight, I manage to not only catch him before he slides from his horse, but I also have enough strength to shove him upright until he's facedown against the animal's neck.

The only death I smell is the earthy scent of the Eastlander, which means that Alexus is only wounded, but I don't know where. His hand is tacky with blood, and I'm trying not to panic. He's not dead yet, but if he dies—if I can't keep him breathing—then I'm alone. The very thing I hoped to prevent by being with him in the first place.

Calm, Raina. Think.

I wipe the sweat from my forehead and feel for the pulse at his neck. It's sluggish and weakening. I have to find and stop the bleeding, or I *will* smell his death.

But gods. The night is thick, an ocean of ink. Contours are all I see thanks to the few buds of light struggling to remain aglow at the road's edge, and even those distort if I gaze at one spot too long.

I run my hands over Alexus's cold body—his powerful thigh, his wide back, his muscled side, his corded arm, his baldric and sword hilt. I slide a hand along his chest too, from curve to curve, feeling his heartbeat, but there's no sign of blood.

I go to his other side and am instantly met with that telltale metallic scent. It mingles with the smell of the Eastlander's death still lingering in my nostrils.

My hands tremble harder. The rush from fighting turns into remorse over killing a man but dissipates into wicked realization. Alexus's britches are wet, sticky, and torn. I flit my fingertips over the gash, assessing the open meat where blood pulses free. The stab wound is deep, maybe to the bone, and perhaps far too close to valuable vessels. He'll bleed out soon if I leave him like this.

I sigh. How many times will I save the Witch Collector's life?

The answer is a whisper across my mind: *As many times as it takes to reach Nephele.*

"*Loria, Loria, una wil shonia, tu vannum vortra, tu nomweh ilia vo drenith wen grenah.*"

I form the words, and with an image of my will—which is a whole Alexus—I begin weaving the glittering red strands of his injury back together to stop the bleeding.

But something catches my attention as I sing and weave. It's so unusual that I almost stop, but I force myself to keep going. The strands of the flesh are different from the strands of life or even of a spell. They're often easier to control, though in truth, I've only ever worked with minor injuries. I've closed my own wounds a time or two, healed a little cut on Tuck's paw, a nasty forge blister on Finn's arm while he slept, and stitched a parchment cut on Mother's finger once when she wasn't looking.

What's odd is that the strands of Alexus's flesh have frayed edges, something I've never seen before. Even more curious, I swear I see multiple threads, though the duplicates aren't precisely the same as the originals. They're more of a vestige, the residue of glimmering shadows.

His life strands were like this as well. So much has happened that my mind didn't unearth the memory until now, when his life once again rests in my hands. I'm not seasoned in healing or saving people from death, and I have to wonder what it means.

When I finish, I rest my head on Alexus's shoulder, fighting heavy eyelids and the pull of a darkened spirit. I saved his life, yes, but I also ended another. I'm not sure if this disaster I'm still walking in has revealed that I'm a merciful giver of life, as murderous as the Prince of the East, or that I'm something selfish in between—like the Frost King.

Wintry snow swirls, building on my lashes, making me think of him. For as long as I can remember, I've pictured Colden Moeshka as a burly man with a frozen crown sitting on an icy throne, a rime-coated white beard hanging to his waist. In my imagination, he'd blow a chilled wind through the wood, his breath freezing and falling to the ground in crystals and snowflakes. It sounds ridiculous, but I don't know how else to envision him.

I see him now, on the backs of my eyelids, but his face is soon replaced by another—a crimson-shadowed adversary I never expected.

Lifting my head, I shake off the thought and touch the place on Alexus's leg where the gash had been, only to feel smooth skin. I slide my hand back up his chest, trying to ignore how perfectly and powerfully built he feels, and rest my palm over his heart. His skin is chilled from the cold, but his pulse is stronger, thrumming against my fingertips.

He will live. And right now, that is everything.

I feel for Alexus's pack in the darkness and free the flask I'd seen back at the stream. Whatever waits inside is so stout that one whiff burns my nostrils. I turn it up anyway. The liquid scorches my throat and settles in my aching chest like a warm fire, reviving and relaxing me.

My mind buzzes with questions about why the Eastlander was there, waiting, how he knew *we* would be there, or if he was perhaps only searching for a way out. I doubt I'll ever know, but the fact that he was just *there*, at the perfect time, unsettles me.

After I'm done with the flask, I secure Alexus to Mannus using the rope from Littledenn. His sword keeps weighing him to one side, so I strap it to the saddle. Once I've covered him with the gambeson, I lead the animals onward.

The thought to bed down enters my mind, to huddle with Alexus until he wakes, maybe even until morning, but it's best if we keep moving. It's so cold here, and the wood seems impossible and terrifying to enter.

Magick is *everywhere*. I've never walked inside a construct, and neither have the horses. That fact—along with worry about what might lie beyond the heavy darkness surrounding us—fills every step with expectation. Nothing awful ever comes, though, save for shivering and a few crow caws, and thankfully, the horses don't give me too much trouble.

It feels like ages pass before bluish light tints the wood like a wintry twilight. The path is clearly visible now, covered in snow and frost. Its gentle curve gives off a muted glow in the darkness.

By the time we round the bend, my hands, feet, and face are so chilled I can hardly feel them anymore, but my discomfort is the least of my concerns. Ahead, the path ends, and what lies beyond turns my blood to ice.

I stop the horses, my legs leaden and numb. My heart lodges itself in the base of my throat.

A frozen lake.

The dense forest wall of the tunnel widens, stretching along the lakeshore for as far as the eye can see. This must be a distortion of magick, a trick for the eye, because the lake goes on forever, east and west. Odd, because to my knowledge, there is no lake in Frostwater Wood.

Turning back to the stretch of ice before me, I try to calculate the distance to the other side—at least a few hundred yards. But the distance isn't what worries me. I've been to Hampstead Loch in the winter, played on its solid, crystalline expanse.

This lake is riddled with cracks. Frigid slush struggles to flow beneath the shattered pale blue surface, just waiting to swallow someone once they break through. Unless I can summon the energy and power to part a solid body of water or build wings to fly us over, our only option is to travel across.

A whistling wind whips around the lake and tears away my hood. The gust is so loud it almost drowns out the groan behind me. Almost.

"Raina."

It isn't lost on me that I'm Alexus's first thought upon waking. I wrestle with how that makes me feel, how the sound of his voice brings me a strange assurance, but only for a moment, because he's suddenly thrashing, his broad body straining against the ropes that hold him bound.

I hurry to his side, clasp his face between my hands, and make him look at me. The second he meets my gaze, his eyes clear, and he settles. His long, dark hair is wild, his green eyes a silvery jade beneath this pearly, icy light. The gambeson has fallen to the ground, and snow clings to his tunic and beard.

Closing his eyes, he rests the weight of his head against my palm before looking at me once more. "You're all right."

I nod, swallowing a foreign tightness in my throat, and let my hands fall away. I busy my frozen fingers with untying the ropes.

When he's free, Alexus reaches for his wounded thigh, only to find frozen blood on his leathers but no mark.

He looks up, brow scrunched. "I didn't dream what happened."

"No," I sign and shake my head.

"You...healed me, then?"

I shrug. *"It was that or let you die."*

He stares at me as though he doesn't know what to think, like I've sprouted a horn between my eyes.

"So you not only see things and conquer death, but you can heal too."

Something Nephele *didn't* tell him. That knowledge gives me a sliver of hope that she won't be utterly unrecognizable once I reach Winterhold.

"I can," I answer, too cold to even think about denying it. My fingers can't sustain an argument right now. With a rigid hand, I motion toward the lake. *"And you said I would never survive this wood without you. So what do we do now, Oh Wise One?"*

He dismounts, keeping a firm grip on Mannus's reins for support. His movements are slow and a little wobbly at first. He *did* lose a good bit of blood. Add in the frigid weather, and I'm sure he still needs time to regain his strength. Time is a luxury we don't have, though.

Studying the blue-white ice that looks like a shattered sheet of glass, he sighs. "Damn. Not good."

That seems like a severe understatement.

"At least we have a little light now," he adds. "And I'm no stranger to ice."

That is the only positive thing about our current situation. Well, that and neither of us is dead yet.

"You know this is a snare set by your Witch Walkers, yes?" I ask him. And though I'm not a bit happy about the lake, I admit that it's a clever obstacle for the land of the Frost King. The Eastlanders must've made it across, though, because there's no sign of them even having been here.

Unless they're the reason for the fissures in the ice.

"Of course I know. This entire construct is a trap." He steps to the water's edge and toes an ice floe. "But we can't stay here. And don't even think about asking me to backtrack. If the way in was a way out, that East-lander would've found it. He'd been in here for a while."

If that's even why the Eastlander was there in the first place. He was waiting.

Like a hunter.

Gods, I was lucky to gain the upper hand. I had but a moment to prepare. Everything after that was impulse and instinct, born of fear.

Cold as I am, heat flushes up my neck and spreads over my face. Chilled sweat beads on my upper lip.

"The magick will let us out," I sign, trying not to breathe so hard. *"Like you said. It will provide a way."*

I think about when Alexus called this place a hopeful tomb, and I glance back to the ice. A tomb for the Eastlanders might very likely be a tomb for us as well.

Alexus folds his hand around my shoulder. "It *will*, Raina. I swear it."

Another frosty wind blows. I throw the hood of my cloak back up and bury myself as far inside the wool as possible, hiding my hands in the slight warmth beneath my arms. I *am* a stranger to ice—and to cold this severe too. I can't imagine surviving these elements for the rest of the night, much less the week it would take to cross the forest and reach Winterhold under normal conditions. It will take longer now. But how long? How large is the construct?

Alexus snatches the gambeson from the ground and wraps it around me. I'm trembling hard, but I still shake my head and pull away. He may be used to harsh winter weather, but that doesn't mean he should be exposed to the elements with no more than a thin tunic and bloody leather britches.

He draws the soft armor tight around me regardless, and I pour every bit of my frustration into my stare. He moves nearer, holding the gambe-son's collar on either side, just beneath my chin.

Head tilted, he leans close, his dark hair falling around his serious face. "You've saved my life twice, Raina Bloodgood. Wise or not, I'm eternally indebted to you. The very least I can do is keep you warm."

I suppose it isn't awful to have a man like Alexus Thibault indebted to me, but I want nothing more from him than his aid in reaching my sister. I certainly don't want this closeness or the way his nearness makes my heart beat harder. I don't want to act like a stupid little girl from the vale caught up in a beautiful man's presence, sucked in by his absorbing gaze. I'm a grown woman who can think around such nonsense.

I remind myself of this fact and that he is not just any man. But I must be delirious from the cold because right now, being held like this, I find every single thing about him intoxicating.

Flushed, I step back, and he lets me go. I keep the gambeson, but only because I don't want him touching me again. I do, however, remember the blanket from Littledenn rolled up on Mannus's back.

I free it from the saddle, shake it out, and step toward Alexus, about to wrap the cover around him the way he wrapped the gambeson around me. I hesitate, though, choosing to keep my distance, and hand it to him instead.

"Thank you. I feel better already." He drapes the blanket over his shoulders and looks around once more, his green gaze hanging on the lake. "We have to cross to the other side. Unless you have a different suggestion. Your magick, perhaps?"

I shake my head. His cloak bunches in the gambeson's sleeves when I slip my arms inside, and though the barrier to the wind feels so damn good, my fingers are still too cold for forming lyrics.

The look on his face tells me that he understands there's nothing I can do. Even if he gives me the words for a spell, my hands are nearly frozen stiff, and I'm spent from fighting and healing and walking in this unbearable weather—in too-small shoes no less. With his help, I could likely figure something out once rested, but we don't have time to wait it out.

Alexus gathers the rope I'd used to tie him earlier and nuzzles Mannus's nose as the animal's ears flick back and forth with nervous energy. Tuck is agitated, too, pawing the ground like she wants to run, yet there's nowhere to go.

"We take the horses," Alexus says. "I cannot leave them."

My stomach tightens with dread. He's right, and it would destroy me to leave Mannus and Tuck behind too, but...

"They will require influence," I tell him.

The thought of the animals fighting us or stamping the ice sends my pulse racing. It's dangerous enough with their weight. That risk makes our circumstances so much more dangerous. There's little to be done for it except to hope the ice holds, because once we're out there, any disaster won't leave time for magick.

Alexus strokes a hand over his horse's head and down his long neck. "Can you try? Maybe a simple calming spell?"

I struggle, gasping at the pain in my knuckles. My fingers are so unbearably stiff that they feel brittle. Thankfully, the words for bringing ease aren't complex, a small construction of only three words I've used before.

Mala, mulco, calla.

On the third attempt, my fingers soften and bend around the shape of the ancient, elegant language, forming a tiny ball of white light. I repeat the words thrice more and push the uncomplicated construction toward the horses.

It disperses into glimmering threads above them, trickling like rain and vanishing into their manes with the falling snow. In seconds, they settle.

Lowering my hands, I notice that Alexus's eyes are fixed on me, unblinking, as if I've bewitched him. His lashes flutter, and he clears his throat.

"*What?*" I slip my hands back to the warmth under my arms.

"Nothing," he replies with a small shake of his head. "Your magick is just really beautiful."

I tighten my fingers, unsure how to respond, not wanting to say anything because my hands are so cold. Thankfully, Alexus takes the reins and leads us toward the lakeshore's edge. Side by side, we stand where tumbled stones meet frost and ice, staring over the glacial terrain. We share a glance, a moment of understanding for what we're about to do.

Then we step onto the ice.

17

ALEXUS

When I was a boy, my father brought me to a small mountain village outside what is now called Hampstead Loch. We met a fur trader there, a man who also dealt in sealskin. He guided us to a camp many miles away, and later we made the journey to the furthest reaches of the Northland Break, where a wooded forest gave way to the Iceland Plains.

The first thing that stands out in my mind about that trip is walking along the coastline, watching the dark sea with its white crests roiling toward the shore. The second is when my foot broke through a weak place in the ice, and utter terror swallowed me whole.

I was lucky. My diligent father had hold of my hand and yanked me to safety, but not before the water reached my waist. He carried me for miles, and I remember thinking that I might lose my legs from the cold.

I didn't, and though I live in the Northlands now and have visited the villages along the plains hundreds of times since, I always avoid the outer reaches. I imagine Fate is smiling in the shadows now, because it has given me yet another chance to brave the ice.

I wipe my hand across my forehead, trying very hard to believe my own words—that the magick will not harm us. But faith is an arduous effort at the moment. I'm still a bit weak, and I clutch Mannus's reins with frigid hands. He follows behind me, wary but steady.

Perhaps it was *I* who needed the calming spell, because every clop of the horses' hooves sends a cringe of anxiety through me, especially as we near the center of the lake.

We just need to reach the other side.

"Step lightly," I remind Raina. "Watch for cracks and thin surface." Though I know she already is. She walks ahead, leading her mare, a dark, hooded figure floating through the blue-tinted night. I can reach her easier this way if the ice gives.

Unless it takes our horses and me down too.

That thought is more sobering than the cold wind, and I silently scold myself for thinking it at all. Nephele and the others must sense me. They won't let the ice give.

And yet the ice cracks, a line zigzagging between Raina and me, accompanied by a splintering noise that makes my stomach drop.

We freeze, and the cracking stops. For a long moment, there is only deafening silence across the lake, until our panting breaths and a roaring heartbeat fill my ears. Raina turns a slow glance over her shoulder, blue eyes wide.

I nod. "Keep going."

We have to.

Each step forward is excruciatingly slow and careful, apprehension tightening every muscle and every move. I'm mentally measuring our distance to the other side—only another hundred strides or so—when Raina comes to another abrupt standstill. I stop, my heart thundering.

"What's wrong?" We don't have far to go, but in my worry, I've gotten too close to her. She inches around and points at the ice. "Is it cracking?" I ask. "Be still."

My mind is a whirl of panic. I'm reaching for the rope looped at my side before I realize that Raina is shaking her head, still pointing.

I look down. Take a judicious half-step closer.

A warrior's face stares at us from beneath the ice. I glance around, only to see more faces and horses too.

The Witch Walker magick created a tomb, all right. Eastlanders lurk beneath the surface, their last moments of fear forever frozen on their icebound faces. I pray to the Ancient Ones that this part of the construct swallowed the entirety of the prince's army—him included.

"Get off this patch of ice," I tell Raina. "It's too thin."

Cautiously, she skirts her mare around the icy burial ground. I follow, guiding Mannus, trying not to look at the faces anymore. They're the faces of the enemy, but there was a time when those of the East were good. A time before the love of their god and his old greed corrupted them and their kings. Something in me still foolishly hopes for a return to peace.

Real peace.

It's a long trek, but after a time, we finally clear the warriors' icy tomb, and we're within strides of the opposite lakeshore. I'm confident that Nephele must sense us now because if she hadn't, would the ice have held?

Raina steps to surer land, tugging the mare with her. I'm right behind, leading Mannus, thankful when rocks and snow crunch underfoot.

My faith is restored until a woman hurtles out of the darkness near the trees—screaming a war cry—and launches herself right at me.

Before I can dodge her attack or even think to grab my sword from the saddle, she's on me like a starving dog. I hit the ice and slide across the lake on my back.

The woman sits astride me, teeth bared and eyes wild. Her light brown skin, covered in pink cuts, gleams with a sheen of cold sweat as she points a knife at my face.

My knife—that I never felt her take.

I grab her wrist to keep her from pushing the blade into my skull, and she bears down. She's strong. Powerful enough to make this difficult.

Control is critical, so I wrap a leg around her waist and flip her over, pinning her arms against the frozen water beneath us. Her hand fists tighter on my blade, and she pushes against my hold.

I slam her wrist to the ice repeatedly until she relents, noting the sound of my weapon skating and scraping across the lake.

Damn it all. She made me break a sweat.

She bucks her hips, once again stronger than she looks, and I'm weaker than I believed. My hands are so numb that my grip loosens, and my left hand slips on the slick ice.

On the edge of my vision, I catch movement, but not before she lands a blow. Her fist connects with my temple, a hit so hard it sends me sprawling backward into Mannus's legs. Startled, he whickers and bolts for land, taking my sword with him.

Trying to get up, I gaze at the ice and stare straight into the dead eyes of a drowned warrior. There's even an outline of the red and gold Eastlander flag, that haunting ever-watchful eye in the center.

The lake didn't take them all, though. At least two survived—the bastard who drove his knife into my thigh and this beast of a woman.

When I meet her glaring eyes, she stomps the fragile ice layer with a heavy, booted foot, over and over, in a voice that makes my skin tighten.

"Your journey ends here, Witch Collector."

I rise into a crouching stance, ice cracking beneath our weight. Deep inside, my darkness awakes, aching for freedom, singing promises of aid. I shut it down and focus, releasing my fear, then lower my head and charge.

If I'm going down, this bitch is coming with me.

We collide, and the breath leaves her body in a *whoosh*. The impact sends us sliding again, this time toward the shoreline.

Toward Raina.

She stands a handful of strides away, unmoving on the bank in the gambeson, chest heaving. Her hood is thrown back, dagger frozen in her hand. Her eyes are bright with alarm, pupils sparkling like she holds fire within.

Ever the virago.

I open my mouth to call her name, to forbid her from coming out on the ice, but the Eastlander woman rams the heel of her hand into my chin.

Seeing stars, I struggle to my feet, grabbing a fistful of her long, dark hair on the way. I haul her to her knees and set her head inside my arm just right, choking off her air.

I will never forget this is part of my past, my body operating from muscle memory, so naturally a killer. A quick twist is all it will take.

But as my vision clears, I hesitate.

The woman smells like death, and her eyes are milky and clouded. She claws at my forearm, teeth bared as she stares up at me with a gaze so penetrating it's as though she's pouring herself inside me.

A dark, unsettling look crosses her face, but for the first time, I can see around more than my rattled head. She may be wearing boots, but she's also wearing the remains of a dress. Not bronze leathers. She's stunning—

and young—a handful of years younger than Raina. When I look beyond the thorn wounds and that ferocious sneer, there's something familiar there—but also something wholly wrong.

A sound snags my attention, and I look up, just as Raina skids across the ice. She rams into my side and knocks the wild girl from my hold. The hit flips me off my feet. I land on my back again with a hard *thud*, sending the breath from my lungs in a rush.

Gods' balls, I've had enough of this.

I jerk up and get to my knees, primed to react, only to find Raina and the hellion who tried to kill me embracing on the ice. The girl glances my way and startles like she's only now seeing me. Her eyes aren't hazy anymore; they've gone dark as night. She blinks, bewildered. It's as though she was in a trance before and is now awake.

Raina releases the girl and signs so fast that I can't understand her words. When she finishes, they admire one another's hands—Raina's witch's marks are bright, but the girl's hands bear no sign of her craft. Raina smooths the girl's tangled black hair, her cheeks glistening with happy tears. They bump forearms and press their foreheads together. The girl whispers something I can't hear, and Raina presses a sign to the girl's chest.

Raina smiles. *Really* smiles. The kind of smile that brightens her whole face. It's a rare thing, and the sight makes my heart squeeze, almost painfully.

Gods. She is so beautiful.

She faces me, brows raised in a sweet, innocent expression, clinging to the other girl's strong shoulders like she's showing me a prize. The relief and joy emanating from both of them is undeniable.

It dawns on me who the wild girl is—now that I'm not on the defensive. Her witch's marks are gone, though they used to shine silver with rust-colored edges. There's something else wrong that I can't quite place, something darker than this girl has any right to possess.

She's a fighter, but she's no Eastlander. She's from Silver Hollow.

The blacksmith's daughter.

18

RAINA

I can't process the girl I'm seeing. Helena is here. In the wood.
Alive.

We sit huddled together beneath a tree, sheltered from the snow-fall by its widespread branches, every limb densely packed with soft green needles and snow. I wrapped Hel in the gambeson to warm her bones. She's still wearing the golden dress she'd looked so beautiful in the night of the harvest supper. The garment hangs in tatters and shreds, the filthy fabric incapable of shielding her skin from frostbite, though she snagged a pair of boots somewhere along the way. She smells of some sort of stench, something likely picked up in the wood or maybe from the village.

And her cuts. There are so many. From thorns, I think. I'll heal them when she's sleeping, or maybe I should just tell her the truth and be done with it. As for her missing witch's marks, neither of us has an explanation. For the first time, glistening color paints my once-unmarked skin, and hers is smooth and blank as a new piece of parchment.

While the horses stand close by, at the farthest reach of the tree's protection from the heavy snowfall, Alexus stalks the lakeshore and surrounding wood. I glance at him, thankful that he's giving Helena and me privacy to speak.

I turn back to her, though I sense Alexus's nervous energy on the fringes of my attention, feel it with his every crunching footfall in the snow. I'm on edge, too, my skin humming with anticipation and shock—neither of which I can shake.

Gods' stars, he nearly killed Helena. I know he didn't realize who she was, and in truth, she attacked him like a rabid animal, but I can't stop thinking about what nearly happened.

I almost lost her. Twice.

"I was with Finn and Saira one minute," she says, "and then they were *gone*, swallowed by fire and smoke. It was chaos, Raina. I searched and searched for them, and for Mother and the twins, but a gray-haired East-lander, the one they call General Vexx, started a fight with me and—" She touches a deep cut above her brow, dried with old blood, and draws an unsteady breath. "He hit me, and everything went dark. When I came to, I was draped over the back of another Eastlander's horse. A big man. Young though, with hair like fire. My hands were tied. The army had just crossed into Frostwater Wood, and we rode here because there was no other way. This magick..." she scrutinizes the construct "...is like nothing I've ever seen."

"It is Nephele," I tell her. *"And the witches at Winterhold. They have learned vast magick and are protecting the king. Alexus says their magick will know us, that we will remain safe."*

My words are meant to ease her, but my faith in such things still isn't strong. If the magick knows us, why does snow build around us by the inch? Why is it so cold we can hardly move? Why no shelter? No clear way through this wood?

Hel glances over her shoulder with a wary gleam in her eyes. "I can see that now. The ice just...opened. One second, it was stable. The next, it started fracturing. The water below sucked most of the Eastlanders down, but not all. Many made it across the ice, including Vexx. The warrior I was with is a giant, and I'm not a small woman. I was so scared that we might break through the ice, incapable of doing anything but watching others fall in, the lake closing around them and refreezing." She grits her teeth, her temple flexing with the movement. It's as though she's clamping off an incoming memory. "I hate them for what they did to the valley, but watching warriors pound against the ice, begging to get out—" She looks at me with those dark and haunted eyes. "I will *never* forget that."

"No, but that was not your fault. You cannot bear the burden of the Eastlanders' deaths."

I take her shaking hands in mine and press my forehead against hers. I wish I could heed my own advice, but I bear the burden of our valley's massacre—those innocent *and* guilty—too well.

A thought strikes me. *"Was there a man with a wounded face?"* I ask. *"The prince?"*

"No, not that I saw."

Inexpressible relief sweeps through me. It isn't a definite answer to the prince being dead or alive, but his absence is a good sign.

"There are mountains beyond here," Helena continues. A hard shiver rolls through her. "And a mostly overgrown path that diverges into two routes. To the right, mountains. It's an awful ride. There's s-so much snow, and...white wolves. Luckily, I got bucked off the Eastlander's horse and ran. He caught me, but I fought him like an-an unholy terror."

"You got away, though." I feel thankful for all those tussles Hel and Finn had when we were growing up, and even more so for her love of the blade.

She nods, her brows pinching together. "Though I think the Eastlander let me. I can't be sure. He could've easily subdued me, yet he failed. I ran until I saw the light of the lake, only stopping l-long enough to cut away my bindings on a jagged rock. I ended up here again. I braved the lake, tried t-to g-go back home. But there was a guard stationed t-there, and the wood allowed n-no exit."

"You saw him?" I ask. *"And he let you live?"*

Her eyes go distant, and she bites her lip. "I don't remember what happened. I don't remember a lot of the past couple of days."

She exhales a long sigh, and the stench that clings to her wafts from her body and breath. I noticed the odor the moment we embraced on the ice, but now, the longer I'm near her, the stronger it gets. It reminds me of the old hunk of brimstone father kept in his trunk, found near a hot spring south of Hampstead Loch. The amber rock—its surface rough with craggy amber stones—always smelled so acrid, even though the scent faded over the years.

"Do you recall what happened after you saw the Eastlander?" I sign.

"I came back here and hid in the wood—" she scrubs at her face like its presence bothers her "—and tried not to freeze to death while I thought about what to do. I slept for a while. Then I woke to the s-sound of a horse snorting. I saw what looked like two people and horses crossing the l-lake. I was so s-sure you were an illusion, that the cold had finally gotten to me. But you came closer, and I recognized you and *him*," she tilts her head at Alexus, who's heading toward the horses. "And, I don't know, something in my mind...snapped." Her eyes shimmer, and her chin trembles. "Again, I don't r-really even remember it. You're sure I attacked him?"

Alexus scoffs and tugs at the blanket draped over his shoulders—his only protection against the wind and snow. He keeps staring out at the ice where his dagger sits, freezing to the lake.

Ignoring him, I nod and caress Helena's cheek, scooting closer for warmth, hoping to soothe. She's so jittery, her words and speech so broken. And that scent...

"You are in such a state. It is no wonder you cannot remember."

"I think I j-just couldn't lose anyone else. Not again. I-I'm sorry." She tosses those last two words over her shoulder at Alexus, and he grunts an acknowledging response.

"I understand." I squeeze Helena's hand. *"But I am here, and Alexus is fine. We are all okay."*

The twisted part of this situation is that—though I'm so glad she did the right thing—at least the right thing in my eyes, I'm equally as happy that she didn't kill Alexus. When I watched them fighting on the ice, the fear that she might hurt him made me just as panicked as when I watched him tighten his arm around her neck. Helena was so fierce, wilder and more violent than I've ever seen her.

And still, Alexus hesitated.

Helena leans close and briefly shifts her eyes in his direction. "You c-call him by his name now? Last week you were stabbing a scarecrow in h-his honor." Though she lowers her voice, her question comes out wrapped in her usual husky tone that carries.

Alexus turns a glance in my direction, no doubt wondering how I might reply to this girl who doesn't know what to think about the fact that I haven't killed him yet. Though I didn't tell her of my plan, my anger toward the two most influential men in the Northlands has never been a secret. There was certainly no hiding my animosity when she told me to pretend that scarecrow was him.

"He was the only other person who survived. Or so I believed. I needed him to bring me to Winterhold. To find Nephele."

It dawns on me that Helena probably doesn't know anything about what's happening between the Eastland Territories and the Frost King, and I'll explain, but not right now. Right now, the weather is worsening. The wind picks up, whipping us with bitter lashes and sleet. My hands tingle like phantom limbs, and my lips are so numb it's like they're no longer on my face.

Clutching the blanket at his chest with one hand, Alexus guides the horses nearer with the other. The animals tug against the reins, uneasy. My calming spell is fading.

"We can't stay here any longer," Alexus says. His face is slightly wind-burnt, his lips a paler shade than their usual red. "We'll start losing fingers and toes if we don't find shelter."

Helena snaps her head around. She drags a hand along her thigh as though reaching for a sword that isn't there.

"There is no shelter," she says, spittle flying, her voice deepening. "I've been beyond here."

Tuck blows a burst of air through her nose, and a twitch ripples down her back. Mannus shakes his head and steps ahead of the mare like a guardian.

Something isn't right. There's an odd tension in the air. Even the horses sense it.

I look at Hel, incredulous. She isn't totally innocent, but for the most part, she's obedient. The most defiant things she's ever done have been her steady practice of sword-swinging in the thicket by the stream and sneaking off from occasional suppers to let Emmitt rattle her world in his father's hayloft. To speak to the Witch Collector in such a manner—a man considered the right hand of the continent's immortal king—is *not* like her.

It's like me, but not her.

Again, I toss the niggle to the back of my mind. She's just unraveled, and the horses are only shaken. Understandable given our circumstances.

Alexus's nostrils flare at her words as he steadies the stallion and mare. "Would you rather sit here and freeze into statues? Or move and live?"

Hel stares at me, and I detect a war brewing behind her eyes when there isn't an occasion for such conflict. Her dark irises lighten, reflecting the falling snow.

"We should go," I tell her.

An odd shadow passes over her face, and an irritated huff trips off her lips. She stands abruptly, stiff, her shoulders squared hard, her chin lifted. Even the simple act of *being* is different from her norm, lacking the elegant grace of a gifted swordswoman that accompanies Helena's every waking minute.

She stabs her arms through the gambeson's sleeves and fastens the toggles from neck to waist with the steadiest of hands. She acts like she's not cold anymore, not in the least.

Face hard, she snatches Tuck's reins from Alexus and swings a long leg up and over the horse. "Raina rides with me."

Another tremble quivers through Tuck from mane to tail, the whites of her eyes visible. Alexus's gaze shifts, meeting mine in question.

His face seems to say, *Is everything all right here?*

I feel unsure but also convinced that Helena is just a young, sheltered woman experiencing trauma amid absolute calamity. I understand that far better than I want to, so I craft another calming spell for the horses and take my friend's offered hand.

19

RAINA

We're going to die here.

My bodice and Alexus's cloak are the only barriers between me and the wintry precipitation that falls heavier and heavier with every passing hour. We've been riding for two solid days, at least. I can't tell because there's no concept of time here. No sun, no moon, no dusk, no dawn. Just misery and aching muscles that have long since frozen stiff.

We rested once, many hours ago, before we reached this path. Now, the horses' hooves are shod in ice, their strides much slower and labored. Snow sits on my shoulders, and frost coats my face.

I tried to summon my magick, to think of any spell that might help us. I even imagined walking a circle of protection, trying to conjure a hut made from forest limbs. But walking would be treacherous in the deep snow along the path's edge, and my hands have grown even less flexible than they were at the lake. The necessary intricate movements for a complex spell are impossible to perform.

As for the wood, it appears the construct only allows for two passages, just like Helena said. Directly into the mountains or around them.

"There are dark things in those hills," she reminds us, and Alexus agrees to stay to the dense woodland that skirts the range instead.

I have to agree with him now about my *other routes* idea. Mountains are difficult enough to pass without the added dangers of this ice-bound magick.

The old oil lamp Alexus found at Littledenn hangs from his hand. The wavering flame gives off enough soft illumination through its amber glass that we travel inside an orb of golden light. Worry for Eastlander's spotting us has long passed, our dire need of light the larger worry. The world outside our faint little bubble is dark but white with cold. The snow and ice that glazes every limb and needle and leaf emits the faintest eerie glow —a forest made of silver and shadows.

The wood lies shrouded in absolute silence—beautiful but alarming. Occasionally, the flutter of wings rustles high in the trees, a caw creeps from a nest, or the distant cry of a white wolf howls through the wood. I can't shake the sense of being watched or followed, so I keep an eye on the path at our backs. It's all part of the construct, Alexus says, meant for confusion, deception, and fear. Like the darkness when we first entered the tunnel. Like the lake.

Mission accomplished, Witch Walkers.

Teeth chattering, I hold onto Hel's waist, crushing our bodies together as we ride. Heat is a precious thing, and I cling to any I can find. It's difficult, though. Her putrid odor stings my nostrils, making me wonder if I'm imagining the smell.

From Mannus's back, Alexus glances at us, pressing his knuckles beneath his nose before letting out a rough cough that's more like a gag.

It isn't just me.

We keep riding. I force my eyes to remain open, searching for any sign of a place we might shelter. No matter how far we travel, though, there are only tangled, thick trees rising high into the sky on either side of the winding path.

Eventually, I give in and close my eyes, resting my head on Hel's shoulder. I'm so terribly frigid, down to the iced marrow in my bones, that I'm uncertain if I'll wake up should I fall asleep.

My thoughts drift to Nephele.

Tuetha tah, if you can hear me, help us. Bring us through this wood, bring us to Winterhold. Please do not let me die here.

I repeat the words in my mind like a song. What else can I do to make her hear me? This construct is so far beyond my comprehension. No strands hang in the ether or even within my mind's grasp. The inner workings of this magick are hidden away, making it impossible to reach out to her by simply plucking a few threads.

More time passes, perhaps an hour or two. It's so hard to stay awake, so every now and then, I mentally recite my plea to my sister. Having a task, even if only in my mind, helps me keep from giving in. Sleep seems like such a comfort. Such relief.

I close my eyes, and for too long, they stay closed.

A face fades into my mind's eye, on the edge of a dream. Once handsome, the face now bears a gaping slash.

The Prince of the East stares at me, eyes narrowed in curious study. Nothing lies beyond him, only a scarlet halo of swirling shadows.

The carved corners of his mouth turn in a deep scowl. "Hello, Keeper," he says. "I see you."

I jerk awake, heart racing, and blink away the sight of him. Gods, that felt so real. His voice was so clear.

But it was just a dream.

Wasn't it?

I swallow hard, remembering something faint. Something distant. The prince called me *Keeper* after I cut him open. Surely dreaming of him is only my mind conjuring that same moment, reshaping it into a new torture.

A long sigh pushes out of me, leaving a frozen breath cloud hanging in my wake. It's snowing so hard that I can barely see the pale light of the lamp, and the horses are moving with such labored steps.

Unaware, I've tightened my arms around Helena's waist like a vise, and so I loosen my hold. Hel doesn't seem to notice. She doesn't shake like me either, and her shoulders aren't slumped from my weight. Somehow, she's unaffected by the cold, and so very warm. It must be the gambeson.

I sit up straighter to give her some relief and press the signs for *All right?* into her thigh. She barely flinches and makes no reply.

It's just the cold, I tell myself. The kind of cold that makes teeth feel like they might shatter and renders the skin and brain too numb to comprehend something like the pressure of a sign.

"There's a path cleared ahead," Alexus calls. "We're bedding down. It's getting impossible to see."

Bedding down sounds impossible too. In this snowstorm? And what would've made a path large enough for Alexus to see his way through the wood?

Helena agrees, her sigh sounding more like a hiss. But soon, we're leading the horses off the path into the trees, Alexus leading the way with his dim light.

I glance over Hel's shoulder, worried about the horses making it through the deep drifts. All that's visible ahead is a gray haze and packed snow, like more horses have already tread this ground—which doesn't ease my worries. Nothing about this scenario is wise, and I want to say so, but what good would it do? It isn't like we can turn back and go home.

Alexus draws Mannus to a halt, and the soft circle of lamplight moves toward Helena and me. When I can finally make out Alexus's face, it's like he's been painted in the tones of the night, all color leached by the cold.

He looks at Hel and holds his lamp high. His dark hair whips in the snowy wind. "You have fire magick, yes?"

She bristles, and after a moment, says, "I'm not good at fire magick."

Alexus arches his brow. "You don't have to be good. I just need you to help me get a fire going." He looks at me and jerks his chin toward Mannus. "There's a rocky overhang over there. I'm hoping this is Nephele's doing."

He walks away, and Helena huffs.

"Foolish man," she says in a manner that isn't her at all.

Alexus stops, broad shoulders stiffening, and turns back, lifting the lamp again. "I'm wiser than you think, girl. You would do well to remember that."

Sometime later, the horses are standing beneath the tallest part of a stone shelter, shielded from the snow and most of the wind. I begin clearing a place for a fire a few strides away, under the lower end of the ledge, while Alexus gathers wood and brush. Helena sits huddled on the ground, silent.

When I'm done clearing snow, I take a seat a few feet from her, feeling a little unsettled by the way the lamplight casts our silhouettes on the stone wall at our backs and sends wavering, fingerlike shadows reaching through the trees. I want to believe that this shelter is my sister's gift, but I don't feel her presence.

Alexus dumps the kindling on the cleared ground and, shielding the oil lamp, works at taking flame from the wick using the wool from the tinder box. It will make a grand start to a fire if the damp wood catches, but a harsh wind sucks away Alexus's stolen light. He tries again, and again the wind blows the flame to nothing.

"Gods' death," he curses, closing the glass door on the lamp. "I can't risk losing the only light we have." He sits at my side, staring across the pile of twigs and broken limbs at my friend. "*Fulmanesh*," he says after a while, directing his voice at Helena. "That's the word for summoning fire. *Iyuma* if it needs urging."

She knows this. *I* even know this, not that I've ever handled a fire thread in my life. Witch Walkers are born with specific skills that manifest at different times and in different ways for all of us. But many forms of magick can be learned, however. Like Finn's family learning fire magick. I've never been keen on learning to manipulate any more threads than I already contend with. But Helena loves fire magick, even if she hasn't excelled. And yet, at Alexus's words, she just sits there, biting her lip, staring into nothingness while we freeze.

"I told you, Witch Collector," she says through clenched teeth. "I'm no good at fire."

Her dark gaze lifts from beneath heavy black lashes, and there's an odd tilt to her head. Without another word, she stands, still wrapped in the gambeson, so tall that—like Alexus—she has to stoop beneath the ledge's low ceiling. She heads to the far edge of the stony haven and sits against the rocks, scooting down on the ground and turning her back to us, like she's going to sleep.

I haven't thought about her missing witch's marks much until now. They were there the last time I saw her, lighting her skin like she held fire within. Now there's nothing on her visible skin, and she's acting more than strange.

Worried, I start toward her. Alexus grabs my wrist, his hand falling away when I face him.

"*Let her rest,*" he signs. "*Perhaps she needs to sleep it off.*"

"We need fire," I reply. My fingers are so stiff they hurt, my joints throbbing.

I know my friend is struggling. I am too. But she didn't even offer to help. Didn't even try.

"We'll get fire, Raina." His voice is as soft as the falling snow. "Even if we have to conjure it ourselves."

After a tug of the blanket tighter over his shoulders, he tries building a fire with the contents of the tinder box again. The cold is so intense without Helena and Tuck's heat that the pain in my fingers spreads through the rest of me. Even though Hel has the gambeson, I can't imagine how she's lying there so very still. Even Alexus's fingers tremble as he fumbles with the flint and wool to no avail.

He closes up the tinder box and scrubs his arms beneath the blanket. "I can show you how to summon fire. You might not like it, but I can show you. One time, that's all it takes. After that, with some practice, you should be able to seek out fire threads for yourself."

I'm so frigid, yet heat rises inside me, warming my face.

"I know what must be done to see them," I manage to tell him.

So much in our world of magick is about connection. Connection to the universe, our inner selves, our inner peace, the world around us.

And connection to each other.

Alexus's eyebrows dart up. "Yet you don't know how to summon fire? Who taught you how to see the threads but didn't take the time to help you master them? Or is this another skill I had no idea you possess?"

He considers me and then glances at Helena, and I can read his mind. But it wasn't her.

I would never admit this—to Alexus of all people—but I helped Finn numerous times, back before I realized that he could harvest fire threads well enough without my aid. He only wanted an excuse to be close to me, and it worked. He never offered to teach me anything.

"Not a skill, and I cannot see them," I clarify. *"I only know what is necessary to do so."*

"Or you think you do," he replies, one brow still raised. "I fear you might've had an inadequate experience." He opens his arms, holding the blanket like wings, and spreads his bent legs. "Come here. Let me show you."

Gods. This is as bad as sleeping next to him, and the very last thing on all of Tiressian soil that I want to do—except die. So with reluctance in my every move, I get up and go to him.

Alexus slides until his back is against the stone behind us, and I fit myself between his legs. As if it's the most natural thing to do, he folds me in his arms, covering me with the blanket, which isn't much guard against the cold. It's coated in frost like everything else.

At first, I think there's no way this will work, but soon, a fragment of warmth builds between us. Even that sliver of heat is utter bliss.

"You can relax." His voice is low, quiet so Helena can sleep. "This is far easier if you're not stiff as a tree. As long as you don't try stabbing me like you did that scarecrow."

I glare at him, then jerk a hand from beneath his blanket and sign. *"I am frozen."*

What I wouldn't do for a wolf skin right now.

He lets out a small laugh that rumbles into me. We both know my discomfort isn't just from the cold. I simply don't want to be this close to him.

"Frozen or not," he whispers, "we need heat or fire if I'm to help you harvest the strands. So you might as well get comfortable. Body heat it is."

I glance at the lamp and widen my eyes. That seems like a better idea for harvesting fire threads than cuddling with the Witch Collector. I eventually figured this out with Finn, though I can't say the closeness from his beginner fire magick days didn't lead to us becoming more than friends.

"No lamp," Alexus replies. "If it blows out, we'll be in total darkness, and believe me, collecting fire threads from body heat isn't something you want to do in the dark if you're worried about touching me. Now sit back and cooperate. The faster we gather the threads, the faster you can warm yourself by a fire and not against me." He leans close, lowering his voice even more. "Since I'm clearly so horrible to be near. Your friend is a wretch and smells like an unemptied chamber pot, and you chose to ride with her anyway. I'm not sure how to feel about that." I glare at him from over my shoulder, but he just smiles and gently takes my shoulders and tugs. "Come on. Stifle your pride. It's bitter out here." When I still hesitate, he says, "Am I truly so awful that you would rather die than be near me?"

Does he not know who he is to me?

With a roll of my eyes, I give in and lean back against him, but only because our shared warmth makes me needy for more. We're both shivering, but the shaking eases once we're closer.

He touches my arm through the cloak and rubs his hand from wrist to shoulder to create more heat. I turn to my side, doing the same to him, if stiffly. I want this over, but as the heat between us builds, the urgency to be away from him isn't so strong.

Finally, I do relax, all to the rhythm of his palm making soothing circles on my back. Around us, the wind howls, and every now and then, snowflakes swirl into our little shelter. He curves protectively around me when they do, and I hate that I find it such a kind action.

"Close your eyes and keep them closed." His voice is still so low and deep. "Then touch my chest. Right over my heart."

I lift my hand but pause. Finn and I never did this. He always said he only required closeness, body heat. Granted, there was touching. Plenty. Not that I minded at the time.

But there was never any talk of hearts.

After a moment of hesitation, I rest my hand in the dip at the center of Alexus's chest. His pulse pounds steadily beneath my touch.

"Imagine strings," he says. "That if you move your fingers delicately, like playing the harp, you can lure those strings right through my skin and into your grasp. You can do this with flames too. Some witches, mages, and sorcerers can even harness fire threads from storms. There's much power in the air during a storm. Heat and light. Fire threads can even be gathered using glass and sunlight. You just have to focus and summon them. They will come."

My magick has always been so hidden. It's strange to share it—with the Witch Collector of all people. I'm letting him *teach* me, and though I've never cared much about expanding my knowledge before, I now find that I want to learn, even under his guidance.

I flutter my fingers against his chest, delicately, like he said. The movement is simple, not that I've ever played the harp, but I've seen it done, and so I mimic the flow through my fingertips, focusing, noting how the connection between us grows warmer and warmer.

Looking up at Alexus, I'm reminded of when we rode together in the vale after the attack, how his heat comforted me even then.

"Close your eyes, you little rebel." A smile tugs the corner of his mouth, and when the dim lamplight casts a shadow in his dimple, maybe a grin tugs my lips too. "Now, *fulmanesh*," he whispers. "*Fulmanesh, iyuma tu lima, opressa volz nomio, retam tu shahl.*"

My pulse picks up at the sound of his voice, the way he sings the Elikesh so smoothly. This lyric consists of more words than what Finn usually uses, but I know each one.

"Think of my heartbeat," Alexus continues. "The force of life within me. Reach for the deepest part of me. Keep strumming, just like you are now. Then close your eyes and repeat those words in your mind. *Fulmanesh, iyuma tu lima, opressa volz nomio, retam tu shahl.*"

I don't trust trying to hear the words. That's still such a foreign notion for me. So instead, I sign the words against his chest, repeating them over and over.

"Fulmanesh, iyuma tu lima, opressa volz nomio, retam tu shahl."

Fire of my heart, come that I may see you, warm my weary bones, be my place of rest.

On the third time, Alexus lets out a broken breath, his hand resting on my wrist. "Do you see the threads yet?"

I do. These threads are bolder than any bonfire. They're the color of flame, so stunning to behold. But like every other thread belonging to this man, there are more strands than there should be, and some are damaged, shredded at the edges like they've been run through the sharpest teeth.

I nod in answer, and he whispers, "Good. Now give me your hand."

When I pull my fingers from his chest, I feel his heat, like the threads are attached to my fingertips. Like I'm drawing them from his core.

Another broken breath leaves him. He cups my hand. "Very good. Again. In your mind only. *Fulmanesh*. Think it."

Fulmanesh. Fulmanesh, fulmanesh, fulmanesh. Iyuma.

There's no warning. No crackling surge of power in the air. No budding warmth. Just a sudden heat over the middle of my palm.

I open my eyes and jerk upright, stunned to find flickering fire an inch above my hand. It isn't much, no larger than the lamp flame, but it's something. And somehow, it doesn't burn. It's just there, ready to be controlled.

Finn never did this. Never held fire, not that I know about anyway. He always just willed an already-made flame to burn higher.

Wide-eyed, I look at Alexus. He jumps up, losing his blanket in the process, and takes the tinder from the tin. Squatting, he stuffs it between two pieces of wood.

"Now." He looks at me pointedly. "This is the hard part. Just send the fire over here." He motions with his hand.

Send it over *there?* Gaping, I stare at him with as much of an incredulous look as I can force onto my face.

He rises and stalks across the small space between us and settles behind me on his knees. Again, he cups my hand and directs it toward the pile of twigs. "It's mental. You *will* the fire where you want it to go. Like most any magick, it will do what you want once you've harnessed it."

Will. I've willed lives back together. I can will fire, surely.

I close my eyes and see the flame in my hand dripping molten over the kindling. I imagine a blazing fire rising and myself hovering over it, warming my frozen hands. I envision glowing embers crumbling to ash, the open heat giving rise to new flame.

"Think of the thing you want most in this world," Alexus says against my ear. "This can strengthen your magick. It's where true power comes from. We often hold the most will for our strongest desires."

My mind is never blank, especially these last few days, but in that moment, there's nothing. Nothing possible, anyway. What I want most in this world are things I can't have. My mother. My father. My sister. My village.

To reverse time.

The winds blow stronger, and a blast of snow whips my hair against my face, stinging my cheeks and eyes. I try to hold on to the fire like I held on to the sword magick, try to keep my mind focused. But another sharp gust cuts through me, and I still can't see anything in my mind's eye, the thing I want most.

I don't know what I want most anymore. Revenge? To kill the Prince of the East? To find my sister? To live? To die and be done with this frozen world? I have too many desires, and they all feel out of reach or wrong.

Overwhelmed, I open my eyes. The flame is gone. On the rising edge of panic, I face Alexus, breathing hard.

"*I can try again,*" I tell him.

He blinks at me, snowflakes settling and dying on his face. "What happened? You were doing so well."

I was, but then...

Shaking my head, I turn away from him and draw my knees to my chest.

He runs his hand over my back. "It's all right, Raina. I imagine we'll have plenty of cold to practice in these next few nights."

He goes back to the kindling and tinder box, and I sneak a glance his way. His hands shake harder now, the world outside our little stone fort a wall of whirling white. He's persistent, and that's a good thing, because finally, after a time, the flint strikes and a tiny flame catches and holds.

Tirelessly, he works, trying to build the flames higher while I think the words *Fulmanesh, iyuma,* over and over. I don't believe it helps, though.

Eventually, there's enough fire that my skin begins to warm. The small blaze fights the wind and snow and wins. Alexus blows out the lamplight to save the oil, tosses his blanket over his shoulders, and sits closer to the fire. I check on Hel just to make sure she's breathing. She is—harder and faster than normal—and her hand is warmer than it has any right to be. I worry it might be fever, so I heal her cuts and wounds—including the gash General Vexx pounded above her eye.

When I finish, I return to the fire and sit near Alexus, holding my hands near the heat as the creep of exhaustion rises over me. I'm worried about Hel, but I'm not sure what more I can do. Sometimes, even with all this magick inside me, I feel so powerless.

"Sorry," I sign, my fingers beginning to thaw. *"I tried."*

Alexus nudges me with his shoulder. "I told you. It's all right. We're going to live." He gestures at the fire with a blanket-covered fist. "You came so close. It isn't easy, fire magick. You made it look that way, though."

"Until I lost it."

He shrugs. "Again, we'll live to try another day."

"Fire magick would have been useful in the vale. All those winters."

"I'm sure. But magick like that has a tendency to spread, taught from parent to child, friend to friend, mentor to student." He pauses, as though unsure about his next words. "Fire in a village can be dangerous."

Biting my lip, I shake off the image that comes to mind and focus my thoughts elsewhere.

"Your ability," he says. "You're a Seer, a Healer, and a Resurrectionist? What is that like?"

I make a face. *"Seer, yes. Healer, yes. But Resurrectionist? No. Is there such a thing?"*

He laughs, but his face falls more serious. "But on the green, I saw you..."

He pauses, though I know what he was going to say.

"I heal, but I have never brought anything or anyone back from the dead. I have saved animals from dying, and you, but that is the extent. I am not very skilled. I thought my magick was secret. I taught myself."

At first, he looks regretful, like he realizes he made me think of Mother yet again, but there's a hint of surprise to his expression too.

"You've done well to make it this far with such complex abilities without a teacher," he says. "And yes, being a Resurrectionist is a thing. It's usually a darker type of magick and a form of necromancy. I wasn't sure about you. The line between healing and resurrecting is often thin. It seemed that was what you were doing—or trying to do—with your mother."

Resurrection. I can see the temptation. Being able to bring back someone you love? To rescue their soul from the Shadow World?

I shake my head, clearing away that thought, and let the moment pass. I can't sleep, tired as I am, and an odd desire to keep talking to Alexus takes over.

"Do you still believe the Witch Walkers' magick will not harm us?" I ask.

I have every doubt in that theory at this point.

"I do. I think the problem is that some of this is not their magick. Like the flowers dying when we entered the wood. My witches wouldn't have us enduring such miserable conditions either. Unless the Eastlanders are closer than we think."

"Then who is doing it?" I fist my fingers and bite my cheek. Like before, I know what he's going to say before the words leave his lips.

"The prince, most likely. The question is, how does he even know we're here? And did he leave that Eastlander behind to kill us? Or was that an unlucky clash with a rogue warrior?"

I clamp my eyes closed for a moment. It's not the prince. The Eastlanders must have a sorcerer in their midst. That's all. Someone with a tremendous amount of skill.

"Helena mentioned a general. General Vexx?" I spell the name. *"It could be him."*

Alexus tilts his head, and his eyes reveal a contemplative thought. "Possibly. Unfortunately, I don't think we can know until we come face to face with whomever it is."

That's nothing I want to think about, so again, I divert that line of thought. There's a question burning inside me that I have to ask, and it has nothing to do with the prince.

"What happened to your magick?" I sign. *"Why can you no longer use it?"*

I imagine that he would be lethal if he could. He knows Elikesh so intimately, so completely, all the finer details, like he's studied every word from every angle.

After a heavy sigh, he says, "It died. A long time ago."

I didn't even know magick *could* die.

"When you were a child?"

He looks up from my hands, and there, under the firelight, something moves in his eyes. I swear I see darkness there sometimes, bottomless and liquid.

Otherworldly.

"Something like that." He leans back and lies flat on the cold ground, staring at the stone ledge above us. "Enough questions for tonight. You must be tired. Get some rest while you can."

Much as I want to, I don't press him for more information about his magick or his past. I'm curious, even more so thanks to his cryptic answer, but he's right. I'm bone-tired, my hands too. And even if I wasn't, I'm fairly certain he just ended our conversation.

When I lie back, the ground is as miserable as expected. There might be heat tonight—or today, whichever it is here—but without the gambeson there will be no comfort, and I'm sure I'll never rest like this.

Beyond our shelter, a crow caws and a wolf howls, sending a chill across my skin. I can hear Alexus breathing, though, even from a few feet away. The steady rhythm calms me, and I think about his words, repeating each syllable in my mind, fluttering my fingers like I'd done when I drew threads from his chest. *Fire of my heart, come that I may see you, warm my weary bones, be my place of rest.*

Within minutes, after so many hours awake, I tuck my arm under my head and drift to sleep, the memory of Alexus Thibault's heartbeat throbbing in my fingertips.

20

RAINA

When I wake, it's only because I hear a rat in the root cellar.

After opening my eyes, it takes a moment to gather my bearings. I'm not in the cottage, and that sound is no rat. There's no root cellar anymore either. I'm in a dark, snowy world where time is nothing and survival is everything.

I'm also not in my bed with Mother. I'm on the chilly ground, folded up inside the Witch Collector's arms, covered by his blanket. My head is nestled firmly against his muscled chest, my arms tight around his waist. Even our legs found their way to one another in the night, weaved like we've slept together for years.

I was already still—I was half-asleep—but I become even more motionless, locking down every muscle, even stilling my breath, like I can shrink from this moment without him noticing.

"Good morning." That deep voice crawls over me, through me, and something firm presses against my stomach.

Gods! I slam my eyes shut and squeeze my eyelids tight. One of Alexus's laughs—the low, deep kind that rumbles—radiates into me, sending a strange sensation straight to my stomach, making it flip.

"Breathe, Raina. It's all right. The world isn't going to crumble because you touched me. A lot, I might add, but still." Unexpectedly, he dips his head, his beard and lips tickling my ear. "Also, you're very warm, and I rather enjoyed your company if that's not obvious, but now that you're awake, could you please disentangle your legs from mine? If I don't piss, we're both going to be in trouble."

My face has never burned as severely as it burns right now.

Mortified, I pull away and sit up, scrubbing my cheeks, only to meet Helena's icy stare from across our shelter. She pokes at the ashes with a stick, jostling what's left of the kindling. The sweet smell of woodsmoke lingers in the air, but it doesn't mask the sulfuric aroma wafting off her.

Bent over to protect his head from the overhang, Alexus wraps the blanket around my shoulders, giving me the last remnants of our heat.

"What?" I sign to Helena once his back is turned and he's stalking toward the forest. *"You abandoned me."*

She raises a brow, not unlike Hel, but her lack of words is startling. She's usually filled with witty comebacks or snide remarks, yet there's nothing but silence between us.

Alexus can't go far—to the edge of the dying firelight is all. The snow is deep beyond our shelter, and though it's lighter than when we fell asleep, it's still dark, like late dusk.

Scrubbing my neck, I look his way, noticing the loosening of his trousers from behind.

"He is your enemy."

I snap my head around, caught in my voyeurism, but also surprised by Hel's words and the sound of her voice.

"I am fully aware," I reply.

Her dark eyebrow arches higher, and her nostrils flare. "Are you?"

Alexus returns and checks the oil lamp. "I'm not sure how long we slept," he says. "Feels like forever. We should get back on the path while it's not pitch dark out. Take advantage of the light and cover some ground."

He creeps to the rear of the overhang where rock meets rock. Clusters of grass have broken through the stones there, brown and dead. He jerks them free of their roots with ease and heads to feed the horses. When he returns, he has the flask, an apple, and half the loaf of stale bread. Carefully, he nestles the bread and apple on a rock in the embers to warm.

"The skins of water are frozen solid, but this—" he shakes the flask "—should be fine."

In a short time, we're enjoying our first food in days. Toasted bread with warmed apple mush. It isn't a lot, but it's enough to ease the pain cramping my stomach.

I don't want to leave the heat. In truth, I'd like nothing more than to tend the fire until it's roaring, forget about Helena's odd behavior, and curl back up against Alexus. I cannot believe I'm thinking such a thing, but I'm cold and hungry, tired of not having a roof over my head or stew in my belly or a bed under my back. I miss everything about the cottage and the vale.

Everything.

I say nothing, though, and soon, we're struggling through deep snow, the horses making every effort to travel back the way we came. I ride with Helena, and Alexus leads the way.

Not far from camp, it becomes evident what stamped down the snow enough to reveal the path.

It wasn't Nephele.

Alexus stops and dismounts. About a dozen Eastlanders and their horses lie half-buried in the snow, scattered beneath the trees. We couldn't see them before, but now, with more light, they're impossible to miss. They must've gotten lost, or maybe they were wet from the lake and froze to death here. They look like statues, all shades of black, gray, and white, leaving yet another image of death in my mind.

They could be us. Might *still* be us, eventually.

Alexus digs around in the snow, feeling for weapons. My stomach turns as stains of blood and torn flesh become visible.

He glances up. "Look away. Wolves have been here."

I bury my face in the hood of his cloak and stare at the ground while he continues digging, until he comes within sight. He's freed a curved knife and stuffs it in his boot, replacing the dagger he lost on the lake.

We leave then, making it to the path faster than I expect. Again, we travel the way Helena says, avoiding the mountains, but after several hours, the snowfall blurs the world once more, and the miserable cold in my bones returns.

We keep going, struggling to see through the blizzard swirling around us. Alexus stops and tries lighting the lamp using flint, steel, and tinder, but he can't get a spark to catch with such strong wind. Eventually—using the

blanket to shield the wind and snow—the lamp lights, giving off soft illumination. We ride on, but we won't have that light for long. The lamp has
little oil.

Like before, I call out to Nephele from my mind. *Tuetha tah, if you can
hear me, help us. Bring us through this wood, bring us to Winterhold. Please do not
let me die here.* I try again, in Elikesh, every single word.

Nothing happens, and I find myself fighting back tears.

But my attention snags on a bough hanging over the path. The tree it
belongs to is massive and crooked, bent hard to the right, with knotty bark
that looks like a face peeking through the snow. I noticed it earlier. It's the
same tree.

I'm not the only one who notices.

"We're going in circles." Alexus draws back on Mannus's reins. "We
need to turn around. Head for the fork in the path and take the route
toward the mountains. You've walked that ground, Helena. Can you lead
the way?"

"Why don't you confer with your witches?" She stops the mare, jerking
on the reins too hard, her voice cutting with a razor's edge. "I can't know
how they manipulate this construct."

I watch Alexus from beneath my hood, watch him lift the lamp to
better see her. His chilly stare lingers on Hel, but he slides his eyes my way
and speaks to me alone.

"We aren't continuing like this." He raises his voice over the whistling
wind. "I've been more than patient with our *guide*, but this stops now. Are
you with me or not?"

Alexus Thibault is still such a stranger, but I know beyond doubt that
what he didn't say is that if I'm *not* with him, I'm on my own.

Before I can take my hands from Helena's waist to reply, she answers
for me.

"Of course, she's not with you. She's with *me*. And we're not going into
those mountains, Witch Collector."

I can't pinpoint what it is that strikes me so wrong—her words, obviously, and her tone. But there are so many other warning bells ringing when
I consider the last several hours with Helena as a whole.

I finally let go of my friend and swing down from the horse. My boots
sink into the snow up to my ankles.

An expression of irritated surprise takes over Hel's face. Her lip curls back on one side, her nostrils go wide, and the skin around her eyes draws tight.

"Get back on this horse, girl." Her words strain around clenched teeth, words that Helena would *never* speak to me.

Tuck snorts and jerks her head, stamping in the thick snow. But that isn't what roots my feet on that horrible, wintry path. It isn't even Helena's eyes, clouded by a white haze that moves and slithers, swallowing her pupils.

It's the scarlet-tinted shadows that leak from her body.

Whorls of foul darkness suddenly seep from her mouth and nose and radiate from her skin. Save for the stench, it reminds me of the Prince of the East.

I take a step away, and another, stopping only when something metal crashes behind me, followed by the thud of boots striking snow.

A nervous glance reveals the still-burning oil lamp on the ground and Alexus standing steady behind me.

He slips his hand across my hips to my waist and draws me close while the ring of his sword hisses through the night. "Leave the girl. Return to the Shadow World you came from, wraith."

My heart stutters. It can't be. Wraiths are just scary stories passed around bonfires in the summertime. There are no gods left to walk the Shadow World to free such an abomination.

Except...maybe a god wasn't needed this time. Maybe the guilty party is the one man made of shadow himself.

The thing inside Helena tosses her head back and laughs, the sound an ear-splitting shriek. "My *prince* wouldn't be very pleased to find that I disobeyed him."

No. I shake my head. It can't be.

The shadow dismounts Helena's body in that same awkward, stiff manner, wearing her skin like a cloak. It comes ever closer, smiling, but then stops and removes the gambeson, tossing it aside. Like before, it slides Helena's hand along her thigh, but this time, it drags Hel's destroyed dress up a sleek, dark leg until the buckle of one of Finn's dagger belts comes into view.

Fast as a heartbeat, the wraith unsheathes a weapon.

A long moment passes as I grasp what I'm seeing, all wrapped up in shadows, the reason the waters showed me so little back at the stream.

The pit of my stomach bottoms out, because according to this demon, the Prince of the East is indeed not dead.

But also because his shadow wraith holds my father's knife.

ALEXUS

I charge forward—to do *what* I'm uncertain—but Raina flings her arms wide, blocking me like a shield. I try to step around her—I'm not the one who's weaponless—but she shoves me back, eyes wild and commanding.

She pounds a sign against my chest, hard enough to bruise. I cover her hand with mine, feeling the letters.

Obey.

It takes everything in me to listen and keep my feet rooted where I stand. Shadow wraiths are part of Tiressia's ancient history that no longer belongs in our world. Wraiths haven't roamed our lands for centuries, the connection to the Shadow World severed by Urdin, God of the Western Drifts. Yet one is here, doing the bidding of a dangerous man.

I glance around. How did the prince know we were in the forest? Did his magick sense us?

"My prince says that I'm not meant to kill you, pretty Raina. Your time to die is not now. I am to take you to my lord." The thing points Helena's dagger at me instead. "But I get to kill *him* if I must." It takes a step, raising Helena's angled brow over her cat-like gaze. "And I must."

Raina looks at me from the corner of her eyes and flutters her fingers. Instinctively, I know what she's asking for.

My sword.

There's only one way to destroy a wraith. Raina has to kill Helena—quick and precise—to trap the wraith within. If she fails, if the girl clings to life a moment too long, the wraith could slip inside one of us instead.

The last thing I need is something else inside me.

There are no Elikesh words to whisper to send this demon back to the Nether Reaches of the Shadow World, so I hand Raina my weapon. This is something I must let her face. It's *her* friend's life. This wraith is hers to kill.

But though she readies the blade and prepares her stance, I still fear she won't be able to do what must be done. The wraith doubts her too. It laughs, a vile sound echoing through the wood.

"You'll never do it," the thing says, the lamplight illuminating Helena in a way that makes her look gaunt and grim. "You'll never kill your dear, young friend."

It tilts Helena's head at an abnormal slant, and the stare coming from the girl's eyes changes. The white storm hovering over her pupils dissipates, and her irises darken to their normal state.

But sweet gods, her face. It changes, contorting on the edge of a rising scream while the rest of her body remains stiff and still as ice. Her brow crumples with cold fear, and terror flashes across her features, widening her eyes, trembling in her chin.

When her scream tears loose, rupturing the frosty air of the quiet forest, it's Helena. The sound—disturbing as it is agonizing—is wholly her, aware and present, echoing without a hint of the perverse possession living inside.

"Raina, please! Help me!"

Tears slide hot and fast down the girl's dark cheeks as she strains, struggling against the thing keeping her imprisoned. She bristles, and her shoulders jerk violently, her feet moving her body forward with lumbering steps, like maybe she's winning the fight.

Or maybe the wraith is taunting us. Taunting Raina. Letting her glimpse enough of her friend to make the necessary end more difficult.

Raina flexes her fingers around the hilt, chest rising and falling fast with rapid breaths. I can sense her indecision. Her uncertainty. The impossibility of the moment.

She doesn't succumb to the lure. Instead, she shifts her weight from foot to foot as Helena inches closer.

This wraith won't let me escape easily, and it won't let Raina simply walk away. It will use Helena to achieve its goal, whatever that may be. The Prince of the East wants the threat of my existence removed, but he has plans for Raina, too, it seems.

And that will not do.

While the wraith has given up a bit of its hold, I bend down, going for the curved knife in my boot. If Raina can't stop this thing, I will.

But I don't get the chance.

The wraith sweeps Helena's arm through the air, and with such little effort, knocks Raina out of the way, sending her tumbling along the snowy path. The horses spook and take off in the same direction while the wraith rushes me like it did at the lake. It sheathes its knife and grabs my blanket, managing to fist my tunic too, and slings me through the air like I'm no more than an annoying branch under its feet.

I slam into a tree at the path's edge, pain zipping up my spine and ringing my skull before I collapse face-first in the snow.

There isn't even time to lift my head before I'm flipped over, my wrists pinned to the ground. Helena's face stares down at me, lips drawn back in a hungry snarl. She's not a small girl—built to be a fighter, not a waif—but she isn't *this* strong.

Shadows bleed from her, filling her eye sockets and nostrils and mouth with red smoke. Those scarlet shadows wriggle and squirm, coiling and spiraling toward me.

I press the back of my head into the snow and jerk my hips to buck her off me, but there's nowhere to go, and she doesn't budge.

Instead, she leans close and kisses me deeply.

At first, I gag around her invading tongue, her nipping teeth, even her soft but hungry lips. She smells and tastes of pungent death and the bowels of the Nether Reaches. But something inside me changes. The smell burning my nose and searing my throat vanishes, and my disgust and fury slip away, leaving me filled with wanting.

Helena lets go of my wrists and grasps my face, bearing down on me harder. I don't fight her anymore. I can't—because I don't want to.

Need builds inside me, a need to inhale her, to let her flood me, filling my every cell with her presence. Wanting more, I slide my hands up her body and thread my fingers into the black curtain of her hair. I fist the silkiness and crush her to me, my own hunger taking over, craving something dark and carnal only she can give. I'm thirsting, and her mouth is a fount, my only relief.

She drags her teeth across my lower lip, easily bringing blood from the wound Raina gave me at the stream. Drawing back, she licks crimson from her mouth, and in that small expanse of time, I'm left with an ache inside my chest but also a moment of realization.

"Oh, it *is* you," the thing says. "I wasn't sure. Didn't believe. But I taste the shade within you, sorcerer."

The wraith's spirit spreads out in a cloud and folds around me like a nebulous hand. When it uses Helena to kiss me again, I'm helpless to fight, even though I can feel its oily presence pouring into me, crawling and curling beneath my skin, obscuring all the light until I fall, plunging into a bottomless abyss.

It's no abyss, though. I'm tumbling backward through the years, a long lifetime of memories passing by as illusory as ever.

The falling slows, and there, in this place of nothingness, I'm met with the darkest parts of myself. They're illuminated in bold and breathtaking light, the moments of my life that will surely one day see me bound to the pits of the Shadow World, along with all the other monsters.

I try to fight it, to claw my way free.

I can't endure this.

That thing gives me no choice, though, forcing me to watch as every life I've ever taken slips from existence—including the woman who once held my heart so completely, and the son she bore in my name.

It's like I'm there all over again, standing knee-deep in mid-summer crops, hearing their screams chase over the vale. I run, sickle in hand, desperation clenching my heart while the hot sun beats down upon my back.

I see the slice of the blades before I can reach them, the bloody slits smiling at their throats, their empty eyes watching a blue sky for the last time. I feel my love's auburn hair in my hands, my son's tiny body cradled in my arms.

I didn't save them. I'm the reason they were killed at all. A man with magick who wanted to be a nobody farmer yet tangled with the wrong king. Over time, I've forgotten the details of their precious faces, but now, in this infernal creation of a shadow wraith, they stare back at me with excruciating clarity.

Misery washes through me, intense and violent. The shadow folds around the deepest part of me, the part I must keep locked away at all costs. There's a prison inside me, and the shadow rattles the cage, agitating the thing my magick has held captive for so long.

No. No, no, no.

Don't stir him, I plead. *Don't weaken me. Nephele, please. I beg you. Where are you?*

From somewhere beyond, I sense pain, knowing inherently that it isn't mine. It's only mingled with my consciousness. Suddenly, I'm falling again, this time toward a dim but present light surrounded by shadow.

I open my eyes to find Helena still atop me. A grimaced of disbelief twists her face, and her hand is raised, her bleeding palm folded around the edge of my sword like she caught it mid-swing.

Because she did.

Raina stands above us, hands tight around the hilt, rage hot in her eyes.

With the taste of the Shadow World still thick in my mouth, I rise on my elbows, but before any of us can make another move, the earth quakes, and the wood beyond the shadow wraith shifts.

I squint into the ghostly wood, unsure what I'm seeing. Even the shadow wraith turns a glance over Helena's shoulder. Raina looks too.

The dense tree line opens, one tree after another unfurling from the tangle, creaking back to where it belongs. A groan fills the night, the sound of wood waking, followed by unnatural sighs whispering through the air on a hushed moan.

The earth shakes again, so hard the wraith tumbles off me. Raina's knees give, and she falls at my side. I curl my arm around her waist, pull her close, and hold tight as deep drifts of snow dislodge, the vibrations causing the dense layers to break apart and settle, scattering through the wood.

Trying to stand on human feet, the wraith grips the narrow limbs of two saplings an arm's length away. The ground settles, but panic hangs like a mask from Helena's face, as though the wraith knows more than us.

It tries to run, but the saplings come to life, snaking around Helena's legs before the wraith can take her far, bringing the girl's body to its knees at my feet.

Gnarled roots of a dozen trees rip from the ground and flail in the air, scattering frozen dirt through the forest. Leaves fall from branches, and birds flee their nests as the roots land like twisted wooden talons, stabbing into the now-thin snow. They creep toward the wraith, almost taunting, like the demon taunted us.

I feel her then—Nephele—her magick warm and reassuring against my skin. Raina looks at me, eyes round. She feels her too.

A soil-covered root reaches out and coils around Helena's waist. The wraith fights the woody grip, kicking wildly, but when it can't break free, it looks back at me with evil shining in Helena's eyes. Suddenly, it clamps a hand around my ankle.

With extraordinary strength and an unnatural moan, the wraith yanks me from Raina's arms, taking me with it when more roots latch on to Hel's body and drag us deeper into the wood. The wraith screams, a wail that curdles my blood.

I flip to my front and claw at the ground, grasping for anything until I finally stop sliding, and Helena's hands let go.

Panting, I turn over, and Raina rushes to my side. She clutches my tunic and arm, her breaths hard and fast as my own. Ahead, in that silver-outlined dimness, the wraith kneels inside a cage made of roots and seedlings. It thrashes against a dark vine wrapped around Helena's wrists and mouth, a vine that stifles the wraith's cries.

But it's no longer the wraith prostrate before us. It's Helena. She's close enough that I can make out the abject horror etching deep lines in her face, the panic burning bright in her eyes. The wraith has let her through once again—to torment us.

But gods, how it must torment Helena.

Raina lurches into the wood. I stumble to my feet and run after her, hooking an arm around her waist a second before she reaches Nephele's makeshift prison. She twists and turns, jerking against me, but I hold fast.

There's nothing we can do for Helena now, not if we want to live.

"Listen to me, Raina." I shift her around and catch her wild gaze with a steady stare. "This is Nephele's doing," I tell her. "I know you feel her.

She's doing this because Helena isn't Helena anymore. She would've killed me and taken you to the prince had Nephele not intervened, and you have no idea what that would've meant for your future."

Raina pushes out of my arms. *"What is she then?"* she signs. *"She is not that* thing *lurking inside her."* She steals a glance over her shoulder at her sobbing friend, sitting helplessly in her cage. When Raina looks back at me, tears stream down her dirt-streaked face. *"I have lost everything. I cannot lose her too. I will not let the Prince of the East take her from me. I refuse."*

She stalks around the wood, studying the ground, the treetops, fisting her hands in her hair. I can see her anguish, her desperation to find anything, think of anything, do anything that might help Helena.

As more tears flow, her inconsolable weeping ensnares my heart. A sense of defeat pulses from her, a sense that she's coming to terms with her powerlessness in this situation.

It almost breaks me.

I go to her and take her face in my hands. "Stop. Look at me." When she meets my gaze, her furor eases. Her panting remains, but her cold hands wrap around my wrists like I'm the only thing keeping her tethered to this world. I press my forehead against hers. "Just breathe."

Her gasping slows, and the snow stops falling around us. I swear the wood feels warmer too.

Moments later, I muster my calmest, softest voice. "If there were any other way to protect us, Nephele would take it. She would spare your friend this torture. You know she would. This cage has to be all she can manage. You must believe it's for the best. That wraith won't let Helena die. It needs her alive if it plans to remain in this world. Nephele will also do anything she can to ease the conditions, though having a wraith inside her makes Helena far more tolerant to extremes. We, however, do not have that advantage. We cannot stay here, and we cannot free your friend of this wraith in a way that won't harm her." I pull back and wipe away the tear tracks from Raina's face with my thumbs, memorizing the feel of her skin, the curves of her face. "But we *will* find a way," I tell her. "And we *will* return. I swear that to you. I need you to trust me. Please."

She stares at me like she's seeing me for the first time. I understand that she knows little about the wisdom and talents of the witches at Winterhold, and I know that I'm the last man she ever thought she would have to depend on, but I need her to know that I can be the kind of man who's worthy of her trust. That I already am.

After a heartbeat, she nods and slips from my grasp.

"Why is he doing this?" she asks.

I let out a long breath and drag my hand through my hair. Her question is vague, and I let it remain that way. *This* could refer to many things, things we can't get into right now. So I give her a vague truth. It's all I can do.

"I don't know. I don't even know *how* he's doing it, but he is."

He shouldn't have this power. Wielding wraiths was an old practice of the Summerland magi. A few Eastland sorcerers managed the skill, but that was centuries ago, before Urdin sealed the Shadow World.

"I want to say goodbye," she signs.

I can't help but eye her warily. I'm the one who needs to trust, I suppose.

"Just be careful. That wraith isn't commanded to harm you but keep your distance regardless." I flex my hand, the skin still tingling from touching Raina so intimately. "I'll gather the horses."

Minutes later, I return with Mannus, the mare, our broken lamp, and my sword, too worried to do anything but make haste. Raina sits on her knees in the snow next to the rootbound cage.

"I will come back for you," Raina tells the girl. *"I will come back, and we will take our revenge. Together. The Prince of the East will pay for this. For everything. On my honor."*

A cringe comes over me when she slips her arm through a gap in the roots. The wraith is still buried, though, and Helena only leans closer, allowing Raina to press the same sign they shared at the lake into her chest. Except this time, I realize that it's not one but *two* signs, for ancient Elikesh words.

Tuetha tah.

My sister.

Helena's brow furrows, and a choked-off sob resounds from her throat. The same desperation that lives inside Raina radiates from her friend, yet she still gives Raina the slightest nod of understanding—one that says she believes in Raina and her promises of salvation and retribution.

Raina forces herself away from the cage and stands, wiping her cheeks. When she faces me, seething, I believe her too.

As we mount the horses, the wraith returns.

"You will never escape him!" That eerie voice is a scream, a sound that makes the skin on the back of my neck prickle.

Raina and I face the wooden cage as the wraith presses Helena's face between two branches. The vine that covered her mouth and wrists moments before now struggles to crawl back up Helena's body, as if something is fighting it.

"Call to your witches all you want, Collector." The wraith wears a wicked grin. "Beg your ancient gods for help. But it's the Prince of the East to whom Tiressia will eventually pray. He sees. He knows. Even *your* secrets are not safe."

With a glance toward the sky, sinking dread fills me. *It is you,* the wraith said when it tasted my blood.

I close my eyes. If the wraith knows who I am, perhaps the prince knows too. I'm not sure what that means for Tiressia or me, but it can't be good. The Prince of the East means to rule this empire, and he's executing his plan—one I have yet to fully comprehend.

And I have no idea how to stop him.

22

RAINA

I ride between Alexus's legs, nestled against him, the God Knife hidden in my boot. When Alexus left to gather the horses, I spotted the knife in the upturned earth near Helena's cage. It's so warm now, where it was bitterly cold for so long. Though I sense that change in the weapon, and it feels more alive, I find myself far less sure if the God Knife is as powerful as Father always said or if Mother was the one who was right. Because I slid that blade into the face of the Prince of the East, and even still, he lives.

Not for long, though. Somehow, someway, I'm going to get out of this construct, and God Knife or no God Knife, I'm going to destroy him.

It's been so long since we left Helena. Three days at least. Maybe more. My hands grew too cold to man the reins shortly after we turned for the mountains, and my hands are my lifeline. And so here I am, huddled against a man I thought I hated, letting him hold me tight, hour after frigid hour, easing me with the curve of his body, breathing his warmth into my neck. Any discomfort at being so near him has vanished. The God Knife hides a few feet from my hand, but I can't imagine using it to harm Alexus now. We aren't anything like strangers anymore, and certainly nothing like enemies.

Compassionate like friends. Tender like lovers.

I'm learning the shape of his body. How he sleeps. The sound of his breathing. And I'm thankful for all of it—the gentle way he runs his hands along my thighs to build heat inside me, the way he clasps my hands and holds them against his chest when they tremble, how he nuzzles his lips into the crook of my neck when he needs to warm them. It doesn't bother me. Instead, it feels oddly right, like we fit together in every way.

And that confuses me to the point that I have to stop thinking about it.

The gambeson isn't large enough to fold around both of us entirely and provides little comfort as we fight to remain awake. Poor Tuck follows behind, tied off and covered in the blanket from Littledenn.

Our lamp is broken, but the sky provides more light than before. It's an odd color now, reminding me of the soft pink shade of my mother's roses, like a morning sunrise, if a sunrise-sky never changed. We can't know how many Eastlanders might be waiting in the surrounding forest or what animals might be waiting to spring, so the light is a blessing.

Every so often, we stop to rest for a few hours, usually curled together against a tree. Then we get back to the path and trudge onward.

We haven't talked about what happened. Whatever the wraith did to Alexus, it rattled him. He rode in a daze for several hours after, his mind in another world. But when my grief for my friend became too much, he shook off his own unease and held me, wiped my tears and whispered kindness into my ears as another cresting wave arrived.

As we travel, Alexus fills the time by telling me stories about distant lands that I'm sure must be fiction, and he speaks to me in Elikesh, reciting what sounds like poems that are so beautiful they easily lull me to sleep. Another few times, we pause our riding to move our legs and nibble on what we can from the pack. The cold has ruined the apples, though we still feed the mush and skins to the horses. We've already drained the flask, leaving us longing for the drink's warmth in the pits of our bellies.

We're wearing down fast. We need real sustenance and sleep and fire, or this construct could become our final resting place.

When we set to riding again, I beg Nephele to send aid soon, to find some enchantment that will weave everything we need into this godsforsaken construct. The snow and blistering winds have all but stopped, and Alexus swears the cold has relented, but we're both still struggling. My eyes keep closing of their own volition, an awful fate, because when my eyes are closed, I see all the things that led me to this moment, beginning with the God Knife being delivered to our cottage door. After that, I see my scheming and thieving, my hidden preparations, and the little white lie I told my mother the morning of Collecting Day.

It only gets worse from there.

I'm also met with the devastating truth of our circumstance when I close my eyes. Three times since we left Helena in the wood, the Prince of the East has found me. He stares at me from my dreams like a figment, but I know he's here, very much alive, and I know he's watching.

I just don't know how, and I don't know why.

Two thoughts swirl in my mind. *Keeper.* Why had he called me that on the green? The word repeats in the back of my brain, but it holds no meaning. The other thought takes me back to the stream. Alexus said a rumor reached Winterhold that the Prince of the East meant to break King Regner's treaty and invade the Northlands, all because he wants the Frost King. At the time, I couldn't have cared less what he meant to do with the king, but now, I understand that the Prince of the East has a larger mission.

And I need to know what it is.

We stop once more, and this time, huddled under a tree, I can't sleep, even though Alexus holds me close, sharing his heat. I warm my hands between our bodies until I feel like I can manage a few sentences. It's the same question I asked before I had to leave Helena, but one I've avoided since for fear of conjuring the enemy. But I can't avoid it anymore.

"Why is the prince doing this? What does he want with the king? A real answer this time."

Alexus scrubs his brow. "Those are two different questions. I truly can't say that I know *why* he's doing this. I don't know his ultimate goal. I have ideas, but the longer I'm in this construct, the less certain I am about anything I thought I knew. Like Helena. Whether he used her to slow us down or stop us all together, I'm uncertain. The wraith wanted to kill me, not you, and I'm not sure what to make of that, what the prince intends to do with you once he has you." He switches to signing. *"Unless he knows what you are."*

I swallow hard, and my pulse pounds.

"Do you think he knows?" Alexus adds. *"Did he see your witch's marks?"*

I shake my head in earnest, but then I replay every second of our fight on the green. I don't recall the prince ever looking at my marks once they became visible. My hands, neck, and chest markings were uncovered, but at least one hand—the one he focused on—was drenched in his blood. As for my neck and chest, my hair is long and thick.

My mind reels. What if the prince *does* know? When I saw him while riding with Helena, he said *Hello, Keeper. I see you.* I'd felt a sense of being watched—being followed—but nothing had been there.

Or had it?

A dark crow flies from tree to tree along the road's edge, and its eyes fix on me. I curl closer against Alexus and burrow deeper inside his dark cloak, thankful for the protection.

What if *those* are the eyes I've felt? What if his crows saw me healing Alexus? Helena? Maybe he sensed me healing Helena through his wraith.

Gods. What if I end up with the prince after all? His personal Healer and Seer?

While my thoughts melt into sheer panic, Alexus falls asleep, his body softening around mine. So much for my question about the king. I'm not sure I can cope with more information right now anyway.

Another crow flutters overhead, keeping its eyes on me—just for its prince, I'm certain. I can't prevent the little pricks from spying, but at least I know to look for them now. And I swear, at some point, I'm going to kill them with my bare hands.

This time, when my eyes close and the prince appears, there's a feeling that he's searching for something more than me.

"What in Thamaos's name *are* you?" he whispers, reaching out across time and space to touch my face, watching me from gods' know where, even as I rest in Alexus's arms.

What am I? I send the message from my mind. *What the fuck are you?*

Opening my eyes, I shiver from the memory of his closeness. It felt like he was an inch from my face, the warmth of his fingertips lingering like a real touch. Did he ask what I am because he heard Alexus earlier?

The prince's ability to project himself into my consciousness, and the fact that he can disappear on a whim, makes me wonder if he's inside this construct at all. I can't imagine why he would stay here if he can simply vanish into nothingness, unlike we mere mortals who haven't harnessed darkness itself.

Then again, if he's so skilled in traveling through this world like the wind, why invade the vale at all? Why not go straight to Winterhold for the man he wants and whisk him away on a red cloud of death? Why come to me like this, like a ghost? Why can he not simply appear right here on this very path in all his shadow-infested glory?

Is it because he's truly a coward? Is he scared that I might do more than wound him this time?

Coward. I think the word, my body temperature rising from the heat of irritation and low-boiling rage. *Coward,* I repeat, and push the slur as hard as I can into the ether, praying he hears and that I make him angry enough to meet me face to face.

The moment shatters, though, because something across the path catches my eye: indigo light, a braided web of magick floating in the air in a thin clearing beyond the path's edge, nearly hidden by trees.

I close my eyes, worried I'm so exhausted that I'm imagining things. But when I open them, the magick is still there.

I suck in an excited breath, smack Alexus's chest, and point into the wood. He jolts awake, his arms tightening around me.

"What? What is it?" He reaches for his sword.

I point again, and this time, he sees it. Feels it, just like me.

Nephele.

We're on our feet faster than we've moved in days, dusting off the snow, leading both horses toward the clearing—toward the magick. I'm so stiff, but I move with swift steps, too swift, too excited, especially for a woman with a knife that can supposedly kill anyone shoved inside her boot.

I can't help it—my heart races with knowing. I can *feel* my sister, almost like she might be standing in that clearing waiting for me when I get there.

Only she isn't.

What *is* there still makes me smile.

Under the glimmering blue strands of inserted magick, there's kindling. *Dry* kindling. It sits in a pile in the middle of a grassy circle, like a spring meadow has been cut out of a tapestry and placed inside this snow-covered magickal world built by witches from miles and miles away. There are two large logs for sitting and resting, and moonberry bushes grow all around.

Their pale blue fruit is ripe for picking, and the roots hold sweetwater we can gorge on.

Better still, one of the prince's crows—a massive thing—sits on a low-limbed tree, watching me steadily.

The sigh of relief that leaves Alexus is more like a groan of ecstasy, and I can't help but look at him and grin. We're going to rest, fill our bellies and warm our bones, and then I'm going to break my way out of this construct so I can find the Prince of the East and end this.

Strange how everything has changed. How my hatred of the Frost King has been the last thing on my mind for a while. How I'm now smiling at the man that I wanted to kidnap a handful of mornings ago and aching for the death of another man I've only just met. Now, when I try to decipher who my real enemies are in this game, I'm no longer so sure. The game is bigger than I ever dreamed, and I'm its newest player.

I walk toward Nephele's skillful refuge and stop next to the crow. Boldly, I meet its gaze and wait until I feel its master rouse behind those beady eyes, curious as always.

When I grab the annoying little soulless scout, neither one of them expects it. Before I snap its neck—with my bare hands, just like I said I would—I push a message from my mind and send it straight to the shadow prince, wherever that bastard son of a demon may be.

Thanks for dinner, you maggot. I'm coming for you.

His voice reaches me on the edge of a laugh. *Best of luck, Keeper. I'll be waiting.*

23

RAINA

"Gods' death, Raina. I could kiss you right now." Alexus sits on the other side of the fire, half-hidden by soft swirls of gray smoke as he gnaws on a roasted crow's wing. Even from here, I can see those full lips, shiny from the fat of dark meat. He drinks from a moon-berry root and looks at me over the dancing embers. "For killing the bird," he adds.

"Of course," I sign. *"For killing the bird."*

My cheeks warm—and not from the flames flickering between us. I know full well that he's only relieved to have a bite to eat, a blazing fire, and a place to rest our weary bones.

I'm not sure why part of me wishes it was something more.

Curled up inside his cloak, I tip back a moonberry root and empty it before placing its husk in a pile with the others I've drained. I'm thankful for the nourishing liquid that quenches my thirst, but also for the roots, fleshy with thick skin. If we clean out the pulp, they'll make excellent storage for the berries, providing protection against the cold. Maybe, along with the berries, they'll keep us from starving, which I'm sure was Nephele's intent.

I lean against the log at my back and let out the longest, deepest sigh. The God Knife lies buried under a tuft of moss beside me, and Mother's bowl sits on a rock near the fire, handfuls of snow melting inside. They're the two things that symbolize what's been digging at me ever since we sat down to eat. I want to check on the Eastlanders and the Prince, and on Helena too, but now, I even feel brave enough to look for Finn. I need the closure of knowing what happened to him, especially after everything I went through with Hel.

As for the God Knife, I can't let go of the niggle in my mind that perhaps I should tell Alexus that it exists. That level of honesty with him should feel so foreign to me, but it doesn't anymore. Instead, I'm left wondering if maybe he knows something about such things. Maybe he can provide insight.

Or maybe telling him will complicate things further.

I'm so tired—too tired to get into *that* tonight. It's a kind of tiredness my body has never experienced but that I have no right to complain about. Before we got the fire going, I healed the frostnip on our fingers, and after Alexus prepared the crow and set it to roasting, we washed our hands and faces. He minded the bird while I tended my feet and the horses' minor cuts and ice-shod hooves. Even those small acts of healing drained me.

Though I feel rejuvenated now, it's hard to feel at ease. Here I lie with food in my stomach, stretched out on warm grass that has no right to exist inside this frozen forest, while a band of Witch Walkers works tirelessly to keep this construct intact, lest the remaining Eastlanders invade their home like they did the village. Then there's Helena, trapped like an animal and suffering the terrors of a demon alone in the cold. The heat in her body had to have come from the wraith, so she's most likely safe from freezing, but I still worry.

I can't help Hel or Winterhold's witches unless I'm whole, so I try my hardest to shut out the guilt I feel for these hours of reprieve.

Dropping my head back, I close my eyes and focus on how wonderful the heat of the fire feels, the way it chased away all the numbness and replaced it with life. But a white wolf howls, and I open them immediately and sit up, the muscles along the back of my neck tight.

I can't stop worrying about seeing the Prince of the East again or being flooded with memories of our burning, dying village or images of Helena fighting her demon or dead men under ice and snow. I'm not sure I'll ever be able to sleep again.

"Helena is out in the open," I sign when Alexus looks up at me from cleaning his hands. *"There are wolves."*

"She's fine, I swear." His eyes are ever the anchor, calming the flutter of worry inside my chest. "Her scent alone is enough to send a pack of wolves in the other direction. But also, *my* scent is all over her. It's the only reason the wolves haven't bothered us. They know to keep their distance. She'll be safe. *We're* safe." He stands and gestures to the ground beside me. "May I?"

I nod, and he sits with his back against the log, long legs bent at the knee.

"You should sleep. You barely slept while we were traveling." He motions toward the fire where the gambeson hangs on two sticks. "It'll be dry now and so warm. It makes a right bed, if you remember."

How can I do anything but grin at him like a fool? There's so much to think about, and yet he's worried about me sleeping and having a 'right' bed.

"I remember," I sign.

It would be impossible to forget.

Before, I wondered how Nephele could be friends with Alexus, but now it isn't hard to imagine. I can't say I understand it, why he takes people from the vale and why they don't hate him for it, but I can't seem to hate him either, much as I wanted to before all of this happened.

I reach across the small space between us and take his hand in mine. There's a bone-deep knowing when it comes to him, and so I'm not surprised when the lines crossing his palm call to me. I'm sure they're not calling to me the way palms called to Mena, but the need to see them closer is real.

I trace Alexus's lines into memory, reveling when he shivers at my touch. I've no idea what they mean, but I wonder.

"Do you read palms?" he asks. "We've a lady at Winterhold, from Penrith, who does."

"No," I sign. *"Not a clue."*

"Minds?"

I laugh and press another *No* into his palm.

He winks and smiles, then lets his head fall back as I tickle his skin. "That's probably a good thing. Though I bet you could if you tried."

Funny how he worries about me knowing what he's feeling and think-ing. First, he asked if I read people's emotions, and now this.

I wish I *could* read him—his emotions, his mind, his palms. Mena always said the lines of the hands define who we are. She labeled me well enough, calling me an idealist with volatile tendencies and someone who struggles with a mundane existence. She called me impulsive, impatient, and imaginative, a restless being who needs freedom to flourish and love to thrive.

I think she was right, but I fear those last two requirements for peace might be impossible anymore.

Alexus exhales and relaxes, as though my touch is all he needs to unwind. Though we've been pressed against one another for days, I would be lying if I said it didn't feel good to touch him outside the mode of sheer survival, just like it felt good when we touched at the stream. His hands are big and calloused, scarred in the way of a swordsman, strong and warm in ways I shouldn't be thinking about.

Delirium. It must be.

But maybe it isn't. Because ever since his words before we left Helena, I can't stop ruminating about how much I *do* trust Alexus, how I knew that I trusted him the moment he asked me to as we stood in the snow. Trust is earned, and though he hasn't had very much time to do so, he's only proven himself as unfailing. If I had to imagine what his palm would tell me, it would be that.

Unfailing.

When I'm grieving, he provides comfort. When I'm angry, he lets me rage but tempers my fury. When I'm frightened, he's right there beside me, facing whatever comes my way. *And sometimes tossing pebbles to scare me.*

I stifle a smile. My mind is in tangles over him.

Shaking my head, I snap out of the spell and rest his hand in my lap. He still has a little frostbite in places and blisters from the reins, so I set to healing him.

He winces and flinches and even hisses a time or two as I weave the tattered threads of his flesh back together. Eventually, he settles, watching my hands as I sing and work. Such a mystery, this man, though he also feels like an open book. Perhaps there are pages and lines I simply haven't had the time to read yet, chapters to lose myself inside. And perhaps I shouldn't want to.

But gods, I do.

Once the strands of his injuries are entwined, I ask, *"Any more wounds?"*

He twists his mouth up to one side as though considering if he should tell me something.

"No shame, just show me. Is it your feet?"

He barks out a laugh, as if what I said were funny, but I meant it. My toes looked horrendous, black-tipped and covered in blisters from too-small shoes. Feet are bad enough without all that damage.

"Frostbite?" I spell out, stifling a laugh myself. *"On your toes?"*

"No," he laughs again. "Somehow, my shameful feet are fine. But this..." He hooks his thumb in the hem of his tunic and tugs the fabric up his long torso. "Is another story."

I swallow hard. Not just because awful scrapes zigzag from navel to collarbone, but because I did *not* need to see this much of him right now. Sometimes I wish my face wasn't so expressive.

This is one of those times.

"When did this happen?" I ask, distracting myself from the dark dusting of hair on his chest and the even darker trail that disappears inside his britches. But I remember when he had to receive these marks, and he sees the recollection on my face.

"Damn thing dragged me a good ways. Rocks and roots and sticks and gods know what else lay beneath the snow and upturned soil. It'll heal fine on its own, though. No need for you to exhaust yourself even more for a few scratches."

I shove my stirring feelings aside and shift to my knees.

"More than scratches. Some are deep, probably painful. It should be easy," I tell him, which isn't a lie. They're not complex wounds, but they've been there for days now, and they don't look good. Even though I feel like I could sleep for a week, eating and drinking have replenished much of my strength, so I begin my work.

His strands are becoming so familiar, and each time I tinker with healing him, the tiny darkness of his stolen death hums and churns and sparks, a little lightning storm inside my heart. It's strange, that connection, that reaching out of energies, but I find I like it, feeling attached to someone other than myself.

It doesn't take long to heal his scrapes. I decide to heal the cut still marring his lip too—the wound *I* gave him. When it's over, I relax and open my eyes.

A yawn awaits, but my mind shuts it down, instead opting to send my hand straight to Alexus's body before I can think to rein myself in.

I dance my fingertips lightly up his healed skin, where a shallow cut traveled over his rippled stomach to the bottom of his chest only moments ago. There are scars I couldn't see before. Strange markings that remind me of runes, raised and rough like someone carved into him with a hot knife.

His midsection flinches at my touch, and he shifts his hips. "Raina."

I freeze at the sound of his husky voice, stopping my inspection over his pounding heart.

Only it wasn't an inspection. It was an exploration. My hand caressing, not analyzing.

When I look up at him, my pulse throbs so hard it's all I hear. Those green eyes stare back at me, dark and promising, and I can no longer make myself care that he's the Witch Collector. All I can see is the man who's been with me for days now, the man who carried me from a fiery village, who washed blood from my hands, who thought of me and me alone when he woke from near-death, a man who kept me warm while he froze.

I see a man. Nothing more and nothing less.

And I want something from him, though I can't tell if I only crave the comfort of closeness or if I'm searching for something more.

He trails his fingertips along my jaw. "It would be best if you didn't look at me like that."

I lean closer and lick my lips. *"Like what?"*

He gives me a piercing look. "Like you want me to kiss you. Because I will."

Softly, I rub my thumb over his healed lip. He slides his hand into my hair, fisting the roots, a pleasant invitation shining in his eyes.

Desire tumbles down my spine and pools low in my belly when he tightens his grip.

I don't move. I just hold his stare, a challenge that I hope I'm up for.

I'm fully aware that I'm testing any resolve either of us might've erected concerning one another, but the barriers I've assembled in defense of hatred no longer seem necessary when it comes to Alexus Thibault.

I know what I want, even if I shouldn't want it.

Even if I'll regret it later.

And right now, I want his mouth on mine—delirious from exhaustion or not. I want to forget. To find some sort of peace—even if only for a little while.

Alexus slides his hand down my side to the back of my knee. In one swift movement, he drags me onto him, my legs straddling his hips. He removes the dagger and belt from my thigh, tossing them aside, and tips the hood of his cloak from my head, untying the laces at my throat. His fingertips forge a fiery path across my collarbone, over my shoulder.

When the cloak falls away, leaving me sitting in leathers and the remains of my dress, a chill courses over me. The air is a mixture of the surrounding cold, the blazing heat of our fire, and the warm comfort of a meadow. It makes my skin feel alive and sensitive, hyper-aware of his every subtle touch.

With his torso still bared to my eye and his hands resting on my hips, Alexus stares up at me like I'm some kind of enchantment. Hesitation dances in his gaze too, and I'm not sure why.

"You are so tempting," he says. "But you need to know something." He takes my hand, presses it to his chest. "There is darkness inside me, Raina. Darkness you will not like."

I trail my palm over the curve of thick muscle, across his hard nipple, down his stomach, making him flinch again.

"There is darkness inside me too," I sign. "Perhaps our darknesses can be friends."

He does have darkness. I've seen it, like I'm seeing it now, moving like a phantom behind his eyes. I heard the wraith too. I know Alexus has secrets.

And I don't care. More than anything, I want him to touch me, and when he finally does—when he runs those deadly hands up my thighs, to my waist, traveling along my ribs to my breasts—the pressure of his grip sends burning desire tearing through my blood.

Alexus folds his arm around me and draws me down, wrapping his fist in my hair again. I plant my hands on the log behind him, but he tugs me closer, until there's no space between us. I can feel every rigid inch of him, and he feels divine. It's a heady moment, making me long for so much more than a kiss.

He brushes his mouth against mine, a whisper-kiss, the contact so gentle yet so painfully forbidden. If only by me. Still, I quiver down to my toes when his lips ghost across mine, like he's savoring every curve, preparing to devour.

He meets my eyes again, another flash of hesitance, of too much thought, but the battle waged in his mind ends, and he truly kisses me.

I don't expect the raw hunger that ignites at the sweet taste of him, but in the time it takes my heart to flutter, I sink my hands into his dark hair, and it's *me* who's devouring. I can't think around anything other than this yearning inside me, this *rush*, the way his heat and hardness tempt me beyond all rationalization, the way his tongue sliding against mine makes me gasp.

I was supposed to kidnap him, not kiss him. Not want him so badly I can barely breathe.

We become a tangle of roaming hands and kisses, any indecision about the situation gone. I tug Alexus's shirt over his head and marvel at the sight of him. Those broad, round shoulders and arms that could hold a woman for days. Then I dip my mouth to his chest, dragging my teeth over his firm, scarred flesh in a soft bite. He groans, that sound of ecstasy that sets fire to my senses.

I've hated being helpless these last days, feeling powerless.

But right now, I feel like a god.

Skillfully, he unthreads the laces at my back, one by one, kissing me all the while until the garment loosens. I sit up, strip free of the bodice and my thin undergarment, and toss them both aside. My witch's marks glow in the firelight, shades of gold, crimson, violet, and silver.

Alexus rests his hands at my waist, stopping me from returning to him. He skims his warm palms over my naked skin, admiring my marks, my curves, every dip and hollow. My body responds, tender parts of me tightening, aching, throbbing, so keenly aware of his eyes on me, his hands learning what takes my breath.

He's breathing so hard, his lips slightly swollen, his hair mussed. It's a lovely sight that I tell myself only makes me swoon because I need relief only he can give. This has nothing to do with anything more than that. Nothing to do with my heart.

Nothing at all.

"Gods, Raina." He closes his hand over my breast in a possessive grasp. "I want you."

I don't intend to make him wait.

It's been a long time since I've been with a man—been with Finn—but instinct becomes my guiding light. I lean down, pressing my naked body against Alexus's bare chest, and trail my tongue along the column of his throat. In response, he whispers my name, a choked, desperate sound, like he can't take much more when we've only just begun.

I love the way my name sounds falling from his lips. I want to make him say it a hundred times more. I want him to beg me to kiss him, beg me to take him, beg me to never stop.

He grazes his rough palms over my shoulders, curves those long fingers around my ribs, and I arch against him, my skin tingling when his touch slides down my back and over my hips.

Digging his fingers into my backside, he presses all that hardness between my legs, making me shiver, making me *want*.

This is desperation, desire so enthralling that I roll my hips over and over, demanding and greedy, feeling like I might die if I don't feel him inside me soon.

He slips his hand between us, tugging at the ties of my trousers. Breaking our kiss, I lift my hips for him, and he slides his hand inside the leathers.

I close my eyes on a gasp, letting him touch me where I want more of him. He's deft with that hand, and in seconds, I'm climbing toward the point of no return.

This shouldn't be happening. It shouldn't be the Witch Collector drawing such damp heat from my body, making my mind numb to anything but the ache he's stoking like a fire. That thought evaporates as he presses his teeth into my shoulder, returning my soft bite from earlier, and dips his hungry mouth to my breast. I move against his touch, chasing the promise that lives in the feverish swirl of his tongue, the rough tip of his finger.

He drags his teeth from my breast and kisses a scorching path to my ear.

"Don't stop. Take what you need." His lips move hot at my throat and then close over my mouth, swallowing my sighs.

I'm on the very edge of euphoria, eyes closed, mouth consuming, when Alexus's handsome face, imprinted on the backs of my eyelids, vanishes. In its place floats the smug, damaged countenance of the Prince of the East.

I jerk away from Alexus, the coiled pleasure inside me unwinding like the threads of a dying life, and the fire within me turns to ice. I keep my eyes closed, holding that connection, determined to do something this time, though I don't know what.

"My, my," the prince says, "you grow more interesting by the minute. What do all these lovely marks mean?" He shakes his head. "Never mind. I'll have time to learn them later. For now, I thought I'd let you know that I figured out what kept pulling me back to your mind. It was something I didn't know existed until I sensed it all over you, but it's something I terribly need back where it belongs, and I intend to make that happen." A laugh bellows out of him, a smoky, obscene sound. "This is goodbye, Keeper, for now. I hate to leave you in this terrible construct, but you'll be safely trapped for when I'm ready for you. And you obviously know how to keep yourself entertained. It's been lovely. And I *do* mean *lovely*. My sincerest thanks for the show." He leans in and raises an evil brow. "But more importantly, thanks for the God Knife."

24

ALEXUS

One moment, Raina is in my arms on the cusp of bliss. The next, she's clambering off me, scrambling across the ground half-naked toward a crow perched on a tuft of moss. The bird takes off, wings flapping wildly, but Raina lunges, hand darting out like a strike of lightning, and grabs the creature by the wing. She flings the crow to the ground, its screeching caw enough to wake the Ancient Ones, and before I can do anything more than sit up, she's driving a knife through its thick chest.

"Gods' balls, what in the bloody blazes?"

I get up and go to her. I'm still raging hard and lingering in a haze of lust, even though the woman I want has crow blood splattered on her bare chest.

Breathing heavy and fast, she jerks her hand back, bringing the knife with it. The sound of the blade leaving the bird is a disgusting squelch in the night.

I haven't seen a blade in Raina's possession since our moments on the village green, save for the Littledenn dagger I gifted her—the one I slipped from her thigh minutes ago. But the blade she held to my throat wasn't on her person when I collected her from the village. Or at least I don't think it was. In truth, I checked her for weapons and only found an empty belt strapped to her thigh.

Helena had a knife, though.

Raina looks up at me, her beautifully marked torso painted in blood. Her glassy eyes are wide and hard, a crimson-slicked knife in one hand, a dead crow pressed beneath the other.

Gods. Virago, indeed.

And yet, I'm still stupidly aroused. Maybe more so.

Shaking it off as best I can, I kick the dead bird away and, after a few moments, crouch before Raina. She's already lowered the blade, shielding it behind her back like she's trying to hide it from me. She takes a deep inhale and sits on her heels, then blows out a long breath.

"Want to talk about it?" I ask with a half-smile, an effort to dismantle some of the crackling energy and tension in the air. "I'm not sure what this was all about," I gesture to the slaughtered crow, "or where you got that knife, but I'm all ears if you'd like to tell me a story."

She glances down at her bloody breasts and back at me.

"Ah, that won't do." I procure a cloth from the pack along with the bowl of melted snow from beside the fire—the bowl she said belonged to her mother. "Join me?" I ask and motion to the log.

Knife still clenched in her hand, she sits with me. She's shaking, though not from fear. Rage rolls off her, and I figure she'll tell me what's wrong when she's ready.

It's strange, washing her like this—her face, hands, *body*—but she lets me, almost like she needs me to.

Outside of the bizarre crow murder, she's still the most beautiful thing I've ever seen. I slide the warm, wet cloth across her tawny skin, still wanting her so much, even though there's a blade in her grasp and fury shadowing her eyes.

I glance at her hand. How white her knuckles are, like she wouldn't let go of that knife for anything. Setting the bowl aside, I retrieve her discarded bodice and undergarment. The heat of her attack is probably still boiling in her blood, but the cold will eventually set in.

Finally, she looks at the knife, then at me, and turns to clean her hand and the blade in the water, drying the weapon on moss. When I step close again, she accepts the bodice but keeps the knife at her side, out of my sight.

I extend a waiting hand. "I can hold the blade for you."

She shakes her head, tucks the knife between her knees, and starts struggling into her clothes.

"At least let me help with the laces?"

She nods, and though it's the last thing I want to do, I sit behind her, straddling the log, and help her dress. The moment we shared has passed, and that's probably best. We're in the middle of a terrible situation, one where emotions can easily twist into unrecognizable feelings. She held a knife to my throat only days ago, almost left me for dead, the only other person in the vale that she knew to be hanging on to a thread of life. This lust, this *attraction*, will lead Raina to a rude awakening once we're safe at Winterhold. There's so much she doesn't know about me. My darkness and her darkness are two very different things. I'm nothing if not one big secret, far from the kind of man she needs in her life.

Knowing that still doesn't make me want her less.

After the last ribbon is tied, she retrieves the thigh belt, straps it on, and swaps out the old dagger for this new blade.

She slips the dagger in her boot and returns to the log, surprising me when she tucks herself between my knees, clasps my face in her hands, and kisses me again. It's a kiss that's so hard and deep I'm left breathless and starving for more when she pulls away and presses her forehead to mine.

Gods, I *ache* for this woman in my bones.

"You can't keep kissing me like that, or we might never leave this place," I tell her. My heart races like I'm a boy again, darkness and secrets be damned. "Worse yet," I add, "I might never learn why you hate crows so much."

It's a bad joke given what happened in the vale, but a moment of levity is needed.

At last, the tension lifts, and a smile tugs the corner of her mouth, though it doesn't reach her eyes.

"The Prince of the East has been following us. Watching. His crows."

It takes a moment for her words to sink in, but then...

I close my eyes on a sigh, feeling like a damned fool. Of course he has.

Of course a prince who can command a flock of crows would use them as spies. There is, after all, an all-seeing eye on his flag.

"But it is more than that," she adds. *"He has been watching* me." She pats her chest.

I frown, not liking the path this story is taking. "Through the birds?"

"Yes. And he comes to me when I sleep."

My blood goes cold. "Why did you not tell me? And what do you mean he *comes* to you?"

She shrugs and taps two fingers against her temple. *"He appears. In my mind. It happened just now. He asked what my marks mean and thanked me for the show, and for..."*

I narrow my eyes when she pauses. "For...what?"

She glances toward her leg—toward that knife—and after a moment of hesitation, unfastens the leather strap of her dagger belt with a trembling hand.

"This blade belonged to my father. He found it on the Malorian seashore. He was a guard witch. He called it a..." Her hands go still again, and she bites her lip, the look on her face one of internal strife.

"You can trust me, Raina." I push a lock of hair behind her ear. "I swear it."

She unsheathes the blade and holds it before me in one hand. With the other she signs, *"A God Knife."*

My mind stumbles around her words, maybe because I'm still torn between desire and utter confusion, but...

I look at the blade. *Really* look at it. There's no blood covering it now. No lovely hand wrapped around its hilt. No stunning woman hiding it from my sight.

My magick, buried and held to task, wails like an animal in a trap.

Shaking, I stare, breaking out in a chilled sweat. It's been so long since I last held the knife, so long that I didn't recognize it at first glance. I don't sense it anymore. The blade is still black as midnight, and the Stone of Ghent still shines, but any bond I ever had with this creation feels broken —at least for me.

"This is impossible." Instinctively, I push away from her. My heart trips over itself, and I can hardly breathe. "There was only ever one God Knife, and it vanished many, many years ago."

I press my hand to my chest, feeling for power that I cannot reach.

She blinks once, watching my reaction so closely. *"But it is real,"* she says. *"You know what a God Knife is."*

I have to fight not to scoff at that.

"Yes, I know what *the* God Knife is." I scrub my hand down my face, certain I'm frozen in a dream. "But *you* shouldn't, and you certainly shouldn't have it."

On impulse, I reach for the knife, but Raina is too fast. She's up and two strides away—knife sheathed in her thigh belt—before my hand can get so close as an inch from the hilt.

My mind still feels like I've fallen into a broken reality, even more broken than the one I'm in, trying to move all the pieces back to their correct places so I can make sense of what this means.

One of the pieces slides into place.

"Was that the knife you put to my throat? Have you had it all this time?"

She nods but then shakes her head like she's confused as to how to answer. There's no denial on her face, and why would there be? She owes me nothing, and she certainly owed me nothing before.

"Helena had it. I thought I lost it in the fire. I took it from near her cage."

I never saw it. Never took the time to notice. The shadow wraith used *my* dagger when it came after me on the ice, but when it attacked in the wood? So much was happening, and so fast, that I can't remember what knife the girl held. All I know is that the wraith had permission from its prince to end my life, and it called me 'sorcerer,' tasted the shade within me. That thing—and very possibly the Prince of the East—knows more about me than most anyone.

Heart pounding, I stand, hands raised in placation as another piece of our situation sinks and settles in my mind, followed by another and another until I'm imagining all sorts of fall out. Raina has no idea the power she's holding, how this weapon could turn the tide of our entire world if it falls into the wrong hands.

And the wrong hands are working very, very hard to acquire it.

"So you have the God Knife." I keep my voice steady as I sort through my chaotic thoughts. "And the Prince of the East knows it exists."

She nods, brows pinched.

"And he sent his crow here to retrieve it. Because he can see us?"

Again, she nods.

I cover my mouth with my hand, drag my fingertips through my beard.

"Perhaps it does not matter," she signs, *"or perhaps the knife is not as real as I have believed."*

I stare at her, dumbfounded, though I realize that her lack of understanding is not her fault.

"I cut the prince with this knife," she adds. *"After he stabbed you."* She draws a line on her face, from temple to chin. *"And he is still alive."*

Of course he is, though I can't understand why he didn't take it from her when he had the chance.

Before I can inquire further, she says, *"He said that he sensed it all over me, that it kept drawing him back to me. He wants the knife back where it belongs."*

I don't know what that means. The last place the prince should want the knife is back where it belongs. It is of no use to him that way.

"He also said that this is goodbye, for now. That we are trapped until he is ready for me. He called me Keeper. He called me that before, on the green. What does it mean?"

Keeper. I rummage around in the recesses of my mind for anything that could give that word meaning in this instance. There were Keepers in the Summerlands—in the Hall of Holies—magi who protected the ancient scrolls and wisdom housed there. Raina is no mage, no Summerlander. Neither were her parents.

"I truly don't know what it means. Maybe tell me how your father came to have the knife. In detail."

She tries, but her father withheld so much, and much of what he knew of the knife was polluted by centuries of twisted lore. However, one thing stands out.

Yes, daughter. I keep it. Because I must.

I study the blade once more, clearing away my shock so I can focus. At first glance, there's nothing. Everyday eyes would see no magickal working at all—the spell on the blade was designed that way, I imagine. It requires single-minded concentration, but I can see the magick emanating from the weapon when I look hard enough. The enchantment is weak and old in normal years for most any kind of incantation, but I can read it all the same. There are so many binding spells in the world of magick, and this is yet another.

Keeper. Now it's beginning to make sense. Her father had no choice when it came to the God Knife. Someone cursed him with the task of keeping care of the blade, a curse that—though weak—has latched onto Raina. The prince didn't take it because he couldn't. Even now, when I peer into the ether around the knife, faint tendrils of magick cling to Raina's lovely hand and wrist like claws.

Which is why the prince sent the crow. Raina was distracted. She let her guard down. Put the knife aside.

And he saw.

I glance around the camp, another very critical piece of the puzzle sliding into place.

Helena.

I don't know how the girl came to have the knife after what happened between Raina and me on the green, but the Prince of the East learned that she'd procured it and tried to use an unwieldy shadow wraith to bring him the blade. If he's after what I think he's after, he will not stop until he has it. Though the statement about him wanting it back where it belongs still confuses me.

Raina takes a firm step closer. *"Why is he doing this? Tell me."*

This is the third time she's asked, and this time, I won't hold back—as soon as it's safer to do so.

"I will tell you," I sign, in case something or someone is listening. *"But first, we must get out of the open. This camp was a reprieve. Gifted by your sister. She knew we would need our strength for what lies ahead. You thwarted the prince's efforts. He might make certain we are trapped here, but he will also send something worse than a crow after the knife. We cannot sit and pray that he will not retaliate."*

Understanding dawns on her face, and I can see in her darting eyes that she grasps the severity of the moment, even without further details.

This time, it's me who takes a firm step closer. "I need you to let me have the knife, Raina."

I don't know if this is wise. It might be safer with her than with me, but I can't imagine how, and I just want to feel it, to see if the connection is truly lost.

She steps back, watching me with those sharp eyes.

Again, I lift my hands. "We cannot let the prince take this blade. It is the key to much devastation. And believe me when I tell you that, of the two of us, my darkness is the darkness the Prince of the East will not want to face." When she still hesitates, I drop to my knee, surrendering before her. "You were ready to trust me with your body, Raina. Trust me with this."

The tension in her jaw feathers as she stares down at me, but her clenched cheek finally relaxes. Though it takes several moments, she extends the knife between us.

I'm trembling like a newborn foal when I wrap my hand around the warm hilt.

My blood thrums with awareness, the heat from the stone sending a blaze straight to my heart and across my skin. That hasn't happened in so long that the rush of it is almost as intense as the pleasure I would've known had Raina ravished me minutes before.

I close my eyes and inhale a deep breath, gasping around the bond that hums and re-forms in my blood.

"Hello, drallag," the blade whispers.

25

RAINA

We ride steadily on the snowy path, our caution a vibration in the air. I've known fear. Those moments standing on the green, waiting for the Eastlanders to attack, and the time after, when violence and fire took all, were pure terror. I also felt it while watching Helena, consumed by a shadow wraith. When I swung that sword, the knowledge that it was her or us was one of the most painful moments of my life. I feel that way now, my insides as twisted as some of the trees in this construct. It's as though I'm standing on the precipice of a nightmare, so close to falling and never landing.

All I need is someone—or some*thing*—to tip me over the edge.

A tingle crawls along my spine, and I glance over my shoulder. I feel a presence. It started a while after we left the refuge, but there's nothing but dark woods and snow. Ahead, nothing but more dark woods, snow, and looming mountains.

And Alexus Thibault, a man I wasn't sure could even feel genuine fear until several hours ago. Now his fear is my fear, because if he's scared, I'm fairly certain I should be as well. I'm just not entirely sure what it is I'm supposed to fear most—the Prince of the East, the worry for what lies ahead, or the secrets of my companion.

Buried in the gambeson, I keep my tired eyes peeled to the tree line, swinging my gaze back and forth with an occasional glance at the sky. For the last few hours, the color has gradually shifted from the soft pink that reminded me of my mother's flowers to a deep, grim red—a shade that sadly reminds me of her too. The whole world is cast in this bloody moonlight glow, reflecting off the snow.

The white wolves are out, prowling in the shadows, and crows follow us through the trees. I'm past the point of exhaustion and have arrived at the place where I'm questioning everything. Is this real? Or is this some illusion thanks to the distressed state of my mind and body?

The unholy melody of baying howls and gurgling croaks, along with a cold snap of wind, reminds me that this is very real.

It also feels like a warning.

I wriggle my feet in my boots, the press of warm steel reassuring. In my left boot resides the old dagger from Littledenn. In the right, the curved Eastlander blade that Alexus found in the snow. He gave it to me in exchange for the God Knife and dagger belt. It was the right thing to do, but there are moments like now, however brief and cutting, when I question my judgment.

But I trust him. Even with his words of darkness. Even though he knows things he's yet to share. And even though he's the Witch Collector —I feel safer with him leading the way, God Knife in his grasp.

More than anything, I believe him when he speaks of his darkness. I don't know what it is, but the truth of its existence is undeniable. When Alexus saw the God Knife—*truly* saw it—the green in his eyes turned black and liquid, that primal stare boring into my soul like he could enter me if he gazed long enough. Otherworldly, I'd called it before.

It's more than that, though. I just can't define it.

Yet.

We come to a crest in the wood, and Alexus halts Mannus. He throws a fist in the air to stop me as well. I take a deep breath, smelling burning wood.

Soundlessly, he removes his sword and scabbard and fastens them to Mannus's back. When he dismounts, it's eerie how quiet he is, how every movement and step is as silent as snowfall.

He creeps up the path with long, careful strides—a cloaked, menacing figure—then he stalks along the path's edge, his back against the rocky hillside.

I close my eyes and focus my hearing.

Voices. They're faint, like murmurs around a campfire, but they're there.

Is this what Nephele hoped to protect us from?

When I open my eyes, Alexus approaches, still hauntingly quiet. He folds his hands around my waist and lifts me off Tuck. Gripping my arms, he bends down and looks me in the eyes.

"*Eastlanders,*" he signs. "*About twenty. Camped on the path. The prince is not with them.*"

"*To the woods,*" I say, pointing.

Because what are our options? As for the prince, I'm worried that he could be anywhere in an instant, so the fact that he isn't warming his bones with his men isn't exactly soothing.

Alexus shakes his head. "*I know where we are now. Too near the mountains. The landscape is too rugged.*"

I glance back the way we came. "*We cannot turn back.*"

"*No.*" Sighing softly, he shakes his dark head again, and his broad shoulders fall. "*The only way forward is through.*" Gently, he presses his forehead against mine and whispers, "I will take care of them. Just stay here."

I grab his cloak before he can pull away. "*They should not have to die for us to live.*"

My stomach churns, sick with knowing what he means to do. If he even can. He alone cannot take down twenty men, Eastlanders at that. Can he? The God Knife hasn't proven itself as the divine weapon I once believed, though he seems to think it's a critical piece in this game we're playing.

He tilts my chin, and even under this red haze, I can see that the pretty green of his eyes has turned black.

"Believe me, this is the last thing I want to do," he says. "But you've seen what these people are capable of. They will not spare us, Raina. They will kill us or take us to their prince. Or worse. Make no mistake."

He tosses up his hood, shadowing his face, and kisses me. I don't know why his hands on my cheeks or the press of his lips feels so shocking. Perhaps because it also feels so natural—so impossibly right—when it should feel anything but those two things. It's a tender kiss, but it makes me weak all the same, scattering my mind like I'm sure he knew it would.

"Do as I say," he whispers against my mouth. "Do not follow me. Your life depends on it. I will come back for you, but no matter what you see, no matter what you hear, do not follow. Swear it."

I hate every bit of this, but I press the word *Promise* against his chest, not missing the way his heart pounds like a war drum beneath my touch.

It turns out I'm more of a liar than I ever knew, because minutes later, the earth quakes and rumbles like a star fell from the sky and crashed in the middle of this godsforsaken forest. Then I'm tying our horrified horses to a tree, stripping off the cumbersome gambeson, freeing both my blades, and creeping up the path in the cold, just as Alexus did.

A momentary white light splits the wood, stopping me in my tracks. The horrible groan of trees falling and snapping—a thousand at the same time—shatters the night, followed by men screaming in misery.

Their screams die at once, and the wood falls to absolute silence and stillness that makes my blood turn to ice. The wolves have stopped crying, and the crows have abandoned the trees.

The rocky hillside digs against my back, the jagged stones loosening as I move. One snags my bodice—under my arm—slicing through the fabric covering my ribs. I wince at the sharp pain. I'm cut, I think, but I'm more worried about every noisy pebble that falls, setting my pulse racing. I'm a liar breaking a promise, but I must know if Alexus is okay.

Finally, I'm at the cliff's edge, panting around my anxiety. It takes all I have to gather my defiant bravery and peer around the rocks.

My heart lurches in my chest, slamming to a stop before speeding up all over again. The Eastlander campsite—no, the path and even part of the wood—looks exactly like my imagination conjured.

Like a star crashed in Frostwater Wood.

There's a crater in the middle of the forest, obliterating the path and surrounding landscape. As for the Eastlanders, there's no sign of them, though dark stains splatter the open earth, and bits of wet flesh hang from the limbs of broken trees.

In the middle of it all is Alexus, kneeling like a fallen god.

Even from here, I can see that he's in pain. He rests his weight on one fist while the other hand pounds his chest like he's driving a stake through his heart. He gasps so hard his back bows with the effort.

I hurry down the hill, stumbling and sliding to the shallow crater. The moment I reach the basin, I'm running. When I reach him, I drop my weapon and fall to my knees, slipping my arm across his back, hoping to help him when I'm not even sure what in gods' death happened.

At my touch, he jerks his head up. Black veins web the blanched skin around his eyes which are still that same liquid darkness, only now it's not only his irises. Even the whites of his eyes have been overtaken.

"Go!" he roars, and the deep, reverberating sound of his voice is bone-rattling enough that the echo hits my core in ominous waves. It's so arresting that I'm shaking, and I almost obey.

Almost.

I feel magick. Not Nephele's magick. Not Witch Walker magick. It's unlike anything I've ever experienced, kissing my skin like that charge in the air the first few times I ever met Alexus Thibault's stare. Only stronger.

Every hair on my body stands on end, and chills run up and down my arms, but not out of fear. The magick in the air is silky to the touch, so cold, and thick enough to taste. It tastes like him—like honey and cloves—and like something else. The wood perhaps, where magick now permeates the soil, the roots, the trees, the leaves.

In reverent form, Alexus presses his forehead to the ground, palms flattened to raw earth, and rocks back and forth, chanting. His voice is too low for me to make out the words, but they're Elikesh, ancient and beautiful, and I know their cadence.

A plea, not a prayer.

I'm not sure how long we sit there, him chanting, me watching and listening, helplessly, but eventually, his rocking slows, his words fade, and he collapses in on himself. His cloak falls to the side, revealing the God Knife, still safely sheathed at his thigh inside Finn's dagger belt.

I roll him to his back and touch his face, wiping away the snowflakes that settle on his eyes and in his beard. The black veins around his eyes have faded, leaving behind purplish bruising in their stead, and his tunic is untied, revealing his reddened chest.

After a moment, he blinks up at me and cups my hand, pressing my palm to his cheek. I expect him to be furious—to scream at me again. But he isn't, and he doesn't. He looks relieved, like a man who just survived something I can't begin to understand.

"Are you all right?" he asks, and I nod. "Good. Help me stand?"

I do, though I'm not sure how much help I am. Alexus is two of me, and whatever he did to those men weakened him a great deal.

With his arm wrapped around my shoulders and my blades secured, we trudge back up the hill toward the crest, but I pause, leaning him against the rocky hillside once we get that far.

"You killed twenty men."

He nods and rubs his eyes, squinting at me like they burn. "Yes. I did."

"Alone."

"Yes."

"In an unnatural way."

A half-nod. "That depends. Magick is not unnatural."

"It is if your magick died a long time ago."

Magick that he didn't employ during the Eastlander attack, nor with the wraith, and I have to wonder why.

"Yes. I offered the Eastlanders a reprieve. They did not accept. And so I did what I had to do." He sighs. "Do you hate me again?"

Again. Because I so clearly lost that particular battle.

"No," I answer, and I mean it, even though there are remains of dead warriors glittering in the crimson light hovering over the wood. While more unnecessary death is the last thing I need weighing down my already overburdened conscience, it was us or them, and I'm beginning to understand the misery of that situation.

They had a choice. They chose wrong. I'm only glad I didn't see it happen.

"Good." He winces. "I don't hate you either, for breaking your promise and seeing things you weren't meant to see. You could've been hurt. Killed, even. That could be you in those trees, all because you don't listen."

He gives me an irritation-laced glare, the same look he wore when he tricked me before we entered the construct. Only now, it's half as severe.

I arch a brow. *"But I was not injured or killed. And now, I require a thorough explanation. Not this moment, but soon."*

Still breathing hard, he glances beyond the destroyed path. "How about within the hour? There's a stretch of caves ahead, in the ravine I'd hoped to avoid. But perhaps it's the best route. We're farther north than I realized. We can get out of sight, get warm, rest, and I'll tell you all that I can."

This seems far too easy, though I hear his boundaries plain enough: All that I can.

Still, I'll take it. This man has secrets. He's willing to talk, and I'm tired of being in the dark. Besides, I can be more than persuasive.

He's a little steadier now, so we make our way through the snow toward Mannus and Tuck. I catch him staring at me, paying no attention to the path before him, a glint of amusement sparkling in his glassy eyes that are slowly returning to their normal shade.

"Are you always this disobedient?" he asks.

I just smile, and for a few minutes, as we walk, I let myself live in the strange sense of normalcy that settles over us, just Alexus and me, shoulder to shoulder. No thoughts of magick or the prince or the king or dead Eastlanders at our back. No whispers across my mind reminding me who he is and that there's a very good chance that he's more than I ever dreamed. It's just us and the snow, and the need for the ordinary, that mundane existence that Mena said I struggle with.

Yet right now, I ache for the mundane, for the dream I'd had on Collecting Day. I imagine being somewhere else, far away from all of this horror. Me and my family and friends, and maybe Alexus. I don't want to fight. I don't want to be at odds with a magickal, mythical prince who might end me. I just want simple and easy. Long walks and stargazing in a world that doesn't feel like it might crumble any moment.

I look at Alexus again. His face is serious and, when he stops and pulls me to him, kissing me, his body trembling with the rush of a one-sided battle, I taste what remains of his power. The potent flavor is as sweet as fresh honey on my tongue.

Dark. Promising. Consuming.

And I know, beyond any doubt, that I've tumbled headfirst into the worst kind of trouble.

And that everything—*everything*—is about to change.

26

RAINA

The trek to the caves is dangerous, taking us down a steep hill and into a dry gorge northeast of Hampstead Loch. We ride together on Mannus's reliable back, pulling Tuck behind. Both animals are so tired that the short journey is even more of a battle. As for me, my side hurts from where I snagged it on the rocks, and I think I might be bleeding a little, but performing a healing on such treacherous terrain is impossible.

The ground flattens once we reach the ravine, making the ride more manageable, though the barren riverbed is rocky and littered with boulders. Overhead, the sky looks like it's painted with blood and speckled with snow.

A wind whips and whistles through the bluffs and nearly rips away the gambeson I cling to for dear life. I tug it tight and tuck my chin to my chest against the gust, causing me to miss the veins of electricity that arc above. But I still feel the power and see the flicker of light.

I've never witnessed lightning amidst snowfall, much less silent lightning, but every so often, a white flash bolts across the red sky. It's enough to make me cringe with every streak, but eventually, it fades and the wind stills, and I drift. True sleep has eluded me for too many days, and my body finally gives in.

When I wake, I'm slow at coming back to life. The first thing I grasp is that I think I heard a wolf howling. Secondly, I'm in a cavern, lying on the gambeson. A dying fire and my mother's dish—filled with melted snow for scrying—wait a few feet away.

Alexus's arms are around me, one slung over my waist, holding me tight against him while the other rests beneath my head for comfort, our fingers entwined. The old blanket covers us, and his warm, steady breath stirs my hair. His beard has grown a little in these last few days, and it tickles my ear. So little has given me reason to smile in the last several days, but this closeness is so calming that I let a satisfied grin unfurl.

The fire Alexus must've built after bringing me inside the cave has burned to embers, so I think we've slept for a long while. I don't feel completely rested, but I no longer feel like I might die from the lack of sleep either.

The cave isn't what I imagined. There's light—and not only from our fire. The faint glow from the crimson sky shines through a small space between two finger-like formations protruding from the ceiling. The cavern's innards are deep and tall enough that Alexus was able to bring the horses inside. They rest at the rear of the cave, lying down, exhausted.

Lastly, it strikes me that the Prince of the East didn't come to me while I slept. Perhaps he really is gone, though I'm not sure he would've left without the God Knife. He thought he had it, but Alexus was right. I destroyed his moment of gloating. He won't let that stand if he can help it.

I sigh. I can't think about the prince right now. Don't *want* to think about him. I just want to lie here, absorbing Alexus's body heat while he rests, thinking about the way his heart beats against my back, the rhythm in time with my own.

"You should be sleeping." His voice sends a delicious shiver through me.

I squeeze his hand, not wanting to let go to speak.

He leans down and presses a tender kiss to my neck, making every inch of my skin come alive.

"I need to add kindling to the fire," he says against my ear. "Or it will get very cold very quickly."

Yet he relaxes and then doesn't move. I suppose neither of us wants to lose this peaceful moment.

My father made a snow globe once, for my mother. He used stardrop petals and water from the stream, poured inside a blown glass orb he fired at the kiln. I remember shaking it and watching the stardrops fall like snowflakes, wishing that all the snow in the world could be captured inside that little vessel. Eventually, the petals turned brown, and dark film coated the inside of the glass. This sliver of solitude feels like one of those stardrop petals, trapped inside a snow globe with a million other moments that have been overshadowed by death, fear, loss, and even interrupted desire.

I don't want interruptions right now, so we stay like that, curled against one another.

"Your father was a Keeper," Alexus eventually whispers.

I turn over, facing him. *"What?"*

He keeps his voice low. "There's magick. Layered on the God Knife. It's old and weak but still at work doing what it was meant to do, which was bind the blade to your father so he could keep it safe and out of the hands of the wrong people."

I have no words. I can only stare and blink, stunned. I don't even know what a Keeper is, not really, but this is still an unexpected revelation.

"When he told you that he kept the knife because he must," Alexus continues, "he wasn't lying. I don't know if he asked for it or was unaware, but someone bound the blade to your father, and now that spell clings even to you."

I press a hand to my chest. That doesn't sound good at all. I don't want to be bound to anything that has to do with the gods.

"I'm fairly certain it's Summerlander magic," he continues, "though an ancient form. Maybe someone visiting the port when your father found it? A mage?"

I wave my hand and shrug. I don't have this knowledge.

"Well, regardless, I've racked my brain about everything that's happened. It shouldn't have been possible for the prince to read the Summerlander enchantment on the blade. The magick of the magi is some of the most archaic conjuring in the world, dating back to Loria herself."

"The Eastlanders used it in the vale, though," I sign. *"With their arrows."*

"Yes, and I still can't sort out how. It's one thing to harness fire threads. It's an entirely different magick to cause fire to incinerate from the inside out. Only those with an intimate knowledge of ancient magick systems can read such archaic Summerland workings. They teach it, in the City of Ruin, but only to the very magickly gifted. But, I think, somehow, the prince saw the spell when he attacked you on the green and knew he couldn't take the knife as long as it was in your possession. Otherwise, he would've tried harder than he did. Of course, later, the blade *wasn't* in your possession because Helena somehow found it, so he used her to bring it to him. And even later, you hid the blade in the moss, severing any protection, and he sent his crow on a hunting expedition."

If the binding magick should've been impossible for the prince to see, how could Alexus see it? And when did Helena come across the knife? She didn't mention that in her explanation of what happened. More importantly...

I jerk up. *"I should have the knife. So he cannot take it."*

"Easy." Alexus rises on an elbow, rubbing my arm to calm me. "It's strapped to my thigh, and I'm better protection than any Keeper." He winks. "Even you."

I'm not sure he's right.

"Finn took the knife from me," I tell him. It had been strapped to my thigh the night of the harvest supper, and yet Finn slipped it from the dagger belt like the best of thieves.

Alexus narrows his eyes. "Who's Finn?"

Heat blooms across my chest and chases up my neck, followed by another cresting wave that I fight with all that I have. I've tried so hard not to think of him, but here he is, rising up like a ghost while I lie beside another man.

"Is Finn the special someone you lost?" Alexus asks. I don't even have to nod for him to know that he was. "I'm so sorry, Raina. How did he take the knife? Why?"

I glance away from his inquiring stare. *"We were dancing at the harvest supper. Calling down the moon. He was only pestering me."*

"So you'd lost your connection to the here and now. I'm not sure how Finn knew to go for the knife when you weren't linked to reality, but... smart man."

Finn didn't know. Of that, I'm sure. He only knew he could still make me weak enough to trick me.

I examine my hands and think about what Alexus said about the prince. *"Why would the magick cling to* me *if it was my father who was bound?"*

He shrugs. "It depends on how the spell was crafted. Magick of that sort has many nuances, and every witch has different methods, especially Summerlanders. It could've been a duty cast on your father and his children and his children's children, and when he passed, you were the child who finally claimed it. Having not been there when the knife was enchanted, that's my best guess."

With distance between us, the air winding through the cavern's entrance grows too chill.

"A little help with the fire?" Alexus says, and I nod. "Most of the wood I found was damp, some of it very wet, as were the pine needles and leaves. All you need to do is summon the threads from the embers. Your magick will remember what to do. Just use your words."

He leaves me and tosses the last of the gathered brush into the fire, save for the twig he uses as a fire poker. I sit up and rub my eyes, still wrapping my mind around the notion of my father being a Keeper. Then I'm drawing fire threads from ash—badly—but it's something I never thought I'd be able to do. With *Fulmanesh, iyuma* repeating on my fingertips, however, I manage to raise a tiny fire from wet brush and smoldering cinders.

Wearing a proud expression, Alexus comes to sit with me, pack in hand. Ever chivalrous, he folds the blanket around me and moves to his knees to slip off my boots, down to my hosen. Gently, he places my feet on a flat rock close to the fire to warm. The heat and his touch feel so luxurious that I close my eyes, just for a moment, and sigh.

Sitting back, he pulls out the tin mug and a couple of moonberry roots I hurriedly packed before we left Nephele's refuge. One is nothing but a protective husk filled with fruit, the other still brimming with sweetwater, although the liquid is frozen solid now.

"Hungry?" He gestures with the fruit-filled root. "I can roast these. I fed the horses the last of the apples."

I give a quick nod in reply, but in truth, I want answers more than food.

Alexus nestles the sweetwater root between two stones to thaw, then spreads the fruit on a flat rock and slides it close to the flames. He holds the Eastlander blade over the fire to clean the steel before laying it on the circle of stones.

He keeps glancing at the cavern's entrance. It *was* a wolf that I heard earlier. An entire pack howls in the distance, likely descending upon the bloody feast left in the wood.

At least the crows have stayed away. I tell myself that they're too startled to come anywhere near Alexus Thibault again. I should probably follow their lead, yet I'm more trapped than I've ever been. And not because of the construct and not because of the prince.

Alexus lets out a tired groan, a sound that's somewhere between resignation and dread. "I don't suppose you're going to eat first and talk about all the other stuff later? I'll keep watch."

I raise a brow as sharply as I can. *"Not a chance. Tell me how you did what you did. Why did you not use that magick before?"*

Setting the pack aside, he stares into the fire. I study his profile, the way the firelight casts shadows along the sharp lines of his face and dances in his eyes.

"My magick is contained," he finally says, placing his elbows on his knees. "Asleep, in a sense. I can no longer access it with ease. It's...sort of tangled with another source of magick. A power I never asked for. When I unleash that power, even a small amount, some of my old magick comes with it. I'm not good at controlling the force of such a release, so I never do it, unless I know it's all right to destroy everything in my immediate vicinity. Which is why I didn't employ that particular ability when the Eastlanders stormed the valley, nor when the wraith attacked. It's also why I asked you not to follow me. Not so much because I didn't want you to know, but because I wanted you safe."

My face warms. *"If you had said it like that, I would have listened."*

"No, you wouldn't have, because that's who you are. It's part of your fire." The corner of his mouth curls up, and he nudges me with his shoulder. "You little rebel."

I smile and tuck my hair behind my ear. I like it when he says that. He says it in a way that's...accepting. No judgment. No voice of reason trying to convince me that it's better to be anything else but the way that I am, a person who doesn't always do as she's told. He says it like he's learned to like that part of me. No one else—not even my parents or Finn—made me feel as though it was all right to be flawed, and even that perhaps my flaws might also be my strengths.

"Where did you get this power?" I sign.

His face goes hard, and his eyes darken, but not in the way of magick. They darken with memory, like he's seeing things he doesn't want to reveal.

He scrubs a hand through his long hair. "Where to begin."

"From the beginning."

"Ah. So simple, yet you know not what you ask. There are so many beginnings, Raina, and they all flow into one long story."

"Then tell me each one," I reply.

A pause tightens the air, but finally, his eyes go distant, and he begins.

☙❧

"I SUPPOSE A GOOD PLACE TO START IS WITH COLDEN MOESHKA, AND A tale of the gods."

I don't know what I expected, but it isn't this.

"Before he graced the throne as the Frost King, and long before the Northlands were a neutral kingdom, Colden Moeshka was a young warrior for Neri, God of the North, in the Land Wars a little over three hundred years ago. Just a boy at the time. Barely twenty, I think."

I blink, confused. This is a tale of the Frost King. We're supposed to be talking about Alexus. Still, I'm surprised by this information for other reasons too. I've heard about the Land Wars, only from history passed down through legend, but I've never imagined the king as anything but a king. Certainly not a warrior and most definitely not a boy.

"And how did he become the dreaded Frost King?"

Alexus gives me a half-smile that quickly fades to seriousness. "He and a small army were sent to guard the Summerland queen's gates during the war. Toward the end, when a small front to the north had been conquered, they found themselves battling a retinue of Eastlanders attempting a sneak attack. Colden and his warriors were outnumbered, but Colden is a fury and a leader. His small northern band destroyed the enemy outside the queen's gates. When it was over, the queen sent for those who remained, to thank them." He studies his clasped hands. "It did not end well."

"What happened?"

"Everything," he replies. "You see, the Land Wars were never about the lands. They were about the jealousy, lust, and bitterness of the gods. Neri wanted Asha. And Thamaos, God of the East, wanted Asha's beloved Summerlands. Neri offered his army to Asha and her queen, but at a cost. Not only did he make a devout enemy of Thamaos, but in exchange for his aid, he wanted Asha's heart. She agreed because Neri was strong and handsome, and even though he had no earthly queen or king to rule his northern warriors, they served him anyway. Worshipped him, even."

I can't help but roll my eyes. Some things never change.

"Asha knew that kind of loyalty would be to her advantage in saving the Summerlands from Thamaos," Alexus goes on. "So she promised her heart and body to Neri, becoming his lover. And for that, many lost their lives, and the lives of a few were forever changed."

Though we're only inches apart, I move closer to him. I enjoy the story, but I'd be lying if I said I didn't also enjoy the soothing sound of his voice.

"Go on," I insist, tugging the blanket tighter around me.

"The wars raged for a long time before Colden was sent to fight. Northern men and Summerlanders fought the Eastern armies until little remained of the enemy. Things grew quiet for a time, and Asha, being the seductress that she was, tired of Neri. So when that final battle happened outside the queen's gates, and Colden and the other surviving northern warriors were brought to the throne at Mount Ulra, Asha was there, without the ruling eyes of other gods, and in her loneliness, one of the men caught her attention."

I stiffen. *"Colden Moeshka?"*

"Yes, Colden Moeshka." Alexus turns our fruit with his stick. "Asha fell for him instantly. Relations between gods and mortals were forbidden, but Asha was foolish. The queen let her have her way with Colden, because even though the Summerlanders owed him their lives, no earthly ruler would dare defy their land's god or goddess.

So Asha beguiled Colden with the Fever Lilac, a flower whose roots contain the powers of desire. Summerlanders grind the root into a golden powder and paint brides' and bridegrooms' bodies on their wedding night. The flower only solidified his lust for her, though, not love, because Colden never gave his heart to Asha. In fact, during his first days at Mount Ulra, before Asha deceived him into her bed, his soul came alight for Summerland's budding princess, a young girl named Fia."

"Fia Drumera? The Fire Queen of the Summerlands?" I feel like I'm hearing royal gossip, only Tiressia's royal fiction has never been quite so intriguing.

Alexus holds up a finger. "Just wait. Don't get ahead. It gets better."

I smother a small smile as he gets up and rips away the end of the moonberry root with his teeth, then squeezes the partially thawed sweetwater into the tin mug to warm.

"When no more Fever Lilacs could be found," he says, returning to my side, "Colden came to his senses, and he was not happy. Colden looks innocent, Raina. In truth, he's exquisitely beautiful. You'll know what I mean when you see him. His appearance is misleading. He is not a fragile man to be trifled with. As for Asha," he continues, "well, she miscalculated the man she'd tricked into her bed. While he'd been entranced by her flowers, she did a horrible thing. In what she believed to be infinite power, she rendered Colden immortal, a godly gift, so that he might be with her forever. And he hated her for it. So much that he almost killed her, but instead, he chained her to a cliff on Mount Ulra, in iron fetters, that he might flee and return to Neri's protection. He hoped that if she lived, perhaps her curse could be undone."

All of a sudden, I can't help but question everything I've ever learned about the Frost King. All my years, I've been told that his immortality was a gift from Neri. Not a curse by Asha.

He was violated. His life stolen.

"Why iron fetters?"

"Because iron stifles godly power. When placed on the extremities—the neck, the wrists, the ankles—it binds. It can even burn the skin and seep into a god's veins, rendering them as useless as any human." He cocks his brow again. "Colden escaped Asha's clutches, gathered his fellow warriors, and returned to the north where, in his rage, he began building a village. A place where he might seal himself off from the world."

"Winterhold."

"The very same. Colden and his men worked for months in the cold, right under Neri's vengeful eyes. The God of the North was jealous of Colden, though he made no sign of it until later. A few years passed. In that short time, Colden considered death, but his friends challenged him against taking his own life."

Confused yet again, I shake my head and sign. *"I thought he was immortal."*

After a lick of his fingertips, Alexus snatches the mug from beside the fire and sets it on the stones to cool. "Immortality is a curious thing. One can live forever until someone manages to kill them. Magick can certainly compete with death, but nothing is eternal. Not even a life given by a goddess. And though Colden loathed his circumstance, little more is unbearable as the thought of losing a life you once loved, especially by your own hand."

I press my hand to my chest, my heart aching at the impossible decision that must've faced Colden every day of his long life. Much as I have hated even the thought of him, I can pity that.

"What happened to Asha?"

"The Land Wars ended. For a time, anyway. The gods tried to force Asha to remove Colden Moeshka's curse, but she refused. Her punishment, therefore, for bedding a mortal and granting him a godly gift, was that she would never—no matter what magick she attempted—be able to make him love her."

"And she was furious."

"Very. But what could she do?"

Alexus rescues the stone holding the roasting berries. He sits the flat rock on the ground and lifts my feet, turning me so that my legs are tucked between his, our knees bent, his encasing mine. He takes up the curved knife and begins slicing our fruit.

"A few more years passed," he goes on, "then one day, the recently crowned queen, Fia Drumera, sent men to the vale to find Colden and give him a message. She wanted to make amends for her goddess's wrongdoings and celebrate Colden once again for the sacrifice cast upon his people. It was essential to maintain peace with a man quickly becoming something of a leader in the north.

The queen's letter swore Asha would not be there; the other gods would not allow it. Colden refused to go, but..." He pauses as something akin to regret flashes across his face, so fast I almost miss it. "In the years since he'd been in the desert," he says, "he'd made a new friend. Someone unlike all his other acquaintances. Someone who hadn't fought alongside him during the war."

With the steadiest of hands, Alexus balances a piece of warm, blistered fruit on the flat of the knife and lifts it to my mouth. I lean forward, and with my teeth, carefully accept.

"Who was the friend?"

"A young man from the valley. They met while the man was hunting in Frostwater Wood. That friend told Colden he should go to the celebration, to honor his fallen men if nothing else. The gods had bound Asha. She was no longer a threat, or so it had been promised. Colden asked the friend to accompany him, and the man agreed, because he'd never been that far south, and it had always been a faraway dream. So they set out."

He reaches for the metal cup and offers it. I accept and take a sip, letting the tin's warmth heat my hands.

"The Summerlands are desert lands, marked by oases. Colden showed his new friend such beauty, the likes of which his eyes had never seen." A hint of a smile curves his lips as he takes a bite of fruit. "The people were kind, the food so sweet and spicy, the water clear and crisp. Then Colden and his friend reached the great wall surrounding the citadel. It was impressive, but the gates—made of gold and ornamented with more jewels than the desert has grains of sand—had to have been forged by the gods. Inside, mud huts were freestanding though many were built into cliffs and under rocky overhangs, in deep caves and even in the side of Mount Ulra. For three days, the people of the Summerlands came together for festivities. There was music and laughter, wine and dance." He looks at me sidelong. "And Fia."

My eyes widen. Tales of the gods and the City of Ruin are fascinating enough, but to learn truths about the Frost King and the Fire Queen has me spellbound. I feel just as entranced as I used to when my father told me stories as a child.

Alexus returns to slicing our steaming food. "The moment Colden saw Fia, he became moonstruck all over again—a foolish notion for a man who might outlive everyone he would ever know. But Fia felt the same. The two were inseparable the first couple of days of the celebration, and on that third night, Fia danced with Colden until the poor man could barely see beyond the stars in his eyes. He'd found joy again, and he wanted to cling to it. With the rest of the world distracted, Fia led Colden to her dwelling."

"For what?" I sign. Instantly, I regret the words, my fingers recoiling.

Alexus grins. "What do you think? She wanted him." He looks at me pointedly. "You know how desire can be. Completely consuming."

My face burns as unbidden images and thoughts cross my mind, images and thoughts that Alexus is undoubtedly watching play across my eyes.

"The story would've been sad regardless," he continues, thankfully, "because Colden was in love with Fia, and he bore a curse only Asha could break. And Queen Drumera, well, the new queen was betraying Asha with the man the goddess still desired, a man despised by every god for his immortality. Colden knew this was a dangerous game, yet he couldn't leave Fia's arms. And that was their doom."

His dark hair falls across his face as he spears another sliver of moon-berry fruit and slips it carefully into my mouth.

"On that third night," he says, "Asha betrayed Queen Drumera's request and arrived for the celebration only to find Colden missing, as was Fia. When Asha found them together, Mount Ulra and every surrounding dwelling trembled. Colden went to her, an attempt to calm her anger, but in her fury and jealousy, Asha cast him away, forbidding him to step foot in the City of Ruin ever again lest he crumble to dust. He didn't even have time to kiss Fia goodbye, let alone tell her what Asha had done. Little did they know that Neri loomed near, observing his old lover consumed with the likes of a mere man. Later, Neri approached Asha with another offer."

With his knife, Alexus points at me and narrows his eyes in a way that makes it clear he's absorbed in his storytelling.

"Asha could never have Colden Moeshka," he says, "and Colden Moeshka could not enter the City of Ruin, but who would stop Fia Drumera from leaving her throne and seeking the man of the north? So Neri made Asha a deal. If she gave him her heart once again, this time for eternity, he would do the thing she could not. He would make Fia Drumera immortal as well, but worse, he would cast within her the element of fire and in Colden Moeshka the element of frost, that they may never—for all their infinite days—come together again."

I sit back, saddened for these people I've never met. People who have lived only as legends to me. Does my sister know this story of her lover?

And if so, does she not care that his heart once burned so brightly for another? That it might still?

"The Eastlanders have learned this tale," Alexus says. "It's been kept secret for over three centuries. It's the reason the gods destroyed themselves. Thanks to Thamaos's influence, Neri and Asha were condemned and buried at Mount Ulra, where they might spend eternity together in their shame. After their deaths, Thamaos wanted to claim their lands, but the one decent god of Tiressia, Urdin of the Western Drifts, blamed Thamaos for everything. Thamaos knew Urdin would be a problem, so he did a thing that you and I may regret, even three centuries later."

"What? What did he do?"

A solemn expression falls over Alexus's face. "Thamaos, unlike Neri, was a believer in choosing a king or queen to rule his lands. He treated them like servants, their purpose to deal with the pathetic Tiressians in his way. He put a man named King Gherahn in power."

I've heard this name, again, from lore.

"And King Gherahn," Alexus continues, "employed the sorcerers of the land for the Land Wars. His pre-eminent sorcerer was a young man from the Tribe of Ghent. They called him Un Drallag."

Again, I nod, more urgently this time, recognizing the name from my father's stories. I'm beginning to see the different tales weaving together.

"Un Drallag." I spell the name in Elikesh, though I never imagined him being a young man. *"The sorcerer who created the God Knife,"* I add.

Alexus's eyes light up. "Yes. You know this part?"

I shrug. *"Father told me a little. That Un Drallag fashioned the knife from the bone of a long-dead god. Thamaos?"*

"Yes, but Thamaos was very much alive when the knife was made. He cut himself open and tore out his own rib, offering it to Un Drallag for the creation of a weapon, so that he might defeat Urdin when the time came. But he failed. A battle ensued along the Jade River, close to Fia Drumera's gates. Thamaos took Urdin from behind and drove the God Knife into his chest. But before Urdin died, he shoved the blade through his own body, driving it out his back and into Thamaos's heart. The last two gods of Tiressia died that day. Summerlanders came, and the final deities of our lands were buried at the Grove of the Gods."

A gasp leaves me. *"The Grove truly exists? I thought it was a myth. We all did."*

Alexus runs a hand over his beard. "It's a very real place. Ancient as Loria. Gods of other lands are even buried there. The Prince of the East knows this, as have other eastern rulers before him, but Fia Drumera has managed to keep the Eastlanders at bay. Now, however, they've learned that the queen's greatest weakness might just be the isolated King of Winterhold, who will turn to nothing more than desert sand if they bring him across the Jade River. This is why I'm so selective about who I collect from the valley, and it's why they don't return home. They have a choice, but they know it's best for all of Tiressia if they stay and learn and protect. After they're told the importance of guarding Colden, they understand why we cannot tell the whole vale. Some secrets can change the world, and those we love most can be terribly tempting."

I curl my fingers tight as my throat closes. I can't say that I would be so noble, but knowing this gives me some sense of peace about the matter, about why Nephele never came home.

"Colden Moeshka is his own force to be reckoned with," Alexus continues. "As restitution, the gods gave Colden and Fia a certain degree of command over their elements. He can breathe an icy fog. Freeze an enemy with a touch. If the Eastlanders manage to take him, I worry they will use him against the Fire Queen, so that they might access the Grove and the magick she has protected for so long."

"What could the Prince of the East even do?" I ask. *"The gods are dead."*

Furrowing his brow, Alexus switches to speaking with his hands. *"At Nephele's refuge, you asked me what the prince wanted with the knife. It is said that a god can rise, Raina. Remember what I told you about resurrection?"*

So many things rush into my mind at once. Alexus's words about resurrection, yes, but also my father's words about the God Knife. *It can kill anyone and anything, the blessed and the cursed, the forever living and the risen dead —even other gods.*

The risen dead.

"A resurrection was performed with an Ancient One centuries ago," Alexus says, quietly. "The story tells of rituals and Healers, not unlike yourself, using the hair of a dead god to bring them back from the afterlife. Some worshippers saved locks of the god's tresses, not realizing their treasure could be used in a rite to restore life. All that was needed was a god remnant and an intact grave."

A chill runs across my skin as I glance at the God Knife strapped to his thigh. *"Are you saying that...Thamaos could be resurrected?"*

"I fear that is exactly what the Prince of the East plans to do, especially now that the knife has been found."

My mind pitches from thought to thought. *"What does that mean? For us? If the prince succeeds?"*

"Thamaos wanted absolute rule, and he did not care how many lives were destroyed for him to attain it. I am certain he is even angrier than before, having spent centuries in the pits of the underworld. If he is brought back from the grave, he will not stop until every person living in this shattered empire bows to him. He would start a war in Tiressia first and foremost, to bring down Fia. After that, I do not know. The world is much bigger than Tiressia. There are other lands to conquer, other rulers to dominate, even a few living godlings. He could change the entire world as we know it, unless I stop the prince from taking Colden to the Summerlands and keep this—" he pats the knife "—safe."

A sudden feeling of loyalty washes over me. For Tiressia and its people. For Alexus. Even parts of our world that are only stories to me. Can I find my sister and help Alexus too? Help him save Colden Moeshka and protect a queen I've never even seen?

"When the god battle was over," Alexus continues, "King Gherahn demanded that Un Drallag travel to the Summerlands and retrieve the God Knife. It was said to be lost in the Jade River or in the sands where it might never be found again. The sorcerer went to the coast, but in truth, he was tired. He had a wife by then, a child on the way. He wanted a life that was more than the one he lived under the king's thumb as a spy, an assassin, a weapon. So he abandoned the only home he had ever known and fled to the northland valley where he'd been a spy once upon a time. The God Knife was never located, but Un Drallag could feel it calling to him. There is such power in this knife, Raina." He touches it. "It would be better if it didn't exist, but there are no gods left to destroy it."

Dread pools in my stomach. *"My father said that the blade harkens to the one from whose body it was made. Is the blade calling to Thamaos now?"*

That thought terrifies me, that I might've been carrying around a relic that summons a dead and dangerous god.

"No, that isn't true," he replies, tilting his head, looking at me like he needs his next words to sink deep. *"The blade calls to its maker, Raina,"* he signs.

After a pregnant moment, he reaches over his head, grabs a fistful of his tunic, and strips off his shirt. With the fabric wadded in his hands, he leans forward again, elbows on his knees, and pulls his long hair to one side.

His back is beautifully made, wide and tapered like wings, like I noticed at the stream. But the skin from his shoulders to his waist is marked with scars, rough and raised, like those on his chest.

The firelight catches on the silvery skin, shimmering. Emboldened, I drop the blanket from my shoulders and move to my knees. There, nestled between his legs, I touch one of the runes on his shoulder blade. He flinches at first, but chills rise the more I admire.

Because it *is* admiration. His marks look like they were painful to receive—branded or carved—but they've left him looking like an artifact, something to be studied, understood, deciphered.

I want to know the history behind each line.

"Do you recognize them?" He looks up, searching my face for some response that I clearly don't have to offer.

I shake my head. *"Only that they are runes."*

"How closely have you examined the knife?" he asks.

"I know it by heart."

"I am not sure you do," he says, slipping the God Knife free from its sheath. "Let me show you something."

He hands over the knife. Once again, the blade is so warm to the touch.

"Look into the stone," he signs. *"Hold it to the light."*

I've held the God Knife near the candles on my worktable a few times, enough to know what it looks like. I've never stared deep into the amber, though, and when I do, I'm more perplexed than ever. Faint markings that I've never noticed before hide inside the stone. I peer harder and twist the hilt toward the firelight, rolling it between my fingers. A dozen or more runes are either etched into the pommel itself or forged into the stone.

My hands still, and a rush of awareness hits me. The marks are the same as the ones on Alexus's body.

"Those are runes, yes," he signs. *"Elikesh runes. The young man who forged that knife used runes and his own blood to bind him to the blade. Runes can act as an—"* he pauses, like he's hunting for the right word to sign *"—enclosure,"* he finally says. *"They trap necessary magick within objects, like a knife. Or within... people. They can also forge a connection."*

I've heard of such things but only in lore. I've even seen runes—they're engraved on some of the old stones inside the temple. But those methods of magick are ancient and archaic, practiced when the last gods still lived. I don't even think godlings in faraway lands use runes anymore.

Sitting back on my heels, I touch the mark over Alexus's right breast. He takes the knife, re-sheathing it, and clasps my hand in his, pressing my palm against his fire-warmed skin.

"The God Knife calls to Un Drallag, Raina," he whispers. "It's been trying, all these years, to return to its maker's hands. Its haven, its home."

A question flutters across my mind, chased by an answer I'm sure I already know.

Heart racing, I ask anyway, my fingers faltering around my words.

"And has it?" I sign. *"Finally found home?"*

A lump builds in my throat and tension in my fingers as I wait for his reply.

He lifts a hand to my cheek and traces the curve of my jaw, looking at me with those otherworldly eyes. "Yes."

27

RAINA

Alexus Thibault is Un Drallag.

The sorcerer who forged the God Knife. An Eastlander from the Tribe of Ghent.

A three-hundred-year-old man.

My head aches from all the thoughts ricocheting across my mind. His life threads. They're so frayed because they're tattered with age. And the Summerlander magick on the blade—he could see it because he's old enough to have learned to read it, possibly in the Summerlands. And *now* it makes sense why the God Knife warmed against my thigh in the minutes before he charged the green and every other time he was around.

Because it *knew* its maker was near.

I sit so still, staring into his stormy eyes, unsure what to feel. In some way, I'd sensed his antiquity. He exudes permanence, sure and unceasing as the stars in the sky. I've been drawn to that part of him from the moment our eyes first met.

"Say something," he signs.

I touch his sharp cheekbone, caress his strong brow with trembling fingers, then trace my touch across his soft lips. He holds my gaze all the while, letting me study him, letting me think.

"You should be my enemy," I sign.

He's an Eastlander. They've taken so much from Tiressia. So much from *me*.

"Yes. If birthplace decides who is good and who is not, then you should hate me."

But it doesn't, and I know that. I also know that he fled a life he didn't want, duty he did not choose, all to make a better path for himself and his family.

And I, better than anyone, understand that.

Sliding my hands over his shoulders and up his neck into his hair, I lean closer. I don't want to talk anymore. His breath is warm on my lips, and his strong hands make their way up the backs of my thighs. I can feel how fast he's breathing, the hardness of his body against mine as he pulls me near.

His eyes stir with conflict when he looks up at me. I kiss him anyway, and he welcomes the contact, opening that lovely mouth for me, threading his fingers through my hair, pulling me closer until my body presses down on his.

Heat seeking heat.

He trails kisses along my throat and lower, tasting the tender flesh at the neckline of my bodice. Unfortunately, he breaks the kiss, and a groan resonates in the back of his throat.

"Raina." He smooths my hair back from my face and holds my cheeks in his hands. "You don't want this. You think you do but believe me when I tell you that you don't." A flash of guilt passes over his eyes. "I've already let this go too far. Let me finish what I need to say, and then you can make your mind, but not before."

My heart sinks. What more can he possibly say? How many secrets can one man hold? I don't want more truths and revelations. I just want all of this to go away, to not feel like I'm being thrust toward some horrific and inevitable collision.

I sit back, wishing there was somewhere to go, but there isn't, and regardless, I become captivated all over again the moment he turns his hand over, revealing more scars on the underside of his forearm.

"These runes bind me to the God Knife." He takes my hand and presses my fingers to the scar on his chest once again. "But these, and the markings on my back, are for something else entire."

I pull my hand away, doing my best to keep my head clear. If the collision is inevitable, let it come.

"Tell me," I say.

"When the wraith had me on the ground—when it kissed me—it showed me all the wrongs I have ever done. There are *many* wrongs, but I swear to you that I have paid for my crimes tenfold."

The tone of his voice rings like a doomsday bell inside my head.

"Un Drallag." He spells the word with his hands. *"Do you know what that name means?"*

"No," I tell him. I'm not sure my father even knew what it meant.

"It means The Gatherer. Under King Gherahn's order, I was forced to roam the Eastern Territory and gather sorcerers for the king's service during the Land Wars. Those who refused..." He casts his gaze toward the fire. "Those who refused died. At my command."

A sick feeling swirls in the pit of my stomach. There are stories of this too. Not of Un Drallag killing his fellow sorcerers, but of the king having his own people put to death for not wanting to fight in a war that meant nothing to them.

Alexus did that. He took people's lives. Not his enemies, and not stealing witches away to another part of the country. Death—certain and final.

"I have earned my title as Witch Collector," he continues. "But the moment I had the chance, I fled that life and came to the valley with my wife and newborn son. We prospered for a time, until the king sent hunters to find us." He meets my watering gaze. "They killed my family before I could do anything to stop them. Helena's wraith made certain I relived that moment and so many others."

I can't make my fingers work, too torn with emotion to respond. I don't know whether to hate him for his past or pity him. The thing is, I have a feeling he isn't finished, that this is not the moment of impact.

Not yet.

"It gets worse," he says, like he knows my thoughts. "I struggled after they were killed and became determined to bring my family back to the land of the living. I spent months traveling the world, ship to ship and shore to shore. I spoke with magi and witches and sorcerers and even a godling, until I finally felt that I could attempt the unthinkable. And I succeeded. Somewhat. I went to the Shadow World, but I did not come out alone."

I close my eyes. The world is spinning.

"Your wife?" I ask, hands trembling. *"Your child?"*

When I open my eyes, he shakes his head and touches the rune on his breast as a few tiny tears pearl in the rings of dark lashes shadowing his eyes.

"My body is a cage, Raina," he signs. *"These runes are a trap. It takes all the magick that I possess, along with these runic boundaries, to keep that power subdued. When I channel it for my own use, like I did on the path, there is a risk that it will escape, that I will not be able to lock it down."* His voice comes out as a whisper. "I almost couldn't contain it earlier. A hundred years ago, I was much better at wielding it, but I've had no need for it in so long that I'm weaker than I want to be. That inability to control this power is why I told you to leave me. I was so scared of hurting you or causing my magick to collapse and letting this thing loose, but it was your presence that made me win the fight."

I stare at him, wondering *what* he could've carried from the underworld that could cause so much damage. Wraiths possess. They don't devastate entire swaths of land and whatever else might get in the way.

"Just say it," I demand, every muscle in my body going taut. *"What is this thing inside you?"*

Without hesitance or preamble, the collision finally comes.

"It is Neri," he signs.

MINUTES LATER, I'M PACING THE LENGTH OF THE CAVERN IN MY SOCKED feet. I feel waylaid, enough that the stupor of a pretty face, mysterious eyes, and a beautiful body—a spell I've been under for days now—has evaporated. I'd wanted to know everything that Alexus just told me—asked for it, even. But my mind can't work things out anymore.

Though we've rested, I'm still sleep-deprived and half-starved, living off a little crow meat, bits of fruit, and sweetwater. My nerves are beyond rattled, and though I feel more lucid than I have in days, my mind is in absolute chaos. Alexus has *Neri*, of all things, inside him. Even if Neri is only partly responsible for the Frost King's rule, he's still a cruel, dead god who should be safely forgotten in the Nether Reaches.

For several excruciating minutes, I'm sure that Alexus is lying, but when I ask if he's being false and he denies it, I feel the truth in him.

He stands and leans against the cave wall, arms crossed over his bare chest, watching me. I stop pacing and toss his shirt at him. *"Put it on."*

I'm angry. Confused. Upset. I don't know what any of this means, but I don't need all those muscles mucking up my thoughts even further. Enough damage has been done as it is. No wonder he seemed ancient. He's been alive for three fucking centuries, and a god—old as a millennium—inhabits him.

I cover my face with my hands and try to steady my breathing.

At least we didn't...

At least he didn't let me...

Neri could've so easily been inside me. I'm not certain how that works, if Neri would have known, but for me, there would've been no coming back from that. I would've felt his terrible presence staining my core for the rest of my days.

I whip around, my hands violent in their command. *"There is more. I know it. Say it."*

"There's no more. All is said that you need to know, and it ended just as I thought it might." He holds up his hands in mock defense, but I see a hint of irritation in his eyes. "And rightfully so. I don't blame you for your disgust. I had a feeling the truth might stop the wandering hands and kisses."

"Then you should have told me before! And I do not have wandering hands!"

Nostrils flaring and tendons straining his neck, he pushes off the wall. "Oh yes. You do. And I tried!" A moment passes, and the tension in his body eases a fraction. "I told you I had darkness inside me. You wanted our darknesses to be *friends,* if I remember correctly. Very *naked* friends, by the way."

He shrugs into his tunic, jerking the fabric down his tensing torso. I just stare at him, too bewildered to know what to do.

"Stop." His voice splits the awkward silence. "Don't look at me like I'm some freak of nature."

"You are *a freak of nature."*

His stare goes dark and cold. "No. I am Tiressia's salvation and damnation, though I have never wanted to be either. I keep Neri bound so that he cannot wreak havoc on the Northlands or any other part of this empire. Three centuries ago, I stumbled out of the Shadow World with a shattered heart, fighting a godsdamn deity who used me to escape his eternal punishment and was ready to tear down the world." His eyes gleam in the firelight. "And I won. A little thanks might be in order."

His words sink in, and I'm left to wonder what would've happened if I'd let Alexus die on the green. Would Neri have died too? Or would he have been released?

"There will be more life after this," he goes on. "You will see your sister, and you'll figure out your future from there. If I'm not too late to save Colden, the kingdom and the vale will rebuild. If I *am* too late, I guess I'm going on a quest to save this empire, and you'll take to the seas and end up with someone who will make you a very happy woman." Sighing, he drags a hand through his hair and rests his hand on his hip. "We just have to get out of this godsforsaken construct first without doing things to one another that we'll regret."

We stand there, breathing hard, like we scaled the cliffs with our bare hands. Before I can reply, an infernal howl tears through the night. The horses sit up, their ears pricking, and Alexus and I look toward the tunnel.

He holds up a placating hand. "It's all right. The wolves are just roaming, hunting for blood after the mess we left in the wood."

Blood.

Slipping my hand beneath my arm, I tuck two fingers inside the hole in my bodice where the rocks dug into my skin. I flinch. The jagged wound stings at my touch, and it's sticky wet.

I hold my bloody hand between Alexus and me and lift my arm to show him the cut.

His face blanches, and he immediately crosses the distance between us and inspects the injury, one hand firm on my waist. "You said you were all right."

I wipe my fingers on my trousers and pull away from him. *"I thought I was."*

Another unearthly howl crawls into the cave, followed by another and another, like the animals are communicating a warning across the ravine.

"I told you before. The wolves won't hurt us. I have the God of the White Wolf inside me, for fuck's sake." He grabs the gambeson, throwing it on. "I'm going to have a look around and gather more brush. You should heal that wound and consult the waters so we can decide what to do from here. You know who to look for."

He moves toward the passageway that leads to the mouth of the cave, but he hesitates. After a moment, he turns and backtracks, coming straight for me.

When he reaches me, he presses me against the cave wall and kisses me with as much fervor as ever before, regardless of his words about futures and regrets.

I should push him away. This will never end well. But I can't. One touch of his tongue to mine, and nothing else matters but us.

He pulls back and runs his thumb over my lips. "Raina Bloodgood, your mouth will be my ruin." Tenderly, he kisses my forehead, then turns to leave. Before he steps into the pool of bloody darkness spilling from the cavern's entrance, he turns a look over his shoulder and holds up a finger. "I'll be back shortly. Stay. Here." He tilts that dark head. "And by all the gods, listen to me this time."

The second he vanishes, I press my fingers to my mouth, wishing I could trap the tingling feeling left behind by every single one of his kisses.

I'm in So. Much. Trouble.

For a while, I sit by the fire, all of this new information simmering and stewing in my mind. Outside the complications with Alexus, the Prince of the East means to conquer the City of Ruin and raise Thamaos. I didn't live when the gods ruled, and I've always been thankful for that. I don't want to live in a world where Thamaos reigns, which means I have to stop that from happening.

I take up my mother's dish. Alexus and I haven't been apart in days, and in his absence, I'm thankful for the distraction of scrying. But before I can begin, my eye catches on Alexus's sword, leaned against the cave wall.

I should take it to him.

No. I *will* stay here. He'll be back soon; I know he will. He's unfailing and unceasing and a host of other words I've painted him with. And, he has the God Knife.

I grab the Eastlander blade and puncture the end of my fingertip. A shiny bead of blood forms and waits to fall as my mind races over my options. I could check on Helena or look for Finn like I'd wanted to before things went sideways, but Alexus is right. I know who I have to look for.

With a turn of my hand, my blood splashes into the water.

"Nahmthalahsh. Show me the Prince of the East."

This time, there are no shadows or smoke or mist, just a moving image unfolding on the water's violet surface.

The prince rides on horseback, a red mantle billowing at his back. About thirty warriors and a flock of crows follow. They're in the wood, but not inside this construct. At least it doesn't *look* like they're inside this construct. They ride hard—on a road, not a path. The trees are lightly covered in white, their autumn leaves and needled branches cradling an early snow. Flurries blow softly in the wind, and the last rays of a setting sun slice through the forest's canopy, the light warm and wavering.

In the near distance, behind a glimmering veil of protection, sits a castle, a dark monolith rising above the evergreens, protruding from the land like one of the mountains to its east and west.

My pulse thunders.

The Prince of the East is about to take Winterhold.

I don't have time to consider what to do. The sound of footsteps and heavy breathing fills the passageway that leads outside.

Fast as I can move, I grab the Eastlander knife and dart to the wall beside the entrance where that pool of bloody darkness spills into the cave. I press my back to the rocks and raise my weapon.

A tall form in a scarlet cloak and bronze leathers creeps from the shadows, hatchet in hand.

I don't hesitate.

With all the strength left in me, I bring down my blade.

28

ALEXUS

The Frostwater ravine runs north and south, just east of Winter Road and far north of my hunting shelter. This great, white crevice—tinted the shade of fevered cheeks—is mostly rock, though evergreen bushes and pine saplings have sprung up from the old riverbed thanks to a rainy early summer. Most of the bushes are buried in snow, and I've scavenged what I could from the thickets growing back the way we came, so walking north is the only option if we're to stay warm here.

I keep moving that way, staring at the rugged cliffs, thinking about everything that just happened between me and Raina, the thing she still doesn't know about me, and how close we are to what feels like freedom, though there's no way to be sure unless I walk to the construct's end. I don't know how far the enchantment reaches or how long the kingdom's Witch Walkers will manage to keep their magick in place.

Or what will happen once we cross into the real world.

I swear the construct is weakening, though. Silent cracks of silver lightning fracture the deep red sky, leaving behind a dark bruise. I wouldn't dare tell Raina, but I fear the red sky is a reflection of the misery the Witch Walkers are enduring, the fissuring a sign of their dwindling control.

We may be free sooner than expected.

Snow still falls, but it's not as cold as when we arrived, feeling more and more like the cold of home—crisp and calming. It's peaceful here too, so I take my time, giving Raina space to think without me clouding her thoughts. I know what that's like. She's all I see, awake or asleep, and that's not how any of this was supposed to go.

Get in. Get Raina. Get home.

Deny my feelings. My heart. My body.

That had been the original plan and the new plan.

And I've failed at both.

Spectacularly.

When I come upon a small thicket of seedlings, I gather what little kindling I can and turn to head toward the cave.

Something crashes into me from behind, knocking the air from my lungs, sending me careening toward a snow-covered boulder. It takes a split second to realize that what struck me is not a *thing* but a *person*.

Kindling scatters across the snow, and I'm plowed into the rock, the weight of another body driving me forward as my arm is wrenched behind me. Breathless, I move to turn over, to fight, but the person holding me stabs a blunt knee into my kidney, pressing my wrist against my spine, all while their other colossal hand seizes my neck, thoroughly pinning me against the stone.

"Be very still, very quiet, and listen," a man whispers. "We're being watched. I don't have much time."

My free hand is splayed on the boulder. I stretch my fingers wide and lift my palm from the snow, an effort to show a silent moment of surrender.

He leans close. "I'm a spy for the king. You don't remember me. I was just a boy when I left Winterhold with my mother for the Eastland Territory. She was from Penrith." His grip tightens, and he speaks through clenched teeth. "I sent a warning that the prince was coming. Why did you not heed?"

Gods. The rumor.

Faces flash across my mind, people who volunteered to work along the spy chain that has become more of a web, in truth. I've escorted scores of

Witch Walkers, Icelanders, and even people from the tiny mining villages of the Mondulak Range to Winterhold. Several later enlisted their services.

This man could be anyone.

"The Prince of the East is on his way to Winterhold, so now you must face General Vexx. And I won't be able to save you." He pauses, breathing hard against my face. "We've been following you ever since you blew up the godsdamn forest. The prince left others behind, but they failed, so he commanded his best battalion—mine, of course—to remain in this hellish place and find this knife you two have so pathetically protected." He lets out a long, annoyed breath. "Warriors are coming down from the cliffs as we speak. Where is the woman? I can only help her if I know where she is."

"What do you want with her?" I strain against his hold, but he only doubles down.

"Not a damn thing. The prince wants her, probably to kill her. She sundered his face with a gash as wide as this ravine. He's going to punish her, I'm sure, and believe me, you do not want her to meet his wrath."

I squeeze my eyes against the image that forms in my mind—of Raina beneath the prince's hands. I would skin him alive, hang him from a tree, and call the wolves.

Boots crunch in the snow. The sound grows closer.

Louder.

It would be so easy to wipe these Eastlanders from existence, but Raina is likely to be buried alive from the ripple effect with this much loose and fallen rock. I have to protect her, but I can't trust this man to be her savior.

"Let me see your face."

"They can smell your fire, Thibault. They can't see it, but they can smell it. They will sniff her out. Unless I get to her beforehand."

I grit my teeth. "Face. First."

He flips me over, and it takes a moment, but his face registers. If he was a boy when he left, and if he knew me, I have long forgotten him.

But I do recognize him. The red-haired Eastlander I faced in Hampstead Loch. The warrior with the bloodless blade who stared me down and rode the other way.

"The name's Rhonin." He glances up, only his eyes, his sharp gaze scanning the ravine. A heartbeat later, he raises a meaty fist and meets my stare. "Sorry about this, but I'm doing you a favor."

Above him, that odd and silent silver lightning splits the red sky.

Then his fist comes down like a hammer, and my world goes black.

29

RAINA

The Eastlander whirls, catching my wrist with a firm hand before I can land my mark. I suck in a deep breath and push harder, but from beneath the cloak, a familiar face stares back at me.

Not an Eastlander.

Helena.

Fear rips through me like a blazing fire, my body locked in indecision. Shadow wraith. That's all I can think as her eyes search mine.

"It's me, Raina. Just me." Her voice is her own, and her eyes are vivid and aware, her wild spirit returned. There's no rotten smell wafting from her, no unnatural quality to her movements, and her skin is as cold as mine.

The tension in my muscles ebbs, disbelief clinging to me like a bad dream.

Her brows knit together, tears welling in her eyes. "Can you just hug me now?" She presses her forehead to mine, and I catch a glimpse of her ochre-tinted witch's marks, flowering up from behind her collar. "Tuetha tah," she whispers, releasing my wrist.

I drop my blade and fold my arms around her shoulders, squeezing her so tightly that she laughs around her tears.

"You're going to break me," she says, and I let her go, smiling so hard that my cheeks ache.

Grabbing her hands, I check for frostbite. There's some, but it's not severe. I can heal it quickly.

I clasp her face. She looks exhausted, and her skin is chapped and reddened from the cold, but otherwise, she looks...whole. Healthy. And though a hint of sadness shadows her eyes, she's *smiling*.

I'd worried that there would be nothing left of her by the time we returned, that the wraith would've turned her mind enough that she no longer remembered who she was. The relief inside me is overwhelming, enough that I can't help but draw her to me and cry.

Once we've both shed a host of tears, I pull back.

"How?" I ask.

She shrugs and wipes at my face, then sniffles and scrubs at her own. "I don't know. Whatever that thing was, it left a day or so after you. Time is impossible to follow here. I felt it leave me like a sucking wind, and off it went, screeching into the wood. After it was gone, the tree that held me withdrew." Her eyes go wide with wonder. "Was that Nephele too? Like the lake?"

Raising my brows, I nod, understanding her dismay, though I fear I'm about to slay her with all the things she needs to know. She's about to learn my secrets and Alexus's too, and stories of shadow wraiths and the Frost King and Fia Drumera and the gods and the God Knife and—the possible end of life as we know it. We could soon live in an age of gods. At least an age of *a* god.

But we won't let that happen. We *won't*.

As long as Alexus can keep Neri contained, that is.

"How did you find me?" I ask, stunned by this girl's fortitude and stalwartness, though I shouldn't be. She's young and naive at times, but a fire lives inside her that few possess. She could be a warrior like no other. She just needs the freedom to let that fire burn.

I suppose she has that freedom now.

"I headed toward the mountains," she answers, "and came upon a group of dead Eastlanders. It wasn't fun, and it wasn't pretty, but I removed one's clothes. I had to, or I was going to freeze to death right there with them." She rubs the place over her brow where a gash had been. "I'd hoped that General Vexx was among the dead, but that wasn't the case." She holds up her hatchet. "At least I filched this."

The Eastlanders we found beneath the trees. I almost killed Helena with one of their blades.

"I came across a campsite," she goes on. "Too fresh to belong to the Eastlanders. They'd been dead for days. After that, I picked up on your trail like Father taught me while tracking deer. There were only two sets of hoof prints where the snow hadn't covered them. I held out hope that it was you. At one point, the tracks led forward, but there was a quake, and the tracks vanished. I kept going, until I came to a hole blown into the earth. There was only one way to pass, so I followed. Not long after, I entered the ravine. I saw smoke rising from this cave. It could've been anyone, but I had to know if it was you."

Amazed by her, I tug my hair over one shoulder, thinking about what it would've been like to have endured the wood alone, but Hel's blinking eyes catch my attention. She touches the backs of my hands, my neck, my chest, her eyes wide, like she's only now noticing my witch's marks. And I suppose she is.

"What in gods' stars, Raina?"

I gesture toward the smoldering fire. *"Come. Sit. We need to talk."*

I tell her everything, beginning with my abilities. I show her my skill at fire magick and healing, drawing out her frostbite and giving her fingers and toes, cuts and bruises, new life, as well as mending the cut on my side. When that's done, I tell her what happened during the attack and everything after. Even how difficult it was to watch that wraith take her away from me. When I tell her about the God Knife and that Alexus is *the* Un Drallag from eastern lore, she stops me, an unsettled look taking over her face as though she's piecing things together that I can't see.

"Raina, the prince's men had that knife. Because of me."

I tilt my head, and she reads my expression, understanding that I need her to explain.

"After I left you at Mena's, I headed for the fallow fields. I had Finn and Saira with me at one point, but we got separated."

I remember this from her tale at the lake, but her memory had been broken, probably because the wraith divided her reality.

"I made it to our cottage," she continues, "but my mother and sisters were already dead. I started toward the fields, but that's when I ran into

Vexx." Again, she touches her brow, remembering. "When I came to, it was still dark. I ran to the green, and you were there, but I thought you were dead. You were lying so still, next to the Witch Collector, and I was...mindless. There was blood everywhere. And that knife, the one with the white hilt, lay on the green. It...called to me. To take it. Not a voice, but a knowing. It was next to your hand, and I wanted some part of you with me, so I took it."

A sigh escapes me, and I press a hand to my face. Gods' death. No wonder I couldn't remember what I did with the knife.

"After that," she says, "I went east and found a way through the barrier they erected, a wedge of an opening filled with thorns. I ran through Frostwater until I couldn't run anymore." She glances at her hands, nervously picking at a nail. "I was devastated. I wanted to make someone pay."

I reach across the space between us and take her hand. I know that feeling. I know what she went through.

"I stumbled upon Vexx's men at the tunnel mouth, and they captured me. When Vexx saw the blade I carried, he confiscated it, but I don't think he knew what he had until later. There was no urgency until the next day, after we made it over the lake. He stalked out of the woods and ordered one of his men to bring him the knife. After that, we traveled harder and faster. They wanted to catch up to the prince; I remember that now. He was ahead with another band. Vexx wanted to kill me or at least leave me behind, but there's a red-haired warrior in that group. Rhonin, they call him. He seems important, though not as important as Vexx. He demanded that Vexx let him keep me."

"And of course, Vexx agreed," I sign.

"Of course."

Disgust roils through me. I want to kill both men, and I don't even know them.

Helena looks up, and that fire of hers flickers in her eyes. "I realized by the way Vexx was acting that the weapon was important. I just didn't know *how* important. Still, I managed to catch all of them unaware in the middle of the night. Even with my hands tied, I stole the knife from Vexx's thigh and ran like the wind."

She smiles, and I smile too. *"And Rhonin let you go?"*

"It seemed that way. He came after me, and there was a moment when he was mere strides away, watching me through the trees. He could've taken me, but he didn't do anything." She shrugs. "He just told me to run."

"And after?"

After was the shadow wraith.

Helena pales. Takes a shaky breath. "All of that is still unclear. I remember seeing you. Being with you and Alexus. And I remember when the wraith left."

The prince had to be watching. He had to know where she was. Why turn back inside the construct when his wraith could force Helena to return the blade? Why endanger his men any further for a hunt? I left the blade unprotected, and he swooped in to take it.

Until Nephele stopped him.

I'm glad Hel doesn't remember; she would struggle with those memories. I pray they stay buried forever.

Speaking of praying, I tell her about Neri. When I finish, she sits in shocked silence.

"Neri is *here*," she says. "Inside the Witch Collector."

I feel guilty. Alexus's stories were difficult for me to absorb, but Helena is coming to terms with even more. I've lied to her and everyone else who knew me for years, yet she seems to forgive that easily. Reconciling what she's always believed about the God of the White Wolf with the truth provided by a man who knows him intimately is what seems to shatter what remains of her belief.

"Neri has been such an important part of my life," she says. "If what Alexus says is true, then..."

Then Neri wasn't such a good, protective god.

"Neri was manipulative and greedy," I sign. *"Toying with the lives of North-landers over his desire for a goddess. He did not give us the Frost King for guidance and authority. He gave us Colden Moeshka, a product of his revenge."*

Resting her elbows on her bent knees, Helena buries her face in her hands. I don't press or say anything more. She's lost so much. Now she's losing the vengeful god to whom she prays.

She looks up and exhales like she's clearing her mind. "We can't let the prince get that knife, and we can't let him reach Colden."

My face falls.

"What?" she says. "What is it? Why that look?"

I glance at the scrying dish. *"Before you arrived, I saw the prince on Winter Road. He was on his way to Winterhold."*

"Well, we can't just sit here." She gets to her feet. "Where's Alexus?"

"Gathering kindling, but he should be back by now."

"He wasn't south. I would've crossed paths with him." With nervous energy rolling off her, she sits again. "I think a storm is coming. There's no thunder out there, but there's lightning. It could get dangerous, and we need him."

The lightning. I forgot.

Grabbing Mother's dish, I hurry outside, returning with a bowl of snow, nestling the vessel in the last of the fading embers. Quickly, I summon the powers of *Fulmanesh*, and in a matter of minutes, I have a bowl of snowmelt. Again, I prick my finger and stir my blood into the warm water.

"Nahmthalahsh. Show me Alexus."

The water swirls and slows, and a picture condenses on the violet surface.

Alexus. Unconscious. His face swollen and bleeding. He's being dragged by the neck of the gambeson through the ravine by a mountain of a man wearing bronze leathers—a man with flaming hair.

A cold sweat breaks on my brow, and my heart kicks in my chest. I blink, praying this vision is wrong.

More men follow with weapons slung over their shoulders. They wear prideful smiles like poachers after a kill. I can't tell which way they're moving, but it must be north like Helena said because the ravine looks different from what I remember.

"Eastlanders," I tell her, my fear and worry morphing into fury. *"They... They have him."* I stand, not sure what I'm about to do, but a cyclone of rage brews inside me.

Helena's eyes glimmer, not with tears but with the promise of a fight. "Well, they aren't going to keep him, now are they?" She gets up and collects her hatchet, my blade, and Alexus's sword. "Which one are you best with?"

"The knife and the hatchet," I answer, as though she doesn't know. She

wanted to give me a choice, but I've sparred with her enough to understand that she needs the sword if heads are about to roll.

She hands me the smaller weapons. "Put your boots on and get your cloak. We're going hunting."

30

ALEXUS

I wake to the crushing impact of a boot striking my ribs.

The kicking eventually ceases, and a gasping cough erupts from my chest, blasting blood and snow into the wind. I'm lying several yards from a fire where a few dozen men sit laughing, watching, and cheering. I've been stripped of my gambeson, my tunic wet and freezing to my skin. I can't see out of my right eye, my throat feels like two hands are clenching it, and my body aches like someone rolled me off the cliffs and let me crash at the bottom of the ravine.

Deep inside me, Neri rages in his cage, rattling my bones.

Another swift kick, this time to my stomach, followed by a stomp to the bend of my knee, sends fresh, hot pain radiating everywhere, enough that the misery nearly sends me back into unconsciousness. Still, I cling to awareness—with desperation.

Raina. She's alone, and she will search for me.

I cannot let that happen.

"Finally coming to," a voice says.

A booted foot nudges my side until I'm forced to roll over, collapsing on my back. I cry out. My leg is damaged, and my body is weighed down.

Above me, that same red sky looms while flurries swirl and descend. A figure leans over me, obstructing the view, and I blink away snow and tears to see him.

"You really should've killed me when you had the chance," he says. A cruel smile simmers on his lips.

I close my eyes and clamp them tight, if only to memorize the merciless regret coursing through me. I knew he was important—by his armor, his flag, his horse.

And still, I didn't take the time to destroy him.

That long, braided gray hair holds the sparse remains of war paint, the vermilion lacquer washed away by snow. His armor is gone, but he wears the bronze leathers of his men and the stench of death.

When he squats beside me, I instinctively reach for the God Knife. Again, my body doesn't move like I will it to, my hands awkward, my movements constricted.

"Looking for this?" He holds up my weapon, twisting his wrist as he scrutinizes the blade. He cuts a sidelong look at me with eyes the color of a snowstorm. "I dare you to try to take it from me. I'm not supposed to kill you until after I have the knife *and* the woman, but seeing what you did to my men, I'm feeling rather ruthless."

"If you saw what I can do," I grit out, spitting blood at his feet, "then you should be terrified right now."

He tosses his head back and laughs. "There's nothing to fear. You're bound, Collector."

I feel it then, the cold weight wrapped around my neck, my wrists, my ankles. I drag a heavy hand up to touch my throat and trail my fingertips over the short length of iron there, pressing into my gullet. Tight cuffs cut into my wrists and ankles, linked together by chains.

Neri isn't raging. He's in misery.

And I'm powerless.

"I know who you are, Un Drallag, and what's inside you," the man who must be General Vexx says. "The prince knows too."

"That's impossible." But obviously, it isn't.

"You'd be amazed by the tales wraiths are willing to share of their homeland. Like Un Drallag traveling into the Nether Reaches when he meant to journey to the Empyreal Fields and coming out with a god weaved into his soul instead. It took the wraith tasting you and entering your memory to be sure it was right about who you were. It *was* three hundred years ago. The prince sensed something unusual on your lady friend, but once the wraith was certain about you being Un Drallag, it made sure the Prince of the East knew exactly what we were dealing with. The dead tell all, my friend."

The Prince of the East knows about me. About Neri. All because of damned wraith.

The general leans close. "I wonder what stories you'll reveal once you cross the Nether Reaches' dark shores. That's where you're going. You know that, I'm sure. The prince has a plan, and it does not include your interference, nor does it include Neri being set free. We need him back where he belongs. In the Shadow World. Thankfully, he's still caged, because *you* somehow survived the prince." He jerks up the side of my tunic. "Without any wounds, I might add."

My mind sticks on two parts of what he just said. When the prince spoke to Raina about needing the thing he sensed on her back where it belongs, he wasn't talking about the God Knife as I'd believed. He was talking about Neri. He sensed Neri all over Raina because of me.

Second...

"What plan?" Again, I spit blood onto the ground, my mouth beginning to refill instantly.

He smiles, like he knew I'd ask. "The plan for the prince to harness the magick at the City of Ruin. The gods' bones must be reunited with their souls. We'll resurrect them from the Shadow World and keep them contained, all while the prince siphons their power. They can't be mucking about all over Loria's creation, though, or we'll never capture them. Which is why we must send Neri back to the Nether Reaches. For now. There *is* a method to the prince's strategy. We will soon have the Frost King, a way to weaken Fia Drumera. The citadel will fall, the Prince of the East will claim the Grove of the Gods, and Tiressia's broken empire will have one ruler."

"One ruler with the power of Thamaos, Neri, Asha, and Urdin. Are you so foolish as to think that this is wise?"

"I'm no fool," he replies. "A fool would believe that Tiressia can thrive divided. The prince means to unify the lands."

"Or so he tells you. Power corrupts. And he's already corrupted as it is. What do you think he will become without limits?"

After a weighted moment, the man stands, ignoring my last words. "Get him up. Let's find her and get this over with, once and for all."

Only half-seeing, I spot the red-haired man—Rhonin—striding my way. With the camp and Vexx at his back, he reaches into his collar and pulls something from behind his bronze leather jacket. Something that dangles from a thick chain around his neck.

Our stares meet, and he winks.

An iron key.

"If this was a favor," I whisper, "Don't help me ever again."

Rhonin lets a smile tempt his mouth, but then he kills it and stuffs the key back to its hiding spot. He and a woman grab me beneath my arms and haul me to my feet.

Nearly choking from the iron band around my throat, I vomit on the snow. It's impossible not to once the world tilts. I don't know how many times Vexx kicked me or what he did to my knee, but he made certain that I would not forget him.

And I won't.

Some of the warriors keep their seats near the fire while others take up swords or hatchets. A few reach for torches that lie tossed in a pile. Most of the pine knots have burned down to half their original size, but they're the very ones the Eastlanders used in the vale. They've been conserving.

They set the torches alight in the campfire's flames, hand one off to General Vexx, and a small band of us walk, Vexx leading the way. His tall, slender form moves like a phantom, his ashen hair whipping in the wind, blending into the wintry landscape.

If I survive this, I'll have his head.

With Rhonin at my side, we make the trek in silence, save for the awful clangor of my chains. The snow muffles the sound when I stumble, which is nearly every step thanks to my throbbing knee. My chains are burdensome, but I'm no god and thankfully feel no burning agony searing my skin. There's only an unsettling vibration in my chest, a trapped windstorm whirling around my heart.

I summon energy, my magick, *anything*, but the iron smothers Neri's power to ashes and my magick along with it. After all these years, the two are so entwined that I can hardly tell them apart anymore.

There are eleven warriors and their general—if I don't count Rhonin—

headed to find Raina. I've no means to fight them, no recourse. And they know it. There isn't an ounce of trepidation in their midst as I'm led deeper into the ravine toward the caves.

Eventually, the smell of woodsmoke tints the air. I force myself not to react, but it doesn't matter. Vexx throws up a fist, nose to the wind, and we come to a halt.

I'm probably going to die soon, because I will never tell them where Raina is, and if they find her on their own, I will end my life trying to save her.

Vexx turns to me, his movements slow and stiff, his eyes hard and cold as he shines his flaming torch in my direction. "Call to her."

The other Eastlanders face me too.

I glare at their leader and scoff. "You might as well end me, because I refuse."

Vexx stares for a long moment before closing the distance between us in a few long strides, until he's mere inches from my face. "*Call* to her. Or I will cut out your three-hundred-year-old tongue. And I'll take my time. Until your woman comes running because she hears your mindless misery."

"She can't reply," I tell him, my throat working against my binds. "She was born voiceless."

He arches a brow. "I don't need her to reply. I need her to show herself. I'll take care of the rest." He unsheathes the God Knife from his thigh and presses the flat of the bone blade to my cheek. "Now call her, or I'll render you as silent as she."

"Just kill me. It doesn't matter how you threaten me. I will not be the reason you find her."

Vexx snarls and presses the blade harder into my cheek.

"Leave him alone." A feminine voice carries on the wind. "I'll take you to her."

Vexx whips his head around. The few torchbearers aim their lights at a figure standing in the middle of the ravine, shrouded in a red cloak. Snow swirls around the statuesque form, and the torches cast competing shadows across the white ground.

Swords unsheathe, and hatchets raise, and Vexx lowers the God Knife from my face.

"Show yourself," he commands, pointing his torch at the hooded figure.

The shadows move. A heartbeat passes.

"Come closer, and I will."

I cock my ear. Is that...

It can't be.

Vexx hesitates but walks forward, God Knife tightly fisted in his hand. He stops a few short strides from the cloaked woman. "Remove your hood, or every warrior here will send their blade sailing straight toward your heart. You have three seconds."

One. Two.

She folds the hood back, and my heart lurches.

Helena.

Beside me, Rhonin tenses, and if I'm not mistaken, even gasps. If the wraith is still within Helena, I cannot tell. She looks much the same, though it's difficult to see the truth with the snow, torchlight, and shadows. The wraith is sneaky, that much I know. I cannot trust the girl before my eyes.

"Well, well," Vexx says. "The Knife Thief. We meet again." He motions to two of his warriors. "Check her for weapons. Don't forget how quick she is."

Helena is so young, barely marked as grown in Northlander terms. And yet the way she stands there, arms lifted at her sides, chin high, spine strong and sure, she seems a thousand years old, confident as any goddess, any queen. There's not a single remnant of unnatural presence, nor any hint of the rattled girl from the lake, and I have to wonder if that was all the wraith's doing, and if this is the *real* Helena.

The warriors strip away her cloak, revealing no weapons. She's no longer dressed in gold, the vulnerable material of her silken gown. Instead, she's clad in the bronze leathers of Vexx's men.

The general clasps his hands behind his back, feet spread wide, studying her. "Did you kill my men and take their clothes?"

A wind catches her hair, blows her scent in my direction. She doesn't smell like flowers, but she doesn't smell like the pit of the world either.

"No," she answers Vexx. "Your men were already dead, but yes, I took their clothes." She looks down at herself and meets his gaze again. "Clearly."

As Vexx closes in, prowling toward her, his warriors step away, and

Helena lowers her arms. She fixes her glittering eyes on Vexx as he approaches.

"Raina Bloodgood is dead," she informs him. "That's the only reason I'll take you to her."

At her words, my knees go weak, but Rhonin pulls me upright. Still, I sway on my feet, a hollowness yawning inside me, swallowing my heart.

Helena must be lying. She *must* be.

Vexx meets her toe to toe, nose to nose. With a light hand, he brushes Helena's jet hair from her face, tucking it back at her temple where he runs a thumb over her angled brow. She flinches at his touch.

"Odd. Last time I saw you, you still bore the bloody mark of my fist." He peers back at me, and for the first time, Helena glances my way. "Funny how injuries keep vanishing," he adds. "I'll have to do a better job next time." Vexx faces Helena. "If you're lying, girl, I will drag you from here to Winterhold behind my horse, and I will enjoy every second. You've cost me enough as it is." With that, he steps back and sweeps his arm in a gesture. "Now. Lead the way, my lady."

Broad shoulders back, Helena turns toward the caves. Vexx positions two warriors at her sides, and he falls just behind. Whatever happened between these two before Helena found Raina and me, it made enemies out of them.

A smothered half-groan, half-sigh rumbles in the back of Rhonin's throat. I look at him as I limp along, glancing where the key hides, but there are men all around—in front of us, behind us, beside us—and he only stares straight ahead, focused on the rugged, snowy landscape.

And Helena.

In the reach of firelight, she climbs the rough and bouldered incline that leads to the very cave where I left Raina.

Vexx tosses a wicked smile over his shoulder. "Be sure to bring Un Drallag."

Pulse thrumming against the cuffs at my wrists, Rhonin nudges me forward. Already, I can feel a hum in the air, the way the atmosphere thins around a coming crisis. I just don't know what that crisis is. I've either shackled my soul to the Nether Reaches even surer by damning Raina to an early death, or something else lies ahead that might see me taking even more lives. Not that it matters.

Whether I like it or not, my soul is irredeemable.

With lumbered steps, we climb until Helena says, "It's just ahead. Follow me."

The second those words leave her mouth, Vexx halts us, his warriors coming to a standstill, each one scattered a few feet from another across the hillside. The two warriors following Helena seize her, and again, she glances at the cave and then at me, this time with wide and worried eyes.

Vexx props a foot on a rock and rests his hands on his hips. He nods to the two warriors flanking her, one of whom holds a torch.

"You two. Onward." He looks pointedly at a man and woman to his right. "And you two, hold her. She stays within sight."

The man and woman grab Helena, twisting her arms behind her back, while the other warriors vanish into the cave's darkness, their light a glowing orb that soon snuffs out. There is no sound. No movement. Just a black abyss in the side of a cliff.

Vexx waits a few minutes, but when the warriors don't return, he motions to someone else. "Go."

Hatchet ready and torch raised, an Eastlander creeps into the darkness with a hint of caution in every step. The torchlight soon extinguishes, and again, nothing.

Vexx looks toward the red sky and roars. He stomps toward the cave and screams into it. "I'm tired of these games! You either come out here and drop your weapons, or this girl's blood *and* yours will flow through this ravine like a river. Don't think I won't do it. I've already acquired the most important part of this mission."

Brandishing the God Knife, he heads toward Helena, staring into her eyes. When he speaks, his voice is loud enough that if Raina *is* still inside that cave, she will hear him.

"Your witch friend has a chance to live," he says. "She can bow before the Prince of the East and beg his mercy for what she did to him. I can't say that he'll oblige, but if the two of you keep toying with *me*, all hope is lost. And as for that bastard," he jerks his head toward me and waggles the God Knife, "his destiny has arrived. Very soon, Un Drallag and Neri will be no more. They'll both return to the Shadow World, and any chance of Thamaos's greatest enemy being set free and allowed to interfere in the prince's plan will have been removed."

Ah. Vexx means to kill me, not that I didn't already know this, but he plans to do it with the God Knife, the only weapon that can kill a god, so that Neri's soul returns to the Shadow World, along with mine. But perhaps the wraith and prince don't know as much about me and the God Knife as they think.

Vexx tilts Helena's chin with one hand, then fists her hair at the crown and yanks her around, her back to his front, facing the cave. Dangerously, he presses the God Knife against her throat.

Aiming his voice toward the cave, he says, "Your call, witch. Does your friend live? Or die?"

For a moment, there is nothing but the snow falling around us, and another silent crack of icy lightning dances across the sky.

Then, from the shadows, a cloaked figure emerges from the cave.

31

RAINA

I step into the construct's dimming crimson light and drop my bloody knife and the Eastlander hatchet. Next, I strip off Alexus's baldric and sword and toss them aside. Lastly, I shed my cloak, so the enemy can see that I'm unarmed. No more innocents will die because of me.

Especially Helena.

This wasn't how things were supposed to happen. We spotted the Eastlanders and their torches—and Alexus—a half-hour ago, but attacking thirteen warriors when we had no upper hand was unwise. We changed course, planning for Helena to lure them into the cave where I'd doused the fire. I would tear into them, one by one, as they entered the passageway.

Alas, the general had other plans.

"Good girl," Vexx says to me. He stands with Helena, craning her head back at a painful angle against his shoulder. The God Knife's tip is pressed to her throat, ready to open a vein. She's alive, for now, and that sends a trickle of hope through me.

The general thrusts his chin at two of his warriors. "Must I tell you every time? Weapons. Hold her. And somebody check the cave."

They kick away my only defense and bend my arms behind me. One of the dead Eastlanders that Vexx's warriors are about to find managed to stab my arm. With my biceps wrenched like this, I can't help but cringe from the pain.

"Raina!"

I follow Alexus's voice. He stands closer to the bottom of the ravine, straining against iron binds while warriors hold him at bay. Iron stifles godly power—Neri's power. I don't know what that means for Alexus's magick, but if he could access it, he would've already done so.

Our gazes meet. He calls out my name once more, but the woman at his side rams her fist into his jaw to silence him.

The general releases Helena and sheathes the God Knife at his hip, watching me closely as he moves my way. Behind him, two women take hold of Helena, forcing her to her knees.

Vexx isn't an overly large man, not much taller than Helena, but his presence is like that of a rising storm over the vale, something I feel more and more the closer he gets. His eyes hold a deathly gleam, sharp and silver as a sword's edge, and his stone-like face—with its weathered skin—has seen many battles, decorated with the scars to prove it.

"All of this—" the general gestures to the Eastlander-dotted hillside "—because of you and your friend." He angles his head, staring at me past the falling snow like he's puzzling me out. "A Witch Walker who can't speak and can't sing. That must've made you quite the disappointment with your people."

"You *pig*!" Helena shouts, wriggling against the women pressing her down. "She has more magick—"

I stop her with a warning glare that could cut ice.

Vexx laughs, curiosity glinting in his eyes. "Does she, now? Interesting." He pushes my hair aside and trails a fingertip down my neck and along my collarbone, tracing my witch's marks.

After a moment, he seems to slip that nugget of information to the back of his brain, then he grabs me by my hair and forces me down the hill. Behind me, the horses nicker and Helena grunts, likely enduring the same fate as me.

We're heading straight for Alexus.

Gods, I want to run to him. His eye is swollen shut, and bloody blooms speckle his tunic. He stands at an odd tilt, like something is wrong with his leg.

Vexx and I are two strides away from the bottom of the ravine when the whole world flickers. It's like the light in a room at night, when a draft has kissed a candle flame.

The snow stops falling, and Vexx stops walking, and we all look up. Helena said a storm was coming, but this is no storm.

Like before, when Alexus and I entered the ravine, white lightning splinters the sky without a single sound. This time, there are a thousand jagged arcs of light shattering the red-tinted atmosphere, spreading like cracks through thin glass. That constant feeling of the construct's magick, the sensation that's been with me for days now, disintegrates, and the glaring light of day breaks through.

A cheer erupts from the Eastlanders, but it takes several moments for my eyes to adjust and my mind to absorb what's happening.

What's *happened*.

The Prince of the East won. He made it to Winterhold—the Witch Walkers couldn't hold out any longer.

"It's about damn time," Vexx says. "This little expedition in the North is all but over now."

I don't get a single moment to bask in the warmth of the sun before Vexx shoves me forward, still holding onto my hair. His elation is evident in his quicker footsteps and the tightening of his grip, the pain and sudden sunlight making my eyes water.

I trip and fall, and a plug of my hair rips from the roots before I land in the snow. Someone—who is not Vexx—hoists me up, pinning my wrists at my back. I shake my head, trudging forward, blinking away the snow from my lashes.

And just like that, I'm standing there, panting, an arm's length from Alexus.

The light of day brutally illuminates his injuries, and my body aches for his. The chains holding him bound are so solid and thick that I don't know how he's still standing.

The way he looks at me almost ends me. I see his fear, and I know that it isn't for himself.

It's for me.

"I'm so sorry, Raina."

I shake my head, hoping he knows that I don't blame him. I just want to be back in that cave, curled with him near the fire, listening to his stories.

Gods, I wish I'd never let him leave.

A tear rolls from my eye as Mannus and sweet Tuck are guided past us, and the women leading Helena bring her to Vexx's opposite side. The general turns to the red-haired giant holding Alexus's arm.

"You can say goodbye to your little friend, Rhonin. She escaped you and nearly cost us everything. Surely you want to punish her."

My heart pounds. Rhonin.

I lean forward, meeting Helena's glassy stare. I pray she was right, that he let her go. I pray that he is not as evil as his general or his prince.

Rhonin looks like he doesn't know what to do or say, a moment of shock passing over his face like a cloud. Alexus peers at him, but Rhonin keeps his eyes fixed on Vexx.

"We can let her go." He glances at what looks to be an early afternoon sky. "We don't have time for this. She's nothing to us. Nothing to our prince or our mission."

Vexx tilts his head and narrows his eyes. "Rhonin, sometimes I wonder if you have the mettle required to even be in this army." He shoves Helena toward the Eastlander. "Either you punish her, or someone else will."

The muscle in Rhonin's jaw feathers. With apparent reluctance, he lets go of Alexus. He has blue eyes, and that cerulean gaze finds Helena, though she's staring at the ground, chest rising and falling fast.

"Fine," Rhonin replies. "But her beating happens in private. I don't like audiences."

Vexx watches his warrior carefully, suspicion leaking from his every pore.

Rhonin snatches Helena's wrist and drags her toward the caves, stalking up the snowy hillside where other warriors remove the bodies of the Eastlanders I killed. Helena fights, like I knew she would, but Rhonin throws her over his shoulder, and the pair vanish into a cave.

With my heart in my throat and rage boiling my blood, I stomp the foot of the man holding me and lunge toward my friend. It's Vexx who claims me, latching onto my hair again, yanking me back so hard that a zing of pain rips through my neck.

He pushes me forward, driving me up the hill in Helena's footsteps until we're back where we started. "Just for that," he says, "we're going to stand right here and let you see her when she comes out. Even if it's for her burial."

If I could free my hands, I would send fire raging across this ravine and end this, but Vexx holds me so tightly, one hand in my hair, the other clenching my wrists, aiming me at the cliff.

Alexus roars as if in protest, but an agonizing sound leaves him, and he goes silent.

The earth rumbles, boulders tremble, and I lose my footing.

Vexx steadies me. Steadies himself.

I can't see Alexus, but I know he somehow did that.

"It's nothing," Vexx calls out to his men, laughing at their fear. "Happens in these mountains all the time." He tries to sound so sure, though I hear unsettled nervousness in him, the way his laughter fades and dies.

Vexx hands me off, like I'm too much to deal with, an interruption to the spectacle involving Helena. I try to see Alexus, but my line of sight is swiftly corrected with a jerk to my head by different hands.

Every Eastlander on the slope by the caves stands in waiting, like salivating monsters, especially Vexx. From the look on his face and the way he stares at the cave's mouth, I can tell that this is a test for the Eastland warrior named Rhonin.

Something comes alive in the air, and there's another moment of pause across the ravine. I don't know what it is, but it resonates in my marrow. It's something I've never felt, a sweeping presence that smells like cold if cold had a scent. It's everywhere at once, stilling even the wind.

A white wolf howls in the distance. Another and another. The Eastlanders shift and cast wary glances from one to the other.

After too many torturous, silent minutes, Helena's scream rings through the ravine, echoing like a death knell. I want to drop to my knees, but I'm held fast, trying to breathe as she wails.

I will kill him and cut out his heart. I will hang his scalp and all its red braids from my belt. I will curse his name so wholly that his every waking moment will become a prayer that he is not found by the likes of me. The Prince of the East and his army will regret that the silent Witch Walker from Silver Hollow lived.

Vexx meets my gaze, a satisfied smile spreading over his face, and Helena's cries fall quiet. After a time, Rhonin stalks out of the cave, dragging a stumbling, sobbing Helena behind him. He glances at the sky with unease, like he notices this new presence moving through the ravine.

The hairs on the back of my neck rise.

Rhonin stands before Vexx, still clinging to Helena who has yet to meet my eyes. Her square shoulders have fallen, and her hair hangs in a black curtain over her face.

"It's over," Rhonin says, his face red and blotchy. "We should go now."

The Eastlander at my back relents his hold, enough that the pain in my neck subsides. It seems he's tired of this too.

Vexx eyes Rhonin, and even *I* feel the tension vibrating between the two men.

The general turns his attention to Helena. Rhonin lets go of her wrist, and she stands there, inches behind him, cowering like a beaten puppy. "You'd make a good soldier, girl," Vexx says. "If we can break you." He takes her chin and lifts her face from behind her hair. "Perhaps now you'll know better than to steal from me."

Her eyes slide sideways, finding me. She has a split lip, and her right eye is bruising. If Rhonin...

Gods. Everything inside me vibrates. I could explode with hatred. Helena has endured so much. She can't endure more. I vow that I won't *let* her endure more, that I'll get us out of this mess and get her far from such peril.

But in the next second, she throws a punch, landing her fist across the general's face. His head snaps, and when he turns his eyes back to Helena, they're filled with rage. In a swift move, he jerks her forward and plants his booted foot into the small of her back, kicking her down the hillside.

Gasping, I lunge for her. This time, I shake loose from my captor's hold, but it's too late. I can only watch in cold horror as Helena tumbles down the rugged, snow-covered slope and collides with a boulder. Her spine bows from the impact, and she falls still and lifeless.

The scent of her coming death reaches me. I inhale deep, absorbing the aroma of a forge fire, sweet wine, and meadow grass in the spring.

I dart toward her before anyone can stop me, imagining her fighting, swinging her sword, living her life somewhere far from the Northlands. I see her bright smile, the heat that lives in her eyes, the flush of sparring and youth in her cheeks.

The moment I'm at her side, I close my eyes, searching for her strands of life. They're there, faint and still golden but fading.

"Loria, Loria, anim alsh tu brethah, vanya tu limm volz, sumayah, anim omio dena wil rheisah," I sign.

I work fast, weaving her beautiful strands in my mind, pouring every bit of myself into the healing until her dimming threads begin to reform. My love, anger, sadness, fear... They all flood my magick.

"Loria, Loria, anim alsh tu brethah, vanya tu limm volz, sumayah, anim omio dena wil rheisah. Loria, Loria, anim alsh tu brethah, vanya tu limm volz, sumayah, anim omio dena wil rheisah."

An arm tightens around my waist. Suddenly, I'm torn from my thoughts, the strands of Helena's existence slipping like threads of silk through my fingers as I'm tossed aside in the snow.

Half-dazed and head swimming, I rise on my elbows, wondering if I did enough.

Vexx and Rhonin hover over Helena.

She's coughing. Breathing. Moving.

Living.

Another tiny death flutters in my chest, an unwanted ending conquered.

Weakly, Helena looks at me with those impossibly dark, brilliant eyes. The wounds on her face—the open and bleeding lip, the bruising eye—are gone.

The general jerks his head around, spearing me with a glare that stabs straight to my core. "You're a Healer?" He moves toward me, hands clenched at his sides, once again delivering the sensation of an approaching storm. "That's why she bore no mark from my fist and why Un Drallag lived, without wounds, after what the prince did to him in the vale." Looking down at me, his eyes narrow. "Did you bring him back from the dead?"

I shake my head. I didn't, and I couldn't have, but I know where this is going. The Eastlanders want Thamaos raised from the dead, by whatever means, and here am I, a woman who just saved her friend from death's grasp.

Vexx will never believe me, no matter what I say, and already, I see his mind working behind his eyes, piecing together all the ways I might be of use. Nephele always said that the power living inside me makes me valuable.

And valuable things get locked away.

I force myself to my feet, wanting to run or head for Alexus, but I'm instantly caught by Rhonin and hauled around to face the general.

His thin lips lift into a slit of a smile. "Oh, am I ever going to be rewarded for this." Vexx looks at Rhonin. "Bring her."

The red-haired brute obeys, handling me like a child's plaything. "What about the other one?" he asks as we head down the hill.

Vexx turns and takes me by the shoulders, sighing with irritation like Helena's life is but an afterthought. "Get up there and slit her throat. I'm really fucking tired of people who won't die."

Rhonin doesn't hesitate. I watch him march away, drawing his blade.

Gods, I *want* to fight! But the exhaustion of healing Helena blurs my vision, turning my limbs to water.

Vexx takes me toward Alexus. He sits crumpled on his knees, swaying like a tree in the wind, the heavy chains tethering him to the dry and wintry riverbed. Behind the links of his fetters, his tunic is torn open, the scarred body beneath now marked by a reddened welt shaped like a bursting star.

The general lets go of me, and finally, blessedly, I collapse in the snow, my legs too weak to hold me anymore as I battle the oblivion that will sweep me into utter darkness.

Vexx stands over me, blocking the sunlight, and nudges my chin with the toe of his boot. "Come, now. Surely you want to say goodbye."

I meet Alexus's gaze, tears rolling from my eyes.

"I will come for you," he promises. "Trust me, Raina."

General Vexx kneels between us, glancing from Alexus to me, unsheathing the God Knife. "Somehow," he says, "I think he's wrong."

The last thing I see before oblivion takes me is Vexx, driving the God Knife into Alexus's heart.

3 2

HELENA

The man named Rhonin brings down his dagger and drives it into the ground beside my chest.

He does it again, for effect. He's good at pretending. He pretended in the wood days ago, letting me run after I fled Vexx, precious God Knife in hand, as though he couldn't catch me.

And he pretended in the cave. He knelt at my feet, willing to do as I bid him, save for what Vexx demanded—anything but that. He would not lift a hand against me, no matter what awaited us. I had to black my own eye with a rock. Bust my own lip. Scream to the top of my lungs and pretend to be the wounded victim the general wanted.

Discreetly, Rhonin slides his blade beneath the sleeve of his leathers and jerks it free. He grips the bend of his elbow and squeezes, letting red blood run over his hand and stain the snow. He glances over his shoulder, and when he turns back to me, his face is ashen, his eyes downcast. With his unwounded hand, he touches a key dangling from his neck and briefly closes his eyes.

"I hate leaving you alone," he whispers, "on foot, no less. But I swear I'll take care of your friend. Avoid Winter Road. Instead, stay north. Get to Winterhold some other way. You'll find shelter there. It can't be far. Maybe a day, day and a half to walk."

He touches my brow with gentle fingers, and a certain sadness saturates his blue eyes, but then he walks away, leaving a crimson trail in his wake, as though the blood that drips from his blade is that of the Knife Thief.

That's what General Vexx called me, earlier, but also in the wood, before the shadow wraith claimed me.

But I can't linger on the thought. As Rhonin stalks away and the rest of the Eastlanders clear the ravine, my mind slips toward irresistible sleep, though I'm aware of an odd sensation brushing up against me.

An icy, silken wind.

And somewhere, a white wolf howls.

⚜

I'M ALONE IN THE RAVINE, STARING AT THE BLACK AND PURPLE SKY AS IT ushers in rising dawn. I haven't seen a real dawn in what seems like ages. I feel frozen in place, but I sit up, aching from sleeping on the frigid ground, my limbs stinging with chilly needles. Otherwise, I'm fine. I'm alive, thanks to Raina and Rhonin, and that's all that matters right now.

Because I have to find her.

I wipe a layer of frost and snow from my face, hair, and leathers and shove to my feet. It takes a moment for my legs to work right and my sight to adjust, but soon I'm stumbling up the white riverbed.

Ahead, bodies lie in the snow. Four.

The first three are the Eastlanders Raina killed in the cave. Vexx didn't grant them the respect of a burial, but worse, he didn't even give them the respect of a deathbed. They lay piled together with limbs at odd angles, their eyes wide open.

I didn't do this for anyone in the village, either. I'd been too distraught, but I'm not too distraught now.

Carefully, I drag the bodies to individual resting places and close their eyelids. I even offer a prayer for their souls.

But my heart isn't in it, much as I wish it could be. War makes devils of people who would've never been devils otherwise, but they were devils to my village all the same.

Standing over the last body, I feel...stunned. His chains are gone, but it's the Witch Collector.

Alexus Thibault. Un Drallag. The immortal man who carried Neri.

Are they both in the Shadow World now?

Willing myself not to cry, I bite the inside of my cheek. Though I didn't truly know him, I mourn Alexus's loss. I'm sure Vexx made Raina watch.

I'm certain he made her watch me die too.

I think of how I can bury the Witch Collector, but the boulders here are too large to carry to cover him, and I've nothing to dig a grave. With as much reverence as I can offer, I roll him to his back, cross his hands over his bloody chest, and sing an old Elikesh prayer for his soul, directing it not to Neri but to Loria and the rest of the Ancient Ones.

They're the only gods I will pray to now.

I still don't recall much of my time with the Collector in the wood, but I do know that he spent three hundred years protecting Tiressia from disaster, and for that, he deserves an eternity in the Empyreal Fields.

After my prayer, I scour the ravine for weapons, but best I can tell, in the dim light, nothing was left behind. Not here at least. I'll need to move northward like Rhonin said, back toward their camp, and hope to find something there.

When I hear my name on the wind at my back, I'm sure I'm imagining things. I stop, tears building on my lashes. I've heard Finn's voice so many times since the fire. When I was with the Eastlanders, I kept expecting my big brother to appear and save me, but he never came. I could hear him laughing at me, telling me to stop being a baby and get up and save myself.

And I tried. I think he would be proud that I've made it this far. I still miss him with my whole, broken heart. I miss my mother, my sisters.

My father.

He might still be out there. Another reason I have to stop crying and keep moving. So I trudge onward, but again, I hear my name, drifting on the wind.

Slowly, I turn a glance over my shoulder and wipe a half-frozen tear from my cheek. In the pale light of early morning, one of the bodies moves.

With his long, dark hair and shredded tunic, the Witch Collector pushes his hulking form to his knees. He struggles to stand, but after a long moment, his body unfurls, shoulders rolling back, feet spread wide, hands fisted like hammers at his sides.

A cold wind snaps through the ravine, and a funnel of snowflakes whirls around Alexus, whipping through his hair and tunic. Behind him, a mist rolls into the gorge, slipping around him. It takes the shape of a man—or perhaps something more than a man. Whatever or whoever it is, it's standing a few feet away from the Witch Collector.

From within the mist, white wolves emerge with predatory grace and howl like they mean to wake the dead.

And the earth rumbles.

III

WINTER ROAD

33

RAINA

I open my eyes to the sound of cawing crows and jerk like I'm falling. At first, I think I'm still draped over the back of the horse that carried me from the ravine and through the forest, but perhaps I'm still dreaming. Only my dream was of Collecting Day, the last day I spent with those I loved.

And that is not where I am now.

I'm in a tent, on my side. The air is bitter cold, freezing my breath in soft plumes, the light gloomy yet bright to my eyes. I turn my ear, listening to the crows and the tent canvas whipping sharply in the wind.

"Ah. I thought you'd never wake, Lovely."

That voice sends a hard shiver through my bones. It isn't the voice I long to hear, but it's familiar, nonetheless.

"Make her face me."

Suddenly, Rhonin looms above. My instinct is to punch him right in his perfectly angular nose, but my wrists are tied in front of me, restrained even further by a rope that connects my hands to my feet.

With one hand, he grabs the knotted mass at my wrists and hauls me up, making me gasp around the pain settled deep in my shoulders and injured arm. Without a second glance, he returns to his station.

At the Prince of the East's left hand.

"Welcome to Winter Road, Raina Bloodgood," the prince says. His face appears gaunt under the faint illumination of a nearby oil lamp, and even in the weak light, his crimson shadows are visible, a twitching and squirming halo.

He sits two feet away on a tall, thick piece of chopped tree trunk, elbows on his knees. He wears the bronze leathers of his men, stained with so much blood they're nearly the color of the Eastlander flag leaning in the corner behind him. His long hands are covered with cuts, like he punched through glass, and his fingertips and ears are black with frostbite. At his right side stands General Vexx, hands behind his back, looking too pleased with himself as he stares down at me with a smug expression that I want to rip from his face.

They're all here. The three men I want to end. So very close and so very different from the men I thought I'd have killed by now when all of this began.

The prince stands then squats in front of me, close enough that I smell the scent of something like ash and the spicy aroma of ground yarrow root, packed into the gash that travels across his face. Black hair stubbles his chin and jawline, but the skin around the wound looks corrupt and fevered.

Inwardly, I laugh. It looks like misery.

I hope it is.

The prince's eyes are soft and roving like he knows me. It dawns on me that he knows me far better than I wish.

He reaches to touch my cheek, but I jerk away. Surprisingly, he lets his hand fall as a wicked grin curves the undamaged corner of his mouth. "You should get very comfortable with me, Raina," he says, voice tender. "We're going to become the closest of friends."

Like our first go around, I spit. This time I hit my mark, right on his ugly face.

Nostrils flaring, he takes a deep breath and exhales slowly, tempering the anger burning in his eyes. Without breaking the stare that pulses between us, he holds his hand out at his side. Vexx hands him a kerchief, and the prince carefully wipes away my disrespect.

"I planned to kill you," he says. "Painfully. But now you have use." Again, he moves to take my chin, and again, I draw back. But this time, he doesn't let me. He ensnares my jaw and—with fingertips digging painfully —yanks me forward so that I'm an inch from his rotting mouth. "The reality you need to understand, Miss Bloodgood, is that you are mine now. Keeper. Healer. I'm sure there are more mysteries to discover behind that beautiful face and all those pretty witch's marks. You can reveal your skills willingly, or I will find ways to unearth them myself. I can be kind, or I can be your worst nightmare. Your choice."

He shoves me away and flicks his hand at his shoulder. Vexx moves to the edge of the tent and draws back the flap, stepping outside where daylight fades from the sky.

How long was I out? I don't recall anything after...

I close my eyes and swallow back tears. Gods, I wish the memory of the ravine wasn't part of me, but it's branded on my spirit, along with so many other awful images that will haunt me for the rest of my life.

At the thought, two tiny flutters at the back of my chest make my heart skip a beat—two tiny darknesses. Though Helena and Alexus are gone, part of them will always be with me.

When I open my eyes, my tears roll free. In the next moment, my breath rushes from my lungs like I've been kicked in the gut.

I might as well have been.

When we were leaving the ravine, I dreamt of Nephele. I saw her screaming, surrounded by flames. She was clinging to Mother, who stood wide-eyed and pale, a spear's tip protruding from her chest. They reached for me. Crying. Pleading with me to help them.

My mother looked forlorn and lost, but Nephele was angry, her eyes filled with accusation. It was so real that even now, just the thought of it makes my skin tingle from the memory of fire and sends my heart lurching against my ribs, a reminder of everything I felt the moment I watched Mother's life leave her body. I've feared what might await me when and if I saw my sister again, when I'd have to tell her that I let our mother die.

Across the tent stands a woman, tall and slender, dressed in sealskin trousers and a blood-stained jacket, the color of a blue beryllus stone—the same color as her eyes. Her hands are bound behind her back, her mouth gagged. An array of multi-colored witch's marks covers the smooth, pale skin of her hands and neck, even the sides of her face, curling at her temples.

Nephele.

I struggle to get my legs under me, my mind screaming her name.

Rhonin grabs my good arm, and for the first time, actually helps me. He lifts me, setting me firmly on my feet, but when I move toward Nephele and her to me, the Prince of the East comes between us, holding up his hands to stop us.

"Oh, come now. Do you really think I'd let you two have a special bonding moment without anything in return?" He tips his head toward me. "How long has it been for you two sisters, eh? I *do* see the resemblance."

I can't stop looking at her. She's so lovely. Long, pale curls, fallen from a loose braid, hang around her fair face. A few lines crinkle her delicate forehead, and she looks beyond exhausted, with purplish bruises shadowing the thin skin beneath her bloodshot eyes. But she is otherwise unchanged. Her eyes are still like Father's, light as a spring sky and so wide that as she looks at me, I swear I see to the bottom of her heart.

My sister. Here. A handful of feet away, yet there might as well be eight more years separating us—thanks to the Prince of the East.

It strikes me then. He shouldn't know that Nephele is *anyone* to me, certainly not my kin. We favor, but she's Father whereas I'm Mother. My features are darker, and my body has more curves and muscle from working where Nephele is lithe and willowy.

How could the prince know?

He yanks the gag from Nephele's mouth, but Vexx is there immediately, pressing the tip of a dagger deep into her cheek. "One utterance of Elikesh. That's all it will take for me to cut out your tongue, witch. You're to speak only when the prince tells you."

Much as I wish otherwise, I fear my sister's magick will not see us out of this. She's drained from holding the construct for days.

The prince repeats his question to Nephele. "How long?"

"Eight years." Her voice is gravelly and ragged from singing magick, her eyes hard as steel as she holds his gaze.

The prince paces a short path, slowly, between us, and slides those insidious eyes at me. "I brought your sister here so that I can make you an offer, Raina. Several of my men died thanks to you and your ilk, and several more are severely wounded. We've a long journey to the coast. I need as many men at my back as possible should there be surprises along the way.

If you want time with your sister, I will allow it—" he glances at Vexx and Rhonin "—with proper supervision. But only if you agree to heal my men and show me what you're made of." He gestures to his face. "And there's me, of course. It's only right that you clean up after yourself, yes?"

I try to lift my hands, to tell him to crawl in a hole and die, but the rope tying my wrists and ankles together doesn't have enough slack.

"You have to free her hands, you cretin," Nephele says.

Vexx digs his blade into her face, and she winces as a shiny drop of blood slips down her cheek.

I move toward her, but Rhonin yanks me back by the laces of my bodice.

The prince stops pacing and faces me. "A simple nod will suffice. Do you agree to my terms?"

I flash a glance at Nephele who gives me an almost imperceptible nod. I don't want to be the reason the prince's wounds heal, and I don't want to be the reason he and his men live to ride across the Northlands and kill another day. But I need my sister. At least long enough to figure out what in gods' death we can do to get out of this.

Finally, I nod. Once.

Vexx stuffs the gag back into Nephele's mouth, and with a look from the prince, Rhonin drags me from the tent.

✣ 34 ✣

RAINA

Rhonin saws a knife through the ropes between my ankles so I can walk with longer strides. He leaves my hands tied and linked to the short rope leading to my feet. He reminds me of someone. Maybe Mena? It's the hair.

When he finishes, he grabs a woolen blanket from a pile, hangs it over my shoulders, and leads me up a small embankment to Winter Road. As we walk, snow crunching beneath our boots, I take in the encampment. To my right, the Prince of the East and his general stroll to a larger tent pitched beneath two tall trees, its canvas glowing in the falling dusk. Obscured figures wait inside, backlit by lamplight. Unwounded warriors, at least fifty, sit around a few scattered fires, roasting various small animals for a meal. They're guarding three wagons nested in a clearing and a few dozen tied horses. Far fewer than they need.

I think of Mannus and Tuck. They have to be here.

Above, heralding the coming night, the prince's spies roost, a thousand beady eyes staring down. How I'd like to *Fulmanesh* every single one of the little pricks.

From the corner of my vision, Nephele's pale hair catches my eye. An Eastlander leads her along the road's edge, then across the wood to one of the wagons. A woman unlocks the doors, and the man throws my sister inside.

Not wagons. Transportable prisons.

Is Colden Moeshka in there too?

To my left, along a snowy path, sounds of pain float through the forest. Rhonin guides me toward those sounds and the injured, and also toward another tent set back in the wood.

"I hope you're not weak-stomached," he says. "It's like a battlefield out here."

I shake my head, but the truth is that I've seen more death and wounds in the last week—or however long I've been trapped inside Frostwater Wood—than I've seen in my whole life. I haven't had time to be sick. I've been functioning within a survival state. But I have enough years in me to know that all of this horror is going to crash down on me at some point.

Those cresting waves.

Torches have been staked into the ground every ten feet or so, creating a path, and to each side, more fires burn. In the pools of firelight, on woolen blankets and against trees, dozens of warriors lie wounded, with no relief save for the wine that a few attendants ladle from a wooden bucket. Stolen from Winterhold, I'm sure. I can smell the bitterness.

Wine won't do much to stave the pain, though. These warriors have broken limbs, disjointed bones, blade wounds, burns, and pieces of iron and steel wedged into muscle.

And frostbite.

No. It's more than frostbite. Some have blackened hands and arms that might need amputation if I cannot weave them back to health.

Damn, Rhonin. The sight makes my stomach queasy.

Alexus's words come back to me. *As restitution, the gods gave Colden and Fia a certain degree of command over their elements. He can breathe an icy fog. Freeze an enemy with a touch.*

The Frost King. If he did this, and I'm confident he did, then surely the Eastlanders couldn't reach him. These men have to be a sign that Colden Moeshka kept himself from becoming a weapon against Fia Drumera. At this point, we need any advantage we can get.

Rhonin and I reach the tent. He flips back the flap and leads me inside.

I can't help but notice how quickly he seals us up, away from the rest of the world.

When he faces me, straightening to his full and towering height, I take a step back. Another. There's a tree stump in this tent and a scorched worktable behind me. Another find from Winterhold, no doubt. Two oil lamps burn instead of one, and a pouch of mender's tools sits on the table.

I am not this kind of healer, I want to tell him, but even if he could read my hands, I wouldn't have had the chance to form the words.

He takes me by the shoulders, oddly careful to avoid my wound, and puts his face close to mine. Too close. It's such a sudden action that I think to headbutt him, but he speaks in the softest whisper.

"Listen very carefully. I'm a spy for the king. I did not harm your friend in that cave. She harmed herself so that we might survive Vexx. And when he sent me to kill her, I did not." He forces the sleeve of his jacket up enough to reveal the end of an angry-looking gash. "I bled into the snow and on my dagger to make it appear that I killed her, but she was alive when I left her in the ravine. I told her to get to Winterhold. I swear my life to the Ancient Ones if I'm not telling the truth." He glances at the tent flap. "I only pray she travels around us instead of crossing our path."

I shake my head in disbelief even after he's finished talking. I keep waiting to hear a lie in his voice or to see one in his gaze, and yet it never comes.

My heart stutters, and relief I struggle to process rushes through me. Helena is alive? And the king has spies. Of course, he does.

The flinty eyes of this giant of a man soften to the point of gentleness. "I wanted to save the Collector too, but I couldn't be in two places at the same time. I didn't know what Vexx planned to do. I'm sorry."

The cavern inside me burns, his words salt to a raw wound.

I'm sorry too. Sorry that I couldn't stop Vexx. That I couldn't do anything but watch.

Rhonin takes my elbow and leads me to the mender's pouch. He kneels beside the cot and folds the leather open, withdrawing a small, simple dagger. A thin sheath covers the blade, and the hilt is slim and short. The whole of it is barely the span of my hand, fingertips to wrist. Perfect for jabbing at close range—or maybe throwing—but little else.

"Here's the plan," he whispers. "The prince is meeting with Vexx and

Killian, his second general, but he wants to be your first healing. Afterward, he's sending Killian south with convoy one. She and other soldiers will escort the first wagon, a handful of Witch Walkers, though not your sister. She's to stay with the prince, as is the king."

I squeeze my eyes shut. Damn it. Colden Moeshka *is* here.

"I know," Rhonin mutters, as though understanding my disappointment. "Word is that the prince unleashed enough fire on Winterhold that the king's ice was of no matter. The Frost King surrendered to save his people. His Witch Walkers were too weak to withstand the prince, but the prince is weaker now. Worn down."

That makes me feel better. Weaker is good.

"Once your work is complete," Rhonin continues, "the prince and Vexx and everyone else will head south. They're meeting important men at Malgros, the same men who got them through the ports in the first place, to get them across the Malorian Sea to Itunnan."

Father used to talk about Itunnan, a port city in the Summerlands. By important men, I assume Rhonin means men in the Northland Watch. Traitors. I don't know how so many Eastlanders could've made it through the port, but the prince clearly thought of a better plan than facing an entire coast of guard witches.

Gods. This can't be happening already.

"The prince plans to let me take you to your sister after you heal him, only for a few minutes, then your duty on this side of the camp begins. He knows your hands must be free for your magick, but don't think he won't have Vexx hovering with a blade at all times, possibly something worse. They're curious about your abilities, but they'd rather see you dead as dust than acting as interference. Do you understand?"

Yes, I understand what he's saying. No, I don't understand what he thinks I'm to do with this information. I nod anyway.

"Later, I'll come for you and your sister. You'll use this dagger to get free of your binds, wound me, and then run." He leans in. "Don't be nice about stabbing me either. It has to look real."

This is the plan?

He eyes my face. "Look, I'm giving you your freedom. It's all I can do. Take it."

His words fall over me like a rush of chilly air.

Freedom.

Rhonin stands and stares down at me, making an innocent face, and shrugs. "This might be cold and uncomfortable, but it's incredibly sharp. You'll need it. Later."

From behind a fallen strand of flaming hair, he winks, again reminding me of Mena. Her daughter was chosen for Winterhold many years before my birth.

Surely Rhonin isn't...

I grimace, sucking in a breath between my clenched teeth as Rhonin carefully slides the tiny dagger into my bodice, until it's nestled between my breasts. The steel is freezing.

He holds my ribcage, shifting my bodice and breasts to hide the hilt, and presumes to tighten the laces at my back. "To prevent the dagger from falling," he says.

Sadness swims through me as I recall a similar moment. This one is just as awkward—the touching—but it isn't intimate in the way it was with Alexus by the stream. I wish I could go back to that moment with the knowledge I have now.

Still, I welcome the contact. If this man wants to give me a weapon, I'm certainly going to let him. The second I get the chance, I'll drive that little blade into the prince's temple, or maybe into that tender spot beneath the chin that Helena always talks about. There's no way I can let him be close enough to heal and not kill him if the opportunity presents itself.

That thought makes me wonder something. Rhonin is a Northland spy. He's become very trusted by the Eastland prince. Why has *he* not killed him?

When I glance up, my eyes snag on his face, blushing seven shades of red. He's as rugged as the Mondulak Range, but the closer I look, the more naivety and innocence I see, two things so incongruent with the rest of him. It provides no answer to my question, but I have no way to ask.

I try, forcing the question into my eyes. I glance down where the dagger hides, and then at the tent flap where I assume the prince will soon appear, and back to Rhonin, shaking my head.

Eyes and faces can say so much more than people believe.

He exhales a breath, reading me easily. "Yes, I've often thought about sacrificing all to stop him, but I never expected any of this. I was called up the ranks for this mission two months ago. I didn't have time for preparations before we left, and the prince has my family within his grasp. My mother, brother, and sister as well." Rhonin points to the sky, keeping his voice low. "Eyes are always watching. I could kill every last Eastlander in this forest, including the prince, and blame it on a Witch Walker attack, but unless I kill every one of his damn crows, his council will know what I've done before I can so much as leave this continent." He sighs, his eyes searching mine, seeking understanding. "My family will not be spared. I need to get home, secure my loved ones away from the prince's palace. Afterward, I can do what must be done. If someone doesn't beat me to it."

Things keep getting worse, but there's a saving grace.

The prince has no hold on me anymore.

Save for Nephele and Helena, I have no one else to lose, and my sisters are in this wood with me.

If *I* kill the prince like I envision, if *I* destroy the Eastlanders, if *I* free the Witch Walkers and the Frost King, these crows can tattle all they want to the Eastern council. Rhonin's family will be spared, the plan to torment Fia Drumera with Colden's demise will be thwarted, the Prince of the East will no longer live, and no gods will rise. The God Knife will still exist, but if I can pilfer it from the prince or this camp, it will remain safe in my Keeper's hand. The snake of the East will lose its head, and I can make it to the Iceland Plains with Nephele and Helena and find passage out of Tiressia before the council becomes a problem.

All that stands in my way is a prince and what's left of his army.

Voices sound from outside the tent—the prince and Vexx. Rhonin places the mender's pouch back where it was and shoves me toward the tree stump near the worktable. He stands at my side, hands clasped before him like a good guard while my heart thuds against the icy dagger.

"Just a little while longer," he whispers. "Then you'll be free, Raina Bloodgood. No victory without sacrifice."

It's impossible not to look up at him, and when I do, I see my old friend in the lines of his face, in the fire of his hair.

Oh, Mena. No victory without sacrifice.

I face forward, my blood stirring anew.

I'm ready.

Let the sacrifice come.

35

RAINA

The Prince of the East sits before me in his bloody leathers, intrigue painted on his face. Behind him, a surprise.

Nephele.

She's still tied, still gagged, and a woman I've never seen holds her elbow. Killian, Rhonin called her. Second general.

"I have questions." The prince gestures over his shoulder. "I thought I'd bring your sister along so I can get answers. As long as you behave with those magickal hands of yours, I won't make you regret that she's here."

Rhonin was right about Vexx hovering. He stands beside me, tying a rope around my neck. No knife to the cheek. No fisting my hair. Instead, he tightens a looped knot, the kind that will only constrict even more if I move the wrong way.

Vexx stands back, holding the rope like he's leashed an unruly hound.

"Her binds, Rhonin," the prince says.

I look prince over. No sign of the God Knife. It isn't on Vexx or Killian either.

Though I can feel Rhonin's hands trembling, he works swiftly, untying the impossible knot of rope that has rubbed my wrists raw. It doesn't matter that Rhonin is nervous. The prince keeps his eyes locked with mine, even after my hands are free.

It's a heavy moment. My thoughts dart everywhere, though I refuse to look away. Desperation will act as a catalyst for impulse if I'm not careful. I might be a rebel, but I need to be a smart one right now. If I reach for the dagger, Vexx will choke me down.

"How does this work?" the prince asks. "I've met many kinds of magick wielders in my day, but never a Healer. Do you know how rare you are?" His words are laced with a sick sort of wonder.

I do know, which is why I tried to keep it secret.

A lot of good that did me.

It's cold, and my hands are stiff and achy from being in binds for so long, but more than anything, I want to talk to my sister. There's nothing the prince can do about what I choose to communicate.

Lifting my hands, I sign. "*I have missed you so much, Nephele. I am sorry I failed you and Mother. I love you, and I will make this right. Tell him that I weave the threads of the wound.*"

The woman, Killian, removes Nephele's gag and holds a knife to her throat.

"Same rules as before," Vexx says.

Nephele's eyes go glassy. Her love for me shines in her gaze.

"Raina weaves the threads of the wound," she translates. Her ragged voice is soft but thick with tears.

"Ah. If only the rest of us could see the threads of wounds. We would live with no fear of pain or death." The prince leans forward and trails a finger up my arm to the sliced, bloody fabric of my sleeve. "Show me."

His touch disgusts me, but it quickly falls away, and I weave my threads, thankful for the chance to heal my wound.

When I lower my hands, he takes my arm and, with two fingers, stretches the material of my torn sleeve wide, revealing smooth, undamaged skin.

"Wonderful," he says, his eyes flicking up to my face. "Now me."

To center myself, I close my eyes, uncertain what I'm going to do—heal him or try to kill him? But then the threads of his wound make themselves known, slithering out from behind swirls of crimson shadows, distracting me from my dilemma.

This can't be right. His threads are...smoldering. Crumbling into flecks of ash and just as fragile. This is what I smelled on him earlier, but the distinct scents are clearer now. I still smell the septic yarrow—it's overpowering—but beneath it hides the aroma of fire, of a sweltering day, of dust and earth.

This is the scent of someone's death, but the Prince of the East is very much alive.

I look closer. The threads of his wound need to be entwined to heal, but they're not just burning. They're all wrong. There are two threads for every instance there should be one, coiled around one another tightly.

I'm too curious not to look at his life threads as well. They're not burning, but they're not golden either. And again, there are two for every one. This time, it doesn't look like any sort of weaving. One of the strands crawls up the other, clinging like a disease. Both bear the pallid colors of decay, but there's something more. There are dozens of loose filaments floating around the main threads, whisper-thin as gossamer, like the dead husks of old strands.

I swear I sense another person, some presence writhing to break free, but that's impossible. Except—it's not.

Alexus's threads had multiples, the residue of glimmering shadows.

Because he contained the soul of a god.

His threads still held the colors of life, though, and they felt precious, threads to be handled with careful hands and careful words. The prince's threads are even more delicate given their state. They feel like—if I try weaving them—they'll burst into ash or completely disintegrate.

I open my eyes, a little repulsed but more than willing to try. If he dissolves into nothing, all the better.

I dance my hands and fingers around the song, aware of the rope chafing my neck all the while. *"Loria, Loria, una wil shonia, tu vannum vortra, tu nomweh ilia vo drenith wen grenah."*

"I can't repeat her words," Nephele says. "Unless you're fine with me speaking Elikesh lyrics."

The prince casts a glance over his shoulder. "No. Let her work."

"Loria, Loria, una wil shonia, tu vannum vortra, tu nomweh ilia vo drenith wen grenah."

The remains of his threads quiver, and then they flutter and rise like floating embers escaping a fire.

Wincing, he touches his cheek.

I can't help but think about the fire magick he and his warriors used on Silver Hollow, the way their arrows burned villagers from the inside out. But how? He's been to the Shadow World, but the afterlife doesn't grant magick or teach ancient workings. What has the prince tangled himself in that he's corrupted his entire existence for a little power?

A strange compulsion comes over me. I reach out and touch the prince's temple. He flinches but doesn't stop me.

An image flashes across my mind, a man in a dank cell, a tower overlooking a foamy, wild sea. He lies on a stone bed in a threadbare shift, unmoving. His skin appears leached of all color and spirit. His cheeks are hollow, his muscles wasted. There is skin, and there are bones, and there's a breath of life, but it isn't much. Just enough to keep him a hair's breadth from losing his soul to the Shadow World.

Gods. *Losing his soul.*

Recoiling, I yank my hand away from the prince and press it to my chest, remembering my father's words. The Prince of the East is a man who somehow steals life and magick from others to grant himself immortality and power his own dark desires.

A man made of shadows, souls, and sin.

The shadows are indeed here, always, and gods know he's filled to the brim with sin.

But he also carries a soul. One who is an unwilling participant. One whose life and magick are being stolen. And if I had to guess, I'd say it's the soul of a Summerlander in a dank cell overlooking the sea.

The prince looks at me and smiles with one side of his mouth, an evil glint in his eyes. "See something you didn't like?"

My heart pounds in my ears. I'm shaken to my core. Those gossamer filaments—are those old souls he's used up?

The prince leans closer. "I felt you. Inside me. Do you rummage around in other people often?"

I'm breathing so hard, trying to wrap my mind around what just happened. I've never been able to see into someone's soul before, but then again, I've never attempted it. There's never been a need. Could I have seen Neri if I'd looked deeper when I healed Alexus?

As the prince sits there, analyzing me, I think of the dagger. It's an inch from my fingertips.

I could do it—kill him. Right now.

I lower my hand a fraction, pearls of cold sweat breaking across my brow.

A sudden commotion outside draws my eyes to the tent flap a second before the clamor of birds fleeing their nests ripples across the canvas. A warrior barges inside, panting, face reddened.

Eyes wide, he bows to his prince. "Forgive me, my lord, but something's wrong. You should come. Now."

With a sigh and groan of irritation, the prince gives me a long once over and then heads outside. Moments later, he returns, a beady-eyed crow perched on his shoulder. Ire fills his stare, his body thrumming.

He lances Vexx with a sharp look. "You and I need to have a little chat." He all but spits the last word before motioning to Rhonin and Killian. "Get these two in the holds and ready the men. We have a rather unexpected visitor on the way." He turns to Killian. "Get the prisoners on the road south. All of them. Immediately."

I glance up at Vexx. He looks bewildered.

And afraid.

The prince's crows have seen something—this unexpected visitor—and it set the eastern lord into a frenzy. I think of Helena. Please, gods, don't let it be her.

Rhonin begins retying the ropes at my wrists—though not as tightly as before—while Vexx removes the noose and follows the prince outside. It's just me, Rhonin, Nephele, and Killian.

I meet Rhonin's stare, pushing all my thoughts onto my face and into my eyes. If he could subdue Killian, Nephele and I could run.

But two more warriors enter the tent. They grab Nephele's arms and lead her into the night while Rhonin finishes securing my binds. He shakes his head, a minuscule movement, warning me that this is not the time for an escape effort.

Killian peers outside. When the woman turns around, her face is grim.

She stalks across the small space and grabs my arm. "Come on. Let's get her to the wagons."

Rhonin tightens his hold on my wrist and levels a cerulean glare on Killian. Everything about him takes on a defensive air. "I'll take her."

She tilts her head, her flat, gray eyes assessing. Not in the least bit intimidated, she drops her free hand to a ring of iron keys dangling at her hip. "*We'll* take her. Because *I'm* carrying her south. Like the prince ordered."

The moment we step beyond the tent, wolves howl, their voices united in one terrible, wailing cry that seems to stretch and stretch. Rhonin and Killian pull up short, and my skin prickles, goosebumps rising along my arms. The energy I felt at the ravine has returned in full force, that unnatural presence rolling in on a cold, white mist hugging the ground, floating over our boots. A chill wind nips at my face and rustles the boughs above us, whistling and meandering through the snowy wood.

Rhonin looks down at me, wary as we start up the torchlit path, the flames struggling to survive the wind. Everything feels wrong, and hesitance traces my steps. Killian glares at me and picks up her pace, all but dragging me. The prince and Vexx are nowhere in sight, but ahead, across Winter Road, the camp is alive, the tall shadows of warriors bustling in the firelight.

As I scan the wood, I notice that the attendants have abandoned their posts in caring for the injured men, their buckets of wine haphazardly discarded along the roadside. I can hardly distinguish the mens' wounded forms in the frosty fog, but I hear their moans plainly.

When we reach the camp, the warriors are ready, eyeing the wood and trees, prepping their weapons, lighting more torches. There's chatter and murmurs—discussion—and enough apprehension tightening the air that it would *ping* if I could pluck it. The prince and Vexx are inside the tent from earlier, their bodies reflected in silhouette behind the canvas. Vexx is on his knees, clearly begging mercy, the prince curled over him in a threatening shape.

I don't know what's happening, but I'm almost thankful that I'll be locked away for it.

We rush past the campfires to the wheeled prisons where warriors hurriedly harness horses, hitching them to wagons. The conveyances are solidly built, wood on all sides reinforced with steel frames. The doors are fastened with heavy chains and padlocks.

Killian starts toward the wagon in the middle.

"Wait." Rhonin thrusts his chin to the right. "That one might be better."

The woman pauses. "I can't imagine how."

"I don't think we need to put her with her sister, is all," Rhonin replies. "And the other wagon is already packed." He jerks me forward. "She's valuable. Valuable enough to be—" he juts his chin to the right again "—in *there*."

An icy finger of dread trails down the back of my neck as I slice a glance at him. Of course, I need to be with my sister. What's he playing at?

Killian mulls over her fellow warrior's words and sets to unlocking the padlock sealing the wagon to my right. My pulse picks up. I feel like I'm being thrown to the wolves.

Behind us, the camp explodes into activity, warriors running toward the path where the injured lay in waiting. Killian yanks the wagon door open, jerks me away from Rhonin's hold, and shoves me inside.

I land splayed across the slatted floorboards in a spill of fractured moonlight. As the chain and lock rattle from the other side of the door, I scramble to my knees and struggle to my feet, darting to the tiny, barred window to see what in gods' death is going on. Rhonin walks away. Killian must be tending to the horses.

Rhonin tosses a glance over his shoulder, and though I wish to the gods that I *could* read minds, I don't need to. He rubs his wrists together and heads toward the tent where I'd seen the prince and Vexx.

I work my hands free of the ropes he left loose and take in the foggy scene—the way the warriors form a wall on the path, facing east, like something is coming from that direction. The direction of the ravine, if I'm correct.

"Grand. Just what I wanted. Company."

On a gasp, I spin around. In the corner, tucked half in shadow, sits a man, long legs bent. Slants of silvery moonlight pour into our little jail, feathering across the dark leather of his trousers.

There are chains—hobbles on his ankles and manacles on his wrists. His hands look lovely. Lovely and deadly. They rest between his legs.

"At least you seem handy," he adds. "A woman who knows her way around a bit of rope. Always a good thing." He pulls his torso forward, an effort under the weight of iron, until the bunched gold-ribboned cuffs of his blue velvet coat shimmer in the light. He looks up at me with the darkest, haunting eyes I've ever beheld. "Unless they threw you in here to kill me."

I take in that pale, golden hair, that sculpted porcelain face, and the iron collar at his throat. Though I've never seen him, and though he's so very far from the image my mind has conjured since I was a child, I know who he is without a second of doubt.

The Frost King.

36

RAINA

"Who are you?" Colden Moeshka stares up at me with a look that frosts my skin.

I stand frozen. Mere days ago, this moment would've been everything. Just him. Just me. Him bound. Me with a hidden dagger.

But nothing is as it was supposed to be. The world feels turned upside down. I meant to kidnap the Witch Collector, not kiss him. And I meant to kill the Frost King, not save him. And yet, here we are.

I touch the hollow of my throat and my lips and shake my head.

Understanding dawns, and his pouty mouth slips into a frown. "Well, well. Raina Bloodgood. I really hoped we'd meet under different circumstances. Somehow, I knew we wouldn't, but no one ever listens to me."

I'm not sure why hearing my name fall from his lips feels so strange, but it does. He knows me from Nephele, just like I know him from Alexus, but this is a man I've wanted dead for *years*. If anyone should be speaking to me with familiarity, it isn't him.

"You look like Nephele. A little." There's an odd pause between us before he glances at the window. "What's going on out there? Where's Alexus?"

The sound of that name makes my chest tighten. I don't want to tell

Colden that the prince's general took the Witch Collector's life, but it feels wrong not to.

"General Vexx killed him," I sign.

A cresting wave threatens, pricking at the backs of my eyes, making my tight chest ache, but I force it down.

From the way Colden watches me, I can tell that nothing I said registers. Alexus might've learned my hand language, and Nephele might've taught it to children at Winterhold, but the Frost King didn't care to learn.

"I don't know your signs," he says, "not well enough for all that, but your face speaks clearly. Something happened to him? Something bad?"

I nod. There's little else I can do. Though the king seems unfazed by the news.

"And what of outside? All the uproar?"

I shrug and turn back to the window. The mist has grown thicker now, prowling across the wood in a menacing eddy. That presence is everywhere, the smell of cold and pine and...something animal.

Before I can get a good look at anything more, the wagon lurches forward, sending me careening into the corner opposite Colden. I grab the rail that wraps around the walls, likely for tying animals.

The jostling eases once the horses take to Winter Road, heading south. I pull myself to the window, only to see the darkened forest flying by at a dizzying rate as we gather speed.

But that mist. It's following. Rushing up alongside. I can taste it. It carries a metallic bite, like sticking your tongue to silver.

Colden battles his chains to get to his knees. He glances at me with one cocked, burnished brow. "A little help would be excellent right about now, or you could just stand there and be of absolutely no use."

My scalp tightens, and the dagger between my breasts feels so tempting.

"Any day now," he adds, swaying with the wobble of the wagon.

Though I'm thoroughly annoyed by the Frost King, even after a few minutes in his presence, I grab his arm and—with all my strength—help his arrogant arse stand.

He drags himself toward the window. A bump in the road causes him to slam into the wall, and that brings me a moment of delight, but he rights himself to look outside.

I stare at him, just like he stared at me, watching the moonlight cascade over his face. Alexus wasn't wrong. He called Colden exquisitely beautiful, and he is. He's as feminine as he is masculine, something stunning in between. He's captivating and breathtaking. Ethereal.

Even if also a complete and utter prig.

"This isn't possible." He peers hard into the night, and I can't help but notice chill bumps rising along his neck and the side of his face. "I don't know what the fuck Alexus did," he adds, "but things are going to go very bad very quickly if I'm seeing what I think I'm seeing. You'd better ready yourself."

I have no idea what he means, and I don't get time to think about it. I free the dagger from my bodice, unsheathe the blade, and in the next breath, we're rolling, tossed from side to side of the wagon like we're weightless. Colden and his chains. Me and my dagger—until I lose it—my body thrown against the ceiling before being thrashed to the floor. Wood groans and splinters and splits, over and over, before we come to a crashing halt.

All I can hear is my pounding heart, and I can't breathe. It takes a minute for my wind to return, a deep gasp filling my lungs with cold air as I cough out bits of earth and wood. Most of the wagon lies around me in pieces, the steel frame warped and bent to one side. Above, the night sky sprawls for forever, snow falling in big, white flakes. But below, that cold mist slinks close, spilling over the road, wisps of white floating through the wreckage.

Hauling myself up, I get to my knees and crawl, slivers of pine stabbing my palms. The horses lie unmoving, and Colden rests near a tree, crumpled in a mess of chains. One of the other wagons, the one ahead of us, is just as destroyed. It's close enough that I can make out bodies scattered everywhere, but some are blessedly moving, getting up.

The wagon behind us rests on its side, leaned against a tree. It's still intact, though the Eastlanders manning the horses are trapped beneath the weight of their wounded animals.

Nephele. Which one was she in?

Voices catch my attention. No—screams. And grunts. Steel clashing against steel. Echoing from the camp. With each passing moment, the sounds grow louder.

The sounds of battle.

Colden isn't far. I clamber toward him, the snow cold on my hands, the mist tangling around my wrists. I don't know who the Eastlanders could be fighting. It must be whoever the prince spoke about—the *visitor*—though that sound certainly isn't coming from a fight with one person.

Which means it can't be Hel. More Witch Walkers? That doesn't feel right either. Even the Frost King felt a moment of fear when he stared out that window.

Regardless, I need a hatchet and loads of newfound brawn. If I can get his chains free, Colden Moeshka might be able to end all of this.

Though he's heavy as an anchor, I pull him over to his back. He lets out a long groan followed by a drawn-out, "*Fuuuuuck.*"

Gods. My dagger is lodged in his shoulder.

He blinks his eyes open and takes me in, then glances at the hilt jutting from his body. "Get that damn thing out of me."

I yank it free, and he barely winces.

"Now, use it to pick the lock on these godsdamn manacles." He struggles to a sitting position, the mist around us rising, and glances behind me. "For the love of devils, hurry."

Oh yes, pick the lock. With a bloody dagger. In a hanging fog. Because that's something I do every day. I can't begin to think straight. Every part of me aches. My mind is as tossed as my body was, and my hands tremble, a leaf in a storm. I'm not even sure if I'm in one piece.

But there's no hatchet, of course, and so I try to pick the lock, sticking the thin dagger into the mechanism as far as it will go. With shaking hands, I twist the metal back and forth, but I have no clue what I'm doing. Or what I'm *supposed* to be doing.

"Magick," Colden bites out. "You're colorful as a damned firework. Surely you have skill. And don't look at me like that. I can all but hear your mind cursing me. Just get these things off me if you want to live."

Maybe he does have to die. We will never survive one another otherwise.

And he clearly doesn't know as much about me as I thought. Marks or no marks, panic is *not* a good motivator. My mind is so blank that I can't even recall the word for scrying, much less a string of Elikesh that might undo a lock.

"Forget it!" He jerks his hands away. "Just run. Find Nephele and run! Go!" His dark eyes lift toward the sky, fixed on something behind me. Those dark irises are shadowed with white, as though he stares into winter itself. He recoils. "This cannot be bloody happening."

Something cold and icy slithers around me, colder than the mist. I go stock-still. Then I follow Colden's line of sight over my shoulder.

The rolling fog rises, high as the trees, and coalesces into the form of a creature that is as tall as Mannus the warhorse.

In the middle of Winter Road stands a naked, nebulous being with white hair down to his waist, pointed ears, and unmistakable lupine features—from slanted amber eyes to fangs tucked behind a curled upper lip. His hands are enormous, and though they have fingers, each digit is dark and claw-tipped, his palms more paw than flesh. He bares the lean, sinewy torso of a man, but he stands on the thickly muscled hind legs of a beast, covered in silky, pristine fur.

I swallow. Hard.

Part man. Part wolf.

Neri.

No wonder the prince ordered the camp into preparations.

Wolves creep from the foggy shadows of the surrounding wood, showing their teeth, growls vibrating in the backs of their throats. There are hundreds—eyes sharp, fangs bared, maws wet with froth. One skulks up beside me until its muzzle is a foot from my face. It lifts its snout, blowing hot breath over me, daring me to move.

I clutch the tiny, bloody dagger Rhonin gave me in a death grip, but every inch of my body might as well be rooted to the ground, implacable fear trapping me in the moment.

Colden glares at the god like he could slaughter him. "You son of a bitch. What did you do to Alexus?"

The mist that formed Neri crystallizes, rendering him corporeal yet still white as snow, his skin glimmering like it's made of stars. He tilts his head, and his amber eyes flare. When he speaks, his voice is so deep and resonating that the forest shudders.

"What did *I* do to *him*?" The God of the North takes long, stalking steps toward us and looms over Colden. He lowers his head, his neck longer than it has any right to be, and catches Colden's face in his clawed grip. "I granted him mercy," he snarls. "Which is far less than he granted me and nothing like what I will grant you." He fists the crossed chains at Colden's chest and heaves him into the air until the Frost King's feet are no longer on the ground. "After three centuries, your time to die at my hand has finally come, Colden Moeshka. And there are no other gods here to stop me this time."

Colden snarls back at the god. "There are worse fates than death. Be creative, at least. You mongrel."

Neri growls, a low rumbling noise, and slams the king to the ground.

Colden's body bounces, the wind leaving his lungs in a gust of frosted breath. Neri waves a hand, and Colden's chains fall away as though unlocked by ghosts. Colden grabs Neri's wrist, sending pale blue lines branching and webbing across the god's pawed hand, ice forming and spreading in chilled vines along the god's forearm.

But Neri laughs, and before the ice can reach his elbow, he flexes his fingers, and the frozen rivulets shatter and fall away.

"I gave you that power, you pathetic human. And I can take it away. This is *my* land," he says through clenched fangs. "I don't seat kings. The only crown in the Northlands belongs to me."

"And yet you'll stand here while the people of 'your land' suffer a miserable eastern prince who means to raise your enemies from the dead."

Neri's face tightens.

"That's what he wants," Colden goes on. "To thrive off their power. Then what will you do? Do you really think he will leave your grave intact for you to return to? If he can't take from you, he will make certain you are no more than this—" he gives Neri a belittling once-over "—mist-made *thing,* for eternity. You can forget being a true god ever again."

A growl leaves Neri, a sound that reverberates across the wood. Fury lights the god's amber eyes, and he presses a massive hand to Colden's chest, just over his heart, digging his blackened claws in too deep.

Heart pounding against my ribs, I bring the dagger up, certain an attack would be a foolish attempt, but I can't let Neri kill Colden.

Neri turns his beast-like eyes on me, and I can't move. Not from terror, though there's plenty of that roiling through my blood. But because he's stopping me, as though all he had to do was *think* about stilling my hand—and the rest of me—and it was done.

The wolf beside me growls and stalks closer, snaps its teeth.

"Just do it!" Colden shouts in Neri's face. "Just end me if that's what you mean to do!"

The god slides his amber gaze back to Colden. The dark and vicious look on Neri's face rattles my soul. It's the savage expression of someone who enjoys torture and means to dole it out.

"There are far worse fates than death," Neri replies, face contorting into a sneer. "Isn't that what you said? Perhaps I shall let you discover how very true that statement is."

Neri pulls his hand away, and with it comes threads.

They're so luminescent that I squint, astonished and trapped in Neri's invisible vise as Colden's body bows off the ground.

He lets out a hair-raising shriek of misery, and the world around us grows colder than ever before. Colder than the frozen lake. Colder than the bitter wood. Colder than death. Cold, everywhere, chasing a painful chill across my skin, brittling my clothes, glinting on shards of splintered wood, even coating my dagger in a glaze of ice.

With a wrathful howl, Neri closes his fist and jerks his arm back, ripping the threads from Colden's soul with so much force his blue velvet coat tears open, golden buttons scattering in the snow. Those threads, ice blue and snow white, coil around Neri and melt into his skin, as though they belong inside him.

But...wait. They do.

Neri made Asha a deal. If she gave him her heart once again, this time for eternity, he would do the thing she could not. He would make Fia Drumera immortal as well, but worse, he would cast within her the element of fire, and in Colden Moeshka the element of frost, that they may never—for all their infinite days—come together again.

Neri just removed the curse he placed three hundred years ago.

And stole the Frost King's power.

37

RAINA

eri cuts his eyes at me again. It's impossible to look away from his snarling, wolfish face.

"Tell him that I *did* save you." He growls behind the words. "Tell him that if not for the great God of the North, he would have lost you on the road south. Tell him that if not for Neri's mercy, you would be nothing more than a bloody stain in the snow. Tell him that I will not save you forever. You can both rot in earthen graves for all I care. The White Wolf's debt is paid. Do *not* summon me."

There's a shrill tinkling sound—like glass shattering on glass—and Neri is gone, leaving behind nothing but a fading, cloudy vapor and a bitter, metallic taste on the back of my tongue. His wolves even retreat, vanishing into the wood, and the white mist he rode in on dissipates through the forest.

His power lets go of me, and I exhale in a rush. Quivering, I shake the blade from my hand, the icy metal sticking to my skin.

I try to puzzle together Neri's words.

He meant for me to tell the Frost King all those things?

Colden groans and gets to his knees, shrugging off his broken chains. Long moments pass as he utters *No, no, no, no, no* over and over before extending a quickly reddening, trembling hand.

He splays his fingers wide and focuses his gaze straight ahead. The veins in his temples and neck pop from the strain, standing out sharply in relief against his fair skin. His whole body shakes with effort.

Nothing happens.

Panting, he drops his head, blowing out a ragged breath. He curls his fingers into a tight grip and pounds a white-knuckled fist against the ground. "Well, fuck all. We're balls deep in trouble now."

Whispers of uneven breathing and the crunch of footfalls across the icy wreckage send me scrambling for my dagger. The cold hilt is in my hand, its sharp tip aimed at a slender neck, in the time it takes a heart to push out a beat.

Just as fast, a hand grips my wrist. I gasp and draw back. I'm on one knee, the person above me wide-eyed as a startled doe.

Nephele.

I shove to my feet and crush her to me, ready to take her and run, like Rhonin said.

"Raina!" She squeezes me tight and pulls away to look at me, smiling, stroking my face with her thumbs. "My sweet girl."

It's been so long, yet she feels the same. Sounds the same. Smells the same. Gods, I've missed her so much. So much that it takes all that I am not to break down into a puddle of tears right here on this godsforsaken road.

How did we get here? Two farmers' daughters from Silver Hollow fighting a truly evil man to save Tiressia? Breathing the same air as an ancient god?

I hug her again. My heart has so many wounds—it's shredded—but I swear, being here with Nephele, hearing her voice, seeing her face, looking into her eyes, has already begun a sort of mending.

Some of the witches from her wagon stumble alongside the road while others help those in need. I look Nephele over. A knot swells on her forehead, above her eye, and there are bruises and cuts, visible in the moonlight. She looks so very tired.

"Are you all right?" I ask. *"Is anyone badly injured?"*

"I am fine," she signs. *"We are fine. Battered and drained, but we have endured worse than a wagon tumble."*

A wagon tumble. Was it an accident? Or...

No. Neri did this. Neri and his mist. He could've killed us. Maybe that's what he intended. Or maybe he was only coming for his nemesis. Either way, Colden was right. Neri left his people here, abandoned, in the wood of his land, with Eastlanders.

I hate him even more than before.

Colden clears his throat. "This is a truly lovely reunion, but I'm fairly certain that the battle for the end of Tiressia is happening just up the way. So if you ladies would care to join me, we still have a fight on our hands."

Amid everything, Nephele darts across the remains of our destroyed wagon where Colden now stands, throws her arms around his neck, and kisses him right on the mouth. Colden smiles, too, even while he embraces and kisses Nephele in return.

There's actual *joy* in his expression. The frigid Frost King, grinning like an imp, even after facing Neri and having his power torn from his chest. It's almost as alarming as seeing the naked God of the North form from fog.

Nephele presses her forehead against Colden's. "I didn't know what happened to you after they took you. And then I saw…" She shakes her head. "I don't know what I saw. I couldn't have seen what I *think* I saw. I must've hit my head harder than I believed."

"I'm fine." He kisses her once more. "You *did* see it. Neri was here, which makes absolutely no sense, but it was real."

"But how is that possible?" Concern edges Nephele's features. "And what did he do to you?"

Part of me wants to stop their conversation and tell Nephele that it's possible because Vexx killed Alexus, their friend. How do they not realize that? Should I tell and risk upsetting them?

Nephele runs her hand over Colden's ruined coat and tunic, tugging the fabric back enough to reveal a portion of a pink starburst blooming on the niveous skin of his torso.

Like the one on Alexus in the ravine.

Colden shrugs his bloody shoulder. "I have no godsdamn clue how it's possible. As for what Neri did? Let's just say that I'm not exactly deadly anymore, but if we can find a sword, that can change. Let's search the East-landers."

Nephele gives Colden a worried look. "He...he removed the curse? That's what I saw him doing?"

Colden nods, raising his brows. "Thus the reason I need all the weapons we can find."

With a new weight settled on her shoulders, Nephele hurries to her wagon while I go looking for Killian. I tuck Rhonin's dagger into a leather loop at the waist of my trousers, my mind racing around too many things to sort.

The second general lies about ten feet from the horses, body half in the road. She's sprawled in such an awful manner that she must be dead. Her short sword is still strapped to her side, so I take it, along with her ring of keys, and meet up with Nephele and a handful of Witch Walkers. Together, we start toward Colden.

He's at the wagon closest to camp, on his knees next to the Eastlanders trapped beneath their horses. It isn't lost on me that—when he breaks the warriors' necks—none of the Witch Walkers flinch. They keep striding toward him, as though all of this is perfectly normal.

Colden snatches a hatchet and uses Killian's keys to unlock the rear of the last wagon. Seven Witch Walkers climb out, uninjured and primed to fight for freedom, but they look haggard, tired as Nephele, and I wonder if any of them—my sister included—can even wield magick right now.

I suppose I'm going to find out because minutes later, we're running into the chilly night, through Frostwater Wood—me, my sister, the Frost King, and strangers I've never met—heading for the eastern side of the camp.

My blood pumps harder and faster the closer we get, our speed increasing. The unknown looms ahead, but I smell the scent of mingled deaths. It makes my eyes water.

Warriors fight on the path, where the wounded waited for my healing. The torchlights that lit the area still burn, illuminating a couple dozen figures, lending an amber tint to the scene, a color that I will forever associate with Neri's eyes and the Stone of Ghent inside the God Knife.

The clash in the near-distance looks like a painting—a war painting—but I can't tell who the Eastlanders are fighting.

Until we break through the trees.

I stumble to a stop at the edge of the forest, heart hurtling into my throat, stealing my air. Colden and Nephele keep moving, straight into the bloodshed, but the weaponless Witch Walkers come to a standstill like me.

Colden slams his hatchet into a warrior's neck and throws the man to the ground as though he is nothing. The body falls, landing amidst so many others, and Colden continues fighting.

I can't begin to count the dead, the fetid aroma of fading life thick and too familiar. Eastlanders cover the snowy path, the white streak in the wood now marred with the red handprint of their deaths. Some of the wounded must've tried to fight.

Above, near the tops of the trees, dozens of silky, fibrous masses float, billowing in the wind. I've never seen anything like it, but I know what those masses are. I feel it on a bone-marrow level.

Souls. Lingering in this world.

Pulse thrumming, I take in the chaos on the path. Raging, the final wave of warriors closes in on Helena, Rhonin, Colden, Nephele, and—

Alexus.

A jolting flush of shock tingles through me, sweeping violently from my head to my toes. I cannot break my stare. Surely I've slipped into a dream, some distortion of reality.

I saw Alexus die. Saw the God Knife enter his chest—the scarred chest now bared to me.

He wears no tunic.

No chains.

No death wound.

Neri. Neri is free. I hadn't been sure what might become of him if something happened to Alexus, but the fact that the northern god stood a mere step from me means that Alexus let him go—in what I'd believed to be death's release.

At the ravine, a mark painted Alexus's chest in an angry, starburst welt —a mark that's still imprinted in his skin and looks like Colden's.

A kiss left behind from a removal of power. Alexus's mark *had* to be caused by Neri's exit. And yet...

The welt had been there before Alexus died.

He freed Neri *before* Vexx stabbed him—when the earth rumbled.

I will come for you, he'd said in the moments before I lost consciousness. *Trust me.*

Gods. I still don't know how it's possible that Alexus Thibault is here, alive, but my blood *sings* for him.

Witch Walkers spread out along the roadside and chant a song of power. Finally, shaking off my shock, I charge into the fray.

It's like being back in the village all over again, only this time, my sister and Helena, the Frost King and Witch Collector, and this new person named Rhonin, whom I might call friend, are with me.

I face off with my first attacker, a warrior I vaguely recall from the ravine. He wields a longer sword, making it hard for me to measure my strikes.

With every twist, stab, and slice, the dark sky, flaming torches, and Elikesh song sends me back to that night, memories rising in a dark tide. My anger and pain build into true rage as I'm forced to remember the moments when I watched my life burn to ash.

But I'm not alone. On the periphery of my vision, my sister wields a spear and Helena her swords, both stabbing, ducking, and lunging with nimble motions. Rhonin is a beast with a dagger, and Colden is a violent force all his own with that hatchet. He and Alexus work off one another, and even though Alexus fights with a wounded knee, their movements still play out in artful form.

The remaining Eastlanders are dwindling, fewer than a dozen left. There are no magick-cast arrows this time. No stolen fire magick to make this easy for them. Their prince is losing his power.

Even in the cold night, sweat slicks my skin as I fight. It's a true battle, clashing swords while maneuvering around fallen bodies and blood-slicked snow.

And this Eastlander is strong. With every swing of his blade, he drives me across the path, forcing me to navigate the littered ground with backward steps, not knowing what lies behind me.

He meets my sword with a swift undercut. I stumble back a step, but then I spin, changing our direction. He pivots, and on the advance, raises his weapon.

I block him, bracing his arm in my hand, and with the distance between us lessened, push my shorter blade into his chest. It takes a second effort to drive the tip through the bone, but I feel his body give, my sword sliding deep with ease. I withdraw my blade, and the warrior falls, the light in his eyes dimming.

When I look up, my gaze catches on two men standing in the wood beneath the trees.

The Prince of the East and Vexx.

They weren't there before.

Though the general looks ashen, fists tight and face drawn in a mask of tempered rage, the prince dons that halo of crimson shadows and wears a sickening grin. It's as if seeing his men die is blood sport.

He lifts his chin and reaches toward the sky, fluttering his fingers. One of the souls drifts down from the treetops, surrendering as commanded. It hovers over him, a helpless husk.

The prince opens his mouth, and...

Inhales it.

A wave of ecstasy comes over him, chest rising and falling fast, his rapture evident. His eyes close, he licks his lips, and I want to vomit.

When it's over, the prince lowers his face, and his hooded gaze meets mine.

I lift my sword, on guard.

At first, there's a moment of surprise in his eyes as he takes me in—I'm not supposed to be here, let alone with a weapon—but his malicious smile returns and spreads.

With a flick of his hand, fire blooms around him, though consuming nothing.

It's a wall.

A shield.

I can smell the Summerland mage's magick in the air, laced with his prolonged death, that same scent from earlier in the tent. The aroma of fire, of a sweltering day, of dust and earth.

The prince and I stare one another down. He stands there, a pillar of stone untouched by flame, amusement bright on his face. To him, we are nothing and he is all.

He moves up the embankment, Vexx on his heels, circling the scene, hands clasped behind his back as a trail of scarlet shadows follows. The two men walk right past the singing Witch Walkers. No one else looks at or tracks them. Because they can't see them.

But I can.

I turn, breathing hard, keeping my eyes on the prowling prince even as my friends and sister fight only footsteps away. This moment reminds me of all the times he came to me, a mirage, watching from some other plane.

Coward. I push that thought through the air the way I did days ago. I pray he hears it, feels it, knows it. He *is* a coward, letting his men die, hiding in the wings, doing *nothing*, standing behind his shield of fire stolen from someone else's magick. Someone else's *soul*. All while draped in the cloak of his Shadow World, too scared to face his enemies on his own.

A glimpse of Nephele snags my attention. She jabs her spear into a warrior's mouth and jerks it out, but then she goes still. Eyes wide. Blinking. She clutches her throat, gasping like an invisible hand has a hold of her neck.

Before I can get to her—or the prince—an Eastlander advances on me. Her moves are so swift that I struggle to match each strike.

I stagger back and almost lose my footing on the embankment, but the Witch Walkers' song reaches me once more from the fringes of the wood. They lift their voices, singing down power, unaware that a devil lurks so near.

Pure energy falls over me, warm as summer sunlight amid all this cold, awakening something primal deep inside.

Awakening something else too.

With every swing of my blade, the tiny deaths I've stolen swell, filling me with a flood I'm not sure I can contain. My heart throbs, brimming with sorrow, misery, hatred, fear, disgust, anguish, adoration, serenity, craving. There are so many emotions that I can't discern them all, but they boil over, a fount of infinite connection to feelings that were never even mine.

I lunge forward, my grip on Killian's sword tight and unrelenting, and with sure footing, thrust my blade into the woman's middle.

Before I can free my weapon, another Eastlander crashes into me. I stumble, and he takes the advantage, lifting his dagger, firelight glinting off its razor-sharp edges and in his equally sharp eyes.

When he brings his arm down, I grab his wrist. He carries so much force that I must release the sword and use both hands to hold him off.

He bears down, pressing me to a knee before him.

"Lunthada comida, bladen tu dresniah, krovek volz gentrilah!"

Alexus. I can't see him, but I can hear him, that velvet voice giving me life, reminding me what I'm capable of.

Lunthada comida, bladen tu dresniah, krovek volz gentrilah. Lunthada comida, bladen tu dresniah, krovek volz gentrilah.

I think the words, holding them in my mind, and closing my eyes, I reach for all of that emotion, knowing what I want to happen. Willing it to be so. Envisioning it.

The blade I made when we entered Frostwater Wood—I see it now, see it thrusting up through the Eastlander's stomach into his chest.

Lunthada comida, bladen tu dresniah, krovek volz gentrilah!

The pressure weighing down on me slackens, and a crude gasp leaves the man's body, a gush of wet breath across my face. I open my eyes to find him staring over me with an empty, lifeless gaze, a sword of amethyst light protruding from his gaping mouth.

When his death scent hits me, I lose any mental hold I had on my magick, the sword drifting away, purplish dust mingling with the still-falling snowflakes. The Eastlander topples, and I dodge his weight, slipping in his blood and falling flat on my back.

A noise reaches my ears as I stare at the sky.

Laughter.

I turn my head only to see the Prince of the East. His mockery lies on the edge of another sound—the rising cry of a flock of cawing crows.

The birds burst from the trees, flying high into the dark night, beyond the place where speckles of glowing, floating embers and twirling snowflakes whirl hand in hand. They fly to where the souls of the dead gather.

And inhale them—one by one.

I bolt upright, slipping in blood and snow, landing on my elbow with a bone-jarring *thud*. I look up and meet Alexus's green eyes, shining in the night. He's three strides away, Helena at his back. They each fight with two short swords they must've taken from the dead warriors at their feet.

But Nephele is nowhere.

When Alexus's attacker rears back his hatchet, Alexus raises and crosses his blades over his head and, with deadly force, slices them down, their sharp edges tearing across and through the warrior's body. Blood sprays the snowy path, and innards fall, more crimson to add to this white graveyard.

The man collapses—the last of the Eastlanders—and in the next blink, Alexus is with me, drawing me to my feet, clutching me.

He fists in my hair, and his lips crush mine. "You beautiful virago," he says against my mouth. "I'm so godsdamned happy to see you."

I kiss him again. Touch his cold chest. Feel his pounding heart. Just to make sure he's really here. He's smiling, the way Nephele smiled at Colden. His dimple appears, the sight sending enough relief into my heart to heal it forever.

But how is he here? How?

He reads the question in my eyes. "Your father told you legends. The God Knife didn't kill the prince when you cut him because it cannot kill with a simple swipe. Though it is a god remnant and dangerous in the wrong hands, the blade I forged is only lethal to living gods because it can penetrate their bones. That's all." He presses my hand to his chest where the blade had penetrated to the hilt. "It isn't lethal to me," he says, "because a clever sorcerer knows better than to create a weapon that can be used against him. I mark what's mine. The God Knife knows me. It bears my rune. My name."

Another kiss, deeper and so intense that I'm gasping when he pulls away.

"Get down!" Helena screams.

The crows turn and swoop, hundreds diving toward us in an unnatural attack. Because they *are* unnatural. These things are not birds. They're demons who steal the souls of men.

Just like their maker.

And I'm done with these bastards. All of them.

"Fulmanesh. Fulmanesh, fulmanesh, fulmanesh, fulmanesh, iyuma."

I form the words with my hands, drawing from the torch fire around us, channeling all my power into lighting these little pricks up like fireflies.

The second the fire forms in my hands, I will it skyward. The crows retreat, but I throw my arms out at my sides, spread my stance, and dig deep into my darkness, making those little deaths flutter with delight.

The prince's winged demons catch my flame. The sounds that leave them are unholy screeches clawing my bones. Instinctively, I clamp my fingers into fists and squeeze until my fingernails cut into my skin.

The flames flash higher but then extinguish, and the birds collapse in on themselves, darkness into darkness. Ash falls from the sky like raining death.

Alexus stares at me in wonder, his eyes darkening with a look I learned far too well that night in Nephele's refuge, one of ignited passion.

Victory rushes through me. In the heat of the moment, with confidence and power thrumming in my veins, I turn toward the Prince of the East.

But he isn't there. Neither is Vexx.

I spin around, scanning the wood, searching.

Vexx is escaping into the forest. I start to chase him, but a surge of hot wind blasts down the path.

Alexus throws his arm up and leans over me, a shield against the heat, and the Witch Walker magick I'd felt so abundantly vanishes, their song falling silent.

Alexus and I straighten, and I turn, as though my mind knows exactly where I need to look to find the man I'd searched for moments before.

My gaze comes to rest on the Prince of the East's still-scarred face. He stands on the eastern side of the path, twenty feet from the slaughter, near the tent where I saw inside his disgusting soul.

Nephele is with him, on her knees, the God Knife's black edge laid across the pale column of her throat.

38

RAINA

Wherever the prince was before, watching me from beyond, he is not there now. Now, he's here, like he stepped from one world to another.

From invisible to visible.

Alexus, Rhonin, Colden, and Helena stare with eyes wide—at me, at one another, at the prince, at Nephele. The scene is as quiet as midnight in the vale midwinter, save for the rushing of our breaths.

The last ash from the crows settles over the wood, coloring the white world gray. Cinders crumble to dust in my hair, on my skin, on my clothes, the death scent heavy in my lungs. Damp forest, pungent rot, and burnt feathers.

But there's more. New scents. New deaths.

The Witch Walkers are gone. The snow where they stood is gone too, replaced by a dark stain of ash that trails along the fringe of the wood then fades.

"Raina Bloodgood," the prince says. "Did you really think that you could take from me so brazenly and not pay?"

It takes a moment for his meaning to sink in. He isn't talking about Nephele.

That hot wind. Summerlander magick.

He destroyed the Witch Walkers. Burned them to ash the way I burned his crows.

Colden raises his hatchet. Aims. "You bastard."

The prince *tsks,* his hand tightly wound in Nephele's hair. "Now that would be very foolish, especially for a *king.*" He trails the tip of the bone blade up the side of my sister's face to her temple and angles it just right for penetration. "Unless you want this talented witch of yours to make her way to the Shadow World sooner rather than later."

He means it. His shadows coil around Nephele, binding her hands, closing over her mouth. I'd wondered why he didn't just ride in on his red cloud and take Colden from Winterhold instead of going to the trouble to sneak an army across the Northlands.

But now I think I know why. The prince must be close to what he wants if he means to take it. It's why he couldn't just find me in the wood and steal the knife. His magick is not so simple as sifting across the world and arriving wherever he wishes. Other than watching him move through shadows here in the wood, I've only ever seen him vanish. All magick has limitations, and I have to wonder if this is his.

It must be, and that leaves me with the worry that if the prince decides to leave us, he'll take Nephele with him—and she won't be able to fight. Not only has he silenced her voice, but he's somehow subduing her power.

Her witch's marks are gone.

"What do you want?" I sign in a flurry, too scared to move toward him but knowing I need to maintain some semblance of control over the situation.

Alexus stands beside me, rigid and on guard, every thick muscle in his torso tensing. "She asked, *What do you want?*"

Smiling like a fiend, the prince answers. "Well, for starters, I want *you,* Raina Bloodgood. I didn't at first, but now, as we've discussed, you have use. I also want Neri sent back to the Shadow World, but someone made sure that can't happen. Not easily, anyway." He gives Alexus a sharp glare. "All because he wanted to save the little witch from Silver Hollow who's caught his ancient eye. You set a god free for a woman you hardly know."

Gods and stars. That's what Neri meant when he said to tell *him* that he *did* save me. He wasn't speaking of Colden. He made a deal with Alexus —his freedom from Alexus's prison in exchange for my safety.

The prince sets his eyes on Rhonin and Helena. "And oh, how I wanted this God Knife once I knew it existed. And now I have it, no thanks to you two, thief and spy." He slides his gaze to Colden. "Then there's the infamous Frost King. A pawn in a game I plan to win. I want you too, though I sense no power inside you anymore. Just useless immortality. What's the point in living forever if you're boring? Do you even have skill?"

Colden scoffs, a deadly grin forming on his face. He stands rigid, ready to lunge any moment. "Let Nephele go, and I'll show you just how much skill I have, you pathetic piece of shit."

The prince laughs and jerks Nephele's head back. "I can't do that because, you see, I need power. The mage who has fed me for quite some time is fading. I require a new source of life. It could've been one of my own." He glares at Alexus again. "Un Drallag, the mighty Eastland sorcerer, would've provided enough power to make me something next to a god. Sadly, all that magick is dormant for now. Isn't it, Alexi of Ghent?"

Alexus clenches his jaw. "It won't be asleep forever, and when it awakes, I swear you're going to regret ever coming here—if you even live through this night."

Damn. There's not enough power in any of us to keep this moment from escalating.

"I need a source of life who's young," the prince says. "Someone who will thrive longer than the old mage. Someone with enough magick in her veins to enchant an entire forest." The prince looks down at Nephele, caresses her unmarked cheek with the God Knife. "Don't even pretend that most of that vast magick wasn't all you."

Heart hammering, I take a step. The prince's mage is dying, which means the eastern lord is in a weakened state. He *needs* Nephele—not just later, but *now*.

I peer into my sister's soul. The threads of her life glimmer golden, but a bloody infection creeps along their edges.

He's siphoning her magick. He's going to tangle the vibrant threads of her life with his poisoned, decaying tatters, use her up until she's nothing but a shell chained to a stone table in a tower or a disregarded husk of spirit floating in the night sky.

I cannot let that happen.

The prince's eyes are on Nephele, but her wide and steady gaze fixes on me. After all these years, I can still read her face, but I refuse to answer the stern glint in her watery stare, the pinched determination in her mouth. She's telling me to end her so that he cannot use her.

But I just got her back. Over my dead body will I lose her again. We're smarter than this. Better. Stronger.

Faster.

With a slight shake of my head, I arch my brow and let my thoughts radiate from my face to give her a warning. I've been stealthy all my life, and my aim is sharp, so I slip the tiny dagger from the loop at my waist and bolt toward her, leaping over bodies, my arm primed for a throw.

In that sliver of a moment, so many things happen. Helena screams my name, and Alexus reaches for me. His fingertips slip off the bloody fabric at my elbow.

I fling the blade down the path with all my strength.

The Prince of the East looks up. Leans left. Flares his shadows.

My blade sails right through them, then he and Nephele vanish in a plume of red smoke.

The crimson shadows remain, and I'm moving too fast to stop. They fling out, monstrous tentacles latching onto me.

An arm clamps around my waist, yanking me to a halt. Whoever has hold of me twists, trying to pull me in the other direction, but the shadows wrap around my ankles and tear me away, slamming me to the earth, knocking the wind from my chest.

When I look up, Colden's wild stare meets mine. After everything—after all the nights I lay awake thinking of how I would one day kill him—the Frost King tried to save me.

Scarlet shadows whirl up and fall, wrapping around him like a fist, dragging him toward a blood-colored cloud. In a blink, he disappears.

There's a hard tug on my body, and I dig my fingers into the ash-covered path at the exact moment that Alexus runs and slides, calling my name, reaching for my hand.

But I'm sucked away into a red mist.

39

RAINA

There's nothing. Nothing but darkness. My murky vision corrects —or *tries* to correct—the blurry world around me.

I blink into focus. The world isn't blurred; it's filled with moving shadows.

Wicked pain crawls up the base of my skull. I'm on my hands and knees on black, rocky ground, surrounded by souls, like the husks that floated above the wood. There are thousands, billowing against a dismal, cloudless slate-gray sky. Even if they don't have eyes, their attention pierces me.

Keeper, they hiss. *Seer. Healer. Resurrectionist. Murderer.*

Witch.

Beyond them lies a craggy mountain that goes on forever. It's guarded by a gate, a massive creation, neither steel nor stone, but something my mind can't give name to.

Because I don't belong here.

I know it.

The souls know it.

This *place* knows it.

A wraithlike being in a red cloak ushers souls through the gate. Some go left. Some go right. Some go straight through. Then he looks up with two glowing orbs for eyes and spies me.

Trespasser.

I try to get up, to run, but everything is all wrong. It's like I'm moving through water, my motions dragged down by some invisible weight.

I turn. Nephele and Colden are behind me, on their sides, still secured by crimson shadows. Both wear expressions of panic. I want to go to them, but a shadow loops around my middle, holding me tight. It's struggling, because I'm tethered elsewhere, a tremendous pressure on my insides, in my chest—around my *heart*. Like something's pulling the organ in two.

More crimson shadows glide across the ground in bright tendrils. I sit back and jerk my hands away as one creeps over my shoulder.

Then comes that chilling, jaw-clenching laughter, slipping in with the shadows, curling up and over and into my ears.

The Prince of the East looms like a jailer, like someone who *does* belong here, God Knife strapped to his hip.

"Welcome to the Shadow World, you three," he says, the seeping gash in his face a reminder that this is not a dream. "We can't stay long. This place likes to keep interlopers, so I only use it as a means to an end when I absolutely must. The question is, where to go from here?"

Colden jerks up like a snake and strikes out at the prince. The shadows holding the king bound coil tighter and tighter until he cries out, his body flung back to the hard ground.

"Try that again," the prince says, "and you'll wish you were next in line with the dead. I have to keep you alive, but I don't have to make it a comfortable existence. You would do well to remember that."

I close my eyes, trying to steady my thundering heart, but something happens. Something strange.

I might as well be one of the souls hovering over Frostwater Wood, because suddenly, I'm there. I can see the bloody path, a red slit cleaving the white forest.

Swooping like the prince's crows, I move closer, a bird's eye view. My body is there, on Winter Road. And yet...I'm here. In the Shadow World.

Alexus sits in the snow, his wounded leg outstretched. I'm lying before him, my head resting in his lap. Helena and Rhonin kneel at my sides. The look on Hel's face is one of conflict and desperation as she hands Alexus a dagger—Rhonin's dagger. The blade I threw at the prince.

With the steadiest of hands, Alexus presses the sharp tip to the thick muscle of his chest, a smooth patch of skin next to the runes I'd so eagerly dragged my teeth across the night we almost took one another, runes I'd touched with tender fingers in the cave.

He carves a sign into his skin, two bleeding, parallel grooves with a single dot in the middle, joined by a V-shaped line.

Lowering the dagger, he pushes my hair away from my neck and runs his hand over the swell of my breast. Then he cuts me, just under my collarbone, making the same mark. Thin rivulets of blood spill from the wound.

He gets to his knees, wincing from the pain in his leg. Reverently, he threads our fingers together and lowers his forehead to mine, rocking gently, a similar ritual as the one he performed that night in the wood when he killed all those men. He's pleading—or praying. I can't tell which, but I feel him so wholly.

He's trying to bring me back to the other side.

I open my eyes, my heart pounding harder. But I'm still in the Shadow World.

The prince stares at me, runs his eyes over me, his smug smile falling. "Un Drallag never gives up, does he? Well, two can play at this game."

He walks away, flicking a hand over his shoulder. His shadows writhe, and me, Nephele, and Colden are drawn upon once more, being bled from the earth—through the Shadow World toward some great divide, fading further from the Northlands. Further from safety. Further from home.

This realm is only a stop. A path. A portal.

A risk, but still a way for a man made of shadows, souls, and sins to escape with what he wants.

But where is he taking us?

One of the tiny darknesses inside my chest hums and churns and sparks, a little lightning storm fluttering around my heart. It's strange, that connection, that reaching out of energies, but I cling to it.

Cling to *him*.

Alexus.

I reach for Nephele's hand and then Colden's, even though they're bound in shadows. I seek the heat and light of Alexus's stolen death, the white-hot power living there, the bond that's connecting us even now.

I'm weak and tired, but I can't let the prince have Colden and Nephele. Have *me*.

I must fight.

I think of the sword of amethyst light. I know I can conjure it.

Lunthada comida, bladen tu dresniah, krovek volz gentrilah. I think the words over and over again, but nothing happens. Too much fear intrudes my mind. Or maybe my magick is no good here.

The prince turns a dark look over his shoulder and angles his head. I feel his contempt from across the red, shadowy distance between us. I have to dig deeper. Down to the deepest part of me, the force of life within.

Swallowing all fear, I look for my own threads, the threads of *my* heart. Like the ones I pulled from Alexus the night he taught me to summon flame.

Fulmanesh, iyuma tu lima, opressa volz nomio, retam tu shahl.

Fire of my heart, come that I may see you, warm my weary bones, be my place of rest.

I carry the song in my heart. Hear it. I won't let it fall silent.

Flames form, a flickering ball of heat roaring before me. The prince heads my way, malevolence and violence rippling off him in waves. I imagine this blazing fire rising and pouring down on him, envision him burning like he burned my village. But first, I must make the fire do what I want it to do.

Alexus's words come back to me. *Think of the thing you want most in this world. It's where true power comes from. We often hold the most will for our strongest desires.*

This time there's no hesitation. I know what I want most.

I want peace. To be surrounded by those I love. For them to be safe. To know joy. To know passion. To know serenity.

That's it. That's all. Peace—in all things.

The fire obeys.

With *fulmanesh, iyuma* in my mind, flames race along the rocky ground, consuming the crimson shadows between me and the Prince of the East. Those same flames roar around him, not like the shield he made in the wood, but a wildfire wreathing him in torturous heat, licking up his bronze leathers, melting them to his skin, kissing his damaged face.

He roars and flails, throwing himself to the ground to pound out the flames, sounds of misery echoing across this waiting place filled with souls —a place that feels like it wants to either swallow us whole or spit us out.

The tether to my heart tugs again. Harder. Colden and Nephele are still in my grip. I close my eyes and will us away from this Shadow World. I can see the wood, and gods, how I long to feel the snow and Alexus's voice drifting over my skin.

But when I open my eyes, we're *still* here.

The Prince of the East rises and steps past the fire, stalking toward me, dragging flames with him, chest heaving as he stares at me like some sort of creature, some monster that is more walking corpse than man.

His face has changed, and not from the fire. It's old. Older than old. Sunken and colorless, like the man in the cell by the sea. His eyes are voids, something from the deepest, darkest parts of the Nether Reaches.

He brings his hands together and then swoops them out at his sides as though he's parting a river. Colden and Nephele are ripped from my hold.

The prince lunges for me. One burned hand closes around my throat. He shoves me down, my back to the rocky ground, his hollowed face an inch from mine, reeking like rot and ruin. For such a withered thing, he's solid and immovable, wholly unnatural.

Swiftly, he unsheathes the God Knife. "What did I tell you when I stood over you in your village?"

I don't need to search my memory. That night is so permanent in my mind, branded on my soul.

We'll meet again, Keeper, he'd said. *And when we do, I'm going to drive that knife into your heart and inhale your soul.*

Clamping my hands over his, I bring my knee up between his legs, praying that he is, in fact, somewhat human. It's enough that he draws back for a fraction of a second and stumbles, but the God Knife slips from my reach.

I force myself to my feet, his shadows and the odd weight of this world trying to drag me back down. He looks at me, and I know he *wants* to kill me, regardless of what power I can offer him. He'll probably inhale my soul right here, with the entire Shadow World watching.

Air shudders out of me on the edges of fury. I need him dead, and I need that God Knife.

I charge him, teeth bared. The prince does the same, his empty eyes wide and wild.

But I'm moving too slow, like I'm not real. Like this place isn't real.

Just before we clash, the prince spins, grabbing my arm, and kicks my feet out from under me, landing me flat on my back with a jolt that rattles my every bone. He comes at me, but I ram the heel of my palm into his nose, sending him staggering back.

We have to get out.

I grab Colden under the arms and drag him closer to Nephele. Dropping to my knees, I clasp both their hands, keeping my eyes on the prince.

He starts my way, and I pray that I can do this, though I don't even know what *this* is.

Before I can do anything, however, the prince bursts into a red cloud and reappears before my eyes. He falls on me like a mountain lion on a doe, straddling me.

Red, riotous shadows seethe from him. They stretch and crawl and creep toward Colden and Nephele, bloody, nebulous rivers flowing across cracked earth.

In an instant, those same shadows writhe around my sister and her king, trying to tear them from my grip again, but I hold fast. I strain and pull, gritting my teeth, clinging to their hands.

The tether around my heart tightens—Alexus, working to bring us back home.

This time, I will not let go.

"Such a disappointment." The prince raises the God Knife once more. "I tried to spare you. You could've been of such great use to me. Now I must leave you in the Shadow World while I head for the Summerlands to raise the gods and bring this empire to its knees."

Gods. Not just Thamaos.

The prince leans close and brushes his decaying lips against my cheek. "At least your soul will restore me. I bet it tastes like smoke and starlight."

I close my eyes. I refuse to witness the murderous look that must shine in his dead eyes as he rears back. I only feel Alexus—his tether and our runes pulling me even as the icy God Knife buries to the hilt between my breasts, just like Vexx did to Alexus.

Gasping, I snap my eyes open. The pain is unfathomable, a bright, burning thing tearing through me, melting the bones around my heart.

I'm dying. I must be.

But it isn't the knife. The knife isn't even there. I'm surrounded by darkness, thick as ink. The only light comes from the burning lines and grooves of the rune on my chest. The sigil burrows into me, spreading heat through my veins, its power claiming me.

I'm in this in-between place, the void between two worlds. Alexus marked me, and now I feel his summons, his voice a whisper in the back of my mind. Colden and Nephele aren't with me, but I can still feel them, at the edge of my grasp.

"Just let me go!" Colden screams. "Save Nephele! This is the only way!"

Though he sounds a million miles away, they're so close, their hands in mine. I refuse to let go. I'm strong enough. I can do this!

But I'm not given the chance.

The fingers clutched in my left hand, fingers I know belong to the King of the Northlands, pry loose from my grip.

The second he's gone, the moment I feel him sucked away, I cry out for him in my mind. There is no victory without sacrifice, but this isn't how the story was supposed to end. I wasn't supposed to fail. The prince wasn't supposed to win. The Frost King wasn't supposed to be willing to give all —for us.

For me. For my sister. For his people.

On a sob, I grab the other hand still clenched in my grasp—Nephele. With all that I am, I heave and heave until I'm no longer alone in the dark.

I cling to my sister, both of us crying and shivering in this abyss. Closing my eyes, I focus on Alexus's prayers, on his tender voice and the promise of his rune, and let him guide me back to the light.

✣ 40 ✣

ALEXUS

My magick hasn't flowed freely in three hundred years. Tonight, only a thin thread of power trickles in my blood, but it's enough.

And it feels extraordinary.

Humming in my veins.

Coming alive in my bones.

When it finally wakes completely, even the mountains will know.

Raina lies in my arms. The prince almost took her from me, but a clever sorcerer marks what's his. Raina Bloodgood now bears my rune.

My power.

My seal.

My name.

Alexi of Ghent.

Shared with *her*.

Her eyes flutter open for a brief moment as snow falls around us. She's too weak to sign, but I know her face, every expression. I can read her thoughts in that furrowed brow, see them floating in her deep blue eyes.

"No," I whisper. "I didn't save you. I only helped you save yourself."

I touch the rune on her chest and press my lips to it. The truth is that this woman is saving me. She saved me on the green, in the wood, in the ravine, and she's saving me right now, just by breathing.

Her eyes close, but her heart still pounds beneath my touch. In another life, I would've tried to know her. I would've admired her and read her poems written by my own hand. I would've walked with her through fields of stardrops, danced with her in the stream.

But this is not another life.

And I'm beginning to wonder if it has to be.

❧ IV ❧
WINTERHOLD

41

RAINA

The first time I rouse, I see nothing but a snowy sky, and it hurts to breathe. I'm alone, but then a body folds around mine, warm and comforting, and for a heartbeat, I think it's my mother. But a little death thrums inside my chest, nestled away in a deep corner of my heart. It's him. The sureness of that fact brings overwhelming relief that sweeps me back to darkness. He is exactly where he belongs.

With me.

His deep voice meets my ears. "Come, little beauty," and I'm dimly aware of being carried away, Frostwater Wood fading from sight.

THE SECOND TIME I OPEN MY EYES, A LONG, BLACK CLOAK SWEEPS OVER me like a blanket. The world is still white, and I think I'm in the vale in winter, the pale light of morning breaking through the clouds. I'm atop a horse, strong arms cradling me while holding fast to the reins. I hear the *chink chink clink* of a bridle, the soft thud of hooves, and I notice an unmistakable sway, rocking me back to sleep.

Before I succumb, I look at the bearded face of the man who holds me, and he meets my stare. My head rests on his shoulder, his mouth so close that the warmth of his breath brushes against my lips.

"It's all right. I'm here. Rest."

My heart pounds, something inside me fearing that this can't be real while another part of me prays to the moon that it is. He shouldn't be here, but he is, and if it's a dream, I want to cling to it a while longer.

My eyes close—I've no command over them anymore—and I drift, curling against the Witch Collector's heat.

ALEXUS.

His name playing over and over in my head tugs me awake the third time. I open my eyes, and it takes a moment to realize where I am.

And that I'm still breathing.

I lie in an elegant bed with four intricately carved posts, a black brocade canopy with matching bed curtains. The room is so warm. It's the size of the cottage, with a fire blazing in a stone hearth. I'm no longer wearing my bloody bodice or leathers or borrowed boots. I'm dressed in a chiffon shift the color of a blush. My hair is still damp and smells of jasmine and lilac.

I remember everything. The ravine. Winter Road. The Shadow World. Seeing Winterhold—in person—for the first time. Being stripped, bathed, and mended by strangers while in a daze. Explaining to Alexus, Helena, and Rhonin as much as I could about what happened. Holding Nephele by the fire as she cried for the loss of her village, her mother, her king.

Reaching for Alexus when it was over.

Asking him to stay.

Healing his wounds.

His body curling around mine.

Instinctively, I run my hand across the bed behind me. Much to my disappointment, the sheets are cold and empty. Alexus and I only slept when he was here, too exhausted to even talk, much less anything else. I find myself regretting that I didn't find the energy for something more before reality rushed to greet us.

I lost the Northland king and the God Knife to the enemy, Vexx fled the wood unscathed, and the Prince of the East and Neri are free. Matters could be worse. I have to keep reminding myself of that fact.

The fight isn't over.

Though I'm achy, I toss aside the coverlet and get up. Deep, silvery moonlight floods the room through a massive arched window. I hadn't been clear-headed enough to take it all in before. This must be a former library-turned-guest chambers. There are books everywhere. Tall bookcases have been built into every wall, spanning from slate floor to coffered ceiling, each shelf crammed to its fullest.

Being from the vale, the closest thing I've seen to a library was Mena's stash of books she brought from Penrith years ago, volumes collected from her trips to the coast when she was young. She owned twelve books—a trove. My parents kept a shelf of six works that I read a thousand times. I've certainly never seen any number of books like *this*.

I could live here.

An ornate wooden desk sits a few strides from the bed, positioned at an angle, facing the view beyond the glass. The desktop is covered with fine parchment and scrolls, organized by size, and an array of inkpots and quills, a wax burner, and a seal.

I pick up the seal and study its impression. It's the same sigil I bear on my skin.

Alexus's mark. His seal.

These are his chambers.

Carefully, I slip my hand into the slit at the neck of my gown and touch the mark that burned itself into my body, branded Alexus's name onto my bones. It's part of me now, much as my soul. On that path in the wood, he'd awoken enough of his magick to create a link between us, keeping me in the here and now. He gave me something to hold onto in my darkest hour. Some*one* to hold onto. Because of him, I'd been strong enough to straddle two worlds.

I return the seal and ghost my hand across an unrolled scroll, feeling the soft rise of Elikesh words Alexus must've begun writing some time ago. The ink is dry, the table a little dusty from disuse. I don't recognize the handwriting, of course, but its elegance calls to me.

There's a tunic draped over the chair.

I touch it. Hold it to my nose. Take a deep breath.

Everything smells like him, that scent of rich spices, dark wood, and the sweet aroma of ancient magick. I turn back to the bed. Even the linens smell of him, and not just because he laid with me for a while. But because that bed knows his body intimately. It makes me want to curl back up and never leave.

I pluck a book from his desk and clutch it to my chest. He reads. And writes. Things I would've possibly guessed but didn't know. There's still so much to learn about him, and I want that chance, scared as that makes me feel.

At the window, I stare over the snowy village that has fallen quiet for the night. One could almost think nothing happened here, if this were the only perspective. The white rooftops and smoke curling from chimneys remind me of home.

But lovely and serene as the scene may appear, if I turn to the left, the tops of the stables and granary are also visible, burned during the attack to nothing but wooden skeletons. I remember the destroyed main gate, the bodies strewn across the courtyard when we arrived, and at least a dozen wounded Witch Walkers being cared for in the main hall when Alexus carried me inside.

Thoughts arise, my mind speculating the worst scenarios. I don't want to imagine the destruction that took place, the way fire had to dominate ice. I don't want to think about more bloodshed, much less look its damage in the eye, but I should go downstairs and see how I can be of use with the injured. Try to find Alexus. Nephele. Helena.

Before I can turn around, a deep voice fills the room. "Do you like books?"

Startled, I face my visitor.

Alexus stands in the doorway, watching me, leaning his long body against the frame. One booted foot crosses the other, his cloak hanging over his arm. I never heard the door open, too lost in my thoughts.

My stomach ties itself into a knot. I've seen the sadness he wears before, that forlorn expression when he returned from Littledenn at the stream. I don't know where he's been today or what he's faced with the people of Winterhold, but it has affected him deeply.

He pushes off the molding and steps across the threshold, closing the door behind him. I swallow hard when the lock clicks and he tosses his cloak on a chair, then moves deeper into the room.

My heart hammers. I haven't answered him, and I'm still clutching one of his books to my chest. I slip it under my arm, shrug like a fool, and find my words.

"I love books," I sign. *"Though there are not many in the vale."*

A cloud drifts over his face, one of guilt, his eyes aglow in the firelight as he passes the hearth.

"I thought I might be needed," I continue, trying to make the discomfort between us evaporate, though I'm aware that most of that discomfort is coming from me. *"For healing,"* I add. *"I was going to check downstairs. Find Nephele and Helena."*

"Nephele checked on you an hour ago, but you were still asleep. She's resting now. Everyone is resting. If you're up to mending cuts and burns in the morning, well enough, but it's best if we give the castle time to grieve and rest tonight." He sits on the edge of the bed closest to me, runs his palms down his leather-clad thighs, and lets out a sigh. "Come here. Please."

I slip the book back to my chest like a shield. I don't know why I'm so nervous. We've been together for days, have hardly left one another's side. I laid in that bed with him. I've kissed him. Touched him.

I crave him.

Yet I'm terrified.

Slowly, I go to him. He looks up at me with those bold, green eyes and reaches for the book still clasped to my body. Finally, I let go, and he sets it aside on the bed.

His gaze travels over me, and I'm suddenly aware that my thin gown hides little. Alexus settles his strong hands on my hips and drops his forehead to my chest, his grip on me tightening.

Tears rush up inside me for reasons I can't explain, a well-erected dam threatening to yield. He's said so little, yet I feel his grief, his worry, his fear, his *want* seeping into me.

I slide my hands into his hair, and he meets my eyes again, his stare glassy.

"We need to talk."

Those are not the words I wanted to hear. *I want you. I need you. Let me have you.* Those were the things I'd hoped he'd say.

He touches my neck and slides his fingertips along my throat, sending a hard chill tumbling down my spine. He tugs the thin fabric of my gown aside, revealing the rune he cut into my body. Tenderly, he presses his warm lips to the skin just below the wound.

It takes my breath, that kiss. The reverence. The connection.

He pushes my hair behind my ear. "I've worried all day that you might hate me for this."

I shake my head. *"Should I?"*

"Maybe. Unless we reverse the rune, you will always be tied to me. Your heart will seek to find me until your last breath. And that was not something I had the right to do."

"Reverse the rune?" I sign.

"It's a ritual of sorts," he says. "If you decide you want that, just tell me."

I touch the mark on my chest, and then untie his tunic and pull it open, feeling his rune too.

"We were already connected," I tell him. *"Because of the death I stole. I can feel it. Feel you. Inside me. That bond would not let go in the Shadow World. You were my tether. Even before the rune."*

"And do you have this bond with Helena? You saved her too."

"I feel her little death inside me, yes. But there was a difference when I was in the Shadow World. Perhaps because you were the one trying to bring me back."

"Or because I've been to the Shadow World myself," he says.

He holds my stare for a long moment, like he's curious, then returns his hands to my hips, fingers tight, the closeness between us thick and tempting.

"You're doing it again," he says, the smallest of smiles tipping one corner of his mouth.

I frown. *"Doing what?"*

"Looking at me like you want me to kiss you."

I sign nothing. Instead, I slip my arms around his neck and thread my fingers through his hair once more.

If I'm obvious, so be it.

Alexus closes his eyes, a weary moan sounding from the back of his throat. When he looks at me again, I lean closer, ready to be brave, to give in to what we both want.

But he stops me.

"I need to tell you something. Something important."

I can't help but pull back and exhale a shuddering sigh. I know this tone.

"How can there be anything else to tell?" I ask him.

"Raina." His voice is so soft. So pained. "I want you, more than anything."

I take a shallow breath. If this is what he needed to tell me, then stars and gods, I'm ready. But he keeps going, and that tone is still there, threading through his voice like each word is a punishment to speak.

"I want to lay you down by the fire," he says. "I want to take you for the rest of this night, wipe away every thought from your mind except thoughts of pleasure. But just like in the wood, I can't let that happen until I've been honest with you. There's one thing I didn't tell you in the cave. One thing you need to know about me. Especially now."

I'd thought of him as such an open book, even considered that there were pages and lines I simply hadn't had the time to read yet, chapters I wanted to lose myself inside. Just moments ago, I wanted this, to learn more about him.

And yet, nothing about this moment feels like I thought it might.

He brushes his fingertips across my temple. "Remember when I told you the story of Colden and Fia? Remember his friend?"

I nod, wondering whatever came to be of the man from the valley, and hoping beyond hope that a man from centuries earlier has nothing to do with us.

"A handful of years after the gods died," Alexus says, "that friend traveled back to the Summerlands to see the queen. He was in a dark place, and guilt that he'd played a role in Colden's curse had overcome him. Had he not persuaded Colden to go to that celebration, he and the queen would have never come together. The man from the valley unknowingly walked the man who would become his dearest friend into a circumstance that turned Colden into a being with ice in his veins and frost on his breath, a thing that could never see or touch the woman he loved ever again. Everything—even his humanity—had been taken from him." Alexus pauses, and his throat moves hard. "Fia agreed to see the friend. He asked her to help him live forever, that he might show his loyalty to his new king and be worthy of forgiveness. He felt he had nothing. Honor was all."

Emotion wraps around my throat. Another puzzle, though already too clear.

"In her worry for Colden," he continues, "the queen advised that the friend seek the most powerful clan of her magi. He did, and though they couldn't grant him immortality, they could bind him to someone else's eternal life. His wife and son had been killed in a recent attack on their village, so he let the magi work their magick." He pauses, emptiness smothering the vivid light of his eyes. "I haven't left the service of Colden Moeshka since."

It takes a moment for his words, clear and direct as they are, to soak into my mind. I think back to seeing him at the stream, the way he knew about releasing the stardrops for the dead, the way his face darkened every time he mentioned Colden's friend.

He's immortal. Something I knew, in a sense. He's Un Drallag the Sorcerer. Alexi of Ghent, the prince called him. I knew he'd been alive for three hundred years. I just haven't had time to wonder *why*.

"This is not news," I tell him, trying on a weak smile.

"I suppose not, but eternal life for me is very different, Raina. I'm *bound* to Colden's immortality. The magi who created the spellwork between Colden and I are gone, and their unified magick is still strong. There is no undoing it. Are you understanding what I'm saying?"

My chest tightens, and I feel sick, though the sudden flood of feelings attacking me makes no sense. It's as though my body knows something my mind has yet to grasp.

"No, I do not understand. You and I are bound—"

"Yes, but the bond we share is only a connection. A link. If I lose my life, you do not lose yours. For Colden and me... We are two halves of the same whole, Raina. My immortality only goes so far as the king's."

There's no keeping the truth from sinking in now.

"No." The word forms on my fingers without thought.

I say it again and again as understanding rattles my heart.

Alexus stands and takes my face in his hands. The look in his eyes and the expression twisting his handsome features answer every question racing through my mind, sealing my heart in cold dread. I close my eyes and search for the threads of his life, expecting to see them as they should be now that Neri is gone.

But no. Alexus still bears multiple threads. Glimmering shadows.

Colden's life. And now mine.

I pull away from him and flee the room, unsure where I'm going. The fear of losing a man I met only days ago should not hold so much power over me, yet it consumes. The cresting wave I've denied any power rises, and this time, it's going to sweep me under.

Alexus Thibault is bound to the Frost King unto death. If Colden Moeshka loses his life at the hands of the Prince of the East, he will take Alexus with him.

And there won't be a damn thing I can do to stop it.

42

RAINA

T he next morning, Nephele wakes me.

"Hey, Sunshine." She uses my old nickname, but the light of it doesn't reach her eyes. "Alexus called a meeting, and he'd like you to attend. Let's get you dressed."

I sit up and scrub my face, dragging my hands through my hair. After stumbling awkwardly into Rhonin's room the night before, I found a dark nook at the end of the hall and hid, crying until there were no tears left to lose.

When the wave passed, I blessedly found Nephele's chambers. She and Helena shared the bed with me. Neither pried about why I'd abandoned Alexus in the middle of the night or why I couldn't stop shuddering with aftershocks. Helena held me, though, and I clung to her, so thankful that she was there.

"Where is Hel?" I ask my sister.

Nephele begins rummaging through her wardrobe. "Downstairs with Rhonin. Preparing for the meeting. They're very strategic people, those two. I think they'll make great friends." With a tunic in hand, she sits on the edge of the bed. The whites of her eyes are clearer today, but I still see sadness—that I caused. "Do you want to talk about last night?" she asks.

I'm not ready to tell her that my heart aches because Alexus's life hangs in the balance or that I fear her dear friend captivated me the moment I first looked upon his face. I can't tell her that I thought of a million ways to save Colden Moeshka last night, nor that I had to stop myself from sneaking out of the castle and stealing a horse to ride toward the Summerlands alone. She's been through so much. Her heart is broken. She doesn't need to bear my heartache as well.

"It has been a harrowing few days," I sign. *"I am only tired."*

"Yes." She glances at her hands, fidgeting with the ties on the tunic. "Colden doesn't believe that Fia will bend. It's been so long. They don't hold the same feelings anymore. He wasn't scared of the Eastlanders for that reason." She takes my hand. "I know that Alexus will do his damnedest to get Colden back, and I hold every confidence that the prince, no matter what magick he holds, will not defeat Fia Drumera. Tiressia will not fall into his hands."

These words are for her own comfort, and perhaps mine too, but I'm not convinced. She may know about the Summerland mage, and the Prince of the East may have touched her magick, but she hasn't seen inside his soul. She doesn't realize how virulent he truly is.

She looks up. "Listen. I saw Alexus this morning. He stopped to make sure you were all right. I don't know what happened between you two last night or in the wood, but I could sense the magnetism you share. It was clear in the construct." She flits her delicate fingertips across the rune visible in the slit of my gown. "He marked you. That is no small thing, Raina. He *claimed* you. Alexus has never claimed anyone. It's an ancient rite. It means that he shared his power with you. If you don't want that, you can tell him. It can be changed."

I don't know what to say because I don't know what I want. Alexus said I could reverse the rune, but I don't truly understand the implications of all that's happened yet. I only know that it feels right to have Alexus Thibault's mark on my skin, though now I must ask myself if I'm being foolish. I've opened myself to a man who has already changed me so much. I can't imagine what will happen if I let this go further.

Worse still, part of me wants to find out.

Half an hour later, Nephele and I stroll downstairs and enter a magnificent three-story library with twenty times the number of books that fill Alexus's room. I'm wearing my sister's clothes, a red affair I don't very much like. It reminds me of the prince—of blood and death—and I'm so tired of thinking about those three things.

Alexus sits at the head of a long, gleaming table. His hair is tied at the nape of his neck, and he's clad in black, a dark knight if I've ever seen one. I look away the moment his gaze caresses me from crown to toe. The mark on my chest warms at his nearness, reminding me that I'm his in an odd sort of way.

A dozen men and women sit around the sprawling table. Another dozen stand along the edges of the fire-warmed room, including Helena and Rhonin. Every spine is rigid, faces pale.

Nephele and I sit, and Alexus begins a speech about how powerful the Eastern enemy has grown, about how these leaders can't blame themselves for the invasion. They did all they could to stop the Eastland army, but the Prince of the East—with his stolen fire magick—drew Colden Moeshka out of hiding, a king surrendering to save his people from further destruction.

"Finding and taking back the king will not be an easy journey or task," Alexus says. "It's a long way to the coast. If we plan to enter the Summerlands, we'll be forced to face the traitors of the Northland Watch in Malgros, and if we make it past them, we'll have to endure the sea. There's no passage for Northlanders, and if we make it across, the Summerland ports are heavily surveilled. We'll need to be very convincing, very clever, have a windfall of luck, or perhaps all three."

"What if the king isn't in the Summerlands?"

I'm surprised when Helena speaks up, though I suppose I shouldn't be. She'd wanted to be part of the Northland Watch for a reason.

"Raina can check the waters," Hel continues. "See where he is."

When she pauses, Rhonin speaks. "The prince likely took the king to the Eastland Territory, to his palace, especially if his power is weak or gone altogether. He doesn't have Nephele, and the king has no magick for the prince to steal. He must find someone to replace his mage, or his plan falls apart. We could go straight to the source. Attack while he's vulnerable."

Alexus eyes the pair appreciatively. "I like your thinking, but right now, there aren't enough of us to take on the Eastlanders in their homeland. The prince will go to the Summerlands. He must, at some point, if his mission remains. We will have a much better chance against him if I reach

Queen Drumera first." Solemnly, he looks around the room. "So many of you have given your lives to this land, in some form or another, and though it pains me to ask you to give more, I wouldn't want to face this undertaking with anyone else. The grooms are preparing our packs and horses to leave come morning. I ask that you all spend the day in consultation with your families and consider accompanying me on the journey to the Summerlands. Save for Nephele and Raina."

The second I stiffen in my seat, Nephele grips my knee, uttering my name through closed teeth, the way Mother used to when warning me to hold my tongue at the dinner table.

I clench my jaw, my glare cutting, sharp as any knife.

Alexus holds up a hand. "You've only just found each other. I won't stand in your way if either of you wants to leave." He looks at me pointedly. "This is what you wanted."

I can feel Rhonin and Helena's attention—this mission needs a Seer—but I keep my stare trained on Alexus, something tight coiling in my chest.

This *is* what I wanted. From the very beginning. To find Nephele and take my family away from war, away from the Frost King, away from the Northlands. Rhonin offered me freedom too, and I'd thought I could seize it, thought that I could run away from everything.

But this time, I hesitate. Because Finn was right. The kind of freedom I long for doesn't exist, no matter where I go. Not in a world where the Prince of the East has any power and Neri the White Wolf roams free.

I turn to Nephele, perhaps for her to make the decision for me. She shakes her head, a plea of forgiveness painted on her face. Even if I'd made it to Winterhold while Mother still lived, Nephele wouldn't have fled. She has a new loyalty now, and it isn't to me.

Abruptly, I rise, my chair clattering to the floor behind me. Nephele reaches for my wrist, but I jerk away from my sister's touch. Alexus stands and opens his mouth to speak, but this time it's me who holds up a hand, silencing the Witch Collector, my soul torn for so many reasons I can't parse them all.

I march toward the library door, feeling Alexus right behind me, but I turn before I leave. He's so close, towering before me. His nearness takes my breath and heats the mark on my chest.

He lowers his voice, his words meant only for me, though every eye and ear behind him focuses on us both.

"I will not ask you to ride into battle for a man you don't consider your king, Raina. If you'd rather make your way to the Western Drifts or even off this break, I cannot fault you."

What was it he'd said? In the cave?

There will be more life after this. You will see your sister, and you'll figure out your future from there. If I'm not too late to save Colden, the kingdom and the vale will rebuild. If I am too late, I guess I'm going on a quest to save this empire, and you'll take to the seas and end up with someone who will make you a very happy woman.

He's never imagined any other outcome. But why would he?

Tears prick my eyes, and heat rushes up my neck and across my face. I don't know why this angers me so. I only know that I'm scared of what I'm feeling, scared that my already-wounded heart feels at risk for more indescribable loss.

But I form the words burning at the tips of my fingers anyway.

"I would be riding into battle for Colden Moeshka, the man who gave all for my sister and me. I would be riding into battle for the future of Tiressia." I turn to leave but face him once more. With my hands, I pound out a truth I need him to understand, a truth that's quickly becoming more than I can stand. *"And I would be riding into battle for you."*

43

RAINA

There's a window in Nephele's bedchamber, covered by a solid shutter to keep out the cold. I open it, make certain no one is below, and toss out the bloody water from the makeshift scrying dish my sister gave me. I've watched the waters for the Prince of the East and Colden most of the day. The prince is shrouded in shadow, almost like he's hiding from me, and the king is in a dirty cell somewhere, the location impossible for me to recognize. Though I sense his frustration and anger, he isn't in pain or misery. That's the best information I can provide Nephele and Alexus for now.

I gaze over Winterhold's darkening yet busy courtyard. More people live here than I imagined, something I questioned Nephele about earlier when she brought me a bowl of stew and bread. Not all are Witch Walkers. Many came from the Icelands far north of here, seeking the protection of the king and the company of a bustling village. Tonight, they're readying for the departure of their Witch Collector and his retinue that will hopefully rescue their king.

At noon, Alexus spoke to the villagers about Neri, how to watch for his wolves and sense his chilly presence. No one can know what the northern god is up to or what he'll do now that he's free of Alexus's prison. We just have to hope he doesn't cause problems, and that he leaves the people of

Winterhold in peace. But with Colden gone and Alexus away, I can't help but wonder if Neri won't try to rule—even without the shell of his human form. He said the only crown in the Northlands belongs to him, and now I suppose he has the chance to claim it.

My eyes catch on Alexus as he leaves what remains of the stables. After speaking to the people about Neri, Alexus and Rhonin rode north to visit some of the families of those he'd asked to make the Summerland journey, and now, when night settles over the land, they've finally returned.

I've thought of him since morning, my mind at war about what to do. His cloak and hair billow in the snowy wind, his every stride sure and strong but heavy with an invisible burden I know he carries. He glances at my window, and though I think better of it, I don't move away. My anger has been tempered. I don't want to argue.

But I also don't want to hurt anymore.

With a nod in my direction, he disappears into the main hall.

Nephele and I decided that we will be in the band of Witch Walkers and any others who leave Winterhold come morning. A decision I made on my own, however, was to protect my heart, to stifle this growing presence between Alexus and me that thrives like its own entity. I'll keep the rune for now, at least until I know more about what it entails, but I cannot put my heart in such precarious hands as those of Alexus Thibault. What lives between us is only there because we survived so much together—just like he said in the cave.

I just need to tell him how I feel.

I'm waiting by his door when he turns down the hall. I'm dressed for bed, my sleeping gown covered by a blue velvet robe. He's carrying his traveling cloak, a striking figure in a black tunic and dark leather trousers. When he lifts his eyes, the sight of me halts his steps, but after a moment, he continues, if a little more hesitantly.

He pauses at the entrance to his chamber, stripping a pair of gloves from his hands. Without a word, he opens his door, swinging it wide, and gestures for me to enter.

I step inside, sweeping a glance over the room as his scent envelopes me. The maidservants have stoked the fire for the night, and nests of candles—placed atop elegant silver stands—burn in each corner.

I rehearsed my words for hours, yet when I face Alexus, I don't know what to say. He takes a step toward me, and suddenly he's inches away.

I breathe him in, and all the air in my lungs evaporates. Being near him like this is all it takes to send a rush of knowing through me.

I've lied to myself all day.

"I'm sorry," he says. "I know you've endured enough since meeting me. I didn't mean to bring you more suffering, but I had to tell you the truth about me and Colden."

I shake my head and stare at my fidgeting fingers.

"I know," is all I say.

"And I wasn't trying to push you away this morning in the library," he adds. "I only wanted you to know that I don't expect you to go any further than this."

"I know that too."

He takes my hand, and after a weighted moment, presses a kiss to my palm. With a question in his eyes, he stares at me, his mouth lingering and so warm as he slowly presses kisses down my wrist.

My body comes alive when he touches me, but when his lips are on my skin, I feel as though the universe moves through me. It's divine. Better than calling down the moon.

But I can't bear it.

I jerk away, my heart pounding out a frantic rhythm. I bite my lip and lie for reasons I cannot completely discern, even as tears well in my eyes.

"I do not want this," I sign, and I don't. I want *him,* but I don't want to risk my heart more pain. *"Wherever we go from here, it must be as friends and fellow fighters. Nothing more."*

He stands before me frozen, but his eyes glisten, making my heart hurt.

"Neither of us asked for this," he says, his stare intent. "Neither of us expected to find ourselves fighting desire at every turn. Yet I've battled my want of you since that night in your village." He leans closer, so close I smell the lavender soap on his skin. He touches his mouth to my ear. "You can call me *friend* a thousand times, Raina, but I know you feel this."

This. This *heat.* This *yearning.* This *longing.*

Destroying me from the inside.

He pulls away and grazes the backs of his fingers along my cheek, drifts the ghost of a touch down my neck and across my shoulder. An involuntary shiver chases through my bones, and my breasts tighten.

"Tell me again that I am no more than a friend." He trails his touch down the front of my robe, stopping over my restless heart. "Tell me that I am just the Witch Collector, and I'll walk you back to your room and never mention what I feel for you ever again."

My hands are fisted at my sides. I unfurl my fingers, intent on forming more lies, but I can do nothing less than touch him. I clutch his tunic, feeling like I can't breathe, uncertain about what comes next.

Alexus settles his hands at my waist and draws me against him, making me dizzy with want.

"What are you scared of?" he asks, his voice so soft. "What is it you fear when it comes to me?"

I look up at him, and a thousand answers chase through my mind. The truth boils down to one thing, though, a truth I can't hold inside anymore.

"That I will never let myself know what it is to be yours. That I will deny myself this. *Deny myself* you. *Out of fear."* I pat his chest before continuing. *"Because I am so scared of losing anyone else."*

Alexus gives me the sweetest look, his expression tender. He slips his hand beneath my hair, across the back of my neck, tilting my head up, his thumb caressing my cheek.

"That's what you want?" He leans in, his breath warm against my mouth. "To know what it is to be mine?"

I close my eyes and clench my teeth, nodding, finding steadiness in his hold and against the solidity of his body as he flutters kisses across my jaw.

He takes my chin in his hand. "Will you let me show you?"

In answer, I nod and press my body against his.

"Protection?" he whispers. "I've taken nothing. I didn't know that I would have the need."

I nod once more. I drink a tonic made by Mena every full moon, as do many villagers of a certain age, people of all stripes. The last thing I need in my life right now is a child.

With a look of relief, Alexus brings his mouth down and touches his lips to mine. At first, his kiss is gentle and attentive, but soon it becomes wholly penetrating, his tongue stroking mine with fluid grace and startling precision. He takes his time, mapping out every curve like he's committing this moment—and me—to memory.

There's a pause, a split second when I feel him smile, and I sense overwhelming joy radiating from his being. I smile, too, and shift my hips against him as I run my hands up his back, craving his touch, the feel of his naked skin on mine.

He groans and deepens the kiss, sliding his hands into my hair, holding me in place. His grip is gentle but firm as he claims me with his lips, his skillful tongue granting assurance as to what's to come.

Gods, I feel so much in this kiss. It's exhilarating and makes my knees weak, but at the same time, there's so much affection and care in this man, in the way he kisses and touches, so much promise that the woman who will leave this room will not be the same woman who entered.

His need for me presses against my stomach. Unable to wait another second, I trace my hands beneath his tunic and break our kiss just long enough to pull the garment over his head and discard it on the rugs beneath our feet. His body is so beautiful—so sculpted and powerful—that I couldn't look away if the moon fell from the sky.

I dance my fingertips along every bronzed curve, cut, and rune, exploring not only with my hands but also with my mouth. His nipples harden when I flick my tongue over them, but when I kiss the skin beneath the new rune on his chest, he moans and rakes his fingers roughly through my hair, holding on as though he might float away if I stop.

He slips his hand down and twists the sash at my waist, giving it a tug. "Off."

A breath catches in my throat, and I nod my permission. In a beat of my pounding heart, the robe lies in a blue velvet pool at my feet.

Alexus kicks off his boots and peels off his leathers, leaving him standing on the most beautiful long, strong legs I've ever seen, wearing nothing but a thin pair of braies that hide nothing of his desire.

He comes for me, kissing me, curving his warm hands around my ribs. A moment later, he cups my breasts, kneading, teasing, and caressing.

"You feel so right in my hands," he whispers, kissing my mouth again before ducking his head low. Through the thin fabric of my shift, he drags his teeth achingly slow over my nipples, biting just hard enough to take my breath. With a delicate touch, I drag my fingernails down his back and draw him closer.

There is no love without fear.

I can't call this love—not yet—but I have to wonder if it could become something extraordinary. Eventually. I'll never know if I let this night pass me by.

Something comes over me, the same something that guided me in the wood—in the refuge. I give in and push Alexus toward the bed. Eyes holding mine, he sits and pulls me onto his lap, his hands sliding up my thighs, over my naked hips, gripping me, heating my flesh everywhere he touches.

I want more. I want this. I want *him*.

I want to finish what we started days ago.

Gathering my gown, I pull it over my head, baring my body. His eyes go dark as he takes me in, but then he lowers his mouth to my breast again, his tongue and teeth sending molten pleasure to my core. He trails his hand down my spine, over my hips, and lower, readying me, making me throb as I push against his touch.

He stares up at me, a wicked little smile curling one corner of his mouth. "I was going to be gentle."

I shake my head and sign his words back to him, the words he'd spoken at the stream. *"Sometimes, a rough hand is best."*

Holding my gaze, he slips a finger inside me, pushing deep, making me gasp. Pulse pounding in my ears, I urge him down to the bed and bury my hands in all that dark hair, kissing him harder and hungrier than I've ever kissed anyone before. His touch remains, his skillful fingers brushing over me, tormenting.

I've never ached like this. Never felt like I might die from need. Never burned for another as I burn for him.

Nothing but his thin braies separates us, and already, the friction and pressure is intoxicating. Brazenly, I shift so that I can slide my hand between us. I untie the laces and tug the fabric down, enough that I can clutch him in my hand. He touched me so perfectly in the wood. I'm only returning the favor.

"Gods, Raina." With every stroke, my name is an ache given life, hanging from the edge of a ragged breath.

Alexus raises his hips. Together, we clumsily shove his braies down his thighs, and he kicks the garment aside. The action only presses his rigid length against me—without any barrier. He's so hard, so perfect.

Slick with desire, I move against him and swallow his fevered groan with a kiss.

"*Want.*" I press that word into the skin over his heart.

Alexus Thibault pulls away from my mouth and says the three words that are my undoing. "Then take me."

Bracing myself on his broad, rounded shoulders, I sink onto him and gasp. There's so little of me and so much of him, yet there will somehow never be enough.

Rocking gently, I draw a deep moan from his chest.

"And I thought your mouth would be my ruin." Breathing hard, he shuts his eyes for the span of a heartbeat, and then stares into my eyes. "I might not survive this."

A smile tempts my mouth. I felt like a god when I straddled him in the wood, and I feel that same way now.

I bite my lip as he carefully rolls his hips, each shallow thrust matching the pace I've set. I can see the tension in him, the way the tendons in his neck strain, the way the vein across his shoulder swells as he clutches my hips.

He's holding back. For me.

Soon my body complies to his movements, opening to him, *for* him—

And I am lost.

There is nothing gentle about anything I do to him from this moment forward. I'm ravenous, heat coiling inside me, the tightest, sweetest ache making me move with relentless abandon.

Alexus skims his hands up my body, wraps his fists in my hair, angling my head back with enough force in his grip that a chill covers every inch of my skin.

"Take me," he commands. "Take all of me."

The soft, dark hair on his chest tortures the tips of my breasts as I move, my rhythm driven by the soft bites he presses along the side of my neck, the way he licks and sucks the places where his teeth might've left a mark. For one long moment, I think I might fall apart from this alone.

But then he closes his mouth over the tip of my breast and presses his teeth around my nipple, sucking. Watching me, he flicks his tongue and raises his hips, pressing into me so deeply that I drop my head back, my body falling still as I try to breathe around the fullness.

He grips my waist and turns us over, flipping me on my stomach. I shiver when he slides his warm hands down my back and drags those rough palms over the curves of my hips and down my legs, all the way to my ankles before he returns and does it all again. The third time he spreads my legs and draws me to my knees, my torso still flattened to the bed.

"You are so beautiful, Raina." He holds me there, his fingers pressed firmly into my hips as he trails kisses down my spine, lower and lower, until—

He tastes me.

I clench the bedcovers and bite down on the thick brocade fabric. He turns me mindless, plunging his tongue into me and over me until I can barely think around the desire he won't let me release.

It makes me ache, and desire overwhelms me. One second, I'm pressing back against him, grinding my hips, needing his tongue deeper. The next moment, he's touching me, opening me, sliding his fingers inside me, his tongue still ravaging my body, and I'm clawing at the bed linens to get away.

A throaty little laugh leaves him as he grips my hips and draws me back to his hungry mouth.

How easily I surrender.

He groans—feasting, savoring, devouring. The vibration of his voice over my tender, aching flesh sends a chill chasing across my skin, coaxing me toward a climax I so desperately need.

This is worship. Alexus Thibault has lain me on his altar and praised every inch of me.

Just when I think I can bear no more, he presses soft kisses to my thighs, trails his tongue up the curve of my backside, and then kneels behind me. Slowly, he enters me, little by little, every inch its own unbearable torture.

Greedy, I shift my hips and push against him, until he's buried deep. My reward is *him,* the lewd curse that trips off his lips, and his shuddering gasp.

With my heart pounding, he curls his arm around my waist and lifts me up against him, my back to his front.

The rune on my chest warms as he lifts his hand to that gentle heat, delicately touching his mark as he moves his hips.

"There is magick even in this," he whispers against my ear. "If you close your eyes, if you search, you'll see the threads of my desire for you. We're connected now. You just need to draw the threads inside you. We can tangle our magick. Even though mine is weak, it will still make this night like nothing you've ever known."

Gods. Tangling our magick? I do as told.

The threads are easier to find than I imagined. They burn brightly as a star, and when I reach for them with my mind, they seep into me like sunlight.

"Got them?" he asks, and I nod. "Good. I'm going to kiss you now," he whispers, tilting my head until his breath is on my lips. "And I swear to every god who has ever lived, you're going to feel me everywhere."

He brushes his mouth over mine, the taste of us sweet on his lips. Hungry, he sweeps his tongue deep, kissing me with the same passion as when he kissed between my legs.

A glimmer of magick and pleasure skitters over my skin, making my body clench around Alexus's hardness. The intensity almost shatters me, the binding of our power, tangling and twisting like lengths of silver silk. I hadn't thought two people could be any closer than the intimacy that happens during lovemaking, but I feel Alexus Thibault throughout every speck of stardust that makes me *me*.

He turns my chin forward. Our glistening reflection and his penetrating emerald gaze stare back at me in the window.

"Look how breathtaking you are." He traces the witch's marks spiraling around my breast, then lowers his hand to the most sensitive part of me. "Watch what you do to me."

There's nothing in the world but us then. Nothing but the way we fit together—bodies *and* magick—the way he takes me so thoroughly. One moment he's clutching my breast, and the next, he's teasing me between my legs, his magick singing in my blood. It's a cruel dance, one he prolongs, sending me to the brink of rapture again and again, our every movement captured in the glass across the room.

I am clay beneath his skilled hands, changing, as though he's molding me. Not back to the woman I was, but to someone new, someone damaged but unbroken, wounded and yet healed. I'd feared how he might change me, and yet he reminds me of who I am and who I can be with every caress, every kiss, every thrust, our magick entwined, bright as a beacon, showing me parts of myself long-buried, parts of myself unknown. I like who I am with him.

Who I'm becoming.

Arching back, I wrap my arm around his neck and writhe on him, that ache inside me building to a breaking point.

He moves harder, murmuring my name like a holy enchantment. This time, he doesn't stop touching me. Masterfully, he rolls his fingertip across that bundle of nerves and lingers. Those merciless circles and his pounding rhythm begin to unravel me. He moves faster, thrusting so hard and so deep that I can taste his magick, sense it gliding across my skin.

I don't know where he ends and I begin.

He's too much. Too consuming.

He's everything.

"Come for me," he begs on a shredded breath, touching me. Touching *us*. "Let me feel you come for me."

My body obeys.

Pleasure cuts through me, lightning flashing like fire in my veins, my core filling with liquid heat as I spasm around his hardness. It's as though I slip outside myself, the connection to ecstasy so intense and thrilling that —for those long, wonder-filled moments—that's all I feel.

Utter bliss.

No sooner than I begin the quivering fall back to reality, Alexus presses his hand over my heart, his other arm tightening around my waist. There's so much power in him, even though contained. Even now it's almost unbearable, but I still want to set it free. I want to experience what it's like when he's inside me and brimming with magick.

"Stop me if I hurt you," he whispers against my neck.

My stomach tightens with anticipation. I shake my head—because there's no way I'll stop him—and again, his smile tickles my skin.

He lowers his strong hands to my hips and euphoria rises once more. His release builds, throbbing inside me.

Dark desire washes through my veins as I train my eyes on the window. The fierceness of his claiming is stunning to watch, his muscles tensing and flexing as he thrusts and thrusts, each onslaught jolting my body, stoking my arousal anew.

His fingers bite into my hips, and in the window, with snow falling beyond, he tips his head back and moans. All that silky black hair slips over his shoulder as a strained "gods" leaves his lips.

I cover his hands with mine, squeezing, because he's carrying us away again, and I can do nothing more than hold on and let him.

Gasping, I take all he has to give, until he cries out my name. His sinewy body shudders hard against mine, and I shatter a second time, quivering with pleasure.

When it's over, we collapse, sweat-slicked and exhausted, wrapped in one another's arms and one another's magick. We lie side by side, staring into each other's eyes for a long time—gently caressing, exploring, touching—the crackling fire and our slowing breaths the only sounds in the room.

Alexus kisses my fingertips, and then cups my cheek before pressing his lips to my mouth. It's a slow, sweet kiss, deliberate and unhurried. I love it, but I pull away.

"You cannot keep kissing me like that, or we might never leave this place," I sign, throwing his words from the wood back at him.

A gorgeous, heart-stopping smile unfurls across his face. "Well, you see, *that,*" he says against my lips, "is what it is to be mine, and I intend to show you several more times tonight if that's all right."

I smile too. A genuine smile. A smile I feel in my heart, my soul.

I touch his dimple and drag my fingertips through his beard before pulling him on top of me.

"Promise?" I sign.

He presses his reply into the skin over my heart. *"I promise."*

44

RAINA

There is no love without fear, but no one told me that fear feasts on those with something to lose. That's been my problem all along, and though everything looks very different now when I gaze at my life, that part remains steadfast and true.

I imagine it always will.

The starkness of this certainty settles deep as I lay before the fire with Alexus's head at rest upon my breast. His long body is wrapped around mine, so still and tranquil, clinging to the remnants of our lovemaking. My mind drifts so easily to the worry that—at any moment—that gentle heartbeat of his could cease, and I can do nothing to stop it. I don't know how to reconcile this. Accepting that this is our fate unless we defeat the Prince of the East with a handful of Witch Walkers is beyond my reach.

Alexus doesn't seem to live under the weight of such concerns. When he wakes, he takes me again, until my mind is blank of anything other than the passion we share. But we cannot remain in the dreamworld of his bedchamber forever.

Too soon, I'm standing with Helena in the main hall, watching servants carry the last of the packs and blankets outside. We're dressed in leathers, thick wool tunics, heavy fur-lined cloaks, and sealskin gloves. Our boots are tall with daggers strapped to both sides, and we each wear a baldric across our chests, complete with swords that fit our hands perfectly.

I can't help but glance at Hel, looking like the warrior she's meant to be. Every hour here brings some new change that makes my old life less and less recognizable, but I'm beginning to feel like these changes somehow fit.

Helena jerks her head for me to follow, and we turn down the impressive hall leading to the kitchens. We pass a half dozen tapestries, each at least thirty hands high, depicting war in a desert. The Land Wars. The wars that led Colden Moeshka to a life he never expected—that of an immortal king.

Hel opens the door leading to the main kitchen, and we slip inside. No one is here but us.

"What is this about?" I ask.

She arches a dark brow and guides me across the room. A pitcher and scrying dish filled with water waits on a rough-hewn table.

"Can you look for my father?" she asks. "If he's out there, Raina, that's another pair of fighting hands we need. Possibly seven pairs of fighting hands if the rest of the hunters are all right. They're good with weapons. Good at hunting. Survival. Tracking."

I blow out a long breath. She's right. The hunters from Silver Hollow would be a grand addition to our efforts, but ever since the night of the attack on the village, I've had a terrible suspicion that our hunters fell to the Eastlanders hours before the enemy devastated the vale. I saw Warek. What looked like a man passed out from too much drink could've also been a dead man revealed to me from an unclear angle.

But I must look again. I must be certain.

I slip a dagger from my boot and prick my fingertip. The blood falls, and I swirl the water.

"Nahmthalahsh. Show me the hunters."

The image that forms on the water's violet surface almost takes me to my knees. The hunters are there, in the valley, burying bodies.

Cupping my hands over my mouth, I look at Helena, my eyes wide. I drop my hands and smile, happy tears welling at the rims of my eyes.

"They're there?" Elation spreads across her face. "You see them?"

With a wipe of my eyes, I nod and then turn back to the water, dumping it into a basin and refilling from the pitcher. Another prick. Another drop of blood.

"*Nahmthalahsh. Show me Warek.*"

The water swirls and another violet scene arrives.

Faces. *Obscured* faces. People, walking behind the low-hanging leaves of a tree. I peer harder, and a wind blows, clearing away the leaves.

I gasp and grip the table's edge. Warek walks toward the charred remains of the village, his face saddened and downturned but lined with the same gentleness he was known for in Silver Hollow.

But he is not alone.

With a limp in her step, Mena struggles along behind him, a little girl clinging to her hand—Saira. Tuck the dog trots lazily next to his girl.

And there, beside Helena's father is someone else. His dark face is hard and filled with bitterness, his skin chapped from the cold morning wind and autumn sun. A shovel rests on his strong shoulder.

I close my eyes, and my heart cleaves in two.

Finn.

❧

I STAND WITH MY SISTER IN THE FALLING SNOW, JUST OUTSIDE WHAT'S left of the stables. I would've never imagined her this way, but she looks fierce, her long hair in tight braids against her skull, her body clad in furs and glinting weapons.

We're surrounded by more than two dozen Witch Walkers and North-landers, as well as their families, lovers, and friends, all saying their good-byes. The grooms lead Mannus and Tuck from their stalls against a cold wind, and though my heart is filled with strife, it still swells for the horses who saw Alexus and me through the wood and will carry us through yet another adventure.

Alexus takes their reins, his dark hair and black cloak whipping in the wind. When he sees me, he smiles, but there's a sad edge to it. His last words before we left his chambers were: *If my life is cut short, I will die happy because I had this time with you. But I will fight for more. I will fight for Colden. And I will fight for us.*

Nephele takes me by the shoulders. Tenderness shines in her eyes. "I know you're uncertain about being here, Raina. About this journey. About Finn. So much has happened. And I know that I haven't been around you and Finn in a very long time, but Alexus is one of my truest friends. I see the way he looks at you. That man would burn down the world for Raina Bloodgood, and he's known her barely two weeks." She gives me a small smile and slides her hands down to clasp mine. "I also know that you're in a difficult position. If I can give you any advice, though, it's to listen to your heart." She pauses, then holds my gaze. "Alexus Thibault is a man who doesn't give his love or body freely, Raina. This is different for him. *You* are different for him."

As Alexus approaches, Nephele casts a glance and a smile in his direction and then turns and strides away. She gives me one last look and a wink over her shoulder.

I didn't need the advice. I knew what I had to do the moment I saw Finn's handsome face.

Alexus halts the horses a few feet away from me. An awkward distance builds in the space between us, a distance that would've been unthinkable a few hours ago.

"I heard about the hunters," he says. "And your friends—Rhonin's grandmother. Warek and Finn Owyn." He clears his throat. "I hadn't realized that Finn was Helena's brother, the blacksmith's son." His eyes are soft and kind when he says Finn's name, but uncertainty and turmoil fill his voice. "I'm glad they're all right," he adds. "We're a week's ride from the vale, but with you watching the waters, I'm sure we'll be able to find them should they travel." He pauses, his voice quiet, his eyes sincere. "You owe me nothing, Raina. Finn being alive changes things, I know. And I understand."

"It changes nothing," I tell him.

Because it doesn't. It hasn't. I don't know how I'll ever explain to Finn what I feel for Alexus or how it happened in such a short time. It's only been twelve days since Collecting Day, and yet everything in my world has changed.

I've changed. And I can't stop thinking about Mena's words of wisdom. *Most battles are hard-fought. Something must always be lost if you're ever to gain. Don't fear this. You will never move forward if you never leave things behind.*

I don't want to leave Finn behind. He's been my dearest friend, such an enormous part of my life. But he will not suffer me being with Alexus in any manner. It's one thing for him to see me living my life alone. It will be a wholly different circumstance for him to see me with someone other than him.

And I'm not willing to give up the man standing before me.

"You're sure?" Alexus asks. Uncertainty lines his furrowed brow.

"Surer than I have been about anything in a long time." I step closer and take his hand.

He exhales, his breath clouding in the wintry air, and without a moment's hesitation, pulls me into his arms, bends down, and kisses me as though he hasn't kissed me in an age. My face heats, and when he finally releases me, I duck my head.

"What will the others think?" I sign.

With a smile that is so true it makes his dimple appear, he leans close, his green stare sparkling in the morning light.

"They will think that we are desperate for one another, and they won't be wrong." He kisses me again—deeper, longer. In those few moments, the world falls away. When he breaks the kiss, reality returns. Alexus faces the crowd behind us and whistles loudly to gather everyone's attention. "Mount up," he shouts. "It's time."

He helps me onto Tuck's back, fitting me in the saddle. I tighten my fingers around the reins as Helena, Nephele, and Rhonin ride up alongside.

Rhonin bows his head and presses his fist over his heart. "Thank you for checking the waters, Raina. It means everything."

I nod in return. He's worried for his family, people I cannot see, but his grandmother is alive in the vale, and that has brought a light to his eyes that I haven't seen since I met him.

Helena grins and glances at Rhonin. "How far we've come. Enemies one day, riding across an entire break together the next."

I see no worry in her eyes. I haven't told her, but I think she knows where my heart has landed when it comes to her brother. Her love for me isn't designed around Finn, though. She wants me to be happy, and if that means kissing the Witch Collector until I turn blue, I know that's what she wants for me.

The Witch Walkers say goodbye to their loved ones, and then we cross through Winterhold's gates and face Frostwater Wood. I've no notion what lies ahead, but I believe that the days leading to this moment were meant to prepare me.

Alexus guides us, and I ride close, but he halts Mannus and takes a deep inhale of frost-filled air coming from the north.

He looks at me over his shoulder, his eyes so devastatingly bold against the snowy backdrop.

"And you're certain you're ready for this?" he asks. "This is only the beginning."

I ride up until he's but an arm's length away. *"I am certain,"* I sign, my determination as solid as the icy ground beneath me. *"We have a king to save."*

⁂

Thank you for reading! Did you enjoy? Please add your review because nothing helps an author more and encourages readers to take a chance on a book than a review.

And don't miss more of the Witch Walker series with book two, CITY OF RUIN, coming soon from Charissa Weaks!

Until then discover THE GIRL WHO BELONGED TO THE SEA, by City Owl Author, Katherine Quinn. Turn the page for a sneak peek!

You can also sign up for the City Owl Press newsletter to receive notice of all book releases!

SNEAK PEEK OF THE GIRL WHO BELONGED TO THE SEA

BY KATHERINE QUINN

Margrete Wood had been locked inside her father's iron contraption so many times that she *should* have been used to its rusted spikes, pungent rot, and the absence of light once he shut the door. It was her *penance* for misbehaving, he claimed. A way to cleanse her soul. But it was no more than a coffin. A vicious device he used for control.

When her father slammed the door, trapping her where dreams went to die, Margrete prayed to all the gods she could think of. Arios, the God of Spring and New Beginnings, and Delia, Goddess of Wisdom and Protector of the Pure of Heart. She even prayed to the wrathful God of War and Vengeance, Charion.

Yet only when she envisioned the sea, wild and unapologetically savage, did she receive any kind of answer at all. Trapped in the dark with nothing but her sinking hope, she chased after the elusive sound of the waves. It was soft at first, nothing but the gentle thrum of the waters meeting the shore.

Margrete closed her eyes and held on to that melody like a lifeline. Soon her body trembled and her heartbeat slowed, and then the song swelled.

The moment the waves became a roar in her ears, she released her prayers with a heart-wrenching hope. She wished to be far from her father. Begged for a life that was not her own. Pleaded to be *free*.

When the door to her box opened hours later, her father's wicked face staring back at her, the ethereal song came to an abrupt end. While he'd done his best to weaken her, to rob her of her courage, Margrete left that day clinging to a scrap of hope her father couldn't touch.

The sea had whispered a reply, a single, haunting word.

Soon.

❦

It had been five days since Margrete emerged from the box and left her father's study. Five long days and *still* her body buzzed with apprehension and promise.

Almost as if the God of the Sea had truly heeded her prayers.

Now, she was being called back to the study, urged on by Adina, her lady's maid, who snapped at her heels like an anxious hound. And hurry she did, for every wrong Margrete committed, each act of rebellion, would not only be *her* punishment to bear. Not since her father turned his attention to her younger sister, Bridget, or Birdie, as Margrete fondly nicknamed her.

A thin layer of perspiration dampened her skin by the time she arrived. Lifting a closed fist, she knocked on the heavy wooden door, biting her lower lip as she awaited a reply.

"Come."

Margrete flinched, her father's voice unusually light. Pushing inside, she found the notorious sea captain of Prias lounging in his chair, his booted feet propped against the mahogany desk littered with maps and trade records. His short, flaxen hair and matching beard were sprinkled with age, white streaks interwoven throughout the strands, his square jaw prominent and masculine.

But it was the cutting edge of his gaze that could fell a man with one look.

"Daughter, sit." He waved her over to one of two plush blue seats before him. A devilish smile curled his thin lips, a malicious twinkle sparkling in his steel-gray eyes that promised nothing but torment.

Margrete had always been told that her hazel eyes and golden skin came from her mother. If only she could have met her.

Hesitantly, she slid onto the cushion, her muscles tensing as her father's gaze swept across her body from behind his desk, his forefinger and thumb pinching his graying beard in thought. Uneasy moments ticked by before he spoke, but when he did, she had to grab hold of her chair to keep from falling over.

"You're to be married here, at the keep, in two months' time."

Margrete couldn't help it when a small gasp left her lips, her mouth parting as though a silent scream wished to escape. It was her only reaction, the obedient words she usually reserved for the captain dissipating like dust in a windstorm.

"I see you're quite thrilled with the news, then?" He leaned back in his seat, pulling his muscled legs from the polished wood. "I'll give you a moment to process."

Tiny beads of sweat formed along her brow, the air in the room suddenly too hot, too stuffy. Her heartbeat thundered in her ears, a tumultuous staccato that sounded like angry raindrops during a squall.

"W-who?" she managed to ask, fearful of the answer. Knowing her father, her marriage was to procure some elusive business deal. She would be used for his purposes, however vile they may be, and her opinion on the matter was irrelevant.

"Count Casbian," he said.

"Of Cartus?"

"One and the same." The captain grinned, enjoying the obvious discomfort playing across her features. "Cartus is Marionette's greatest asset for defense, and the count's military position will do well for us. I'm told he's also a favorite amongst the king and queen."

This was about influence. As if conquering the seas wasn't enough, the captain now wished to gain the favor of Marionette's rulers through the count.

"And he *is* quite young," he added, "which is lucky for you. Meaning you won't soon be made a widow."

She didn't allow her bewilderment to show, but the truth was that she'd believed her reputation suffered too great a blow for any man to look her way after what happened two years ago. Then again, her substantial dowry might persuade suitors to overlook her past indiscretions.

She swallowed down the tears at the memory of her father's young guard, Jacob, who'd been foolish enough to fall in love with her. They'd been caught in the act by the captain himself, and to her horror, her father had thrust his dagger into the very heart that had once belonged to her. She was to remain pure until the captain found a match for his daughter that suited his needs, but thanks to Jacob, any purity vanished.

And yet now, none of that seemed to matter.

Pulling herself together, forcing her chin to lift, Margrete addressed the man who relished in misery with an icy calm. "I see," she began, sitting up straighter in her chair. "And this has already been decided? The count has agreed to this as well?"

"Yes." He didn't hesitate.

"And you didn't consult me." The words were out before she had a chance to rein them in.

Storm clouds brewed in his eyes. "*Consult* you?" He let out a mirthless laugh, his eyes drifting to the corner of the study where his sick contraption hid behind a silk screen. The unspoken threat was obvious. "You should consider yourself lucky I've given you this opportunity." He seethed. "I was never awarded such a thing."

The captain didn't speak of his past, of his parents, except for once, five years ago. Margrete woke in the middle of the night and crept down the stairs, only to overhear him arguing with a man. She hadn't recognized the voice, but before he kicked the stranger out of the keep, her father had told him, 'You can slither back into your hovel and tell our *dearest* parents I'm merely showing them the same kindness they did me.'

The captain caught Margrete that night, and without a word, dragged her to the box and shoved her inside. Only when dawn came did he open the door.

They never spoke of the man again.

"Don't make this hard on yourself, daughter," her father said, shaking the memory from her thoughts. "I'd hate for you to receive another lesson so soon after the last."

Margrete shut her eyes, and just like that, she was back inside the confines of the box. Its metal spikes poked at her skin, the smell of her blood fresh in the air. Her breaths quickened as shadows closed in on all sides. Sometimes he'd leave her in there for hours. After Jacob, she'd been trapped for a full day.

What would he do if she refused him now?

Margrete cleared her throat and opened her eyes, willing away the images that haunted her every waking moment. So many thoughts rushed into her mind that she couldn't think clearly, but one stood out amongst the rest.

Perhaps she didn't need to refuse her father. Marriage to the Count of Cartus would change her life, change *everything*. For better or worse, she couldn't say, but it was a way out of this keep and a way to flee her father's control.

There was just one problem.

"If I'm to marry Casbian, who will watch over Birdie? You're frequently gone, and the keep is no place for a young lady to live alone."

Birdie's mother, Margrete's stepmother, had died four years past, and the poor girl still suffered the loss. She needed her older sister now more than ever. Birdie's sweet disposition would never endure under their father's merciless thumb.

"Bridget will remain here," he said. "Under her governess's supervision."

Where she would be his latest victim.

Margrete's stomach clenched, a nauseating ache forming. She couldn't let that happen. She had to be brave now, had to find a way to shift this situation to one of advantage.

And she knew precisely how.

"I never ask much of you, Father," she said, nearly choking on the word, "but I will ask this of you now. One final gift you can give me as a farewell."

He cocked his head, eyes narrowing as he awaited her proposition.

"I would like Birdie, and her governess, to come to Cartus when the count and I set sail for his home. I cannot bear for her to be isolated and far from family." She paused for a single heartbeat. "And surely it would benefit you to have her stationed in Cartus."

Many influential men and their families settled there, and while Birdie was only seven, her early presence might be advantageous for a power-hungry sea captain—though Margrete had no plans to ever allow her little sister to be used in such a way. Her father highly underestimated her if he believed otherwise.

The captain considered, stroking his trimmed beard as he let time stretch thin. She waited, unmoving in her chair. This was a fear tactic he enjoyed using on his adversaries—silence—but she wasn't in the mood to play his games.

"You actually make quite a good point," he said, relenting, though his jaw ticked. "I will strike a bargain with you then. Marry the count without delay and without any of your *theatrics*, and Bridget will be allowed to leave with you to Cartus."

Margrete nodded, though she hardly felt herself move. The fact that her father conceded to her request so easily had her wondering what else was up his sleeve, what other little secret he kept close to his charred heart.

"Thank you," she said, hating the words. "If that is all, then I will leave you to your work." Margrete knew better than to leave the study without his permission, and she waited for him to wave his hand in dismissal, that malicious smile still twisting his mouth.

"Oh, and daughter," he interrupted before she was halfway to the door. She stopped, glancing over her shoulder. "You'd do well to remember the teachings of last week, because if you disappoint me..." He paused as her heart thundered madly.

Teachings. It was what he called his punishments.

"Oh, I never forget, Father," she said, gathering her long skirts and abandoning the captain to his plans.

I will never forget. And one day, I hope to make you pay.

Don't stop now. Keep reading with your copy of THE GIRL WHO BELONGED TO THE SEA, by City Owl Author, Katherine Quinn.

And don't miss book two of the the Witch Walker series, CITY OF RUIN, coming soon, and find more from Charissa Weaks at www.charissaweaks.com

Don't miss book two of the the Witch Walker series, CITY OF RUIN, coming soon, and find more from Charissa Weaks at www.charissaweaks.com

Until then, discover THE GIRL WHO BELONGED TO THE SEA, by City Owl Author, Katherine Quinn!

ॐ

One woman chosen by the God of the Sea. A king hellbent on saving his mysterious island home. And a forbidden romance that could destroy them all.

Forced to marry the wealthy Count Casbian by her power-hungry father, Margrete turns to the gods, praying for a life free from the men who wish to rule her. Across the sea, a ruthless immortal answers...

Planning to use Margrete to reclaim a powerful relic stolen from his people, Bash, a devilishly handsome king, kidnaps Margrete on the day of her nuptials. Bringing her to his home, the mystical island of Azantian, it isn't long before a devastating secret is revealed—one that ties Margrete to the gods themselves.

Drawn to the spirited woman he's sworn to hate, Bash cannot stay away from Margrete and the passion she ignites within him. When the lines begin to blur, Margrete must make a choice between a fiery love, and saving the realm from the dangerous magic awakening inside of her soul.

The first book of this exciting fantasy trilogy is perfect for readers who love high-seas adventures, swashbuckling heroes, and forbidden, steamy romance. Fans of Danielle L. Jensen's _The Bridge Kingdom_, and Sarah J. Maas's _A Court of Thorns and Roses_ will be enthralled.

ॐ

ACKNOWLEDGMENTS

This book began as a short story that wanted to be a novelette that wanted to be a novella that wanted to be novel. It would've never become the book it is without the support and encouragement from the amazing people below.

First, to my husband. This writing journey of mine has existed around the happenings of our busy lives. There have been many mornings when I woke you at 4am because I had to write something down, and late nights where the light from my laptop kept you awake. There have been dinners with ceaseless book speak, more bookstore trips than I can count, weeks and weekends away for writing conferences and retreats. You've watched me doubt this path, watched me try and fail and try and fail again, and all the while, you only ever told me I could do it. You believed in me even when I didn't believe in myself. I couldn't have done this without your unwavering support. Thank you. I love you. You're my best friend and my rock.

To my daughters—thank you for being the wonderful humans that you are. You have endured the struggle of having a Writing Mom. You tolerate my head being in the clouds 95% of the time and have always given me the space I need to feed my creativity—even though that means living in a house with books EVERYWHERE. You've been my truest cheerleaders, always proud and always encouraging. I adore you all.

To Hannah Banana—for making me read Twilight. Because of you, I remembered my love of story and reading, my passion for books and writing. I saw that passion in you, and it set a fire in me. If not for you, I wouldn't be on this path.

Melinda Collins, my friend and critique partner of ten years, thank you for reading all the crappy drafts of my many stories and for always being the positive voice I need to hear. Thank you for being the White Space Queen, for destroying my unnecessary 'as' usages, and for cutting all the words I miss. We make a great team, and I truly appreciate you and the time you put into this book and all the other work I've created over the years. I'm a better writer because of you. From the bottom of my heart, you rock.

Jodi Henry, my birthday twin, thank you for years of critiquing/reading and sharing ideas through two million words via text messages. Thank you for believing in this story when it was a baby novella. Your kind words gave me the courage to believe in Raina and Alexus and to stop doubting myself enough to get the damn thing published.

To the numerous people in my life who have influenced my writing journey: Susan Bickford—for all our writing retreat and conference fun, Alexia Chantel—for being the sweetest person I know, cheering me on, and making me feel like I can do ALL THE THINGS, Molly Brogan and Ashley R. King—for being amazing humans who make me laugh and reading whatever I send no matter when I send it, the members of Music City Romance Writers—for access to workshops, contests, and the publishing world, the ladies in the Mid-South Historical Novel Society—for being so kind to a fantasy writer with a love of history, the SFF SEVEN—for inviting me to blog and sharing your platform, Andrea Hollis—for letting me borrow fantasy novels back in the day and for being my first editor, April Carroll—for reading my writing when we were supposed to be working, Wendy Jordan Petty—for just loving me and being happy for me no matter what, and Sandy Spencer Coomer—for my time at Rockvale Writer's Colony. I wouldn't have finished this book if not for my time at your beautiful farm.

To my AMAZING Rebel Readers and the readers of The Witch

Collector novella/Once Upon an Enchanted Forest—thank you for your excitement, for your heart-eye emoji comments, for the DMs about the book before it was even out in the world, for those who messaged and emailed me wanting more, for those who beta read, and for all the readers in other countries who have been tracking Raina and Alexus's tale—this one is for you. Readers make the book world go 'round, and I appreciate you all so very much.

And finally, my heartfelt appreciation to the team at City Owl Press. I didn't know this expanded novella would become a four-hundred-page novel when I signed that contract, yet you took the change in stride and have been nothing but supportive and encouraging. I'm thankful to work with such amazing people, including a host of supportive authors who are truly a family.

ABOUT THE AUTHOR

CHARISSA WEAKS is an award-winning author of historical fantasy and speculative fiction. She crafts stories with fantasy, magic, time travel, romance, and history, and the occasional apocalyptic quest. Charissa resides just south of Nashville with her family, two wrinkly English Bulldogs, and the sweetest German Shepherd in existence. To keep up with her writing endeavors, and to gain access to writing freebies and book giveaways, join her newsletter, The Monthly Courant or her Rebel Readers group on Facebook.

www.charissaweaks.com

instagram.com/CharissaWeaksAuthor
facebook.com/CharissaWeaksAuthor
twitter.com/charissaweaks
pinterest.com/CharissaWeaks

ABOUT THE PUBLISHER

City Owl Press is a cutting edge indie publishing company, bringing the world of romance and speculative fiction to discerning readers.

Escape Your World. Get Lost in Ours!

www.cityowlpress.com

facebook.com/YourCityOwlPress

twitter.com/cityowlpress

instagram.com/cityowlbooks

pinterest.com/cityowlpress

Made in the USA
Columbia, SC
25 March 2023

14261298R00221